THE PRICE OF INERTIA

(THE SEVEN SINS, #4)

LILY ZANTE

AUTHOR'S NOTE

The Price of Inertia is the fourth book in **The Seven Sins,** a contemporary romance series of steamy, angsty and emotional stories featuring characters who are loosely connected.

All books in this series are STANDALONE but loosely connected.

Other books in the Seven Sins series:

Underdog (prequel)
The Wrath of Eli
The Problem with Lust
The Lies of Pride
The Price of Inertia
The Other Side of Greed

Sign up for my newsletter and get a FREE book:
https://www.lilyzante.com/news

CHAPTER ONE

WARD

"Don't go dying on me," says Rob, my agent, and probably the only person whose opinion I value.

"I'm not going to die. I'm taking it easy. That's not going to kill me."

"You've been taking it *too* easy."

Easy isn't how I would describe the last few months. I throw him a resentful look. "I've had stuff to deal with."

"Do you have to work from bed? The same bed you sleep in?"

"I'm not in bed now."

"You're not at your desk, either." Rob exhales loudly. "I've given you the time you need, Ward, but you're not making any progress. You're in danger of missing the deadline. This book was supposed to release along with the movie."

I grab a handful of potato chips and shovel them into my mouth.

"So, I've made the decision for you. You're going to Chicago. A change of setting will do you good."

I almost choke, and get up off the couch, dropping my bag of chips in shock. "I'm *not* going to Chicago." *Hell, no.*

"I've rented you a beautiful mansion. It might help."

"How?" How the hell will being in Chicago help me? My satin robe has fallen open. Rob looked at me oddly and made a sarcastic comment when he first saw me. I quite like this. It's comfortable. Far easier to sit and write in this all day than wearing sweatpants. I pull the sash tighter, but not before Rob gets a peek at my flabby torso. He winces and I turn away.

I've packed on a few pounds. My face might have rounded out a bit. I'm in a funk and have been like this for months.

"It's not permanent," Rob insists. "Three, four months. You need to finish the manuscript, Ward. You can't miss your deadline."

I sink back onto the couch. The words don't flow these days. They haven't for a while. For the second time in my life, I'm stuck with my writing. I used to be able to pull words out of thin air and piece together plots that would have my readers keep turning the pages.

I've lost that gift again.

"This is a seven-figure deal and you need to honor it. What you don't want is to risk incurring a penalty. Think of the bad press. Think of the movie that's coming out. Think of the book tour. The publicity. The talk shows. *Think.*"

I hang my head because all the things he's just mentioned weigh me down. Rob has done great things for me. He's been my agent for over a decade, my only agent. He's been more like a mentor, guiding me when I've had no real-life role models. I hate publicity. I hate talk shows. I'm no good at them. I can't talk to people, much less laugh and joke with them, but because of this trilogy, this amazing book and movie deal Rob negotiated for me, I have to do the whole publicity crap.

The first movie in my *Morbid Trilogy* will release by the time the last book comes out but it's this last book that I've hit a wall on. I can't see me making the deadline. I haven't written much. I've tried and struggled, and I have failed.

"You're not doing yourself any favors slobbering in front of the TV all day," Rob complains.

I lift my legs onto the couch and lie back. "It's research."

He stares at the screen. *"Grey's Anatomy?"*

"It's research," I repeat. "Wait till you see what happens to my main character during surgery."

"I'm looking forward to it. When will you get the manuscript to me?"

I say nothing, because I have no idea. Rob shoves his hands in his pockets and paces around my study. "This isn't good, Ward. You being stuck like this again."

My jaw tightens. "It's not like that," I throw back. "I'm not in that same hellhole I was in all those years ago." This isn't like *that*. "Don't worry about the interviews and shit. I'll be okay by then."

"You need to write the book first!" He points at me. "When you clean up, when you take care of yourself, you come up looking good. When you look good, you feel good. It doesn't matter what you say in your interviews because most of those women readers of yours, they like that you brush up real good."

I groan.

"It's a damn shame that you look like a slob right now." He throws me a look that is soaked in disapproval. "When was the last time you shaved, or got a haircut? When was the last time you left the house?"

I lie. "Last week." It was two months ago, when I needed to get into my psychotically deranged murderer's head. I prowled around the streets of New Orleans in the early hours of the morning, trying to get into character.

"Last week?" Rob's tone indicates he doesn't believe me for one moment. "To do what?"

"Have a cup of coffee." Being a writer means that lies come easily. Making stuff up for a living is a skill that comes in handy in real life.

"You expect me to believe that you went outside and sat in a coffee shop and had a cup of coffee, surrounded by people? You? Ward Maddox, the reclusive, hermit author?"

"Yeah, I had coffee. That's what I did." I rest my hand on my stomach and feel the soft, marshmallowy flesh. I have packed on a few pounds too many. "I replotted the ending, then I had to go back and change the middle, and then I hit a bar and restaurant in the evening." I lie again. He knows me too well and will see right through me.

If I could have things my way, I would never leave my writing cave. That's why I bought one of the most expensive and beautiful of houses here. A twelve-bedroom home with chandeliers and fireplaces in each room, stained glass windows and elaborate architecture. This is my castle. A place where I reign, where I am at my happiest.

A place where I feel safe.

Good for nothing piece of shit. That's what my stepdad called me. The bastard would turn in his grave if he could see me now. I wish my mom had come here and seen my home and what I made of myself. She could have lived here, I even asked her to even though she didn't deserve an ounce of my kindness. She turned me down, and we barely saw each another over the years.

"Yeah, sure you did." Rob stares out of the window. "You also brought home a beautiful woman you picked up at said bar and spent the whole night showing her a good time."

Bastard.

Now he's messing with me. I can tell he's annoyed because it's not like him to bring up that stuff. He knows I'm cautious around women. Dating a basket case will do that to you. Sometimes I wonder if I am always drawn to insane people. Or maybe they are drawn to me because of what I write?

Rob stares at me as if he knows everything about me. And the problem is he does. This guy, who is supposed to be my agent, has become the only person I ever have any proper contact with.

"How many pages have you written?"

This is the question I've been dreading. "Six."

"Today?"

I laugh, because that is hilarious. "Today?" Hell, no. "Six in *total*."

His brows squish together like angry caterpillars. "In total?" He massages his temple. "You can't afford to miss your deadline."

I never miss my deadline. Unless I'm in a funk. "I'll get it done." But I've been in this funk for months.

"That's what you said last time." Rob knows what it does to me. He's helped me through it before.

"I will get it done."

He strides towards me. "Damn straight you will. I've made arrangements."

I sit up slowly. He said something about Chicago. No

way am I leaving my house, especially to go *there* of all places. "I'll get it done," I insist. I don't want to hear what he has to say.

He nods. "You will. In Chicago."

"No."

"Yes."

"Hell, no."

Rob scratches his eyebrow. "James Garvey approached me. Wants me to represent him."

"And?" I clench my teeth and wonder why the guy needs a new agent. I can't stop another author from wanting Rob to represent them. But James Garvey hates me too. Considers me to be an upstart. That's because he's in his sixties, and I've just turned forty-one. He and I often compete for the number one slot on the New York Times Bestseller list.

"I'm just letting you know. Say what you want about him, but the guy is prolific He's written three books this year, and he had a heart attack two years ago. He managed it somehow."

I clap my hands together mockingly. "Let's hear it for James Garvey."

Rob looks at me, and his eyes trail down me from top to toe. "If you're not careful, you're going to end up with a heart attack. Maybe even a stroke. Sitting down all day isn't good for you."

"I used to take care of myself." I used to be good. Good diet, I hardly touch alcohol, and I'd work out regularly. That was until my mom got sick and summoned me to her deathbed. I went running, like a fool.

"Then what's gone and happened to you again?" He looks genuinely concerned.

I don't want to talk about it. "If you want to represent Garvey that's your call."

"I don't want to represent too many authors. Sally wants me to slow down and take it easy. We want to vacation more and spend more time with the grandchildren." He makes me feel as if I'm too much trouble. "I don't want you to die on me, Ward. Hearing about Garvey's health scare, and seeing you," he jerks his chin at me, immediately making me feel self-conscious, "it worries me. I've made a decision."

I lift an eyebrow and brace myself because it involves Chicago. He knows I hate that city. I'm surprised that he's suggested it.

"You need to get back on track, Ward. This writer's block you've been fighting has gone on too long. You look out of shape and you sound unmotivated. Freya says you wander around the house all day—"

"You grilled my housekeeper?"

"I can't rely on you to give me all the facts."

I manage to stare at him without blinking. It's frightening how well he knows me.

Freya has been with me for years. The stern but efficient housekeeper is the only person I see on a daily basis. She has the key to the house, and is there by the time I wake up, right through until the evening, when she has my evening meal ready.

Sometimes she brings her ten-year-old grandson along with her. I'm worried she's going to leave me. I don't want to think about replacing her. She's irreplaceable. She doesn't talk much, I barely notice when she's around because she hardly makes a sound. She makes my meals, takes care of my laundry, and cleans all the rooms slowly, one room at a time. I don't want a cleaning company. I don't want a live-in cook, maid or housekeeper. I want my mansion to myself.

"You need to get your act together and finish the book on time, and you need to get into shape for the book tours and interviews, and don't forget the movie premiere."

I groan loudly because that stuff makes me want to retch. The first two books in this trilogy sold millions of copies worldwide. Both are getting made into movies. I should be ecstatic, but I'm not. The publicity, the idea of having to meet other people and pretend to like their company, makes me break out in hives.

"Are you stuck on the plot?"

I'm stuck, but it's not the book. It was facing my mother on her deathbed that did it. She pined for the monster she had married. The man I was supposed to call my dad, but I never did. The man who punished me for it. "You don't need to babysit me, Rob. I'll get over it. I just can't function the way I need to at the moment but I will. I promise you I will."

"Has your magic pen stopped working?" he asks.

"My magic pen is safe and sound." I write everything longhand with my MontBlanc. Notes, first thoughts, basic ideas, the first rough, rough, rough draft. It's all done on paper first.

"I can't lift you up all the time, Ward. It's exhausting, so you're either going to do what I say, or ..."

"Or what?"

"There is no other alternative."

I swipe my hand over my face in exasperation. "You want me to go to Chicago to finish the book there?"

"You've always said your past defined you. Maybe go back and face your demons."

He doesn't know what he's talking about. What makes a child grow up and want to write horror. A stepfather who locked him up in the dark. That's what. But that didn't hurt as much as watching the mother I doted on, who doted on me, change into someone I barely recognized the moment she met him. "Chicago is the last place on Earth I want to visit.'"

"I've rented you a house, nothing as beautiful as this, but I've tried to find you something to your standard. All paid for by you, of course."

"I'd expect nothing less."

"You have bad memories of your time there. You're stuck and, given what's happened, maybe you need to go back to the source of your pain."

"You think, huh?" I pick up the bag of chips from the floor and stick my hand into it.

"And there will be no more of that." Rob nods at my chip bag, then picks up and shakes each of the four empty Coke cans that are lying on the coffee table. "I've got you a personal trainer and I'm still looking into getting you a—"

"A what?"

"A personal trainer, and I'm still looking into getting you a housekeeper."

I draw in a slow and steady breath. "I don't need people. I'm a fucking writer."

"Then write, for goodness' sake, *write*."

"I'll take Freya," I throw back. The only problem is that she'd have to live with me, and I don't want anyone living with me. In fact, the best part of having Freya as my housekeeper is that she goes home every day.

"I've already asked her and she doesn't want to go. She doesn't want to leave New Orleans."

The wily little fox. Rob's been making plans behind my back. "I don't need a personal trainer."

"You've turned into a sloth. You're out of shape. Your face is puffy. When did you last shave?"

I raise a hand to my beard. It's thick and prickly but there is no need for me to shave. Or get a haircut.

"When was the last time you got a haircut?" I knew that would be his next question.

"A couple of months back."

"Try to look presentable. You don't want to scare the new people away."

"I don't think that's necessary. I can work out on my own."

Rob crushes the cans between his hands. "You look like you've been working real hard," he snorts. "You leave next week, and by that time, I'll have found you a housekeeper."

"A housekeeper? I don't need a housekeeper."

"I beg to differ." Rob looks around the room in disgust.

"What I need is a box of donuts," I tell him. I'm being serious, too.

Rob snorts. "You're going to end up looking like a donut if this continues."

"I'm processing things."

"It's been months, Ward. Months. Is this going to be like the last time?"

I close my eyes. The last time I went into freefall, I couldn't write a word for months. I open my eyes and glare at him.

"That's what I thought." He walks towards the door. "Chicago will jolt you into action."

He has no idea. Chicago is full of bad memories.

"Get a haircut. Try to look decent."

CHAPTER TWO

MARI

I've lost everything in the space of a week.

Sitting on a park bench with Jamie, listening to the happy cries of children playing, I wish I could be as carefree and happy as they are.

"It's a lifeline," I say, staring at the sheet of paper with the description of the only job I could find that needed someone urgently. I'm going for an interview tomorrow. "This is so beneath my current pay grade and position," I wail.

"It *was*," Jamie reminds me. "It's only temporary." He accompanied me to the recruitment agency which was my first stop this morning, after he'd helped me move stuff out of my apartment.

"Only temporary," I repeat, feeling the need to reassure myself. Being a housekeeper is not the career move I had in mind, but then, Jamie and I never expected to get laid off when we went to work a few days ago.

"Hey," Jamie nudges me gently. "Think of it like a new start, from everything."

"For you, too." I say, nudging him right back. I'm so grateful for a friend like Jamie. My life has gone to shit in the space of a week. We worked at a small family-run hotel. I was the front desk manager, and Jamie worked behind the scenes, overseeing the hotel's amenities. We had no idea that our boss was taking part in shady money laundering activities. The hotel shut down immediately and all the staff had their contracts terminated.

And not only did I lose my job, and a very well-paid and satisfying job at that, but I found out that Dale, my boyfriend of two years, had been secretly seeing someone else and had gotten her pregnant. I made the mistake of stupidly forgiving him after I found him cheating on me the first time.

Jamie was lucky. He found a job almost the next day, working in the local gym. It's nothing like what he had at the hotel, but at least it's something.

"This will cheer you up." From his backpack, he pulls out a bar of my favorite chocolate. This guy knows all about the small things which make me happy, and right now, I'll grab any slip of happiness that comes my way.

Grinning, I take it from him and waste no time in peeling it open. "Thanks." I offer him some, but he refuses to take it, probably because he knows just how much I love my chocolate.

"I'm going to apply for other jobs in the meantime," I tell him, taking a bite of the chocolate bar.

"Me too. I can do better than where I'm at."

"We can both do better. At least you have a roof over your head."

"You can stay with me for as long as you want, Mari."

He's a good guy. A good friend. Someone I can depend on, unlike the douchebag who was my boyfriend. "You're too kind, but it's not ideal."

"Seriously, you can stay as long as you want."

I ditched Dale, of course. I don't need someone like him in my life, but I wish I'd learned my lesson the first time around. I deserve better. Jamie always says I'm too nice, too forgiving, that I always see the best in people, and that's my downfall. My mom always used to say that, too—back when she was my mom, before the dementia hit and slowly made her forget who I was.

A few days after that? My landlord told me to leave after I couldn't pay the rent for my apartment for the third month running. The well-paid job? I'd started using my income to pay for my mom's nursing home care. She lived with me in my small apartment, but she'd started to have a few falls and then she would get upset when she forgot something. I didn't think anything of it at first, but one day she got lost when coming home from grocery shopping. That's when I took notice.

Over the next few months, she would become irrational and get upset easily. She thought she was seeing people walking around in the house or outside. I was starting to find it difficult.

Then she fell down and broke her arm and while in the hospital, she was diagnosed with stage four dementia. Maybe that's why I couldn't keep an eye on what Dale was up to. I'd stay at his place a lot, but the sicker my mom got, the less I saw him. There was no possibility of him coming to stay at my place. It was tiny as it was. With my mom being there, it was hard.

Still, she was my priority and I nursed her back, but it wasn't easy, what with her new forgetfulness and mood swings. It was when she left the stove on all day that I decided she would be better off in a nursing home. I found a nice assisted-living facility for dementia patients. It was expensive and it didn't take Medicaid, but I had no choice because I didn't want her to be transferred to a state-run nursing home.

It was hard, at first, to explain to her that we couldn't live together anymore. She flits in and out of being 'my mom' and being a stranger. The trick, and the gift, the beauty, is to have her for as long as possible being my mom. And this week, this week out of hell, I was told that she has stage five dementia.

It's good that she's in a nursing home, having someone keep an eye on her all the time is less worrisome for me, but I still worry. She's only been there a few months, and I've been paying to keep her there, thinking that the promotion I was going to get was going to come through. My boss had told me it was. And then the crook himself messed things up for us all.

I'd been paying a third of my rent for the past few months, needing to get my mom settled but my landlord got impatient and threw me out.

"Why so quiet?"

"My life is a shitshow."

"It's not. This, right now, your life and everything that's happened, this is what's supposed to happen. This is where you're supposed to be. Hopefully, you'll learn this time."

I narrow my eyes at him. "Learn what?" I scoff. "Being broke, discovering my mom's dementia is worse than I thought? Losing my job? Having a cheating boyfriend?"

"That you are too nice, too forgiving, too ..." He pauses, then presses his lips together, as if he doesn't want to say.

"Say it."

"You're too reckless, especially when it comes to guys. You can do better. Dale is a jerk. He was a jerk the first time he cheated on you, and now he's a ..." He shakes his head, and I can tell he wants to swear.

"I fell in love," I say, putting the chocolate wrapper in my pocket now that I've gobbled it all up greedily. I was in love. I am reckless, perhaps. I give my heart too easily, without thinking. I don't second-guess when my insides go all mushy, or when someone kisses me and my toes curl. I'm not a hussy, but I can't *not* react at times like this. And Dale was so handsome and wonderful in the beginning.

"Who's it with?" he asks. "The interview tomorrow? A family with kids?"

"I think it's a guy. A businessman." That's what the recruitment consultant told me. She said it was a new job placement that came up and they didn't have many details about it yet. I look at him and widen my eyes, exaggerating my very scared face. "A perv, you think?"

Now Jamie looks worried. "I'll come with you, if you want."

"To the interview? How stupid would that look?"

"The offer's there if you want."

"I'll be okay. I'm a grown woman. It's just an interview. Oh, my goodness!" I squint at the paper with his address as it hits me. "He lives in the Gold Coast area."

Jamie's eyes widen.

The famed Gold Coast is one of Chicago's most prestigious areas. Suddenly, my woes have evaporated and I feel uplifted. In the nightmare of my week, this new revelation is as shiny as a diamond. But Jamie stares at me as if there's an axe murderer standing behind me. "Maybe you shouldn't go alone."

"I'm going, and I'll call you before I go in, and as soon as I come out, okay?"

"Deal."

A red football bounces towards us. I look over to see a bunch of teens yell at us to kick it back so I get up and give the ball a hefty kick. Too bad it shoots off in the wrong direction, about five yards wide of where the guys are.

"And remember, you have a lot going on at the moment. Don't worry about finding a place to stay. You can stay with me for as long as you want."

"Awww." I squeeze his arm slightly. "You're very sweet."

"Just trying to help you out," he mumbles, before moving his arm and looking away.

Now I've upset him. This is a strange thing, us being such good friends. He hasn't been lucky with women either, though as far as I know no one has cheated on him. We went out as a foursome once last year, and I met his girlfriend, but they split up a few months ago and he never really gave me a reason why.

Me sleeping on his couch might raise eyebrows with some of my friends, or even my mom, depending on what sort of mood she's in and if she remembers who I am, but it's the only way my life works right now.

"I worry about you," says Jamie, staring at me pensively.

"Awww, stop that. You have plenty of worries of your own without adding me to the list."

CHAPTER THREE

MARI

I stare at the fancy four-story house and I pray that I get the job. I pay the taxi driver and climb out with my mouth open in awe. It's got one of those limestone facades, cream-colored brickwork, and shiny, sparkling expensive-looking windows. I catch a glimpse of a chandelier sparkling from one of the ground-floor windows.

My whole world has completely topsy-turvied, from having to leave my tiny apartment, to walking in to this glamorous new world.

I could work here for a few months.

I could be a housekeeper.

I ring the doorbell, my heart thumping as if I've sprinted the last mile. I'm not a nervous woman. I'm used to dealing with difficult customers, people who are rich, and feel entitled. While being a housekeeper isn't something I've aspired to, this job is going to be a cinch. Though I won't tell any of my friends, aside from Jamie, about it.

The door opens and a friendly-looking older gentleman opens the door. The skin around his eyes crinkles as he gives me a warm, friendly smile. I feel relieved because he looks normal and nothing like the axe murderer my imagination had served up.

"Hi." I smile back and extend my hand. "Nice to meet you," I say, putting on my best voice. I'm always professional, but a glance at the mansion and now seeing what it looks like inside makes me nervous.

I assume that he is a rich banker type, maybe someone who travels a lot, or is here for a few months. Maybe he has been sent to work here from someplace else, which would explain no mention of a wife or family.

"Pleased to meet you, Miss Evers," he says, shaking my hand before closing the door as I step inside to admire another chandelier which hangs just above me in the large entrance hall. The walls are beige colored, and there is a gorgeous rug on the floor. Everything in here, even the soft wall lighting, reeks of money. "Marianne Evers," I say, forcing myself to stop gawking at the surroundings, "but people call me Mari."

"I'm Rob. Let's go into the kitchen, shall we? This shouldn't take long."

I follow him into a kitchen that is bigger than my entire apartment. The cabinets are a dark blue wood. I've never seen anything like them. Sparkling wine and champagne glasses glisten behind squeaky clean shiny cupboard windows. Silver domed lights hang over the white marble kitchen island.

It looks brand new, squeaky clean and spotless.

"This is beautiful," I say, looking around me. It's a whole new world. I want to live here, I've already decided.

Rob looks at his watch. "When can you start?"

"Excuse me?"

"I read your resume, and the agency confirmed that the hotel you worked at suddenly closed down."

I'm impressed by his research. "I lost my job last week. The hotel where I worked shut down instantly. It put a lot of people out."

"And you were a manager?" he asks. I'm prepared for this. I knew I would be overqualified for the role. "Yes, but I don't mind this job. I need something quickly. I'm adaptable and I'm good at accomplishing things. I'm also resourceful, hard-working, I can—"

"Relax. You seem to be perfect."

My jaw falls open. He barely knows me.

He clears his throat. "My client needs someone quickly," he says, as if he can read my mind.

"Your client?" A chill ices through me. It suddenly strikes me that this guy is not who I will be working for.

"He's here, he's, uh ..." Rob coughs lightly and looks over his shoulder. My heart starts to race. Something feels off. If the client is here, why isn't he interviewing me? And what is Rob's role then? He clears his throat again which sets me further on edge. "My client isn't the easiest person to get along with."

"I thought you were the client?" I say nervously, and then I glance around, expecting someone to jump out.

"I shouldn't even be doing this. I'm a literary agent." He laughs to himself as if he's enjoying his own private joke. "You'll be working for Ward Maddox." He waits, observing my reaction. I'm not sure what I'm supposed to do. The name rings a bell, but only because it sounds slightly odd, strong, unusual. I think I've heard of it before, but I can't place where.

"You don't know of him?" Rob asks. "The horror writer. He wrote *The Dark Woods* and *The Attic*."

I shake my head. I don't read horror. I can't abide gore.

"What do you like to read?"

"Romance, mainly," I say, and then, because I don't want him to judge me, "also thrillers and mysteries." Which is true, but I wish I hadn't felt the need to say that.

"Ward is a best-selling horror writer." He gets up and disappears, before returning with a bunch of hardback books which he lays out on the island.

"Ah, yes." I nod. I've seen those books before. They're distinctive. They were everywhere at one point. "Didn't they make a movie about this?" I say, picking up *The Attic*. I'm trying to remember what the author looks like, but I can't. I don't think I've ever seen him before. Horror isn't my genre, so I would never read these books. I turn to the book's back, expecting to see a picture but there isn't one.

"Of *The Attic*? Yes. And *The Dark Woods*, although that was written many years later, the movie for that releases this year. Ward is currently writing the third book in that trilogy now."

"Oh." I'm going to be working for a horror writer. A famous, best-selling author. *Of horror*. My week couldn't get any more surreal.

"Hopefully, Ward will get his mojo back and finish this book on time." Rob crosses his fingers for luck. "Then we can have another New York Times Bestseller."

I'm sure it's a great thing, but I'm anxious to meet the guy now. A ball of excitement paws through my stomach. This is a great thing. A new journey. "So, I'm going to be a housekeeper for him?"

"Yes."

"You've got the job," he tells me, glancing at his watch again.

"What?" I blurt out, shocked. "Just like that?"

"I need to go. I'm going to be late for my flight."

"But we haven't agreed to terms and conditions."

"I'll have the contract emailed to you when I get home."

"But, but, my hours, my duties, you didn't tell me anything—"

"I'm sorry. This must seem strange to you. It's a strange situation."

"You've said the word 'strange' a few times now. I'm getting scared."

He laughs. "Not backing out, are you?"

"No, but I—"

"Good."

"Can you start now?"

I scoff, out of sheer shock. "I was supposed to find a place to live," I start to explain, but he already looks as if he's in a rush to go.

"I've had a hard time finding someone at such short notice. Someone who could fit the part."

I swallow. "What part?"

"Ward is fussy. He's moody, and temperamental, and keeps to himself. He's rude and short-tempered."

"You're not selling this to me," I say, and feel my heart thumping beneath my ribcage. I look around at the opulence of the mansion, and my brain is figuring out whether this is worth it.

What other choice do I have?

"I need to find a place to stay." It's true. After the interview, I was going to look around and find the cheapest, most habitable place to live in.

Rob tilts his head up. "You don't have anywhere to stay?"

"I lost my job, got thrown out of my apartment, my mom's in a nursing home and ..." I stop myself from humiliation. This guy doesn't want to know my story, and I'm not the kind of woman who willfully doles it out. I don't know what's come over me. I've lost my mind just being here.

"You can stay here."

"What?" My voice is shaky.

"You can stay here. This place is too big for one person. It's got seven bedrooms, eleven bathrooms, a library, a study, a—"

"Eleven bathrooms?" My mind explodes. Who the hell needs eleven bathrooms? And only seven bedrooms? It doesn't make sense.

"This isn't Ward's house. I've rented it for him for a few months. He needs to get the book finished. He'll have a personal trainer coming in every day, and you to cook and make sure the house is clean. You'll barely see him."

"It's just me and him living here?" My heart skips a beat at the thought that I'm going to be living in a sprawling mansion with a horror writer.

"There's a personal trainer, but he won't live here. Ward doesn't like people."

I almost choke in response. "I don't have to live here," I reply. In fact, I don't even need this job. I'll find something else.

"I'll double your salary."

"You'll double my salary?" My heart almost misses a beat. "Why would you do that?"

"I'm not paying you, I'm only the agent. The money is coming from Ward."

"You sound desperate to find a housekeeper."

"This guy is falling to pieces. I can't help him. I don't expect you to help him other than to cook and clean, and between you and the personal trainer—" he pauses, then looks towards the door, "Trevor, he should be finishing up now. Between the two of you, you might just scare Ward enough for him to hide in his writing cave and finish the damn book. That's all I want."

"Double?" I say weakly, partly because I'm speechless that he could double my wages so easily. He might as well have been a genie that popped out of a lamp. I start to wonder if I'll get two more wishes.

"Double, and you stay. Don't worry. I'll figure everything out." He flashes me a cheesy smile. "He's harmless, and a recluse. You won't see him. He's also a slob. Messy and unmotivated. I need you to make sure he eats well and healthily. Trevor is here, hopefully doing a workout but I need to leave this city. I don't have time to find anyone else, and goodness knows Ward's not going to do a thing about it."

The door flies wide open and a man charges in, all hair and wild eyes. "I am *not* listening to that fucking man!" he growls.

Rob lets out a slow exhale as he stands. "Mari, meet Ward Maddox, world famous horror author extraordinaire."

The beast—because this is exactly what he looks like—turns and stares at me and I almost stumble back from the shock of his angry gaze. There's a growth on his face, a good three inches of thick, prickly beard. His hair is long and unruly, longer than a man's hair should be. He pushes it back from his face with a sweep of his hand. Menacing eyes, framed by dark eyebrows stare at me. He's wearing shorts and a t-shirt which make him look flabby next to the other guy who's just walked in. He too is dressed for the gym, but he is toned, and muscular, and fit. The contrast between the two couldn't be more prominent.

"I don't need this," Ward tells Rob in an angry tone. "I have words to write."

"And how many have you written?" Rob asks calmly.

"That's not the point. If I didn't have this bullshit stuck in my schedule—"

"It's an hour," Rob points out. "An hour, right?" he asks the other guy who I assume must be the personal trainer.

"An hour, but I'm happy to do more, just say the word."

"Let's stick with the hour for now," says Rob, expertly ignoring Ward. "Trevor, meet Mari, the new housekeeper."

Before Trevor can move forward to shake my hand, Ward explodes.

"*She's* the new housekeeper?" He doesn't so much look at me as give me the evil eye. His curt reply startles me. First of all because I assumed that all people who were famous were nice, and secondly, because I've done nothing wrong. The guy barely knows me.

"We agreed to this," Rob says calmly. "You need structure."

"This messes up my timetable." Ward gesticulates with his hand, waving it in the direction of me and Trevor. Trevor gives me an apologetic smile.

"Excuse us," Rob walks out with the writer in tow, leaving just me and the gym guy.

"Welcome aboard," Trevor says warmly, then shakes my hand. I take an instant liking to him.

"Is he always like this?" I ask.

"This is my second day. So far, yes. He was like this yesterday."

He's going to be worse than the most difficult customers

I've dealt with at the hotel. Still, I've always been good at my job, and I see Ward Maddox as a challenge. "Are you staying here?" I ask Trevor. I would feel so much safer with someone else under this roof, instead of it being just me and the psycho. Having met him, and knowing that Ward is a horror writer, fills me with dread.

"God, no. I'm only supposed to give him a daily workout on weekdays. I'm supposed to encourage him to get into shape. Encourage him to go for a run or do a workout." He snorts. "It would be a miracle if I could get the guy to get up off the couch." He goes on to tell me about yesterday's botched training session. "At least he got dressed today," Trevor adds. "Yesterday he was floating around in his robe."

"Why does Rob even bother?" I ask, finding the whole thing ridiculous.

Trevor shrugs. "As long as I'm getting paid, I won't complain. I've been paid and the dude hasn't even done one class. What are your duties?"

"To cook and clean." I'm not even sure I want the job now.

"And you're staying here?" Trevor asks, looking worried.

I feel his worry. A knot forms in my belly and I consider my original plan to start looking for an apartment. But then I remember that Rob doubled my salary on the spot, without even batting an eyelid.

I can do this. If the money is this good, I *have* to do this, and it's only a temporary contract. For a few months.

Even I can put up with that caveman for a few months.

CHAPTER FOUR

WARD

"Let me remind you, I'm doing this as a favor because you don't want to deal with these people." Rob's lips clench tightly as he closes the door to my writing room. "Can't you at least open the blinds?" he asks. "How the hell do you write in here when it's so dark?"

"You forced me to move here, at least have the decency to let me choose my writing environment."

This house is too fancy, too bright, too beige and too modern. It's not me. I like darkness. I'm used to it now. My home in New Orleans is stuck back in time. Four-poster beds, beautiful windows, rich, detailed architecture. My writing cave there is dark wood, rich red curtains, a thick blood red carpet. Those things create the perfect setting in which I can write.

I have struggled with the brightness of this room, but at least it has a fire and a couch. I despise the light gray carpet, but if I keep the blinds drawn, and light a few lamps, I can partially create the right mood for me to write in.

Not that it's helped. I've only been here a few days and my skin is crawling with the thought of having to talk to these surplus people I don't need. "Is this really necessary?" I struggle not to explode, and try to keep my voice as neutral as I can.

"It hasn't worked. You've written six pages in how many months?" Rob paces around the room. "Your mother died. I understand this might have raked up all sorts of emotions."

I inhale deeply. I'm dealing with it, in my own way. Shutting down, closing off more than usual. Rob doesn't understand, and what he's done has only made things worse. "Just get rid of them. Please. I can work better if it's just me. I'll get the book finished on time. I'm good with deadlines."

Rob lifts his nose and pins me with a deathly stare. "You can't. You couldn't even get up off the couch, and I have that personal trainer on your back trying to get you to move."

"I hate exercise." I run my hands through my hair which is knotty and long. I've hit rock bottom, even I am aware of this, but I can and I will work through it in my own time.

"It's eleven in the morning and you're still in .... in ... *that* thing." He glares at me as if I'm wearing a thong.

"It's a robe and it's comfortable," I reply defensively.

Rob clenches his fist. "You should know, Ward, that this is not what I'm supposed to do. I'm not supposed to babysit you."

"You don't have to babysit me. I'll get my shit together. I'll get the book done."

"If you wanted to, you would have by now."

I have a better idea. "I'll stay here. You're right, maybe being back in Chicago might help."

"That's better. Go back to your roots and face your past."

That I won't do. "Get rid of those two."

Rob looks at his watch. "Can't do, and I'm not arguing about that. I need to be back in New York. Four days here has been too long." He points a finger at me. "I only did this to help you. You need a manager more than you need me."

"I don't want a manager." Rob has been a godsend, and I don't want to piss him off.

"You have a personal trainer, and you have a housekeeper. When I next see you, I'd better see a new and improved version of you, and I want the first draft finished."

"I can do that. It'll be done. Don't worry."

He moves towards the door and says something that really pisses me off. "By the way, the new housekeeper, she'll be living here."

"What?"

"She needs a place to stay. She said she needed a week to find a place to stay. I told her she could stay here."

He knows I hate people. He knows I hate having anyone around. He *knows*. "Why the hell would you do that?"

"You want the truth? Because I'm worried about you."

"I'm fine." As if having that woman living here is going to help me.

"You were a mess last time, Ward."

"Last time was different." Last time I was in love with a woman who was crazy.

"This is not negotiable."

I follow him out into the entrance hall. "This isn't going to work," I tell him.

"Make it work. Face your demons. Write the damn book."

. . .

MARI

Trevor and I are laughing when the others walk back into the kitchen. I'm holding one of Ward's books and it must look as if we're laughing about that. Feeling guilty, I quickly put the book down.

"Ward is ready for your training session," Rob says. Ward has a scowl on his face. He looks anything but ready. Or maybe he always looks that miserable.

"Good luck," Trevor whispers under his breath as he walks away.

"Is he always this difficult?" I ask when it's just me and Rob. He slips on his jacket and looks as if he's ready to leave.

"He's an acquired taste. He takes some getting used to. Stay out of his way, and he'll stay out of yours." He chuckles. "Get him a box of donuts if you really want to make a good impression."

"But what am I supposed to *do*? What do I cook? Is there a cleaning schedule? Where are the cleaning supplies?"

"You look like a smart woman. You'll figure it out."

I rush after him. "What does he eat? Where do I buy the food? What hours am I supposed to—"

He lets out a groan, and from that one simple sound, I can tell that this guy doesn't have it all figured out. This is as new for him as it is for me. He grabs his briefcase and looks at his watch again. "Take this," he slides a business card out of his jacket pocket. "Call me if you have any questions."

"I have questions now!"

"I have a plane to catch, and I don't want to miss it. I've been stuck here for four days waiting to find a housekeeper. You're perfect for the job."

Lucky me. I feel as if Rob has washed his hands of Ward and dumped his duty to me. I rush towards the door as he prepares to make his exit. He can't leave me alone in this house with that beast.

"I'm not sure I want this job." It's a last-ditch attempt because my fear has overtaken me.

Rob spins around fast. "You have to take this job."

"Why?"

"Because I need you to do this. That guy can be a piece of hard work. He's not always like this, but ..." he shrugs. "His mother died last year and the guy is a mess. He won't talk about it, but he's had stuff to deal with. Problem is he also has a book to finish. This is my way of getting him to finish it. Him getting fit and back in shape wouldn't be a bad thing either," he mumbles.

My head is spinning and a trickle of compassion oozes from my heart. He lost his mom? I feel sorry for him because caring for my mom and losing her to dementia has ripped a hole in my heart.

"Fine then. I'll stay." Let's face it, what other choice do I have?

"It's only temporary. Until he finishes the book."

"Easy enough for you to say."

"Call me if you need anything, or," he pauses then looks at me, "or if you can't get anything out of him."

"You haven't even shown me to my room or taken me around the house. I don't even know where everything is."

He lets out an anguished groan. "I cannot miss my

flight. I'll call Ward and get him to show you around. You might as well bring your things over as soon as possible. Goodbye, and good luck."

I wonder how much of that good luck I'm going to need.

CHAPTER FIVE

MARI

Excitement mingles with fear and apprehension as I make my way back to Jamie's place. I have to start packing. I don't want to take much, even though I could move all of my things into the mansion and the author guy wouldn't even notice.

I think about it for a few seconds and let the idea go. Ward Maddox is a rude, feral, short-tempered man.

I don't want to give him ammunition to get rid of me. As things stand, he already seems to hate me being there.

I throw things into my suitcase and my shoes and toiletries into another bag. I don't want to take a lot, which means most of my life's belongings will stay here at Jamie's place. He hasn't complained one bit. Jamie has been the kindest soul to me, letting me keep most of my stuff here. His apartment isn't as tiny as mine, but that's not the point. The point is I have so much stuff. I had to take everything with me when the landlord told me to leave. I've got a lot of my mom's things with me as well. A part of me thinks she'll come home. In my head, I tell myself that her nursing home stay is temporary. That one day I'll have a better job and I might be able to bring her back home, when I have a home, and then I'll be able to hire a private nurse for her. My imagination goes wild sometimes.

I bet I could match Ward Maddox when it comes to making things up, though I wouldn't want to fill my head with gory things. It has to be shiny, happy things in my world. Unfortunately, right now, my world is anything but that.

I don't want to dwell too much on my current predicament: that I've landed a job in a beautiful home, with a beautiful salary. The nice things are overshadowed by the beast of a man I will be living with.

I can't wait to tell Jamie.

He walks in a few hours later and sees my suitcase by the door.

"What's this?" he asks, glancing at me with a dour face.

"I got the job!"

"Already? This is the interview you went to today?"

I nod excitedly. "Incredible, right?" I clap my hands together, trying to make myself feel good about this even though it dawned on me earlier that I'll be living with a total stranger, and a guy who's not really nice at all. The house might be a luxurious haven but this guy looks scary.

"You were offered the job on the spot?"

"Uh-huh."

"Wow." Jamie takes his backpack off his shoulder and leans against the door, as if the shock of my news isn't what he wanted to hear. I expected more from him. A little bit of excitement for me, given the bad week I've had. But even when I tell him that the guy offered to double my wages, he doesn't flinch. "Aren't you worried about that?" he asks, adding more fuel to the fire that is my worry.

"Guess who the mystery man is?" I ask him, "the guy who I'll be cooking and cleaning for?"

He looks confused. "I have no idea."

"He's someone famous. Someone world famous."

Jamie's eyes widen. "World famous?"

"Not like a movie star or anything. Someone more low-key. You might know of him though."

He looks at me as if I've asked him to marry me.

"Ward Maddox," I pause and let that sink in. Jamie blinks twice.

"*The* Ward Maddox? The guy who wrote *The Attic?* The guy who writes horror?"

I nod, relieved to get some sort of reaction from him. "Isn't it exciting?"

Now he's buoyed up and asks me all sorts of questions. I answer them as best as I can, while leaving out all negative stuff about Ward. I tell him everything about the house, the parts of it that I have seen.

Later, I pack my belongings into my car, but Jamie insists on coming with me to help.

Somehow, having Jamie by my side for as long as possible, is a great comfort to me.

WARD

This situation stinks like a rat's ass.

What the hell am I doing here in this house that isn't even mine?

With two people I barely know?

Screw Rob.

I can replace him in a heartbeat. There are enough New York agents who would gladly take me on.

If only it was that simple.

Rob is more like a friend.

I'm stuck with him or, rather, he's stuck with me.

Screw Rob.

How will I survive the next few months? He's left me with no choice but to get on with it, but he hasn't made it any easier. He likes to think he's helping me, but he's not. This book won't get written any faster even with this new setup.

Like I told Trevor, the trainer guy, I'm up for exercising. I used to do it before. My career will kill me. Sitting at a desk all day long is bad for my health. I'm aware of the problems. I just can't fix everything at once. I can't write and get healthy and fit when I'm in a funk. I told Trevor that I need to take things slowly. He showed me around the entire gym room and told me how each piece of gym equipment is used—like I don't already know. He's a cocky, arrogant guy. I'm not stupid. I see him judging me. Just because he's got the muscles, and I have the flab. I can look like him, I have had that type of physique, maybe not as pumped as him, but not far off. If I choose to put my mind to it, I can get it back, but my mind has been elsewhere, lately.

When your mother stops loving you at a young age, and you live your whole life waiting for her to say she made a mistake, waiting for her to say she was sorry, straining your ears to hear her beg for forgiveness—and none of this happens, it sinks you into a funk so big that nothing and no one can help you dig your way out.

Today's training session was a waste of time. I didn't make any progress, and I didn't really work out. Rob thinks he can click his fingers and I can magically transform and spring into action.

I fucking can't.

After Trevor leaves, I return to my den. There's no need to shower because I haven't worked up a sweat, but now there's something else to worry about. I can't concentrate because *she's* here.

Somewhere.

The new housekeeper. Rob told me to show her to her room and to give her a quick tour of the house.

The bastard.

As much as I love and respect the guy, he's made more work for me. I haven't decided which room to allocate her and I'll wait for her to come to me. At least the house is big and there are plenty of rooms so I won't have to run into her.

I sit down to write but the words don't come easily. Too much has happened today. Rob doesn't understand how much this new setup is going to derail me. I was already struggling to do that simple task—sit down at my desk, put my favorite pen in my hands, and start writing, always on loose sheets of paper, with my notebook of plot points and characters to hand.

I always write a few chapters longhand, then let that sit before I go back and tweak it. Later, I type it up into my computer for what will form my first draft, and I flesh and deepen things as I type. I chisel at some things that are not needed. Working this way, the story transforms, changing, and growing, and becoming a story worth telling. Once the first draft is complete, I'll read it again, and fix it, then read it some more, and fix it some more. I do this for as long as it takes to perfect the idea that was once in my head as it takes form on paper. And during that entire time, nobody but me gets to read it.

But I haven't been able to do this since my mother died.

Those six pages are all that I've managed.

With these new changes to my day, I am determined to finish this book so that I can get back home to my normal routine and get my life back. I look through the loose sheets of paper and read through what I've written.

It's garbage.

Then I look through my notebook hoping for inspiration but the doorbell rings. The interruption knives through my concentration. I glance at the clock and am shocked to see that it is late evening. I've lost track of time. The doorbell rings again, and I ignore it.

The new housekeeper has already failed in her first task. "Mary!" I roar, not wanting to get up. She won't hear me. The house is too big and she could be anywhere. I'm going to need a bell or something to summon her with. Or get a pair of walkie-talkies so that I won't have to physically look for her.

"Answer the goddamn door!" I bellow, my rage simmering as I am forced to leave the cocoon of my study.

I hear a shout and banging on the door. I head towards it and open the damn thing myself. Two curious faces stare back at me. One of those faces belongs to the new housekeeper. What the hell is she doing outside?

"It's Ma-ree," she says.

"What?"

"It's not Mary. Ma-ree."

I blink at this woman telling me how to pronounce her name. This woman who should not be here. This woman I am stuck with as a punishment from Rob who foolishly thinks it will help me to finish my book.

Now there's an incentive if ever I needed one.

"I thought you were inside. Where did you go?" My eyes shift to the guy standing next to her.

"I had to get my stuff. Rob told me to move in as soon as possible."

"I bet he did," I grumble.

"This is Jamie," she says quickly, introducing me to the grinning idiot. He's had a smile on his face the entire time. I sense that any moment now he's going to ask for my autograph or a selfie. Of course, I'll have to decline both.

"Nice to meet you, Mr. Maddox." The guy holds out his hand. I refuse to take it, and I turn away. I have words to write.

Or words to *pretend* to write.

Or a chair to try to sit in and pretend to look busy in.

I walk away to return to my den and leave them talking. She tells him she'll be fine but by the tone of his voice, the guy doesn't seem to think so. Then the door closes, just as I approach the door to my study.

"Wait!" The housekeeper's loud yelp pierces through me, forcing me to turn around.

This.

This is what I did not want.

Or need.

Tight-lipped, I turn around and glare at her.

"These are for you." She hands me a bag which I refuse to take.

"What is it?"

"Take a look, you might like it." She laughs nervously.

I still refuse to take it. "What is it?"

She looks at me, wide-eyed and nervous. I can smell her fear.

"It's something she brought for you," her friend says.

"Donuts. Rob said you liked them," she explains.

I take the bag and peek inside. I recognize the box. It's fancy looking and from one of the most expensive bakeries in the city. I'm curious as to why she went to so much trouble. "Donuts?" I say.

"You like them?" Her eager expression wills me to like them. I dislike neediness in people. I dislike people, full stop, but neediness pisses me off completely. "I don't know."

"Haven't you tried these ones before?" She's eager to please me.

"Can't say I have," I lie.

"These are supposed to be the best—"

"I guess Mr. Maddox will try them in time." Her friend puts a restraining hand on her arm.

The housekeeper steps back, looking disappointed. "I don't know where my room is. Rob said you would show me. This is a beautiful house, by the way. I've never stayed in a place so beautiful be—"

"Please stop talking."

She clamps her mouth shut.

"I can't think with so much noise."

She looks shocked. "But I don't know what my duties are. Rob didn't have time to show me much."

This is the shit I shouldn't be dealing with. I scowl back at her.

"He had to rush off. He said you would do it. He had a flight to catch and he was in a rush, so I—"

"Please! Stop talking." I swipe a hand across my face. The woman will be the death of me before I get to the end of my book. I gape at her as if all the energy has been sucked out of my body, and it has been, *almost*, or will be, *soon*.

What have you done, Rob?

I am not used to living with someone. I'm not used to being around people. I am not used to being told what to do. I live in fictional worlds with fictional characters. It's safer that way. Most of all, I despise having to show this woman around.

I miss Freya. She makes my food and leaves it in the kitchen. The house is always clean. We can go weeks without passing one another even though she comes every week day.

It works.

This isn't going to. For a start, this one talks too much. She's going to kill my concentration.

"If you're busy, writing and all, I can make my own way to my room. Just tell me which one it is. I don't want to bother you too much. Rob said you had a book to ..." She's doing it again, talking too much, but as I watch her silently, her voice trails away. She's getting the hint.

"That's better," I say.

I now have a choice. I can either show her around or go back to my study and stare at the blank page.

So I take the easy option.

CHAPTER SIX

MARI

With my suitcase in my hand, I follow him around like an unwanted dog he is trying to lose. He rushes around, although 'races' is the wrong word, given his heavy build.

The house is beautiful. He shows me around downstairs.

"I expect my writing room to be dusted and cleaned every day, preferably when I'm not in it."

"When will that be?"

"It varies. I can't give you an exact time."

I try not to say something smart and sassy back, even though I'm privately pissed that he expects me to be at his beck and call.

"Don't mess with things on my desk. Leave things as you find them. Don't read anything. I don't want to have to stow things away and get them back out again, it messes with my process."

"Got it."

He leads me into a room which has the biggest TV I've ever seen. This room is littered with chip bags, donut boxes and drink cartons and cans. It's four times bigger than my bedroom was in my last apartment. As I glance across, I can see into the kitchen. "Sometimes I like to relax in here," he says, as I watch and wait to see if he'll bend down to pick up the trash from the floor. He doesn't. "There's a TV in your room."

"Oh, so I can't watch TV in here?"

He looks taken aback. "You're not on vacation. You have a job to do here."

I open my mouth, then close it quickly before I say something else I will regret. He's so rude. I wish I hadn't bothered making a detour into town to get him those donuts. He's so unappreciative and nasty.

A tightness forms in my gut as I follow him out of the TV room and into the entrance hall where I should have left my suitcase instead of dragging it around with me everywhere.

I miss Jamie.

He's a real gentleman.

This man is not.

He shows me the other rooms: the place where all the cleaning supplies are kept, and the pantry, the kitchen. He tells me that he will leave me his credit card on the kitchen island and that I can buy what I need and order groceries, and if I prefer to go out, to look online and find out what stores are nearby. Then he shows me the library before opening another door.

"This is my study." He opens the door quickly, and lets me step inside. It's dark in here and such a contrast to the rest of the house. "I need it polished and clean, every surface spotless. And my desk," he walks over to it and slides a finger along the sleek wood, "my desk has to be neat and tidy." I walk over and find myself paying extreme attention because he seems so serious about the matter. "You must not mess up the order of things." He lines up the papers and pencils and pens again, even though they were already neat. "And you must never read anything." He pins me with a ferocious stare that makes me stop breathing. He's expecting an answer, I realize.

"I won't," I say quickly. "I won't read a thing."

"I want everything back in its place."

I nod.

"My pens and pencils. My MontBlanc. This is my lucky pen." He picks it up and examines it before setting it back down again.

Weird.

"You can open the windows to let in some air while you clean, but I want the room left exactly as you found it."

"Understood."

"I don't know anything about you. Rob hired you and took care of all that, but let me be very clear. You are not to read anything I have written."

"You've already mentioned that."

"I'm telling you again."

I have to force myself not to roll my eyes. "Again, I understand."

He ushers me out before closing the door. Then he marches up the stairs and I stand at the bottom, watching him with simmering resentment. Not once did this man offer to take my suitcase from me. Not once did he offer to assist me.

"What are you waiting for?" he asks, turning around when he's a few steps up. There is tension is his voice.

Always. It's like he's permanently annoyed and bitter. He's made it perfectly clear that my presence here is unwanted, but I need this job.

I can't afford for him to get rid of me on a whim, and with Rob gone, it wouldn't surprise me if this guy tries to look for any opportunity to get rid of me.

How wrong I was. How disappointed Jamie will be when I tell him what this guy is really like. I assumed he would be nice because he was famous and successful, but I was so, so wrong.

"Uh ..." Telling the truth isn't going to help me. "I was admiring the staircase. It's ... it's beautiful, the way it curves around the —"

"Hurry up," he snaps, marching on ahead. "I don't have all day."

I grab my suitcase and bound up the stairs, catching up with him in no time. "I did say you could tell me where my room was and I would find it. I know you have work deadlines and a book to fin—"

"Stop," he growls. "I can't take your constant whimpering."

I have the sudden urge to tell him to shove his job up his huge butt, but I am trapped by my circumstances. My mom depends on me. I'm doing this for her.

And I don't have a better option.

"I'm sorry. I won't talk if it upsets you that mu—"

He turns to me at the top of the stairs. "There you go again." He does a zipping motion with his fingers against his lips. "I can't think when you're constantly yapping."

"But you're not writing now," I protest, noticing his ugly satin robe again. It looks ridiculous and makes him look much older than he is.

"I'm always thinking," he mutters, pointing his finger to

his head. "I'm always thinking of the story. Your voice is like the sound of nails scratching a blackboard."

That's an overdramatic exaggeration. I hate him. I hate him more than I believed was possible. I zip my lips together and resolve not to say another word.

"You only need to clean my room once a week, otherwise you don't need to be on this side of the house."

I nod, then follow him like a sheep as he heads down the other hallway on the left. He opens the first door of many. "Take this one." He flings the door open but doesn't step inside. "I trust it will suffice?"

I step inside, as he switches on the light.

Will this suffice?

My heart leaps for joy. Yes! Yes, it will.

It's huge with the biggest bed I've ever seen, and a dresser, and closets, and another door presumably leading to a bathroom. "This is wonderful!" I cry, my insides jubilant with joy as I walk inside. I set down my suitcase and bags, too excited to speak, but also under strict orders not to.

This is *my* room.

Mine.

For the duration of this prison sentence. Excited, I walk inside and look around and inspect the room. There's a walk-in closet, though I don't have enough clothes to even fill one of the racks. The closets are extra space lined around the room.

Who has this many clothes? Or possessions or things?

I turn around, needing to ask him something, but as I come back out and step into the room, he has disappeared. I run towards the door, and peer down the hallway only to catch a glimpse of the edge of his robe as he turns the corner and disappears.

He didn't tell me what I needed to wear; whether there

was an outfit or uniform I should wear. He hadn't told me anything. I don't know what time he expects breakfast, or what type of food he likes to eat, and ditto the same for lunch and dinner.

I'm in the dark about all of this.

The only thing that makes my stay here palatable is that the house and my room are the most luxurious I've ever had.

It's a shame that the price I must pay for this luxury is to live with that swine.

The next day I wake up bright and early, then lie in bed feeling inexplicably happy. Staring at the ornate lampshade above my head, and the beautiful silky wallpaper around the room, makes me happy. Being surrounded by things of beauty, instead of peeling paint and broken-down things, make for a positive state of mind. I've often had to imagine better things for myself, and the struggle has been real, especially these last few weeks, but today I am really here, living in a multi-million-dollar mansion in the Gold Coast area.

For that privilege alone, I can suffer this position.

I get up and shower and get ready, making the decision to wear what I wore at work: smart clothes, just because I need to feel that I'm 'at work'. Not smart like a blazer, but a blouse and a skirt with my work pumps. Hopefully, I'll find an apron somewhere.

I'm dressed and in the kitchen by 7:00 a.m., rummaging around in the supplies cupboard where I find an apron. I walk past the study because I want to clean 'his' area and get it out of the way. I'm not sure if he's in here though, so I knock and when there is no answer. I go inside and breathe with relief to find the room empty. It's dark and smells of mothballs and mustiness.

How does he find inspiration in such a setting? I walk around the room taking a good look because he didn't show me around properly last night. His desk is messy around the edges, but in the center, papers and books and stationery are lined up neatly. Lamps are dotted around, and there's a long soft leather couch and side table. I start pulling up the blinds and opening the windows to let in the fresh air. Then I return to his desk and start polishing it to perfection, my eyes flickering over his sheets of papers. He has notebooks, and Post-it notes, scraps of paper, a pile of books, and yet some more notebooks on the floor. Handwritten notes litter his desk. I'm careful not to let my eyes stray. He's warned me not to read anything, but I also don't read horror, so this isn't going to be a problem.

Cleaning his study doesn't take long and after that, I decide to get his breakfast ready even though he's given me no indication of his dietary choices. I didn't make office manager so fast by being told what to do. I used my initiative.

The fruit bowl is full and I cut up some fruit for him. Just as I finish arranging the blueberries in a bowl along with the strawberries and a small bowl of yogurt, I hear footsteps. I look up as he walks in. For a moment, there is a flicker of surprise on his face, as if he's forgotten all about me. He's wearing that ridiculous dressing gown again. Satin, gray, and with socks.

It's such an old man's look. "I've prepared some fruit." I remind myself to speak in short sentences.

He blinks.

"I didn't know what you wanted for breakfast."

"Not that." He throws an irritated glance at the bowl of fruit.

"You didn't tell me what you want."

"Coffee," he growls, walking over to the coffee machine. "Make sure this is ready every morning."

"If you had told me, I would—"

"I'm telling you now."

I bite my tongue. "What do you want?" I ask, forcing myself to count slowly to ten, before I say or do something crazy. "For breakfast, and lunch, and dinner?"

"Just coffee." He fills his cup up and disappears.

"That's not helpful," I hiss under my breath.

CHAPTER SEVEN

WARD

"How about we do a few reps?" The trainer guy suggests. "Ten push-ups first, then ten burpees, followed by a minute of mountain climbers? Just for a warm-up."

No way.

"What do you say?" He rubs his hands together as I stand there not moving.

I should be at my desk.

"Can't we do something else?" Something simpler? Like ten minutes on the treadmill. I hate burpees as much as I hate push-ups. Mountain climbers I can do. *Used* to be able to. There's also the fact that getting down on the floor and jumping up then back down again is going to send my rotund belly jiggling even more.

"We've been talking about programs and fitness, Ward, but I think it's time we made a start. Your abs aren't going to magically appear."

I resist the urge to bare my teeth. "I'm aware of that." The smartass is at least twenty years younger than me. I want to see what he's going to be like when he's in his forties. I hate the way he looks at me, as if I'm a huge mass of blubber. But seeing myself in the mirror, standing next to him, even I'm embarrassed.

"Ten push-ups aren't too hard. Try it, you'll be surprised at what you can do."

The contrast could not be starker. My t-shirt hangs over my belly while trainer guy's is flat, hugging his washboard abs. He is lean and toned and his arms have protruding veins and muscles. His t-shirt has no sleeves, in order to better show off his physique. Even the muscles on his legs are defined.

He makes me look like a loser. I take a step away so that I can't see myself in the mirror because comparing our two physiques is the quickest way to depression.

Maybe I should have had that bowl of fruit the housekeeper had prepared. Although the two stale donuts in my study, washed down with my morning brew, tasted much better.

"How about we start with five then?" he suggests when I don't move an inch.

He's gone down from ten to five. Humiliation rips through me.

Good for nothing worthless piece of shit.

My stepfather's voice whispers in my ear. Trevor hasn't said it in those words, but the looks he gives me isn't far off. "Five?" I can manage five push-ups. I get on the floor and start.

Damn.

This is hard, but I'm determined not to give up.

"That's it. You've got it!" He's trying to motivate me but I find his tone patronizing.

I attempt my third one, but it's killing my arms to lower my torso to the floor and get back up again. I can't collapse in a heap on the floor, even though I want to. I'm determined to do ten.

I want to smack him. He, too, talks too much. I lower myself to the floor for number three, and I want to stay there.

"Come on, Ward. You've got this."

I clench my teeth together. I can't do this. I really can't. I'm overweight and I'm struggling because of it.

Who the hell struggles with three push-ups? I used to be fit. *Once.* I used to run and weightlift, a long, long time ago. Now I am riddled by the pressure to produce books, bestsellers no less, because that's what they eventually become. Producing something worthy has a weight that bears down on my spirit. Coupled with the demons I can't always keep buried, it's no wonder I've fallen back into a funk.

"You're nearly there!"

Trainer guy claps his hands together, and I lose the will to live. I must look like such a slob. It doesn't hit me until this moment how unfit and out of shape I am. And when I look down and see my stomach—through the top of my t-shirt—hanging down like a beanbag, I want to die of shame.

I pray that the housekeeper doesn't walk in and see me like this.

I get back up for the fourth push-up and I want to give up. A part of me gave up after the second push-up, but my pride and persistence makes me follow through. Even though it feels as if my arms are on fire, I force myself to press down and come up for the last time.

"Five! Well done."

This patronizing little shit is doing my head in.

I'm going to complete the set of ten he originally gave me.

With a huge grunt, I lower myself do the floor again. "You're doing more! Excellent," he says, as I start my sixth one. I'm in danger of collapsing. This is fucking hard but I am determined not to give up.

Good for nothing worthless piece of shit.

I can't give up. Clamping down on my jaw, trying to muster every ounce of willpower in me, I grit my teeth and manage to complete the set of ten. My heart is racing, as if I've done an hour's worth of high-intensity workout. It is pathetic to feel like this after only ten push-ups. I'm in worse shape than I thought.

"Well done, Ward." He claps his hands together as if I've run the New York Marathon.

My face feels hot. My arms sting from pain. It takes a heroic, almost superhuman bout of determination for me to get back up again.

That killed me.

"Well done. We have a lot of work to do. What are your goals? What do you hope to achieve out of these sessions?"

I'm glad he asked me that now, because if he'd asked me first thing in the morning, I would've said eating donuts and watching daytime TV would have been worthy goals. They're also a good enough excuse for when I struggle to write. For where I am in my career, with the pressure of a movie and the final book of a trilogy to release this year, I'm completely paralyzed into inaction.

"I need to lose weight and get fit, obviously." I feel like a rhino standing next to this guy. I saw the housekeeper looking. Saw her judging.

"We can do that. I've got a program in mind and we'll slowly ramp up to it. I can see we're going to have to go slower than I originally thought."

Fucker.

"I haven't worked out for a while. It will come back."

"Oh, yeah. Sure. You'll be fine once we get into it," he says quickly. "You write most of the time, I imagine, so it's important to have a good mix of cardio to get your heart working. We'll do some muscle toning work." He pointedly stares at my belly. "With a good diet, we'll get rid of those extra pounds in no time."

"Good. Are we done for the day?" I ask. I need to get back to work.

"Yeah. Almost. How about you do fifteen minutes on the treadmill?"

Hell, no. "Sure." I say, walking reluctantly over to the treadmill.

"Any chance of an autograph?"

No. That's my reflex action. That and not answering questions I don't want to answer, but I'm going to be stuck with this guy and that woman for a few months, unfortunately. "Sure, when I'm done here."

MARI

I strain my ears to listen out for sounds of another argument. Ward clearly doesn't like people around him, but he seems to hate the idea of exercise more. I wonder what today's outcome will be, but it seems to be calm and peaceful there as I walk past the door to the gym.

I examine the rooms downstairs so that I can plan my cleaning schedule. I have no idea what his royal highness wants for lunch, and I'm determined to hold my ground and not make something that he's going to turn his nose up at. I'll find out from him first, before I waste my time making him something he won't want, though clearing up the TV room gives me a good idea of this man's diet. I'm not surprised he's in the shape he's in.

Around mid-morning, Trevor wanders into the kitchen, and I'm so pleased to see him. I stop wiping down the countertops. "You survived," I say with a smile. This is only my first proper day here but I'm already missing human interaction.

Trevor holds up his hand with his fingers crossed. "It's early on. Anything could happen. He's hard work."

I nod in agreement. "Are you in a hurry to leave?" I'm about to take a break and it would be good if Trevor could spare me a few moments.

"I'm not in any hurry."

"Good. Have something to eat." I set out Ward's bowl of fruit and a bowl of yogurt and get out two small bowls. "I'm taking a break."

Trevor sniffs his t-shirt. "I'm smelly."

"I'm not going to smell you. I could do with some company, that's all."

We sit and talk, getting to know one another. He tells me about his job, and how much he loves it, how he doesn't consider it to be a job because he is a fitness fanatic anyway and could live in the gym twenty-four-seven. I tell him about my job and how I got laid off so suddenly and how this job was a lifeline. He's sympathetic about my woes and is a great listener. I don't delve into any of the other problems, and keep it all about this sudden change in my life with this new job.

"This must be a complete turnaround from your normal life? Going from being a manager to this."

"It's a complete change. It's temporary, that's what I tell myself. It won't be forever and the money is good. I need all the help I can get right now."

"Sounds like a lucky break to me."

I look around the kitchen. "From eviction to this, all within the same week. That's one way of looking at it."

He smirks. "It beats being homeless, right?" He lifts a spoon to his mouth.

"I was staying with my friend, and I was supposed to take a few days to find a place to live, but Rob seemed pretty desperate for me to start. This wasn't supposed to be a live-in position."

"You'd have to be pretty desperate to put up with living here. *With him*," he whispers.

I dip my spoon into the creamy yogurt, mixing the berries in slowly. "It's weird."

"How was your first night?"

"I slept, so I count that as a good thing but ask me how I feel next week." We grin at one another. "I was listening out for sounds of discord," I confess. "Especially after yesterday, but things were relatively quiet."

He laughs as he scrapes his bowl clean. "That's because that tub of lard was on the floor struggling to give me ten push-ups."

"Shhhh." I hold a finger to my lips, lightly shocked to find Trevor referring to Ward like that.

"Don't worry. He's probably still recovering in the gym."

"He's a writer," I say. "He's really famous."

"I know. I got an autograph from him," he says proudly.

I certainly won't be asking for such a thing. "You asked him to do ten push-ups?"

He grunts. "I asked him to do a set of various reps. He struggled to do five push-ups, then almost killed himself to prove he could do ten."

I wince. "Ouch." I glance at the door, worried that Ward might be lurking around.

Trevor snorts. "It was like watching a baby elephant on the floor, you should have seen him."

I press my lips together as a visual pops up in my head. "He probably hasn't worked out in a while. Rob said he's hit a wall." I'd be depressed if my mom had passed away, so I can understand Ward's head not being in the right place. He must have been close to his mom for him to be so devastated that his agent has had to take such drastic measures to get him to finish his book.

"One thing's for certain, I'll have to go real slow with him. I put him on the treadmill afterwards and he sweated like a pig." Trevor chortles as he takes a blueberry from the bowl and pops it into his mouth.

"I think he's going through a tough time right now."

"Have you seen what he eats? Pure junk."

I dip my spoon into my yogurt. "I offered him this for breakfast, but he turned it down."

"I'm not surprised his belly is the size it is. You should have seen the way it was hanging when he was doing his push—"

"Get. Out."

My head jerks up. Ward is standing at the door, his nostrils flaring. Trevor looks horrified, then embarrassed. His face turns beet red. "I was only ... I didn't mean it ..."

I wish I could disappear into thin air. I open my mouth,

ready to say something in Trevor's favor but the look on Ward's face is more than angry. He looks feral.

"Get OUT!" he roars.

Trevor stands up slowly.

"You're fired," Ward hisses. "Get your things and GET OUT."

"Look, I was out of line and I—"

"GET. OUT." Ward roars, making me jump in my seat. It's like he's dropped a bomb and my body reverberates in the ripple of the aftershocks.

Trevor feels it too. He gets the message. There is no negotiating this. He grabs his bag and leaves, skirting around Ward who's standing in the wide doorway, not moving an inch.

Heat tinges my skin. My insides hollow out.

I didn't say anything.

Did I?

I didn't laugh.

Or did I?

Suddenly I'm not so sure.

I wait, sitting timid as a mouse, awaiting Ward's wrath. In less than a day, I've gone from being a confident hotel manager who loved her job to a meek and quivering housekeeper.

I've hit rock bottom.

Ward glares at me.

In the daylight, staring at his face head on, I see him clearly for the first time. He's swept back his long dark hair, and his eyes bristle with something bordering on rage. He's been humiliated by Trevor, and made fun of, and I was here listening to it. He looks like he's going to explode.

I brace myself, but I don't have anything to hide or

anything to fear, except for losing this job. I didn't call him names.

I summon my hotel manager persona. With a calmness and smoothness I definitely don't feel, I get up and walk towards the refrigerator. I feel the weight of Ward's stare branding into my back.

"What would you like for lunch?" I ask as casually as I can, opening the door and peeking in. The fridge is half empty. There are fizzy drinks and cheese. Not much else.

Thanks, Rob. You really did leave me high and dry.

He doesn't answer, so I force myself to look at him. "Lunch?" I ask him. "You need to tell me what you want for—"

"I suppose you found that funny?"

I coach my nerves to calmness, force myself to speak up. "I didn't laugh."

He fixes me with a death stare. "Lunch?" I ask, hoping to appeal to his appetite.

"I'm not hungry." He walks away leaving me none the wiser. I should count myself lucky. At least he hasn't fired me.

CHAPTER EIGHT

MARI

I make it through the next few days, though it seems to take forever for the weekend to come around. But early on Saturday morning, I head out to Maplewood, my mom's nursing home. It's an hour's drive from Ward's place.

My mom is sitting in the conservatory when I get there. To my extreme joy, she recognizes me as I walk through the large communal living room.

"Marianne." My mother's face shines with happiness, and my heart glows. I smother her, bending down to give her a huge hug, my arms circling around her frail little body.

She used to smell of lavender, but she doesn't smell like that anymore. The scent I associate with her is not here in Maplewood. This is one of the better nursing homes from the many I looked at, but there is no scent of flowers here. More like dry paint, varnish, and mothballs.

I hold onto my mom because I don't want to let go. Letting go might change things, and here, in this moment, she's my mom, and I'm her daughter, and she knows it. I inhale, long and deep, and I cling to her.

"Now, now, Marianne. What's that for?"

I move away and swallow the sob that has slowly climbed its way up from my belly to my throat. "I missed you, Mom. How have you been?"

She leans forward a little, her leathery arms resting on the armrest. "I like it here," she whispers. "The nurses even offer to walk around with me."

I am an only child, and while it's never really bothered me before, now it does. This is when it would have helped to have siblings, with us all living close by so that we could all keep an eye on her and visit every day. I can't do it all alone. Weekends are the only chance I have to come here. "I'll walk with you outside."

Her face lightens up. "Will you?"

Of course I will.

I help her into her cardigan. It's chilly outside and I don't want her to catch anything.

I want to tell her that I have a new job, but I don't want to overwhelm her, give her new things to have to remember. Strange how I've never thought of it like that before, strange how getting older makes you think of these things—that living life and reporting on each day might be 'stuff' that is just another piece of information to have to hold onto.

Instead we reminisce. We talk about my dad, and our vacations when I was younger, and the friends and neighbors we've known over the years. I want to bring back the memories of the life she lived, in those moments when she remembers. I let her talk and tell me whatever she wants as we walk through the calming gardens.

But as the day moves on, she lapses back into episodes of not knowing, of becoming confused, of faltering when she's about to say something. Worst of all is the dead expression in her eyes when she looks at me as if I'm a complete stranger.

The nurse tells me that it's been a long visit, and it's better if I leave and let mom rest. So I say goodbye, and I hug her frail body, trying not to squeeze it with the full force of the love I feel for her. I try not to linger too much, to not inhale deeply as my face brushes her shoulder and I wish I could smell the lavender again. I pull away with my heart in fragments and I leave the nursing home feeling wretched.

I hate to leave her behind. It doesn't matter how nice Maplewood is, the thought of mom there, lost and not knowing who she is or where she is and who I am, is cold and makes me uneasy. A ball of anxiety grows in my stomach as I check my cell phone for messages before I drive back. There's a message from Jamie and it's like a tiny lifeline of happiness. He's asked me to come over for dinner on the way back from my mom's. 'If you're not too busy', he adds.

It's Saturday night. I don't want to mess up his plans. I'd told him that I'd stop by to pick up a few more of my things. I text him:

Only if you have nothing better planned for tonight?

He replies back:

Come over.

No plans.

Dinner with him is exactly what I need.

As I drive back, the hour's journey seems longer. When I was in my apartment, it was forty-five minutes, and where I live now has added on an extra fifteen minutes. I never worried about the distance before. Maybe because my life was different, it was secure and assured. I had my job, and my apartment, and I was in ignorant bliss about my boyfriend. Is it that the fifteen minutes has changed things so much, or that the rug has been pulled out from beneath my feet?

I no longer have the job I loved, no apartment that I can call mine. No boyfriend either, at least, not one who belongs to me. I'm better off without that cheating, lying scumbag who put his penis inside another woman and got her pregnant. I forgave him once before and I should have learned from that mistake. Jamie's analysis of my bad luck with men is spot on. I am reckless. I take risks. I give my heart too easily.

A liar never fully changes.

A leopard never changes its spots.

One thing is clear: men and relationships aren't my concern right now. There's only one thing I need to do while I try to put myself together. I must keep my mom at Maplewood, and take care of her, visit her as much as I can on the weekends. The staff members here are so much better, and she seems better cared for. She might slowly be wandering away from me, but at least she is alive. I must keep her there, and that's the only thing that keeps me working for Ward. I have to put up with him no matter how rude and insolent he is.

I feel slightly better when I arrive at Jamie's place. But when he opens the door, I hug him for the longest time. All of a sudden, I'm overcome with emotion and I grab onto him and nestle my face in the hollow of his neck. He holds me silently, and when the moment stretches out, I pull away.

"Mari?" His eyes sparkle with concern.

My eyes have welled up, and I'm embarrassed. "It's nothing," I say, but I don't sound convincing at all.

"Hey." He hugs me again, then pulls me inside gently. "You're upset because you went to see your mom," he says, putting his arm around my shoulder protectively. "You always get teary."

I nod, because if I say anything, the emotions I've managed to bottle up inside me might explode and gush out in a torrent of tears.

Jamie is warm, and strong, and his hug is the most comfort I've experienced in weeks. Dale and I had been slowly drifting apart but it was weeks before I realized something was wrong. We had stopped making love months ago. That should have told me something.

"Talk to me," he coaxes.

I pull away to retrieve a tissue from my pocket, then blow into it. "Just give me a moment." I turn away and blow loudly into it. I dab at my eyes, feeling silly now that I've had a moment to compose myself.

Thank goodness that it's only Jamie. I don't usually fall to pieces. I'm usually dignified and together. Minor events don't ruffle me, but my life recently has been made up of things that aren't minor.

We go into his living room, and I sink onto his couch. He stares down at me looking worried.

"I'm sorry." I dab at my eyes again. He squats down in front of me. "Your ..." He lifts a finger to my face. "Your mascara is running."

I attempt to wipe it away with my tissue. He makes a face.

"Worse?" I sniffle.

He takes my tissue—even though it's damp with my snot—and finds a dry corner, then wipes my eyes gently.

I breathe out. Since when was Jamie so kind and considerate? I've always thought of him as my work colleague. We've helped one another through tricky phases but this feels different.

I claim my tissue back from him and proceed to tell him about my visit to my mom, and how it upset me. He squeezes my hand and reassures me about her being in the right place and how I've always cared for her. He says all the things that make me feel better. Then I tell him about Trevor losing his job and how shocked I was by Ward's sudden dismissal.

"He did what?" Jamie is shocked. I can almost see his earlier fascination for Ward breaking away. I tell him about the conversation Trevor and I had, and the things Trevor said about Ward.

"I'm shocked that Ward fired him but Trevor was being downright rude." He seems unsure about where to sit, then walks to the couch opposite and sits there instead of next to me.

"Trevor didn't do anything wrong. We were just talking."

"But he was laughing at him, talking about him disrespectfully. I saw Ward. The guy looks pretty tubby and out of shape. He's going to feel humiliated hearing you two talking about him like that."

"I didn't say anything."

"Still, I can't blame him for firing the trainer guy."

I roll my eyes. "He floats around wearing a robe all day! He's not fit, but he's not as big as he looks in that ridiculous thing."

"He's probably feeling self-conscious about his weight and shape. You said his agent more or less shipped him off to a new city and told him to get with it."

"I'm not saying Trevor was right, but he didn't deserve to be fired like that."

"I'd do it."

I look at him in surprise. "You're too nice. You'd give a guy a second chance."

"Would I?"

I nod. Of course he would. Because Jamie is a nice guy. There's not a bad bone in his body. A few of our work colleagues used to think Jamie and I were flirting around one another, even though both of us had partners, but it was never like that. It wasn't flirting, he's just a really nice guy. I've never been attracted to him. He's too nice and I like dangerous men. Maybe that's why I have a track record of picking losers. I like the excitement and my ex was reckless. Maybe that's why he did what he did, and that's why I ended up getting hurt.

"I don't know," I say, shaking my head. I'm unsure about Ward. He's rude and surly and lazy. I don't feel scared, or threatened in any way, but I don't like him as a person. I also can't afford to lose this job. I tell Jamie about my fears, about the mansion being so big and alien, and how I can go the entire day without seeing Ward and that suits me.

Unfortunately, the kitchen has a side that opens up to the room with the huge TV and I can see right into it. Worse, the thing I see from where I stand, is the couch, and if Ward is in there, I'll have a full view of him lying on the sofa, often with a bag of chips in his hand, stuffing his face as he watches TV.

"Sorry," I say, when Jamie looks at his watch. "I've come

here and all I've done is whine and moan about my life. Tell me what's going on with you? How's the new job?"

We swap stories about our weeks and how we have fared since getting laid off. He needs more money. Seems like every working person I know needs more money. Life is just one big never-stopping hamster wheel, unless you're a big-ass author like Ward. I look at his life with envy. The guy works from home, floats around in a satin number, writes when he feels like it and goes on to make millions.

I hate him even more.

"You should make use of the gym," Jamie says.

"The gym?"

"It's there, he's probably not going to use it much. It will help you feel better. You can do your yoga."

I do love my yoga. It calms me, helps me, grounds me.

"Seriously, Mari. Don't waste the opportunity."

He has a point. I'm probably going to need my yoga more than ever now that I'm working for Mr. Grumpy.

A delicious aroma floats through the air, and I'm starving. I didn't even have anything to eat for lunch and now its late evening. "Did you cook?"

"I've made dinner. I figured you might be feeling down."

"Aw, Jamie. You didn't have to do that! We could have gotten take-out. It would have been my treat."

"Well, this is *my* treat. I know it upsets you seeing your mom."

This man understands me, I see that more clearly now that we're not in the confines of our work environment. I want to give him a hug and I get up to do just that but he walks into the kitchen. In a corner on the countertop, I see a few bars of my favorite chocolate. He bought them for me. Before I get a chance to say something, he opens the oven door and pulls out a roast chicken complete with roasted potatoes and vegetables. I go to hug him but now he has his arms full.

"Here," I dart around the table, setting mats out. "Put it here. This is too much, Jamie," I say, as I get out the plates and cutlery.

"Don't go thinking I did this just for you. I have to eat, too."

Except I know that Jamie wouldn't have gone to all this trouble for himself. It's been a while since anyone took care of me, and this, tonight, with Jamie fussing over me, is perfect.

"I'm so lucky that I have you in my life right now." I mean that sincerely. His smile makes up for everything.

The Ward Maddox's of this world have made me cynical, but Jamie restores my faith in humanity.

WARD

"How are you getting along with your new friends?" Rob asks.

I've been staring at my notepad for ages. His phone call is a welcome diversion. "I don't have any friends."

"Yeah. That's never going to change," Rob throws back.

"I fired the personal trainer." I expertly deflect the conversation before he can ask me about my writing.

"You did *what?*"

"I fired him."

I listen to his cries of exasperation and explain exactly what happened. "So I fired him."

"Don't you think you overreacted?"

"If you think I'm going to put up with that crap, you're wrong."

"I should have warned him," Rob grumbles.

"Warned him about what?"

"About how difficult you were. I told Mari, but for some reason I didn't think to warn Trevor."

I find it amusing that he has to warn people about me, although it's the right thing to do. They need to know what they are getting themselves into. "There's no way I'm going to let anyone talk about me like that."

"So, this guy upset you?"

"You sound surprised that I have feelings."

"Sometimes, Ward, I'm not so sure."

Rob can piss me off easily sometimes. "I'm getting the impression that you think this is my fault."

"You're not good around people. I knew this wasn't going to be easy, but I expected the new hires to last longer than a few days."

"The housekeeper's still here," I shoot back.

"I'm surprised that you didn't fire her at the same time."

"She never said anything."

"You'll find a reason soon enough, but go easy on her, will you?"

"You make me sound like a villain from one of my books."

He chuckles. "With you I never know."

I'm curious. "Go easy on her why?"

"She lost her job."

I snort. "I'll try to be gentle."

"I'd appreciate it. She's nice. She accepted the job on the spot. Of course, I had to pay her slightly more to get her to accept."

"How much more?"

Rob coughs lightly. "Double."

I have no idea what double the rate is. I don't even know what the going rate for these people is. I don't care. I'm aware that I need a manager or a PA to help me through my daily life, but I've made a choice not to have people around me. And unwittingly, Rob has fulfilled that role to a degree. It's not his responsibility, and he's gone over and above what he needs to. "I'll try not to fire her."

"This is a big year for you. It's a big gamble, writing the third book in a trilogy almost a decade after the first book. It sets up a lot of expectation."

I groan. Every time he reminds me of this, the pressure intensifies. I wish I could go back to the days when writing was fun. I wasn't so well known then, but I had enough to get by. I didn't need millions. Or the fame, or the loss of my anonymity.

Writing is a chore now. I'm not sure I'll ever get my love for it back.

"Dare I ask about your writing?" he asks. I had a hunch this question was coming, since that's the only reason he ever calls. "How's it going?"

It's not. This week has upended my daily schedule. I've had people in my house to get used to. A new city, and new home. How does he think this is going to be any better?

"Why don't you go back to the house where you lived? Or revisit the children's home?" he suggests.

Is he fucking crazy?

I won't be going to Grampton House, and I won't be going to my childhood home. Ever.

Some places are best left forgotten. Though I've written about some of them. It helped me to reach some sort of closure.

"I don't need to visit any of those places."

Rob lets out a loud exhale. I sense he's fed up. I've tried his patience lately and I'm aware of that. He's only trying to help.

"I was about to write," I tell him, staring at the blank notepad again.

"Don't let me stop you."

I hang up. I need more coffee. I head into the kitchen again and refill my cup, and notice that there's a scrap of paper lying on the table that wasn't there when I woke up.

Salad and quiche are in the fridge.

I'll be back later tonight.

The housekeeper has gone out for the day.

My shoulders sink with the relief of this news. This is just how I like it. I have the place to myself.

No fitness guy.

No irritating housekeeper.

I stare at the scribbled note again and my eye catches the line a few spaces lower down.

Don't wait up.

There's a smiley face after it.

What in the devil's name does she mean 'don't wait up?'

She's trying to be funny, or familiar, but I don't like it. I peer inside the fridge and pull out the food she's left. It doesn't look too bad though my insides roil at the heap of salad. Still, the quiche looks appetizing. I don't imagine for one moment that she baked this. She's no Freya.

But she's trying. I have to give her that. She could have left me a sandwich. I guess Rob must have explained things better to her than he did the personal trainer.

I head straight back to my study and get on with my writing. My story is in a lousy shape right now but my longhand notes aren't complete garbage. I sit up and move my plate out of the way. An idea pops into my head and I start to scribble some notes. The more I write, the more ideas pop up in my head. I write some more and fall back into the story almost seamlessly.

When I next look up, it's evening. I almost choke in surprise. Hours have flown by, and my lunch is untouched. The salad leaves look wilted but I'm starving. I stand up first and stretch, feeling stiff and achy all over.

But I feel good.

I feel *inspired*.

I've written more today than I have in the entire month.

Picking up my plate, I start to eat but the story is so fresh and vibrant, I can't eat for long. I begin typing up the longhand notes and adding to the first draft of my story. The words fly from my fingers faster than I can type them.

This is what it's like when the words flow; when everything comes together and the story pours out of me. It's a wonderful streak, and one that probably won't last for long; it's as rare as it is satisfying. But I'm going to go with this. I know from experience how elusive such things are, so I will ride this out for as long as I can.

When I look up again, it's almost midnight. I finish off what's left of my lunch and I'm so hungry that eating it eight hours later makes no difference to how it tastes.

There's an odor in the room. I sniff. I haven't showered today either and the blinds are still drawn.

Feeling more like a slob than ever, I stand up and roar. It's an animalistic sound but as I walk around, flexing my fingers and loosening my arms by shaking them, my body is tighter than ever. I feel closed up and rigid.

I haven't even walked around the house much, moving from the TV room to the kitchen is what I usually manage.

I run my hand over my flabby belly and cringe. A physique likes Trevor's is what I want. I had it before and I don't see why I can't get it back.

Maybe tomorrow I'll head straight to the gym and do a short workout on my own. I fired the trainer but there's no reason I can't use the gym.

Today has been a good day. I need to shower and go to bed. Just as I'm about to leave my study, I see my plate lying on the table. It's a habit of mine to leave things lying around. But for some reason, I pick it up and head over to the kitchen then stop.

The housekeeper sits at the island with her head in her hands. Her posture is slumped, she looks resigned. I seem to have caught her unawares, in an unguarded moment. She hasn't even seen me, and I don't want to interrupt her because she looks deep in thought. But I'm inside the kitchen now. I tiptoe over to the sink and set down my plate on the countertop. When I turn around, she's looking at me.

"You're up," she says, sounding surprised.

"You told me not to wait up, but I couldn't help myself," I reply dryly.

She gapes at me in confusion yet seems a million miles away. "Your note," I remind her. "You said don't wait up."

"Oh."

I wait for her to ask me if I liked the quiche, or the salad, or anything else. I wait for small talk, only, she doesn't say anything. She's not her usual talkative self. She gets up from her stool and says 'goodnight' and leaves.

The next morning, something isn't right. I think I'm coming down with something because my first thought of the day is to head to the gym.

As I pass by the kitchen, I contemplate having a strong cup of coffee and maybe a donut or two. I've still got some left over from the box Mari gave me. Writing is damn hard work. Some like bars of chocolate, some like alcohol. Me, I like a box of donuts.

I should hit the gym first, then I can reward myself with coffee and donuts. Having made that executive decision, I head into the gym but the sight which greets me is that of Mari, or rather, her upturned butt, high up in the air. I stop in my tracks. She's in a V-shape posture, with her feet and hands planted on a mat and her face turned down. She hasn't seen me, but I have a pretty good view of her. She looks good.

Her butt looks great.

She's wearing a crop top and I can see the sheen of perspiration on her back.

Blood rushes from my head straight to my groin and I feel lightheaded for the few seconds it takes her to notice that I'm gawking at her.

She stands up immediately. "I wasn't expecting you to be here." The disappointment in her voice is hard to ignore.

My body responds to her in a way I am ill prepared for. Excitement darts through me. I want to say something witty, something that will detract from the way I look, something that will make her see me and not the blubbery loser I suddenly feel like.

"I ... I need to ... workout," I say, for once at a loss for words. She wipes the towel across her brow, and my attention falls to her thin and taut arms. I've only seen her in her work clothes, but the skimpy skin-tight cropped leggings and crop top reveal her slim and shapely body.

Standing in my gym shorts and t-shirt, I've never felt so self-conscious of my body before.

Or so turned on in months.

"Do you want me to go?" she asks.

"Go where?"

"Leave. If you'd rather have the gym to yourself."

I would rather have the gym to myself, but only because I feel twenty pounds heavier than I should be and I don't want her to see me. But since she's already here, it would be selfish of me to tell her to leave. "Shouldn't be a problem. It's big enough for both of us."

"I'll get back to it, then," she says, getting ready to get back down on the mat again.

"What was that?"

"Warming up," she replies.

"That was warming up?"

"That was downward dog."

"A downward what?"

"Downward dog," she explains, tucking a stray lock of hair behind her ear. "It's a yoga pose."

I suck my belly in and try to get my belly button as close to my spine as I can, hoping that I can smooth out the curve of my paunch. She picks up her bottle of water and takes a huge gulp from it, still staring at me. She unnerves me. This is my house, albeit rented, yet I feel unsure of myself, especially here in the gym which isn't my domain.

As she continues to drink, I stand there, unsure of what I should do next. I was supposed to do some push-ups, but given that I looked like a beached whale last time, with Trevor standing over me as I killed myself doing them, I decide not to put myself in such an embarrassing position, especially since she's here.

I glance around the room, desperate to find something quickly that I can start using.

The treadmill.

Get on the treadmill.

I head over to that and set a speed that I can handle

easily. Trouble is, she's directly in my line of sight. Now she's straddling a bench and drawing down the weights bar. My attention is drawn to her lithe taut arms as she pulls and lets go of it. I can't help but notice her breasts as she brings the bar to chest level and pushes up.

If I'm not careful, she's soon going to see the evidence of my arousal.

This is awkward.

Worse, compared to her, I'm so out of shape. A picture of her and Trevor laughing about me flashes in front of me. I hate being around people and I hate this most of all—being in the fucking gym, looking like an overweight loser.

I try not to glance at her, but I can't help myself. I look away, trying casually to find another machine I can use that's far from her.

I consider using weights. Giving a display of my strength, and then I wonder why the hell I'm even thinking of something like that. I would look ridiculous. No weights yet. Nothing too fast, and nothing that requires me to do push-ups.

I decide to use the vertical climber machine which Trevor said would be good to use. The beauty of this is that she's not in my direct line of sight and hence won't be the distraction she's currently being.

I'm on it for about five minutes, thinking about my story and trying to plan what chapters I need to focus on later. But my attention is once again diverted by the sight of Mari on the floor, on the same mat again only now she's doing push-ups. I can see her from the reflection in the mirror.

She makes it look really easy, too.

I narrow my eyes wondering if she's doing this on purpose because I fired the trainer. They were both laughing at my pathetic attempts.

My body tenses. Irritated, I look at my machine display. I've barely done much, but I've had enough. I already hate using the gym but the housekeeper being here has pissed me off.

Just as I step off it, she walks past me with her belongings.

"Is that it?" she asks in surprise.

It's the condescending tone in her voice that grates on me more than her fitness level. I can't even lie and say I've been here longer than I have because she was here before me.

"I've figured something out," I tell her, "For my story. I need to write it down before I forget."

I rush out of the gym. It's the fastest I've moved all morning.

CHAPTER TEN

MARI

That was a shock to my system, finding Ward in the gym. Even last night he startled me in the kitchen. That's twice he's popped up when I've least expected to see him. Either I'm lonely and reading the signs wrong, or he's changed.

A little softer.

A little different.

Maybe he feels bad that he fired Trevor.

Maybe he's making an effort to be nicer.

He seemed embarrassed to find me in the gym, but he also seemed uneasy. At first, I was startled when he showed up. This man is a stranger to me, and he could be a psycho for all I know, even if he's a multi-millionaire best-selling author.

I should be afraid, based on his behavior so far, and yet I'm not. In the gym it was a sense of power I felt, not fear.

He might be the master of my destiny in that he's my

boss but in its barest, raw terms, in the gym, Ward Maddox isn't as brutal or as terrifying as he likes to think. I'm not sure if it's because he's unfit, or slightly paunchy. Me showing off and doing those push-ups probably didn't help. Staring into Ward's eyes, I felt jubilant, but when he left as suddenly as he had arrived, a part of me felt I'd gone too far.

I'm about to head into the shower when my phone rings.

It's Rob.

Good, because I have a million questions I still need to ask him.

"What happened with Trevor?" he asks, before I get a chance to say anything. I was wondering when he would find out. I was wondering if I should be the one to tell him.

I tell him what happened. "Thank goodness you're still there. For a moment I was worried that he might have fired you."

I laugh uneasily. "I need this job. I can't afford to lose it." I figure that being downright honest, even if I sound desperate, is the right thing to do.

"Ward can shoot off with his mouth sometimes," Rob says. "I knew he wouldn't find it easy having two new people upset his routine."

I hold my breath, suddenly afraid Rob's going to tell me that it's best if I also leave. "Trevor shouldn't have said those things," I reply, somehow justifying Ward's stance. "He wasn't being complimentary."

"Ward's never been in such bad shape before."

"You'll be surprised to hear that he was in the gym just now."

"What?"

I tell him about the gym session just now, but omit the fact that Ward didn't do much and didn't stay for long.

"I'll be damned," says Rob. "At least something's working."

"He seems to be heeding your advice," I add.

"It's a shame it's not translating over to his written work."

"You'd be surprised. He said he needed to write today and that he'd figured out a few issues with the story." I've suddenly become Ward Maddox's biggest fan.

"Are you serious?" Rob asks.

"That's what he told me."

"He's talking to you?" That Rob has asked this, is telling.

"We were in the gym together."

"Together?" The guy sounds positively shocked.

"I was using the gym, I hope that's okay?"

"Perfectly okay."

"I need to do something. I'm feeling cooped up and there's a lot to get used to." Taking Jamie's advice to hit the gym was good. My yoga session and workout has improved my mood somewhat, but I'm not sure how much of my elation is to do with feeling I've got some sort of power over Ward.

"Of course," says Rob. "You go ahead and don't feel shy."

"Oh, I'm anything but shy," I assure him.

Rob chuckles. "At least it worked. Getting Ward out of New Orleans and somewhere new worked."

"I'd say he's doing fine."

"How is he with you?" Rob asks, and I wonder if I'm being tested.

"He's ... ok—aaaay," I say slowly.

"Good. That's what I want to hear. I can't afford for him to fire you too."

"Me neither."

"I wish he hadn't fired Trevor. He needs a personal trainer. I know Ward. He has highs and lows. I'd feel better if he had someone to come and push him more."

A silence falls because I have no idea what to say.

"I don't have time to look for a replacement personal trainer. Do you know anyone?"

Jamie comes to mind immediately. "I have a friend. He's a fitness fanatic. He used to be in charge of the gym at the hotel before we both got laid off. I'm not sure if he'd be able to do it." But Jamie is in awe of Ward Maddox. He'd definitely be hyped at the prospect of being his trainer. "He's not a personal trainer," I hasten to add, knowing that Ward might be a stickler for detail.

"If he's a fitness fanatic, that's good enough. Ask him. Tell him the money will be good. He only has to come every weekday and kick Ward's butt, and try not to get fired."

"I'll ask him today." I'll ask to meet him this evening. I'm already looking forward to the idea of going out and having someone to talk to.

"Great."

"And now that I have you on the phone, I've got a few questions for you." Questions about my hours, and my duties and what sort of food I should cook for Ward. So far, I've been guessing and just getting on with things, and it's working.

"Fire away."

Rob informs me that Freya, Ward's housekeeper in New Orleans, finished at six o'clock each day and had weekends off but would leave him food. This is more or less what I've been doing.

"Just be nice to him, and do what he says."

"He doesn't say much," I reply. "He keeps out of my

way. I was worried that he'd be a picky eater, but he's becoming better as the days go on."

"It seems you both have an understanding."

I wouldn't go so far as to call it that.

"Are you interested?" I've told Jamie about Rob's proposal.

We're in a bar, having a couple of drinks. There's live music, and the place is busy. I've missed being in the world of people who are laughing and having fun. Ward's house is deathly quiet. I'm not used to it, but then again, being a housekeeper is not my vocation. This is just a stepping stone, I remind myself.

"Working for Ward Maddox?" His eyes are suddenly animated. "Hell, yeah!" Then his face sobers up. "But you said he has a temper. That he's weird. He fired the other guy."

After running into him in the gym today, I feel as if I have a better handle on Ward. I've seen another side to him, and he seems more human. "He's not weird. He's just ... awkward." Brooding and miserable on a good day. Offensive and rude on a bad day. I intend not to have any bad days with him. "He's used to his own space and he's not used to dealing with people."

"That sounds weird."

"I thought you liked him!" I protest. I so badly want Jamie to take this job. For one thing, it means I get to see him every day and it will give me something to look forward to, a little company, a little humor, someone familiar. I also think it will be a good second income for him.

"His books are brilliant. I can't believe you've never read any. Or watched *The Attic*."

"I hate horror." I lean forward across the table. "It's only one hour a day and the money will be good. He's not so bad when you get to know him."

"You've changed your tune quickly," Jamie says.

"I'm trying to sell him to you so that you'll take the job."

"You want me to take the job?" he asks, his eyes dancing with amusement.

"I need company. Ward writes all day. I don't see anyone."

"You want me to take this job on so that you'll get to see me."

He's twisting my words, but in a roundabout way, *yes*. He's not entirely wrong. "It will be like the old days. Kind of."

He seems to be considering it. I want him to say yes because it's isolating, and hard, being alone. Cooped up all day in that house, cleaning and cooking—it's not that I mind it that much, as not interacting with people.

"At least I get to see you," he says, lifting his beer bottle to his mouth. "It will be like old times."

"Yes, it will." I smile, because that's exactly what I have in mind.

"And I could use the extra money," he says, as if he's trying to sell himself on the idea.

"We can't whine about him, though. You don't want him to fire you on your first day."

"I promise to be on my best behavior."

"It's only for a few months. Rob's desperate to find a replacement, so if you're smart, you might be able to negotiate a good rate."

"I don't have your sob story. That's why you're living there, right? Because you have nowhere to stay?"

"I mentioned that I was going to find a place to stay, and he made me an offer."

"I don't want any perks. Sorry." Jamie puts his hand over mine and gives it a squeeze. "I shouldn't have hit so low."

I move my hand away and lift my cocktail glass. "It's okay. This job means I've been distracted and I don't have to think about Dale."

"You still think about Dale?" He sounds annoyed.

"He was my boyfriend."

"He cheated on you. Not once, but twice. He got someone pregnant, Mari. Why are you wasting your energy thinking about him?"

His tone startles me. I had no idea he hated Dale this much. I hate him too, but there are moments, lonely moments, when I lie in bed at night, and I can't help but think of my ex and the good times we had. "You're supposed to make me feel better."

"I'm sorry. But I hate it when you lapse back into the past, Mari. It's like you've forgotten what a dick he was to you. You deserve better."

That brings a smile to my face. "I'm going to stay single for a while. I need to get my head on straight and focus on the important things."

"That's better. Focus on the important things." He sets his bottle down. "Now tell me, what's Ward Maddox really like?"

"You'll find out soon enough. We won't have to work for him for long, though it depends on how long it takes him to finish this book. From what Rob says, he's been struggling with it."

"His mom died recently," Jamie announces.

"How do you know?"

"I read up about him. He's a big deal, Mari. You're working for *the* Ward Maddox."

"So you keep reminding me. You sound like a crazy fan." This guy has never been on my radar and I'm not in awe of his fame.

"He's writing the third book in the *Morbid Trilogy*."

I wince. "There's a lovely sounding name if ever I heard one."

Jamie tut-tuts. "That Attic was the first book, then he wrote The Dark Woods years later. The movie to that is coming out this year."

I feign a long drawn-out yawn.

"Working for this guy is wasted on you."

"I can't help it if I don't know much about him."

"Did you know that he had a girlfriend who died under mysterious circumstances?"

"What?" My eyelids fly open. "When?"

"A long time ago."

"Where they dating?"

"I think they'd just split up."

"What?"

"It was around the time The Attic blew up. It catapulted him into success."

My insides cartwheel and jiggle at the news. My earlier power over Ward fizzles away and is replaced by a sense of foreboding.

"The new book," says Jamie, in a suspenseful voice. "Have you managed to get a sneak peek at a few pages?"

I shake my head. "He's made it clear to me that his desk is off limits."

"Don't you see his work area?"

"I do. I have to clean the study first thing, but he's warned me to not touch anything, or snoop around. The place is littered with junk food wrappers and cans, but the main area on his desk is neatly organized. He has a pen."

"A pen?"

"A MontBlanc pen he seems to cherish."

"A MontBlanc?" Jamie echoes.

Now that I've had ample opportunity to clean his desk, I can see that while it's a mess, the middle of it is pristine. I tell Jamie, "Towards the center, everything is lined up nice and neat. His notebook closed. His sheets of paper all tidily placed underneath. Then he puts his magic pen across the top of the notebook, and six sharpened pencils placed vertically along the righthand edge."

"The freak!"

"You can't call him that," I say. "He's not a freak. Just … lazy." I recall the plethora of things I have to clear up after him daily.

Jamie makes a face as if he's disgusted. "I'm shocked. I had no idea he was such a slob."

"You don't have to clean up after him. You just have to give him a workout."

"I can do that, but I can't start for a couple of weeks."

"A couple of weeks?" I cry, horrified. I'm worried that Rob will get desperate and find someone else for the role. I'll try and work on him. A couple of weeks isn't that far away. "Talk to his agent and explain," I say. "Rob's a good guy. You'll see."

"Now?"

"Yes, now."

I call Rob on my phone. "Hey, Rob, it's me. I have a new personal trainer for Ward. He can't start for a couple of weeks, but he's one of the best. I can vouch for him." I wink at Jamie as I pass the phone to him. Already I feel a little happier about returning to the mansion tonight. It's not home, I don't have a place I can call home right now, and that thought leaves me feeling unsettled.

But at least seeing Jamie every day will be something to look forward to.

CHAPTER ELEVEN

WARD

"I've found you a new trainer," Rob tells me.

"I don't need a new trainer," I protest. "I managed to do a workout myself."

"I heard."

"From who?" Though I have a pretty good idea from who. I don't tell him that I haven't done one since that day I found Mari in the gym. I've avoided that room, and her, for days.

"Mari."

I hope he doesn't have her spying on me. That would be below the belt. I'm aware that he's worried I'll stop writing completely, like before, but that's not going to happen this time. I wonder if that's the purpose for him hiring a live-in housekeeper for me. "What did she say?" I ask, curious.

"That you were working out in the gym. That you'd figured out something with your story. It pleases me to that you're making an effort to be nice."

"It was a passing comment. Not a conversation." *Why in the hell is she talking about me to Rob?*

"Jamie Hurst starts in a few weeks' time. He needs to take care of a couple of things first."

"When was this decided?" I was getting used to the idea of having the mornings to myself, without the added stress of a personal trainer.

"You need someone, Ward. I told you, James Garvey suffered a heart attack. The way you're going, I have reason to worry."

"So you found me a new trainer," I state, wanting to change the conversation.

"Mari found him, actually."

"Mari?"

"Jamie is a friend of hers. They both got laid off at the same time, so try not to fire him."

"Him as well?"

Rob laughs. "You worry me sometimes."

"I worry myself."

"I'm serious. Give the guy a chance."

I hang up, curious now to see what this new trainer friend of Mari's will be like. She's gone out to do some grocery shopping. I know this because she left me another note on the kitchen island telling me. Maybe now is a good time to go to the gym while she's out of the house.

Why am I tiptoeing around her? Why do I care?

There's something about Mari that makes me more self-aware, but I'll be damned if I can figure out what it is. I'm not attracted to her, I barely know her. Then why do I care what she thinks?

She makes me feel like less of a man. I hate for her to see my flabby, unfit body, and I hate that she is fit and slim, and can easily do the things I struggle to.

I never used to be like this. Not in my thirties but hitting forty has brought its own set of problems.

Sitting at my desk, writing, or pretending to write, has many disadvantages. It's not just the emotional mind-crushing feelings of imposter syndrome which riddle me, but the sheer difficulty of writing something that people might want to read. Time and again I wonder if I can actually do this. Always I wonder if I have failed. And apart from the emotional toll, my writing has also taken a toll on my health. My stomach bears the brunt of it.

It makes me angry each time I see a photo of James Garvey looking dapper, distinguished and a picture of success. He's what a real author looks like.

I head into the kitchen and glance at Mari's note again.

Chopped fruit in the fridge. More salad and quinoa for lunch.

I look in the fridge to find the plate of food. It looks bright and colorful, but it doesn't look appetizing. I'm tempted to have a couple of donuts, but I am also embarrassed by my gym encounter with Mari. It shouldn't make a difference, but it does.

I leave the plate of salad and instead reach for the bowl of chopped fruit. I've written four pages this morning and I'm pumped. My characters are taking shape and the plot is thickening.

Something has changed.

I feel motivated to write, and though I'm not back to my usual productive standards, I'm making progress.

Perhaps Rob was right and having a change of scenery and environment is helping a little. Being forced to live with another person has made me self-conscious. I never cared what Freya thought of me. She never intruded on my thoughts. With her, I was never forced to have interactions. Unlike now.

I'm sitting at the island, eating, when the housekeeper walks in.

"Oh." She stops when she sees me, as if she's shocked. I don't normally have my lunch in here. It's always at my desk in the study but for some reason I decided to eat here today.

"I hear your friend starts here soon." I wipe my mouth with a napkin.

"Jamie?" She breaks out into a smile. "He has a few things to straighten out with his current workplace. He's definitely starting?" She sounds hopeful as she runs her hand through her silky hair. It's the color of dark chocolate, with caramel mixed in. Strange how I never noticed that before.

"In a few weeks."

"That's great. You'll like him."

I have my reservations. "Will I?"

"He's nice and friendly, like Trevor ..." She winces, as if she's wandered into hostile territory.

"Trevor was rude and disrespectful."

She starts unpacking the groceries but doesn't answer. It was a rhetorical question. We haven't been in the same room since that time in the gym. This first meeting is a little stilted but there isn't the usual edge.

"You don't ever go out," she states.

"I don't need to. Everything I have is here."

"But going for a walk can be nice. It might help you to get some fresh air."

I don't find her curiosity, or advice, as offensive as I usually would.

"Rob says you and your friend both lost your jobs." I've

never had more than a few words to say to Freya, and I've known her for years. I have no idea why I'm taking the time and trouble to make conversation with Mari now.

"We all got laid off. All the staff. It was horrible. The owner was charged with money laundering offenses. We had no idea any of this was going on." She shivers with disgust. "I never thought my boss was that kind of person."

"People will surprise you in ways you can never imagine."

"You're right. You're absolutely right about that."

I should know. I write about these people all day long.

"Jamie is nothing like Trevor."

"No?" He must mean something to her. I wonder if she's subtly pleading with me not to fire him.

"He's a good guy. Most of my belongings are at his place." She stops suddenly, as if she's said too much.

He *is* her boyfriend.

A thorn pricks at my side. This means they will laugh about me, and talk about me, just not here. They'll do it in private. "You're together?" Why did I ask that? Why did I pry in a way I never do?

"God, no," she cries. "We're just friends."

Even if they are just friends, there's a chance I'll be the butt of their jokes and I won't even know. I get up abruptly, the need to shut myself away pinching my thoughts.

"You're leaving?" she asks, looking startled at my abrupt departure.

"I have words to write."

She nods, as if she understands. "Do you need me to bring you anything? You seem to be making progress." Her smile is light and reassuring. She's making an effort. Trying to be nice and friendly. I should make an effort, too, but now

I wonder if I should head to the gym and do a workout before her friend shows up.

CHAPTER TWELVE

MARI

I can't decide if Ward is becoming more civil, or if I'm getting used to him. Or whether I feel sorry for him, knowing about his mom and his girlfriend. But as the weeks go by, we reach a nice equilibrium.

Being cooped up together gives people no choice but to try to get along. It also helps that the house is huge. We could go the whole day without seeing one another, like we did soon after the gym encounter.

I make it a point to go into his study first thing every morning and give it a good cleaning before he starts. I'm still as careful as ever around him. I'm aware of his short temper and I can't risk losing my job over his tantrums.

The shining light on the landscape is Jamie coming on board. Even though Ward is nicer, it's still lonely and isolating being here. I miss not being in a work environment. Back at the hotel I had plenty of interaction with my work colleagues and the customers. I was surrounded by people, and I never realized how important it was to me until I took this job.

I don't know how Ward does it, sitting indoors all day long. In all the time I've been here, he hasn't been out once. Lately, he's in his study more and spending less time in the TV room. I've noticed that he also doesn't wear that loose-fitting robe of his.

I haven't seen him in it this week. Instead, he's been wearing sweatpants and baggy sweatshirts.

As I walk into his study, I'm surprised to see him and I jump back in shock. "I wasn't expecting you in here so early."

"It came to me," he says, not looking at me. He's scribbling away furiously as if I'm not even here.

"What did?"

"The twist. I slept on it, and I woke up with the perfect twist."

"I'll wait until you're having lunch before I polish the surfaces," I tell him but I pick up his litter from the coffee table and the sofa. He's even got a half-full can of fizzy drink on the mantelpiece above the fireplace. I notice that he's got a fire going. Usually when I come in here, the blinds are always drawn, but with the fire going, there's a dark, cocoon-like ambiance to the room.

He picks up his pen and taps it on the desk repeatedly. He seems somewhere else. I know my place, and it isn't here. He continues to tap away with his pen, and I, curiously, glance over my shoulder at him as I walk away, then trip over something on the floor. A box of cookies. The half-empty bag of chips in my hands goes flying to the floor and some of them fall out, leaving a mess. I scoot down to pick them up.

"Go," he growls.

I look up. "But I've made a mess—"

"*Go*. Before I lose it." It's an order. I jump up at once and leave.

WARD

I stop tapping my pen and flex my fingers before I start writing again. Moments like this are rare, when I wake up with a full scene in my head and the urgency to get it down on paper spurs me on. The problem which had stalled me last night vanished into a wisp of smoke and I was writing down new words, my pen flying, ideas pouring out of my head. Until she walked in.

Mari interrupted the flow. Her bending down to pick up something is a level of interruption I don't need.

I didn't mean to be so short with her, but what ordinary people don't understand is that when words are stuck in my head, they need to come out. They don't come out when I see Mari's pert bottom facing me.

As it is, I've struggled to unsee her in her gym clothes, bent over doing her downward pose.

Freya never distracted me in that way.

No one ever did.

I don't like live-in housekeepers, and one such as Mari is the most dangerous of all.

I try my ritual again. Tapping the pen twenty times on the desk. All writers have a writing ritual. I'm not the only one. Something, *anything*, to get the muse working. Only, this time, she seems to have failed me. I can't pick up from where I was.

When I'm in the flow, words gush out like water from a

dam. I lose track of time, of who I am, of where I am and when I stop, my fingers are stiff.

I was on a streak until she came in. I'd been up early and writing for two hours. I flick through the sheets I have written. It's all here, every single last detail of it.

Getting up, I flex my fingers and I pace around the study. I have to get my writing streak back. After a few more minutes of flexing my fingers, and rotating my shoulders and turning my neck from side to side, I hunker down at my desk and attempt to write again.

MARI

He's been in the study all day and hasn't even come to the kitchen to have his lunch. I debate over whether I should take it to him. The guy needs food and water. But I recall how annoyed he was when I tripped and made a mess on the floor and then started to clean it up.

He needed to be left alone.

I put his lunch back into the fridge and set about with my cleaning duties. Later that evening when I go to make dinner, I see that he still hasn't had his lunch. I debate once more about risking his anger and taking some food in for him. Then I decide against it.

I make a light dinner, in case he might want that instead of his lunch, and head into the gym for a workout.

Jamie and I used to do this in the hotel gym at the end of our shifts, especially on a typically bad day. Ten minutes on the treadmill, five minutes on the vertical climber and five minutes on the rowing machine. It's not easy to make myself do this alone. With Jamie, it never seemed like such hard work because we'd be talking and he'd be making jokes. It says something about my current state of mind and where I am that I've chosen to do a workout instead of going out or watching TV.

Loneliness is hard for me to handle, and boredom doesn't help.

I move onto some light weights, and then I open up my yoga mat in the corner and do a few yoga poses. The stretches and breathing exercises make me calmer, stretch my muscles, and take all the knots and kinks out of my body. I end with my favorite yoga move of all, lying on the mat with my eyes closed, and my legs out and my hands on the side, breathing and trying to clear my mind.

I'm floating.

Floating, floating, floating.

Then I see Ward at his desk, tap, tap, tapping away with his favorite pen.

I try to clear my mind, to erase that image.

But it flashes into my head again.

He's tap, tap, tap, tapping.

I hear a noise and my eyes fly open.

Ward's dark hypnotic eyes stare down at me.

Jesus.

I'm about to bolt upright, except I'm paralyzed and I can't move. A gasp falls out of my lips at the sight of him standing over me. The words '*axe murderer*' flash before my eyes in blood red letters and I stare quickly at his hands.

My heart almost shoots out of my mouth.

"I didn't mean to snap at you," he says.

"What?" I manage to sit up, seeing that he isn't carrying an instrument with which to kill me. But I can't help feeling scared. After all, he crept into here and I didn't even hear him.

Then I remember that his girlfriend died under mysterious circumstances. What does that mean, *mysterious circumstances?*

How long has he been here? Feeling a little underdressed in my sports bra and clingy yoga pants, I hug my knees up towards my chest in the hope that they'll give me some cover. Ward is still standing, towering over me, and I'm sitting hunched up on the mat.

I promise to inspect every inch of the house in thorough detail tomorrow looking for bugs and hidden cameras.

"When I said I was going to lose it." His voice is gruff, and he's wearing the same clothes he wore earlier. "I didn't mean I was going to lose it, my temper. I meant I was going to lose the plot I had in my head."

I blink. He looks rough, and even though his beard is shorter and trimmed, his face looks rough.

His words don't make sense, because I'm so scared. How did he know I'd be in here? Is he following me around? Are there hidden cameras in this place? I shiver. My stomach empties. I stand up slowly, acutely aware that I'm the only one here with him. This man has many moods, and personalities, and he scares the hell out of me. "Did you come looking for me?" I ask, my voice shaky, and sounding like a child's.

As if he can sense my trepidation, he takes a step back. "I came to use the gym."

But do I believe him?

"Have you finished?" he asks, not getting on any of the machines yet. It's as if he's waiting for me to leave.

I take a few calming breaths and start to level my breathing. He wants to use the gym. He didn't come here to spy on me. I remind myself that he's been cooped up in the study all day and that he hadn't eaten lunch. "Have you been writing all day?"

He nods.

"You didn't eat your lunch."

"Lunch?" he asks, as if it's an alien concept. We're standing a foot or two apart, his gaze falls to my stomach. He moves towards the treadmill but doesn't get on it.

"You must have been so into your story that you forgot to eat."

"It happens." The upturned lips look like a weak attempt at a smile. I feel slightly better.

"I didn't mean to snap," he says again, and this time I understand, because my mind is functioning fine now that I'm not scared out of my skin. "You don't have to be so rude," I say, emboldened by his attempt to apologize. "I was only trying to help."

"You interrupted my thoughts."

"I didn't know you were going to be in the study."

"I told you, I had something I had to get down."

"I'm your housekeeper," I say, the anger rising inside me. "I'm only doing as I was told."

I was in a state of calm until he showed up. Now I'm all riled up again. "That's some apology," I say as I turn away. I can't figure this guy out. The air between us flexes and tenses like a muscle. I'm done in here. He can have the gym to himself.

CHAPTER THIRTEEN

WARD

After a knock on my door, Mari sticks her head in. "Sorry to disturb you but the new trainer's here."

"I'm coming." But she's already closed the door and disappeared. Something strange is going on between us. I didn't mean to startle her the other day when I went to use the gym. I also didn't expect her to be in the gym lying on the floor the way she was. I apologized, and I meant it, but we ended up in another disagreement.

I don't understand it at all.

I quickly put my papers to one side and stack my pens and pencils neatly in place. It's time to meet this new trainer and see what he's like.

As I walk down the hallway, I hear the sound of conversation and laughter. A tall and well-built man is talking to Mari. She sees me first and turns silent. Abruptly, the man turns around.

"Mr. Maddox." He seems self-assured, striding towards

me with a grin and an outstretched arm. "I'm Jamie Hurst, your new personal trainer."

"Jamie." I shake his hand harder than I intended, so much so that he almost winces, but he continues smoothly, and goes on to tell me how much he loves my books, and how he's been such a huge fan. How much he loved *The Attic*. I listen but say nothing. I don't need to. He does all the talking, and he's clearly enthused and even in awe of me. Mari never was. I like that about her. I steal a glance at her, but she's looking at the new guy.

She's avoided looking at me, I've noticed. I can't pinpoint what it is, or why, but things have definitely been strange between us. It keeps me on edge, this up and down rollercoaster of me and the housekeeper. My environment is supposed to be calm and peaceful, conducive to creativity, but ever since I've met this woman it has been anything but.

Meanwhile her friend continues to jabber like a chattering monkey. "What do you think, Mr. Maddox?" he asks finally. It's only when I turn to him, I realize I haven't listened to a word he's said.

"Call me 'sir'," I say, more to deflect the fact that I don't have a clue what he's asked me. Mari appears shocked by my request and it gives me a silent chuckle.

"Uh... well. Uh....sir. Are you ready to start?" The trainer seems awkward and I'm pleased with myself for wiping that smugness off his face.

"I'm joking," I tell him.

"About?" Jamie asks.

"About you calling me sir." Mari looks visibly relieved and the trainer's expression eases. "Call me Ward."

"Ward, then."

"No, just Ward."

This elicits a laugh from him.

"Let's get this over and done with." I lead the way to the gym.

MARI

I almost choked when Ward asked Jamie to call him 'sir'. And then I chuckled when he made another attempt at a joke. Both within seconds of one another. Is it possible that Ward Maddox has a sense of humor hidden beneath that hair growth on his face?

Anything is possible with him. He's like a chameleon. Ever-changing. I never know what to expect from him one moment to the next.

I finish vacuuming one of the downstairs rooms and then set about making a list of grocery items. Rob said I could order online, but it takes just as long to get online and order things, and I prefer to have a reason to get out of the house. I'll go shopping with Jamie once he's finished because I'm interested in finding out how the first session went. It will be safer to do a post-workout catch-up with Jamie out of the house.

I prepare Ward's lunch; a healthy sandwich and a smoothie. He actually asked me for it. He'd left a printed-off smoothie recipe on the island this morning.

My back is turned when I hear a knock on the kitchen door.

I turn around and see Jamie. "Good?" I ask him. He nods and doesn't say anything because I've warned him not to.

"I need to get some groceries. Shall we get a coffee?"

"I need to shower," he says, taking a big slug from his water bottle.

"I can put up with your stinky smell for an hour." I'm desperate to escape this house. "Come on." I scribble a note for Ward in case he wonders where I've gone. "I don't have long."

Twenty minutes later, we're sitting in a coffee shop and I've got my favorite iced cup of coffee. I giggle. "How was your first encounter with '*sir*'?"

"I almost had a heart attack," says Jamie, opening his bottle of coconut water.

"He's not usually so ..." I wave my hand in the air because I'm at a loss for how to describe him. "Funny, shall we say."

"You think he's funny?"

"Compared to what I've seen of him, yes, that was funny." Though, the more I think about it, Ward is changing, or maybe I'm getting to know more about him. "How was the session? Did he do everything you asked?"

"He's out of shape, but not too much. He's got a pot belly, but it's not too bad. I was expecting him to be in worse shape given what you'd told me."

"He sits at his desk all day, and probably all night too." I say. "He's like a vampire. I've never seen him leave the house."

"It shows. He's sluggish. He says he wants to tone up and lose weight. Says he wants a six-pack."

"He said that?" I try to imagine Ward with a six-pack but my imagination doesn't stretch that far.

Jamie nods. "He's not going to get a six-pack, but he can definitely lose the belly and tone up. It's not going to be that difficult. He used to work out, he's had a setback, that's all."

"Hmmmm." I try not to dwell on the image of a toned-up Ward.

"He was more talkative than I expected."

This surprises me. "He was?"

"He was nothing like how you made him out to be."

This *really* surprises me. "What did he talk about?"

"Me, and how I lost my job, and what I did before."

"You sucking up to him about his books probably helped."

"I didn't suck up. I was being truthful," Jamie says. "His books are brilliant. You should try and read one."

"I can't stand horror."

"He's brilliant. You'll be amazed," Jamie insists. Him suddenly becoming Ward's biggest fan irritates the hell out of me.

"I'm not going to read horror. *Ever*."

"Do you ever get a chance to see his current work in progress?"

"It's on his desk. Along with his special pen."

Jamie sniggers, yet I can't help but think about Ward and his split personality. He leaves a mess in most places, yet his desk, in the middle is neat and tidy. There are splinters in his outward persona. I think about the joke he made when he asked Jamie to call him 'sir'. Is that a chink in his armor?

"Most writers have a ritual," Jamie states matter-of-factly.

"How do you know?"

"I read about it somewhere."

"You're always full of trivia."

He leans forward across the table and grins wickedly. "I'm more than just muscle, baby." Then, "Lunch?" he asks.

"You said you needed to shower." And I was supposed to be quick. I have yet to go and buy groceries.

"I'm here now. We're here now. Come on, Mari. It will be like in the good old days." I recall the good old days when he and I would have lunch in my office. Take-out from the hotel restaurant on some days, and other days we would go out and get something. Go for a walk. Complain and whine about our jobs. I had reached the highest position I could have in that place and had been thinking about changing jobs. I hadn't expected my next career move to be this.

"How's the job search going?" he asks.

"I haven't found anything. I've been looking on and off, but I haven't had a chance to look properly."

"What do you do all day stuck in that big house?"

"I spend all day cleaning. It's insane, but I find I quite like it." Or maybe I'm just bored.

"What's there to clean? How does that place get dirty?"

"He likes it clean." And what else is there for me to do but clean, in the morning, then have his lunch ready, then I have a few hours before I prepare dinner. Then I'll hit the gym, though ever since that day when Ward was standing over me, I haven't been. "I keep myself busy. It's the only way I get through the day. I'm done by six o'clock and then the day is mine."

"He doesn't summon you during the night to make him a sandwich?"

I find that an odd question, even if it's a boyish attempt at a joke. "No." I get up. "I need to go. He'll be wondering where I am."

"He has tabs on you?"

"I don't usually go out in the middle of the weekday."

"You make it sound like you're in a prison, Mari."

Sometimes it seems like one. I blow him a kiss. "See you tomorrow."

"What happened to lunch?" I hear him say as I head towards the door. I didn't mean to stay so long. It's irrational, this sense of dread I have about it.

I rush off to buy the groceries I need. A short while later, I'm back at the house and I walk in with the grocery bags in my arms. Ward's sitting at the kitchen island with an empty plate and a notebook by his side. It's almost as if he was waiting for me to return.

"I was wondering where you were." He closes his notebook.

"I had to get some chicken. You said you wanted chicken salad tonight for dinner."

He gets up from the stool, displeasure darkening his features. "I went to get chicken," I insist. I can't tell what he's pissed off about. "Did you need me for something? Because I made your lunch."

"I'm not incapable of finding my lunch, or making it myself." He starts to walk away, leaving his lunch plate and glass on the kitchen island. Normally it wouldn't annoy me as much as it does right now.

Then why does he look so disgruntled?

"At least have the decency to face me when I'm talking to you!" I swipe a hand across my chest. Have I really just hollered at him like that?

He turns around and stares at me with an expression so cool—and the opposite of what I expect from him—that I'm temporarily floored.

I put the grocery bags down and wish I hadn't because now I've got nothing to do with my hands.

Don't say something you'll regret.

Don't.

You need this job.

"Can you tell me why you're so annoyed?" I ask, a little more softly.

A muscle tenses along his jaw and the tiny twitch in his skin alerts me to his unease. He says nothing, which only increases my frustration.

"I'm sorry if you're upset," I say. I hate kowtowing down to anyone, least of all him. It's not in my nature, but I don't want to run the risk of him telling me I'm fired.

I want to scream at him. *Say something.*

But he's so cool. So unaffected. So aloof.

I quell the desire to throw something at him but he walks away without saying a word.

This isn't me at all, a meek and subservient woman bowing down to the lord of the manor. That's what this caveman makes me feel like, and I hate it.

CHAPTER FOURTEEN

MARI

I'm not going to be a meek woman and act as if I'm in the wrong. So, the next morning, I make no attempt at polite conversation. In fact, I purposely avoid Ward.

I hate walking around as if I'm skating on thin ice, worried that it will crack and I will fall in and die. I hate feeling weak. It gets me wondering if my recent interactions with men have always been broken. Even with Dale, this wasn't the first time he cheated on me. He'd done it before but I forgave him.

Why?

Because I needed him? Or because I thought he would change? We had it all, great chemistry, great sex. He was great in bed, an amazing kisser and an awesome lover. He was thoughtful and he understood me, or so I thought. He was a good listener, and not all men are. He was the man I thought I could have a future with. I was foolish enough to believe he was husband material, because in a sea of boyfriends where most were losers, Dale stood out. What does this say about me, except that I fall for the wrong guys every time?

Imprisoned in this huge mansion with nothing much to do in my evenings, I nitpick the knotty fabric of our past in an attempt to unravel it. I look for moments and conversations where he might have left a clue, I try to find the exact point in our relationship where he started to look elsewhere because I was not enough. And at the same time, I want to believe that his cheating was a glitch. I want to pretend it never happened. But it did happen. He got someone pregnant and he's with her now.

Ruminating over the carcass of my past, I find nothing but hollow bones and promises.

Now I have plunged into another crazy situation. Ward is complicated. He's my boss, and he's changeable and strange. Sometimes I feel as if I understand him, and then he'll go and do or say something to prove that I have no idea about him at all.

Is the fault with me?

For the next few days, I get up at an ungodly hour to tidy his room, knowing he came down early that day because he had his plot twist in his head. I'd rather not run into him like that again.

Purposefully staying out of Ward's way means that the only person I see is Jamie.

There's a note for me one morning when I enter the kitchen. It's from Ward, of course, and it's the first time he's written me a note. I marvel at the neat handwriting he has for a man.

More salad, please. Quiche is good.

No quinoa.

I throw it away, but going forward, if he leaves me notes, that's what I'll prepare for his meals. Prior to this I'd been guessing and he would eat whatever I made, so this is a first, him dictating to me what he prefers.

"Let's go out tomorrow," Jamie says one Friday. I raise an eyebrow. "You look like you need to get out of this prison."

I catch sight of Ward walking past the kitchen door. "A prison," I hoot with pretend laughter, loud enough that I hope he hears. "That sounds about right." I want to twist that knife right where it hurts.

"You up for it?" Jamie sounds surprised that I've accepted right away.

"I'm definitely up for it." I'm in the mood for having some fun. It's better than staying in this miserable place.

"Where do you want to go?" he asks.

I'm too busy staring at the doorway, waiting to see if Ward is hovering around, eavesdropping.

"Mari," Jamie touches my hand. "Where do you want to go?"

"I don't mind. You pick a place, and then pick me up."

I visit my mom the next morning. She seems fine and alert, and she recognizes me, which is always a big bonus.

I brush her hair, and slip on the new cardigan I've bought her. She used to always feel cold, especially in recent years, and she doesn't tell me anymore, but I worry that she's cold. Would she even think to tell me? I put the new cardigan on her before we go for a walk in the grounds.

She seems a little bit more frail than last time. I don't have a plan, but a wish, and that is to have her come back home. One day when I get a place of my own. Even as I imagine this, the logical part of my brain knows she will be here until the end of her life and I'll never have my mom back at my place.

My place.

I have no place.

But the money for taking care of Ward is a huge help.

Maybe I can rent a place near the nursing home? It's a new idea, and I resolve to start looking for my next job around here.

Lunchtime comes and I sit across the table watching my mom but she's having problems feeding herself. It takes forever for her to lift the spoon from the soup bowl to her mouth, and her hand shakes which in turn spills the soup. I try to hold back, I want to let her do it, but after the fourth time, when she spills half of the soup on her clothes, it becomes too painful for me to watch.

I take over gently, telling her I can help, and I end up feeding my seventy-eight-year-old mom. A thought comes to me, it's one I've been pushing to the back of my mind, but now it's in front of me and I can't avoid it. Now, as I feed my mother, I realize that in the space of a year, the woman I have looked up to all my life, the one I have gone to with my problems and whose advice I have sought, whose shoulder I have cried on, this woman has reverted back in age and time. Now she is more childlike than momlike. I have become the caregiver, where once I was cared for.

Once upon a time, I would have cried on her shoulder and told her about all the ills that had befallen me. I would have told her about Dale and how I lost my job. I wanted to tell her. I wanted to tell her how he broke my heart, but now I can't. She'll never know. She doesn't need to know.

It's not her problem.

It's mine and it hurts. Not Dale and what he did to me, but the sharp and painful understanding that I don't have a mom I can go to anymore. I never realized there was a lease on this contract.

When I leave Maplewood, I am heartbroken all over again.

Meeting Jamie turns out to be the highlight of my day. My week even. As I sit across the table from him in a restaurant that is a little too dimly lit for my liking, I see couples everywhere.

Who else would be here on a Saturday night?

I assumed he would pick the local Greek restaurant where we used to get our lunchtime take-outs from at the end of the month in small celebration of getting our paychecks. He's picked the upscale Italian restaurant where Dale and I came on our last anniversary.

"Why did we come here?" I ask, looking at the Italian menu for the fifth time and I'm still not able to decide what I want. I never could because the food here is so good. Dale used to tell me to order everything. At the Greek place, it would have been a no-brainer. I wish we'd gone there instead, not just because it has no bad memories, but because of the familiarity. There is comfort in older things.

"I thought we'd try somewhere new. Why? Don't you like it?"

"I came here with Dale not so long ago."

Jamie looks sheepish. "Sorry. I didn't know."

I shake my head. "Why would you?"

"This place must be full of bad memories."

I shrug. A lot of places were, in the early days. Being in Ward's house has been like having a clean slate. It's a small thing to be grateful for.

"We can go someplace else," he offers again.

"We can stay here. I'm over him."

"Are you really over him?" Jamie asks.

"Yes. We'll stay here." I can't avoid places just because Dale and I went there. I have to erase those memories and create new ones.

He clears his throat. "I hope you don't mind me saying this—" I look up because he sounds so nervous. It's not like him.

"Saying what?"

"That next time you don't rush head first into something."

"Into something?"

"Make a mistake. Go off with the first man you meet."

I cough out loud, almost choking, because I can't believe he said that. "Jamie!"

"We've been friends a long time," he says, looking even more nervous than he sounds. "I hate seeing you upset, Mari."

I look up. I'm not sure why he felt he needed to give me that advice. Jamie is being different around me. Our friendship used to be easygoing. *Jokey.* We'd talk about work, and the boss, and some up-their-asses difficult customers that we could bitch about out of earshot. Now there are none of those things to talk about.

It feels a little awkward, and it shouldn't. I get that he's lonely too ever since he split up with his girlfriend. But he's also always been there for me. I close my eyes and breathe in.

He's also right.

I met Dale at a club. We had sex the same night. I barely knew a thing about him. He was rebound sex after I split up with a guy who dumped me days before my birthday. I met him at a restaurant, where we were celebrating a friend's engagement.

What he's saying isn't wrong. He's simply looking out for me. I ask him if he's heard back from his girlfriend ever since they split. It was months ago, before Dale and I split. "I don't want to talk about her," he says stiffly, then holds up the menu so I can't see his face.

Ouch.

I understand.

I wouldn't want to talk about Dale either.

The conversation instead turns to our current person of interest that we have in common. Ward Maddox. "How's your new role?" I ask him. "What's the verdict at the end of the first week?"

"He doesn't talk much. I like that." Jamie sips from his beer bottle.

"He's not a man of many words," I agree.

"But he's not as weird as you made out."

"You said his desk setup was weird!"

"I also said writers have a ritual," says Jamie. "He's eager to get into shape. He asked me to put him on a meal plan."

"So that's why I'm getting notes about what he wants to eat?"

"Notes?" Jamie's brow creases.

I tell him how we've been exchanging information by writing notes, how I've been staying out of Ward's way. How he's moody and I have no idea why. I tell him what happened after that first day when I returned from our coffee shop visit, after I had been grocery shopping.

"He was mad at you for going out?"

"I'm not sure what he was mad about."

"Asshole." Jamie looks pissed.

A server stops at our table to take our order but mumbles "I'll give you some more time," and shuffles off. It's just as well seeing that we haven't yet decided on what we're going to order.

I tell Jamie how I've stayed out of Ward's way and made myself scarce so that he has no option but to leave me notes.

"He's pretty normal in our workouts," Jamie says.

"Maybe it's just me, then."

"Some can't handle strong confident women."

"I'm a shell of who I used to be."

Jamie looks surprised.

"That hotel manager dealing diplomatically with customers who broke a vase and didn't want to pay for the damage? Gone. That woman is gone."

Jamie knows me well and disappointment wells in his eyes. "It must be difficult for you to hold your tongue."

"It's a miracle that I haven't bitten it off. I've had to force myself to hold it in many times."

"You're in the wrong job."

"It pays well, so I can't complain." I look at the menu again.

"But it can't be rewarding?"

"It's only temporary. What I can't stand is the way Ward changes. He has mood swings. I can't handle that."

"Asshole."

"You be nice to him and carry on as usual. You don't have to take on my problems. You said you liked him."

"That was before I heard what a douche he'd been to you."

"The money is good. I don't have that much to do. It's

not a labor-intensive role. It's lonely, sure, but I get to see you every day ..." I smile sweetly at him.

"I brighten your day?" He thumbs at himself, his lips curving out into a smile.

"I didn't say that."

"But you meant it," says Jamie, grinning. "Can I hear you say it?"

I roll my eyes. "You make my day better. Okay?" I summon the server over because now I'm starving.

CHAPTER FIFTEEN

WARD

Damn. This. Hell.

I hurl my notepad across the room. I pick up my pen and have a good mind to toss that, too.

She's with him.

I can't focus.

I can't think.

I grip my pen even tighter, my knuckles white, my skin taut.

This is insane.

Fucking insane.

It's none of my business what she does and who she does it with. I shouldn't give a damn. I shouldn't waste any thinking time on her, and what she is up to.

But I can't help myself.

I haven't had this type of problem in years, because I don't get into these types of situations.

Rob and his stupid solution to my writer's block. I love

the guy, but this isn't working. I push out from my chair and stab the digits on my cell phone.

"How long?" I ask, when he picks up.

"What?" Rob's voice is cool and calm. "How long for what?"

"How long do I need to put up with this farce for?"

"What are you talking about?"

"Me, in Chicago, in this goddamn mansion."

"You said it was helping you to write."

"How long?" I growl. I so don't want to stay here. I'm better now. I'm eating better, I'm on a fitness program. I don't reach for the box of donuts each time I struggle to get words down.

It is a miracle.

"I would say it's working, Ward. Wouldn't you agree?"

"It's working, yeah. So let me come home." I miss New Orleans. I miss my bed. "I miss Freya's home cooking."

"You have a problem with Mari?"

I grind down on my teeth. Trust him to zero in on the problem. "No."

"The new trainer?"

"No."

"Then what's the problem?"

A knot forms in my stomach. The problem is that I've let that housekeeper get under my skin. I've seen her in her tight and clingy yoga gear. I've seen her smooth naked stomach. I can't unsee those long thin legs. I can't help but notice the bow-shaped full lips, or the way her silky chestnut hair cascades around her shoulders when she lets it out of her ponytail in the evenings.

I swallow. "I can't settle here. It's the house."

Rob snorts. "The house? Are you kidding me? Ward, what's with you?"

I'm distracted is what's wrong, but it's none of Rob's business what my problem is. His solution clearly isn't working and it's causing me more grief. And *that's* my real bone of contention. "I've been here long enough—"

"You can't come back until the book is done, Ward. The first draft at least. We agreed."

"We didn't agree. You said this was what I needed to do—"

"I said I couldn't babysit you anymore."

"I'm not falling apart," I insist.

"You didn't write for months. You haven't written. In your line of work, that's considered a fail, and this year is—"

I grit my teeth together. "I'm not failing. I'm not falling apart. My mom died. I can handle it."

"You've been making good progress ever since you moved. A change is as good as a – uh... what's the expression?"

I ignore the question. "I'm almost halfway done with the first draft."

"See, it's working. You needed a change of place, of people."

An awkward silence bleeds into the air.

"What's the real problem, Ward?"

Where do I start? That Mari is avoiding me. That she thinks I'm an asshole. That I care what she thinks. But most of all that she hates me. And why the hell do I even care? "I hate Chicago," I reply, thinking about how I have done everything to not step outside the door. This city has given me scars I have tried so hard to forget.

"It's Saturday night, Ward. Take a break. *Do* something."

"I was doing something." I growl. I've been trying to write all day, but knowing that Mari has gone out with the trainer seems to have used up most of my thinking power. It's no use talking to Rob. He won't understand. "I'll get the first draft done, and then I'm coming back."

"Then you can."

I hang up, annoyed. I'm stifled, being in here all day long. Back home I would go for a walk, not every day, but a few times a week. I've become slow and sluggish here. The workouts help.

I run my hand over my stomach. It's becoming flatter. My muscle memory is beginning to kick in. With continued effort and persistence, I feel confident I can start to regain some of my original body shape.

I glance at my watch. She's still not back.

Screw this.

Rob says I can't return until the first draft is done. That's a challenge. He's thrown down the gauntlet. I'll get this first draft done faster than he thinks.

CHAPTER SIXTEEN

MARI

The following day, I don't see Ward or hear from him. There are no notes on the kitchen island when I come downstairs in the morning.

By late afternoon I still haven't heard from him, and his lunch has gone untouched in the fridge.

It's the weekend and I don't clean his desk or do any tidying up because it's my time off. He's asked for me to leave him some food if I can, otherwise it's not a problem. I've been good and have left him food whenever I've gone to see my mom.

Even now, while we're in the middle of our disagreement, I still endeavor to make sure he has food and drink. He's still my boss and it's only because of him that I'm able to pay for my mom's nursing home and treatment.

I have a heart.

I'm not all stone-cold bitch.

I tiptoe towards his study, open the door and peer in.

Two lamps are lit, one on his desk and one on the side table near the fire. He's lying on the couch, on his side, fast asleep.

I step inside quiet as a mouse.

The room is a mess. Papers are everywhere. The floor is littered with plates and bags. The donut boxes are back.

He's had a binge session. A junk food fiesta.

The room smells. I don't know where to start. The sight of the messy table makes me itch. I feel the need to tidy it, and clear the floor, and open the windows.

I fight back the urge to spring clean this hovel. I tiptoe over to the couch. Ward looks peaceful when he's asleep. His brows aren't pushed together, and there are no lines on his forehead. No tightened jaw.

He seems almost ... sweet.

Calm.

Gentle.

He looks a little thinner, too. I peer closer. He's trimmed his beard. The thick growth is gone and it was definitely there when we argued last time. Now there is a light dusting of hair on his face.

He looks almost sexy.

I hold my breath as he shifts further on his side, so that he's almost face down on the couch cushion. I look around for a blanket, or a throw, but find nothing. There's no ottoman either. I can't stand here staring at him. I can't tidy up the room either for fear that he might wake up. Then he'd blame me for interrupting his sleep, and then we'd get into another disagreement.

I also can't leave him to freeze.

Slipping back to my room, I grab a blanket and rush back, hoping he hasn't woken up; I'd hate for him to see me do something nice for him.

But he's still asleep when I return.

I drape the blanket over him gently and pray he doesn't wake up.

WARD

There's a knock on the door. I rub my eyes, and wince as I turn. Another knock follows and before I can answer, Mari sticks her head around.

"Jamie's here. You overslept."

"What?" What day is it?

"Jamie, he's here," she hisses.

It can't be. I was writing. I've been writing. I've lost track of time. "What day is it?"

She peers at me. "Monday," she says slowly, as if I'm an idiot. "Did you sleep here again last night?"

I sit up. A rancid odor reaches my nostrils, making me want to gag. I must stink. Fuck. She can probably smell me. I don't make a pretty sight either. I run my hand through my hair and find knots.

"Coffee," I say, wanting her to go, not wanting her to smell my two-day-old sweat. I've spent the entire weekend here. Once Rob gave me that ultimatum, I worked like a fiend. I've slept here both nights.

"I need to shower. Can he wait?"

"I'll tell him, and I'll have your coffee ready."

She leaves before I have the chance to say anything. I get up, planting my feet on the floor. Where the hell did this blanket come from? I slept here for two nights and I didn't leave the room much. Not to shower. Not to work. Not to seek her out.

I scarfed the entire box of donuts I'd ordered, and I worked my way through a mountain of junk food.

But I got lots of writing done. If this is what it takes, then this is what I have to do. Without doubt, and without intending to, I've given Mari and her trainer friend plenty more fodder to laugh at me about.

To hell with them.

I need to shower, and then have coffee, and then do a class with Jamie.

Back in my room I lather myself all over, and feel the grime and sweat wash away. My body feels different. It's not so loose. Not so soft. My arms feel bigger. I like the weightlifting program Jamie has me on. I run my hand over my belly and prod a couple of fingers in it. It's not as jelly-ish as it was before, but it's not hard, like steel, either. Standing next to Jamie, I would still feel like a rhino.

Is she sleeping with him?

I wash the shampoo out of my hair, try to unravel the knots I find. I need to get this cut. Need to spruce myself up.

I didn't have a blanket in the study.

She must have put that on me.

Which means she must have come looking for me.

Is she sleeping with him?

The thought taunts me, jabbing at me like a betrayed wife. I wonder what time she got back on Saturday night. I heard her in the kitchen, but I didn't want to see her face so I slept in my study on Sunday night as well.

She must be sleeping with him.

I slather myself all over again. Picture Mari and Jamie, and then Mari again in her workout clothes.

My cock hardens.

Thinking about her has that effect.

I'm going to have to jerk myself off again, but I try not to think about her as I do it.

It's creepy.

And wrong.

It's what almost a year of no sex does to a man.

CHAPTER SEVENTEEN

MARI

"He overslept and needs to take a shower," I tell Jamie. "Can you wait?"

"I can wait."

I pour a cup of coffee for him. "You look cute. Nice apron." Jamie grins at the apron I wear sometimes, especially if I'm doing heavy cleaning. Today is my dusting day. I plan to dust the entire house from top to bottom. "His room smells like a pigsty. I want to clean it while he's out. Give me a few minutes."

"And miss the chance to see you dusting? No chance." He follows me into Ward's study.

"You shouldn't be here." Ward wouldn't want him here. I speed up my dusting.

"It's dark in here," he says, walking around. "Aren't you going to let down the blinds?"

"He likes it dark." I tidy up the desk, shifting his items around the desk while giving it a good wipe and polish. I glance up to find Jamie examining Ward's possessions. What's wrong with him? He knows better than to poke around. "Hey, don't touch. Ward doesn't like it."

"Relax. I won't break anything."

"You shouldn't even be here. Ward would get mad if he saw you in here." Ever wary, I polish quickly, moving his things around the desk then putting them back exactly as I found them.

I fold up my blanket and leave it there. He might need it another time, then I run the duster over the leather couch and the coffee table and any surface I can find. I would have polished it properly, pulled up the blinds and let some fresh air in but I'm anxious about Jamie's presence and I want to be done with this room quickly.

"Pick up some of those things, would you?" There's no point him snooping around when he can be of use.

"What a slob." Jamie looks disgusted as he picks up empty bottles of water from everywhere and the empty donut box and junk food wrappers. "No wonder he's out of shape. Have you seen this?"

I frown. Ward has obviously had a relapse these last few days. He was getting better. "He was starting to get better. He must have had a hard time this weekend."

Jamie snorts as he walks over with a couple of cans in each hand. I finish setting everything back carefully, making sure that the pens and pencils line up exactly as Ward had left them.

"What are you doing?"

"They have to be arranged just so," I explain. I see a greasy stain on the corner of the desk, something I've missed, and polish it immediately.

"Just so?" Jamie stares at the display. I must admit, I found it strange at first as well, but now I'm used to it. He sets the cans on the desk then picks up a pen and messes up the pencil display. I slap his hand. "Don't!" I hiss. I grab the pen and set it back, then hand him back his bottles and wipe that area again.

"Is that *the* pen?" He examines it carefully. "So it is. The MontBlanc."

"Stop it, Jamie. Put it back."

"You've gotta be kidding me. Are you serious?" He stares at the desk in astonishment.

"You're the one who said writers have rituals. Well, this is Ward's."

"Weirdo." Jamie shakes his head in disbelief.

"He's not that weird. He's ... it's just the way he is." I try to fight in Ward's corner.

"Just the way he is. A weirdo."

"I don't know why he's the way he is, but he needs things to be in a certain order. You don't understand. Writing isn't easy."

Jamie laughs. "I'm more shocked by the things you're saying than by this guy's craziness."

"Out!" I shoo him out of the room and into the kitchen again. A few moments later, Ward comes in. "Sorry I'm late," he says, sounding too happy for my liking and making me suspicious.

"Hey, no problem," says Jamie. "I was just catching up with Mari. Late night?" he asks. I wait to hear Ward's reply.

He pauses before answering. "I had a lot to catch up on."

"Your new book. How's it going?"

Ward is silent and I want to kick Jamie. Can't he tell that Ward doesn't want to talk about his book?

Ward says nothing, but pours himself a cup of coffee and sips it. Jamie looks at me, obviously finding this awkward, but I can't stop looking at Ward. His hair is wet, the rich dark locks hanging just above his shoulders. I much prefer him with an almost beard. I can see the angles of his face better. He seems so different, less angry, less formidable without his Samson-and-Delilah growth. Though his hair is still long. He's pulled it back into a man bun, like he usually does for the workout, only I never noticed it enough to stare at it so much before. Trimming his beard has made a world of difference to his entire appearance and I can't help but stare at him. I notice he doesn't look at me even once.

"Shall we go?" Ward says, having only taken a few sips of his drink.

He hasn't glanced in my direction once.

WARD

I return to my study after the workout and having taken another shower. I run my hand across my face. If feels different now that I've trimmed. The hair is less dense. I should have shaved the damned thing off. Maybe next time. I'll call a barber over to the house and get a haircut too.

The workout was just what I needed. Something to take my mind off things. Something happens to me when Mari is around. I can't be myself. I can't be me. I wish we could go back to how things were in the beginning.

She was friendly.

I was civil.

Now we have this awkward empty space between us. The more I try *not* to think of her, the more she's in my head. Staying in my study the entire weekend helped, to an extent. Immersing myself in my writing worked. I got a lot done. At this rate, I'm certain I'll get my first draft done much sooner than I envisaged.

I didn't look at her today. I couldn't. She was in the kitchen talking to Jamie but I couldn't bring myself to stare in her direction.

She has an effect on that I can't fathom. It's something I could do without because I have enough people in my head to deal with and I don't need real-life drama.

Mari complicates my life without even knowing.

I open my notepad and reach for my pen. Then I look up, because it's not there.

My fingers search the desk, lifting papers, moving notebooks and Post-it pads out of the way.

My pen is missing.

My frenzied fingers search around the desk, but there is no sign of my pen.

Can't be.

I had it this morning.

No, I overslept this morning.

I had it last night.

Or did I?

Of course I did. I was up until the early hours making more notes.

Where is the goddamn pen?

I hunt around under the desk, then look behind my chair, at the floor behind me, in case I've dropped it.

Fuck.

I need my pen.

I rush over to the couch and find the blanket folded up neatly. I unravel it, expecting the pen to ricochet forth.

There's nothing there.

I search along the couch, underneath it, and all around the coffee table and mantelpiece.

I even look at the coals in the fire.

No fucking pen.

I look around the room. It's tidy. The plates and boxes and junk food trash are gone.

Mari tidied up.

I storm out of my study, hollering. "Mari!"

She comes running. Her face is ashen.

"What is it?" She looks terrified. My voice can be loud when I need it to be.

"My pen. Have you seen it?"

"Your pen?"

"My. Fucking. Pen." It enrages me when my things are misplaced. It's a waste of my time, of my creativity. The effort expended in looking for something which should never have been misplaced in the first place is a fucking time and energy sink.

She looks terrified. "I saw it this morning."

"Then where is it?"

"I don't know." Her eyes widen, the whites more noticeable. I almost feel sorry for her. "How do you not know?"

Her eyebrows squeeze together. "Know what?"

"Where my pen is."

"Because I don't."

"Don't what?"

She lets out a sigh. A veil of confusion clouds her expression. "What do you think we're talking about, Mari?"

"Your pen."

"My pen. That's right. My pen." I open the door, motioning for her to come inside. "My pen which isn't there." I nod my chin in the direction of my desk. She stares at my desk blankly. "Now, what do you expect me to do about it?"

She saw it this morning, she just admitted to it. She was the last person to see my pen. It didn't vanish into thin air. She has misplaced it, mistakenly or otherwise. She stares up at me with her doe-like eyes, her mouth slightly open, looking worried.

"I saw it. I'm sure I saw—"

"It's not there now. Maybe you moved it. Check your pockets."

"I didn't steal it."

"I'm not saying you did. You might have accidentally ..." My words trail away as she gets down on all fours and starts to look under the desk. The sight of her on her knees sends a signal straight to my cock.

It's bad enough that I had her in my head not so long ago, jerking off like a horny-as-hell teen. Now that she's on all fours, my arousal kicks up a notch.

She crawls back but not all the way, and while I'm busy admiring her butt, she lifts her head and I hear a thud. Then a yelp. She's hit her head on the underside of the desk. She touches her head as if she's in pain. I want to ask her if she's okay, but the raging throbbing between my legs makes me hold back.

"It's not here," she says, still kneeling as she glances around on the floor.

Rage overwhelms me. "You saw it last. Find. It."

"I've looked for it and I can't find—"

"I can't write without that pen."

Still touching her head, she reaches for the desk to help her get to standing but she knocks over my glass of juice. The sweet smell of oranges permeates the air as the liquid bleeds out all over my desk, heading towards my papers and notes.

No!

"What the fuck!" I cry and leap forward, scooping up the priceless papers. They are sopping wet underneath.

No!

What the hell has she gone and done now?

"I'm sorry," she whispers, and whips out a whole heap of tissues from the box on my desk then starts soaking the liquid.

"How clumsy are you?" I snarl, looking through my precious papers. All of my weekend's work is wasted.

"I'm sorry." She pulls some more tissues out and wipes furiously. It was a full glass of orange juice. The damage is done. It's even gone all over her blouse.

"You've ruined everything I worked on."

"I'm sorry," she whimpers. "It was an accident. I was trying to help you."

"Help me? You've been nothing but trouble."

"Trouble?" she cries, taking a step back. "You're a nightmare to work for." She stops, presses her lips together and continues to clean up the mess. "I need to wipe this down," she mutters. "It's all sticky and I need to—"

"Don't." Any moment now my bottled-up rage will erupt.

She straightens up. "You don't want me to clean this up?" Her voice is stronger now. The meekness has vanished. She's angry, and stares at me as if she wishes I were dead.

"Leave it."

"Fine. I'll leave it then. If that's what you want."

"That's what I want."

I exhale a long, slow breath. Not only do I not have my pen, but I have to clean up this mess.

She thinks I'm crazy for making such a big deal about my pen. I'm not so sure this was to do with just the pen. Frustration and irritation mingle together to form one angry cocktail.

I've never had a pen go missing like that.

I've never had anyone in my personal space. In all the years I've known Freya, I've never had a pen go missing.

She's not a thief, that much I'm know. It's obvious that Mari has picked it up and misplaced it. I wish she'd own up to it.

CHAPTER EIGHTEEN

MARI

The asshole.

The great, big, fat hairy asshole. He's nothing but a pathetic, vile childish excuse for a man.

The orange juice clings to my arm and chest and feels uncomfortable. I need to change my blouse. I have no idea about his pen. But I banged my head trying to find it. What did I get from him? Nothing. Not even an ounce of sympathy.

I push the door to my bedroom open and rush straight for the bathroom where I take my top off. I wish I could stay here and not have to go back and make his lunch or dinner. I'm tempted to spit in it. I would, if I were that kind of person.

I can't take a shower, so I wet a washcloth then squeeze a blob of shower gel onto it and attempt to remove the stickiness. But my mind is a riot of confusion spiked with hatred.

What just happened downstairs? I replay the scene over and over in my head, shocked that it has come to this. Disgusted by my response, that I became a whimpering, nervous wreck crawling under the desk so desperate to find the pen that I had no part in losing. He accused me. He thinks I had a hand in it. Instead of standing up for myself, I turned into a meek little mouse in front of that huge bully.

How does this man manage to do this to me?

Jackass.

Douchebag.

Prick.

I miss Jamie. I wish I could go and see him right now, and tell him what a monster this man is.

I wish I could leave.

I never expected this role to turn into this. I never expected Ward Maddox to be so nasty. For weeks, I've been picking things up after him, keeping his study clean, tidying up the TV room, cooking for him.

It's your job. You're getting good money for this.

I'm not sure it's worth it. I dry myself, and stare at my expression in the mirror.

I look miserable.

He reduced me to a wreck and I'm so not that woman.

I'm independent and strong, and yet I muzzle my voice in order not to upset him.

I so don't want to be here.

I want to leave.

I *would* leave.

But I'm trapped.

A few months. That's what Rob said. Ward will be finished with his writing in a few months' time. And then I'll be free.

I can do this, I tell myself.

I have to do this because I have no alternative.

WARD

She said I was a nightmare to work for. I have a feeling she wanted to say much more but she's scared I might fire her like I did Trevor. He didn't say anything to my face. He said it behind my back.

She hates me, and she's right.

I am a nightmare to work for.

This is all Rob's fault.

I can be a jerk. I've spent too much time alone by myself, in my own fictional worlds and places of horror and fear. I'm more used to being there than in the real world. It's how I survived being locked up in the attic by the man my mother married. It's how I dealt with her sudden change, her switch in love and loyalty. How I dealt with things when my once doting and loving mom fell completely under this man's spell and forgot all about me.

Mari is right. I am a nightmare, because most of my childhood was a nightmare.

Guilt punches my gut at what just happened. I could have handled it better. I saw the fear in her eyes. I did that to her. *Me.*

I know what it is to fear others, but Mari shouldn't need to fear me.

Annoyed and irritated, I get up and look around for her but she's not in the kitchen or in any of the rooms nearby. I call out her name, but she doesn't answer.

"Mari!" Still, no answer.

I take a moment to consider my options before going upstairs. I should forget this fiasco and get back to my writing. That's my main priority and this—what I'm about to do now—isn't. It's also not easy for someone like me. Facing up, confronting, saying I'm sorry.

But I need to apologize. I was wrong. I got angry. Frustrated, more like. Bottled-up feelings. I've never had to deal with this situation before, with people living with me. Even former girlfriends didn't.

I walk towards her bedroom and find her door slightly ajar. A closet slams shut.

"Mari," I hover outside, but she doesn't answer. She's probably packing her bags to leave.

I push the door open and look inside. She's disappeared. The room is clean and tidy as I would expect. A clean blouse is laid out on the bed.

"Mari." My voice is so low, she probably hasn't heard it. The bathroom door opens and she walks out, in her bra and skirt, then screams at the sight of me.

I can't help it, but my gaze dips lower. Her full, buxom breasts are pushed up high in a black, lacy bra.

Hot damn.

She's wearing that under her work clothes? I'll never be able to erase that image from my mind. I suck in a breath, my cock hardening.

I look away. "Sorry," I mumble. "I didn't mean to scare—"

"What are you doing here?" If looks could kill, I'd be lying dead on the floor right now. Venom shoots from her expression. I expect her to cover herself with her hands or something, but she doesn't. To my surprise, she stands there before sliding her hands to her hips, as if she's proud of her body, and on display.

I'm tempted to grab the blouse on the bed and hand it to her, I'm nearer to it than she is, but I wait for her to do it. The fact that she doesn't piques my curiosity. My manhood throbs.

"I—I ..." I can't form words. I can't think. Every useful cell in my body has congregated to the space between my legs.

"You what?" she asks calmly. The power has switched. There is no trace of the frightened woman from the study. She stands before me in her skirt and bra as if she's on a photoshoot. A flash of knowing flickers in her cool expression.

I want her, and she knows it. "I'm sorry. I came to apologize." It's a battle to not stare at her. I can't seem to drag my gaze away. She's all the things I am not: calm, aloof, defiant.

"You came all the way here to do *that*?"

I want to kiss her. I want to put my mouth to her soft, satin skin. I want to leave a trail of kisses from her face to her neck to her breasts.

"I'm sorry," I say again. She doesn't respond and still makes no attempt to cover up. I warn myself that her sexiness is a siren song I need to take heed of. I haven't had sex for so long that this sight of her is killing me.

My imagination fizzles and spurts. Blood gushes south. "You're almost naked," I comment, because nothing else appropriate comes to mind. I should look away and still I can't. I can't take my eyes off her, and she knows it. Our roles have reversed and she holds power over me in this instant. Right now, I'm not the man she works for. I'm just a man, and the way her chin is tilted confirms that.

"You should get dressed," I say.

"You interrupted me. You're the one who's in my room without permission."

"I knocked on the door."

"I didn't hear. I was in the bathroom washing the juice stains off."

I swallow, because my mind now holds images of her in the shower and me washing her. My gaze runs down her length, taking in her flat stomach, her silky skin, her beautiful breasts. And still she makes no attempt to cover up. I can't stop myself from taking a step closer. The blood in my cock, drained from my brain, has made it hard to think straight.

She doesn't even flinch.

I can't do this. Stepping towards her bed, I snatch her blouse. The silky fabric is soft to touch, it's like holding *nothing*. I hand it to her, praying that she'll take it and spare me the agony of having a hard-on and no release.

She gives me a look of victory, as if she knows the effect she's having on me.

"I'm not used to being around people," I say, my voice tight because it's getting harder to breathe watching her slip her arms into the blouse slowly. She's doing a reverse striptease, and it couldn't be sexier.

"That was obvious from day one." She slowly does up the button on one sleeve cuff, then the other.

"Obvious?" I try not to stare at her chest, which is still on display.

"You're not an easy man to get along with."

"I'm trying to be better."

"For who?"

"For you," I reply, surprising myself with that revelation.

"For me?" She starts to do up her blouse buttons one by

one. It's excruciating to watch and do nothing while my cock grows bigger.

This woman is a torturer, a tease, someone who constantly surprises me. When the people I hang around with the most, the characters I create, my string-controlled marionettes, do as I command, having this wildfire of a woman in my life means I am constantly on edge. It's intoxicating, and frustrating, and I'm struggling to hold it together.

"Are you doing that on purpose?" Because it seems to me that she's playing with me.

"Doing what?" A smile curves along her lips. She knows. She knows what effect she's having on me and she doesn't care. Her gaze dips lower and settles on the tent pole between my legs. If only I'd been wearing my wretched robe. It would have hidden this better. Instead, the soft fabric of my sweatpants reveals everything clearly.

I pause, because I don't have a handle on the situation. I back away. "I'm not going to fire you, in case you were worried about that."

"Fire me for what? I didn't take your pen." She tucks her blouse into her skirt, breaking the spell, whatever it was, this strange thing that happened between us just now.

She's still maintaining she didn't take it. I didn't move it. She's stubborn. "I'm not accusing you of stealing it."

She snaps her head towards me.

"I didn't mean it like that," I say. Fuck. I can't think straight being this close to her, seeing her half naked.

"You're making a lot of accusations."

"I'm also making a lot of apologies."

She clears her throat. "I shouldn't have said that to you, about you being a nightmare to work for." I notice that this isn't an apology. She's not sorry for what she said. She's right.

"I am a nightmare. I admit that I'm not easy to work for." I put my hands into my pockets and wait for her to say something. "Anything else you want to say to me, now that we're at this juncture?"

"How frank can I be?"

"As frank as you want."

"Can you handle it?" she asks.

My cock twitches some more. She's putting more ideas in my head.

"Slob," she throws at me.

I fold my arms. "Go on."

"How about lazy, and filthy, and rude?" Her confidence is at full-throttle. She's trying me. She's saying the things she held back from saying before.

"Anything else?" I ask her. It turns me on even more, having her hurl these words at me, showing me that she's not scared.

"That pretty much sums up what I think of you."

"Are you sure that's it? Because if there's more, I can definitely handle it."

She gives me a caustic smile. "That's all for now." Then, "Why aren't you going to fire me?"

"Do you want me to fire you?"

"No."

"Then why ask?"

"You fired Trevor for less."

"You need the job, and I need a housekeeper."

Her mouth twists.

"So, we're even," I state.

As I head towards my study with the new insults she's

hurled at me, it's not anger that simmers beneath my skin, but arousal.

MARI

I wait a moment after he leaves, and then I draw out my long-held breath. He's closed the door, but I go and stand against it, making sure it's closed and he can't come back in. Not because I'm scared of him, or because I feel threatened, but because my heart is thumping wildly. I try to still it. Try to force my breath to regulate. Try to dismiss the throbbing between my legs.

What did I just do?

How was I so bold and confident, standing in front of him half naked and *wanting* him to see me?

I experienced a type of strength I haven't felt around him. The man who managed to strip me of my confidence *wants* me.

I could see it in the way his dark hooded eyes bore into me. He ravished my body with his stare.

I saw his erection.

Hard to miss something that big.

This is dark, and dangerous, and taboo.

He's Ward Maddox, a reclusive author.

I'm ... a mess.

Dale cheating on me has shaken my self-belief. I've been surviving, driven by the need to move on and put behind me all the bad things that have happened lately, things over which I have no control.

This just now, it gave me power. Having Ward Maddox devour me with his eyes.

I can't tell Jamie. This is private. This is me being provocative, wanting, *needing,* to know that another man finds me attractive. Just thinking about Ward sets my heart racing. Makes my skin tingle with excitement.

Could something have happened between us if he hadn't left the room?

I imagine him taking a step towards me, tugging my hair back and lifting my face, then crushing my lips with his. I imagine his hands skimming over my belly and his lips ...

The sound of my phone ringing snaps me out of my sultry daydream.

It's the nursing home. The air in my lungs is sucked out.

The nursing home staff only call if they have a problem.

CHAPTER NINETEEN

WARD

I walk down the stairs with a boner the size of a truncheon.

I don't need this.

My head is filled with her and it will mess with my writing.

I should go back to New Orleans.

Or get Freya to come here. This never happened with Freya. Or anyone. Mari is a different creature.

She didn't care. She showed no embarrassment or shame. Not that there was anything for her be ashamed about, not with a body like that.

But I didn't expect that from her.

That woman is full of surprises, and that is the hook that reels me in. She might be my housekeeper, but just now, in her bedroom, she was the temptress.

I want to take her over my knee and run my hands over her smooth bottom. I want to trail my fingers all over her body. I want to explore, and suck and kiss her everywhere.

I head back into my study and sit at my desk but I still have no pen, and I still can't write.

I can't function.

I can't create.

Everything is messed up so soon after I had managed to get myself back on track. Now, not only do I have no pen, I have a boner which needs to be taken care of. I also have that image of Mari in my head. It's stuck on auto rewind and doesn't help my dick.

I hold my head in my hands.

She's thrown the biggest wrench in my day.

I'm so hard, it feels painful. I need to take a cold shower or spend the afternoon jerking off, neither of which will help with my word count.

Damn Mari and her beautiful half-naked body.

Damn the power she has over me.

That was one plot twist I didn't see coming.

MARI

My mom has had a fall.

I grab my bag and rush out, heading straight to the nursing home. Why's she at the nursing home and not the hospital? Alarm bells sound, loud and piercing. What if something bad has happened? What if she can't be treated? My brain goes haywire at all the things that could go wrong. I'm driving so fast that I get a speeding ticket on the way which wastes more of my time.

By the time I get there, my mom's lying on her bed. Brenda, one of the nicer caretakers at the home, is fussing over her. I rush right over. "What are you doing here, Marianne?" my mom asks. She sounds okay. She looks unhurt. "It's the wrong day."

"She's fine," Brenda assures me. "You had a bit of a fall, didn't you?" she says to my mom.

"Is that why you're here?" my mom asks me. "Because you're not supposed to be here today." I'm secretly pleased that she is aware of my visiting days and is alert enough to know that this isn't the weekend.

"What did you do, Mom?" I give her a light hug and plant a kiss on the top of her head. My racing heart slows down. A lightness warms my insides. I've been fraught the entire time, dread and worry coursing through my veins from the moment I got the call. Now I can relax. My mom's okay. She's going to be fine.

Brenda leads me outside and tells me that my mom tripped but luckily fell onto her bed, which cushioned her fall and prevented her from hurting herself badly.

"Tripped on what?" I want to know, scared that her reflexes and brain synapses are failing.

"She tripped over her shoe."

I'm so happy to hear that.

"She's going to be fine. We've had the doctor check her over. I called you because I knew you'd want to be here."

"Thanks. You did the right thing." I feel even better about my mom being here because of Brenda. She says my mom reminds her a lot of her own mom, and for that reason I like to think she'll keep an extra careful eye on my mom.

It doesn't matter that it was a minor fall, and that she's okay. This is the best outcome I could have hoped for, and after the kind of morning I've had, I need my mom, and an escape from my place of work more than my mom needs me.

Soon, it's time for lunch, so I stay with my mom and decide to spend the whole day with her now that I'm here.

My courage has returned, and Ward exhibited a side of himself that I haven't seen before. He's not important, and he's not my priority. My mom is.

I return later in the evening. It's only then that the tiredness hits me and my grumbling belly signals my hunger. I didn't eat much at the nursing home earlier.

Was it only this morning that Ward overslept and then we had the pen saga? It seems so much longer than that.

I'm famished and head into the kitchen to make myself a sandwich. It's only when I open the fridge door that I realize I never left Ward any lunch, or dinner, or even a note to say I was going out. I just rushed off and didn't think about him at all.

I don't care. My mom was more important.

But as I start to butter my bread, I jump as I catch sight of Ward in the TV room. I notice the litter on the floor beside him. He's lying on the couch in the TV room and there's something different about him. He turns and stares.

I blink.

Has he learned nothing? He seems to have nosedived back into earlier stuck ways.

Can losing his favorite pen stall him so completely?

I look away and spread the butter evenly on my slice of bread. I focus on making my sandwich as if it's an intricate task that requires all of my attention.

"Hey."

Oh, god, no. He's come to talk to me. I lay the slice of

ham onto my bread, wishing I had something else to do, something that would require more of my concentration so that I wouldn't have to look up.

"You okay?" he asks.

I nod. He seems to want to talk, but I am wary. "I forgot to write a note. I'm sorry. I had to rush off."

"I didn't mean to upset you."

"You didn't." He thinks I left the house because he upset me. His eyes are dark, and the circles underneath are just as dark. He looks disheveled. A mess, compared to how he looked fresh out of the shower this morning.

"Did you write all day?" I can't help but blurt out, because he looks as if he's been cooped up at his desk writing feverishly all day, and it that's the case, then his junk fest is well earned.

"I didn't write. I couldn't."

I wonder what he thought of me being gone for the entire day. I feel the need to explain. "Something came up. I had to rush off. I'm sorry I didn't—"

"You don't have to keep apologizing." His voice is strained, but I can't tell if he's really tired, or annoyed, or just hungry. Or maybe all three.

It has been a day that has shattered my emotions. I am so physically exhausted from the melodrama of the last twelve hours, that all I want to do is be left alone to eat my sandwich in peace, but as I stand here talking to a rough-looking Ward, I can't help but wonder what he's been doing all afternoon.

I glance at the litter on the floor of the TV room. He's eaten, but it's a whole heap of junk food.

"Are you hungry? I can make you something to eat if—"

"I can make it myself. Even though I'm lazy, and a slob, and rude, I can feed myself."

He's calling me out. My words have obviously hit deep. "You were getting good with your healthy eating," I comment, ignoring his pointed remarks.

"I was."

"Then what happened?" Is he blaming me for what happened? For losing his pen and causing a disruption to his creative flow. I need to clarify something. "I didn't steal your pen."

"I didn't say you stole it. I don't have you down for a thief."

"Good, because I'm not." Let me get that straight. I want to know why he's so adamant that I misplaced it, but I'm also too tired to start another fight.

"Where did you go?" he asks. "To see your friend again?" His voice is hoarse and his curiosity surprises me. The questions hang in the sultry charged air between us. I don't want to open up. I don't want him to know anything about me, because I sense a current of something between us, something wild and electrifying. What he's asking isn't run-of-the-mill polite conversation. There is subtext beneath his words.

I don't understand my new pull towards this man, but it's there, the throbbing between my legs starting up again, a slow, low, thrum, subtle enough that I can pretend it doesn't exist, yet potent enough to alert me. I'm heading into dangerous territory if I can't stop myself from reacting to him.

"My friend?"

"Jamie."

I lift my chin and find myself fall, fall, falling into his dark-as-night eyes. I could take up residence in them. Sink deep, deep, deeper and find myself in his core. Maybe then I would get a better understanding of him. It feels like I can chisel away at his exterior for years and still not know the real him.

And yet ... he's seen me almost half naked.

I've seen his boner.

I would give anything to know what he's thinking right now.

This isn't right, or normal, me standing here with a ham sandwich that I am ravenous to eat, and him watching me with a predatory glare.

Food isn't the thing that's on my mind right now. "I didn't go and see Jamie. Why?"

He folds his arms, getting all defensive. "I wondered if you went running to him and told him what happened between us."

"First of all, I don't go running to him, and secondly, nothing happened *between us.*"

We fall silent. I take a bite of my sandwich, but now I'm conscious of chewing, of him watching me eat. "Did you write?" I ask when I've swallowed.

"I can't. I'm stuck."

"You get that stuck without your pen?"

"You wouldn't understand."

"Try me," I say, with a little more need in my voice than I would like.

"Today hasn't been a good day," he replies, but it's not a growl, not what I'm expecting. He seems tired and worn out. As am I.

"It's been a long day," I say, lifting up my plate and my glass of water. I was going to eat here, but he seems to want to hang around.

I can't be around him.

I can't be around him and not feel anything.

I can't.

I need to escape to my bedroom. "Goodnight."

CHAPTER TWENTY

MARI

"How's he been?" Jamie asks me in a hushed voice after his morning session with Ward.

"Who?" I'm in the kitchen fixing lunch. This morning I got up super early and prayed that Ward wouldn't be asleep in his study. I wanted to get his desk tidied before he showed up. There wasn't as much litter in his room either.

Jamie glances over his shoulder, then whispers. "Ward."

"Fine, why?"

He pulls out something from his pocket.

A pen.

It's not just any old pen.

It's *the pen*.

My eyes almost fly out of their sockets. Enraged, I snatch it from him. "What are you doing with this?" I hiss.

"It was a joke. You said the guy had been an ass to you, so I wanted to put him in his place."

"When did I say that?"

"Over dinner the other day."

"You thought taking his pen would be the answer?" I'm so livid I want to hurl the pen at him like a flying missile. He has no idea of the grief his little stunt has caused. The problems it has created. The thing it has started.

"How did he react?"

"How did he react?" I cry, then remember to lower my voice. "Do you have any idea how angry he was?"

Jamie's face turns hard. "Did he blame you?"

"Duh! It was there one minute, and then it wasn't. Who else is he going to blame?"

"He could have mislaid it." Jamie's jaw tightens. "What did he say? Did he threaten to fire you?"

"He didn't say anything. He ... he just got annoyed." I decide to keep the news about the entire saga to myself. "I'll put it back on his desk. Please don't do anything so stupid again. I can fight my own battles."

Jamie leaves and I try to figure out how I'm going to return the pen to Ward without him knowing the truth. He's seen me search for it on the floor, under the desk and on the couch for it. He saw me look all around his room.

I can't just tell him I found it there. Jamie has no idea of the mess he's landed me in. This is a drama I could do without, given everything else that's going on.

My phone rings and I rush to answer it. My heart misses another beat when I hear Brenda's voice. What now?

"Your mom's fine," is the first thing she says. "She wanted to speak to you." I walk away, far away into the entrance hall and listen as my mom thanks me for coming to see her yesterday.

"That's okay, Mom. I was worried."

"You worry too much."

"Just be more careful. Try not to trip."

She laughs. "You'll come again on the weekend?"

"I sure will. Love you."

As I walk back into the kitchen, I freeze at the sight of Ward's back. He's examining the pen. I stop breathing for a few seconds.

"You found it?" he asks, rolling it between his fingers as I slowly return to the salad. I pick up the salad dressing and pour a little in, trying to think of what to say.

"What?" My eyes are riveted on the salad, as if I'm performing some kind of open-heart surgery.

"You know what." His voice is playful. This is both new and alarming. I lift my gaze to his. Amusement dances in his eyes.

"Oh, the pen ..." I murmur, noticing that he has shaved completely. There's no hint of stubble on his face. When did he get that his haircut? I start to think back to last night. Did he get it cut while I was with my mom?

He taps the pen on the island, breaking my reverie. "Yes. The pen."

"I was going to tell you."

"How did it end up here?" The way he cocks his head, the way he doesn't fly into a rage or accuse me, should make me feel relieved. Should make it easier for me to breathe.

But it does neither.

He's waiting for an answer, only I can't give him the right one. "I ... I think I ... I think I might have accidentally picked it up to write you a note." That's the best I can come up with on the spur of the moment.

He lifts an eyebrow. "After I told you not to touch anything on my desk?" There isn't an ounce of anger in his voice.

"I'm sorry. I wasn't thinking. I must have grabbed it by mistake."

"That's what I thought you'd done." His lips turn upwards, just a fraction, but he looks as if he's trying not to smile. "Where did you find it?"

"Here somewhere."

"Where somewhere?"

"Why do you need to know?"

"It's a very important point. I'm a stickler for detail," he says. I'm scared that he knows Jamie took it.

"I can't remember."

"We had a disagreement over this, Mari. You really can't remember?"

"You call what we had a disagreement?" That's putting it mildly.

"What would you call it?" he asks.

"Your behavior? Bullying rudeness, in the first instance."

"Don't hold back."

"I won't."

"I believe you didn't."

My mouth opens but I forgot what I was going to say. Is he referring to me in my underwear? Or the things I called him when I had the chance? I'm trying to deflect his attention from where he thinks I found the pen, but in doing so I've inadvertently walked myself into a blind alley.

"Do you need to borrow it still?" he asks. His eyes glitter with something mischievous and it makes me more alert.

I didn't borrow it. I didn't even take it, but thanks to Jamie, I'm now paying the price for it. "No," I answer. Then, "Your lunch will be ready soon. Did you want me to add chicken to it?"

He narrows his eyes, because he knows I'm steering the conversation away from what he asked me. "You don't usually ask me what I want. Are you offering me an a la carte service?"

"You're the boss. You get to call the shots."

He gives me the tiniest hint of a smile, but it's a naughty, knowing smile, as if we share a secret.

Sweet Jesus. I need a fan to cool down my face. I want to comment on his haircut, but I'm scared he'll make something else of it.

"I don't mind what you cook. You seem to have a knack for knowing what I need."

As he leaves, I suddenly understand why he's not angry, why he's being playful.

He thinks I'm flirting.

He thinks I took the pen on purpose.

He thinks I'm trying to catch his eye.

The look-at-me-in-a-bra stunt I pulled has led him to him to think this. He's shaved today.

Completely.

Just now.

He definitely had his usual five o'clock shadow last night. That much I remember, even if I don't remember the haircut. I was too scared to look at him for too long.

It's the first time I've seen him that he's been clean-shaven. Underneath all that growth lurks a fine figure of a man.

My heart starts to race.

My body's telltale signs of approval.

I am so in trouble.

CHAPTER TWENTY-ONE

WARD

She took the pen and hid it from me and I have no idea why. Some people are drawn to celebrity, but I don't consider myself to be one. Authors aren't in the same bucket as movie stars.

Why would Mari take my pen then pretend she hadn't? She's not the type of woman to play those types of games.

I push this new drama out of my head because I've wasted too long not writing.

I'm also struggling to forget that I've seen her shirtless, and that whenever we talk, there seems to be an undercurrent vibrating in the air between us.

I have to block her out.

I look through my notes and poke at my plot in the same way as I poke at my salad. I scratch my face, and my fingers find smooth skin. No beard, because I shaved it off completely. I liked the comfort of my beard. It was a thing of safety, something to hide behind. It also takes a while to get used to having a lighter head of hair. If Mari noticed, she didn't comment.

Mari and her games.

Women do this sometimes. Mess with your head. My mother did, when I was a child, and then again on her deathbed.

It takes great resolve, but I keep to myself for the next few days. Jamie comes and I have my hourly gym session with him every day, but for the most part, I avoid running into Mari.

Jamie says I'm making good progress. I can see it for myself. To begin with, I can do more than a handful of push-ups easily. I managed thirty today. I'm also back on track with my healthy eating. Jamie says he's surprised because most people don't make such a huge leap in progress. He's surprised that I have. When I set my mind to something, I can pull it off.

How else have I managed to write so many books? It takes patience, and persistence, and a concerted effort, fueled by dogged determination.

It's not just my diet that I'm keeping an eye on, I'm taking to exercise as if my life depends on it. This is what I tell Rob when he calls one day for a progress report.

"Your life does depend on it," he says. He wants to know about the book, because that's all he cares about. I string out the conversation and talk about everything else but the book because I like to wind him up like that.

The first draft is coming along better than I expected. In a few more weeks' time, I'll have written the ending. Then comes the hard task of rewriting it and polishing it and checking to make sure that everything makes sense. But I hope to be back home by that stage.

"Keep it up," Rob tells me. "I look forward to reading the first draft."

I look forward to finishing the first draft.

Two weeks go past and I stay burrowed away in my study, away from Mari. She appears to be avoiding me too.

We can easily go for days without seeing or talking to one another.

The only reason I know she's around is because my food magically appears on time.

MARI

I was worried for no reason. Ward has locked himself away in the study, keeping away from me.

It's better this way.

Sometimes I look back on that time when he came to my room to apologize, and I wonder what I was thinking. I'm not an exhibitionist by any stretch of imagination.

Maybe Dale's betrayal cut deeper than I thought. It dented my pride and took away a huge chunk of my self-esteem. That man broke my heart and I'm not sure I've recovered.

I don't have time for romance. I have no interest in striking out or meeting someone new, but I feel unnoticed, unattractive and forgotten, here in this place, all alone.

I need to be around people. I need to be appreciated, I thrive when I'm told I've done a good job by my peers, my managers, and the customers I serve. This is why working here leaves me so unfulfilled and unappreciated. The desire to be acknowledged and needed is necessary for our delicate human egos.

Although we've kept away from one another, I found myself staring at Ward as he was putting his dishes into the dishwasher. I couldn't help but notice how his arms were more defined. There was a shape to his muscles that hadn't been there before. And since when did he start wearing t-shirts that hugged his body like that?

The transformation that's taking place in front of me is so hard to ignore, he is changing fast before my very eyes. I don't hate him as much as I used to. I'm not even scared of him, and I definitely don't feel nervous around him.

I wish he wouldn't hide away the way he does. My mind strays back to the day I saw the tentpole in his pants. I shake my head and try to throw out the images that tempt me.

But Jamie confirms what I'm seeing. He says Ward is doing really well and he is shocked by the transformation. He makes a comment about Ward's new haircut and beard and jokes that the guy is probably getting ready for publicity once the book releases. The movie is coming out as well. I'd made myself believe that I might be the reason for Ward's new makeover, but Jamie's words now make me doubt that.

I'm being silly. Fantasizing again. Making up stories where there are none. Being weak and filling myself with romantic ideas as usual.

Jamie is one of Ward's fans. Right now, he's reading a book that Ward wrote and he tells me to read it, but like always, I decline to.

It makes me wonder, what possesses a man to write horror?

CHAPTER TWENTY-TWO

MARI

Every day is the same, like Groundhog Day. The only thing I have to look forward to is Jamie's visits.

Visiting my mom on the weekend breaks up some of the monotony. Maybe next weekend, I'll allow myself an evening of drinks and dinner with Jamie. Some normal conversation. A group of our friends are getting together, Jamie tells me. He said that Raleigh, a friend more Jamie's than mine, is going to organize a get-together in a couple of weeks' time. She liked Jamie and I've always wondered if there was a hint of an attraction between them. It would be good to catch up and see everyone and see what they are doing now.

We haven't managed to talk much in recent days because he's doing an extra half an hour, at Ward's request. When he finishes, he has to rush off to make it back to the gym where he works.

I'm in the study early one morning, tidying up Ward's

desk. As I begin to polish his desk, moving his papers and notebooks out of the way, I catch sight of my name scribbled on a sheet of paper.

It's a scribble in his spidery scrawly handwriting:

Mari

I bend over, lowering my head and peering closer.

He wrote this.

My name.

Why?

"What are you doing?"

I jolt my head up as his sharp voice pierces the air. "I ... I ..." I lift my hand, duster and all, trying to figure a way out of this.

Ward walks towards me. There's a sharpness to his features that wasn't there before when his beard hid most of his face. My heart threatens to crash out of my ribcage, my pulse gallops like wild horses.

"I told you to keep your hands off my work."

I quickly put his notebook on top of the papers and try to make his desk look neat and orderly, just how he likes it.

"What were you doing, Mari?" He lifts up his pen, *that* pen, and taps it on the desk as if he's a headmaster waiting for an answer.

I try to straighten up to my full height, to regain some semblance of control, of authority, but his menacing glare makes my insides quiver.

"You wrote my name." I state, lifting my chin in a way that I hope signals defiance.

"You were looking through my papers," he replies, as if that explains everything.

We're facing one another and only the chair, neatly tucked into the desk, stands in our way.

"Why did you write my name?"

He scoffs, as if I've lied. "Did I?"

"Who else would?" I quip cheekily. "I can show you." I go to pull out the sheet of paper.

"*Don't* touch my notes."

My duster falls to the floor and I reach down to get it. I forgot. He doesn't like me snooping around.

Then, in a softer voice, probably because he's reminded of what an ass he can be, he says, "I must have been thinking."

"Of what?" I ask, standing up. His Adam's apple bobs, telling me he's not as calm as he pretends to be. "Am I in trouble?" I want to know. I can't help but think of my job, and my mom, and the expensive nursing home. I've given this man enough chances to fire me.

"In trouble?" His eyes glint in the dim light of the room. "Any reason you would think that?"

"I didn't read any of your papers. I swear I didn't. I saw my name and I ..." I can't think of what to say. Him writing my name means something, doesn't it? Or am I desperately trying to make it mean something?

"But you managed to find a sheet of paper with your name on?" he asks, calmly.

"It was sticking out. I didn't go looking for it. It caught my attention."

"Did it now?"

I blink, and I'm about to ask him what he means but I have lost the ability to think. The nerve endings all over my body throb like a thousand miniscule drums.

This is the wrong reaction for me to have here in this

room standing so close to this man. I've done nothing wrong, I remind myself, and I never took his pen.

"First you take my pen, and now you find a sheet of paper with your name on it. What's going on, Mari?"

I gulp. "You've got it all wrong. I saw my name, and I was curious." I try my power move tactic and take a step towards him. I'm so close now that I accidentally brush my hand across his naked forearm. I shiver, not because he's accused me wrongly, but because the heat and hardness of his arm, of his body, of his muscles, causes a peculiar reaction inside me. He advances a teeny bit, and I retreat but now I'm pushed up against his desk and I have nowhere else to go. If I inch back any further, my bottom will be perched upon it.

"Curious?" he whispers, then makes a counter move and cages me so that my bottom is perched on the desk.

"It was an accident," I managed to splutter.

"An accident?" He rolls the pen between his thumb and forefinger, then lays it flat against my arm and, holding it by the tip, he slides it down. A sigh escapes my lips. Sweet Jesus. I don't understand how a pen can turn my entire body into one big erogenous zone.

"Mari," he says my name as if it's the sexiest word alive. Just hearing it from his lips makes the breath catch in my throat. "You wanted my attention, didn't you? Well, now you have it."

"You ... you think I took your pen on purpose?" My mind blanks under the spell of his scent; a combination of conifers and pines, and zesty lemon wafts over me.

We've never been this close before.

Not like this.

Heat rolls off him and heats my skin. My body shivers in anticipation.

I *should* tell him to stop.

I *should* ask him what he's doing.

But then he might stop and I don't want him to. This slow sensual pen massage holds me captive.

I should say something, because I'm innocent. "It was an accident," I rasp as he continues to run the pen along my arms, over my silk bouse, which is way too showy for being a housekeeper, but this is all I have of my working wardrobe. The sensation is erotic. He's not even touching me but I am so turned on. I'd do anything he asked me to.

"I don't believe in accidents," he murmurs, his attention on the pen as he rolls it over me, then looks to see what effect it's having on me.

"What are you doing?" I manage to say. I'm so aroused, and this is so abnormal, I need a normal question to break us out of this insane yet beautiful foreplay.

"I have no idea." He stops for a microsecond and eyes me. His gaze is wanton. I want to give in. To give myself. How have I never noticed how gorgeous he is? I see him properly for the first time. There's a dusting of stubble across his face. I decide I love this look the best of all; when he looks dangerous with a hint of wicked. Not mountain man with three inches of beard, or clean-shaven with smooth skin, but like this, dark and dangerous and brooding.

I stutter out a gasp and begin to wonder what it would be like without the pen, with just his fingers trailing all over me. He moves the pen lower, stroking my waist, making light movements from my hips to my waist and back up again.

A spiral of electric heat snakes in the base of my belly and moves lower, between my legs.

"Does it feel good?" he asks.

Another gasp escapes my mouth. "Yes ..." The voice I

hear isn't mine. It's low, and velvety, and steeped in desire. Desperation, even.

I *need* him—this big brooding man beast who is deliberately arousing me. And who I am wilfully letting.

He leans further towards me, an inch, maybe two. It is raw and carnal, the energy which drips off him and washes over me. Like a sexual tsunami. Smoldering heat envelops me as I hit the desk. I shuffle and sit back, resting against it. And just as quickly I get scared and try to move off the desk in case I mess up his work. He pushes me gently back.

"Your papers," I protest.

"Screw the papers."

In the next moment he moves the pen to my breast, holding it like a wand, running the tip against my breast, as if he's drawing an outline. My eyes fly wide open, my lips part. I moan as he continues to roll it back and forth, back and forth. Teasing, touching, arousing. Under my silk blouse, my nipple rises to a peak. My mouth falls open. I huff out, bite my lower lip because I don't want him to hear me moan.

"Tell me when to stop, Mari."

I tilt my head back slightly, but I don't have the willpower to close my mouth. This is too sensuous. Too dirty. Too unacceptable.

I love every moment of it.

"You thought I took the pen so that I could entice you?" I ask, as the situation suddenly becomes clear to me.

"Didn't you? You know how much it would annoy me."

I blink.

I want to set him straight. It wasn't a crazy ruse on my part, despite what he thinks. Something in my expression must give him a clue because his expression suddenly cools.

He stops rolling the pen over me. I want to cry out and

tell him to continue. He has no idea of how ready I am for him.

I eye the pen. I want it on my breast again.

His gaze drops to my lips. We're transfixed in a crazy moment of lust and longing.

"What do you do when you get annoyed?" I ask. There is no logic to my question, but he has led me down a tricky path and I want to lead him away from the truth, from Jamie. There is no way he can ever find out that Jamie was responsible. He'd fire him in an instant.

Besides. This isn't such a bad outcome, if this is what he chooses to believe. The air is charged with more than guilt and accusation. We're bound together in a thick cloud of desire and I can't think straight.

So I won't.

Instead, I throw caution to the wind. I turn around and place my hands on the desk, jut out my bottom and ask him in a voice I never knew I possessed. "Are you going to punish me?"

He closes in on me, and I sigh with delight when his hardness presses against my bottom.

He's erect.

And big.

He wants me.

I've turned him on.

I did it before, and I've done it again now.

He wrote my name because he can't stop thinking about me. Nor I him. I occupy a space inside that head of his, and even with his fictional worlds and characters, he still thinks of *me*.

I must mean something to him.

He drops the pen onto the desk, then plants his hand beside mine. The other one slides under my skirt. I suck in a breath, and instinctively jut out my bottom, feel his steel erection poking me even harder. His hand skates over my thighs, then over my panties.

My insides turn to gloop. His touch makes me shiver. When he lifts up my skirt, tucking the hem into my waistband, exposing my panties, my legs turn to jelly.

"Do you want to be punished?"

A horror writer, a relative stranger is asking me this. A man I barely know.

And yes. I want him to punish me.

Jamie's words come and haunt me.

Don't rush head first into something. Don't go for the first man you meet. Don't make a mistake.

I feel as if I know enough about Ward. We connect on some deep, primal, raw level. I may not understand this man completely, but I understand his desire for me.

"Do you?" he growls.

I still don't answer, because I'm gutless. Boneless. A mass of willingness. He pulls my panties to the side, exposing a bare bottom. I whimper. And then he slaps me. It's not hard, not like a slap that makes a noise, but a light, quick slap. One that sends a signal directly to my core.

A gush of heat spreads all over my skin. I whimper some more then turn my head to the side. "Do it again," I beg.

He kneads my buttock then runs his hand over it as if he's admiring every inch of it, and just as I'm about to plead with him to do it again, he slaps it lightly one more time.

It's the most turned on I've ever been.

"This is why you took the pen, no?" he rasps so close to my ear that I can feel his hot breath. I buck against his hardness, needing to press against his shaft.

"Mari," he whispers. Butterflies threaten to erupt from my belly. He has me bent over in the most beautiful position, with his body pressed tightly against mine. I widen my stance so that I can feel more of his cock against me. Even wearing clothes, there is enough heat and hardness from him, against my slickness. It is beautifully sweet, and torturously taboo.

"How did we end up like this?" he whispers, sending shivers dancing along my neck and back.

"My name," I manage to stutter. "You scribbled my name."

"I was thinking about you." His hot breath against my cheek intoxicates me. He presses hard against me again, eliciting another moan from me. "I can't help it. Ever since that day ..." He doesn't need to spell it out. "That's how I see you in my dreams."

I sigh as he strokes my thigh. "Do you think about me?" he asks.

I can't lie. "Sometimes."

He shivers out a breath before nipping my earlobe and making me cry out from the sheer unexpectedness of it.

It's too much. I push back, try to straighten up and he lets me. I turn around to face him. We're both flushed, our faces red and heated. I gaze at him, needing to read his thoughts, wishing I could tell what he was thinking.

What now?

I need to gauge what's going on behind those eyes. His gaze never moves from my lips and I wonder when we will kiss.

But the doorbell rings.

He stares at me before putting his hand to my waist—I don't flinch, it's like my body wants more—and he pulls out the hem of my skirt so that my skirt is hanging down and I am decent once more.

My chest is still heaving but my disgruntled nerve endings are pissed that he's stopped stroking me.

I look at him with longing, and at the same time I try to smooth a hand over my hair, smooth down my blouse and skirt. "Jamie's late," I say, making myself presentable as quickly as I can. My eyes fall to his huge bulge between his legs.

"You won't be ready to do a workout with that in the way," I quip. I bite my lip, wishing, wanting, desiring that we had found some sort of release.

"It's not Jamie. I told him not to come today. It's Rob."

"Rob?" I cry, running another hand over my hair. "What's he doing here?"

"Take care of him," he says gruffly. "Give him a beer or something."

"A beer? This early in the—"

"I didn't expect him here so soon. Give him anything."

"And you?" I'm so aroused, glancing down I notice my erect nipples peaking under my blouse.

"I need to take care of something," he grumbles, not looking at me.

CHAPTER TWENTY-THREE

WARD

This woman is going to kill me. If anyone's going to die from blue balls, it's me. She makes me *do* things. Behave in ways I never thought I would. We all have fantasies, but she makes me want to play mine out. She presses my buttons, and I can't resist her.

In the safety of my room, I jerk off again, all the time thinking of Mari bent over my writing desk. I can still smell her sweet flowery scent, can still recall the way I touched her.

I haven't been with a woman, much less spent intimate time with one, for so long. My memory fogs over at my past fleeting encounters. I have never come on to a woman like that. I've never jerked off so much either. My characters fill my brain. My plot twists and turns feed my imagination. I have no time in my life, or space in my head, to divert to anything but my writing.

Yet Mari has crawled into my brain. She has filled my

head and taken over my thoughts so that I can't think of anything or anyone but her. I'm not prone to obsession, but obsess about this woman I do.

I've crossed a line somewhere. She brazenly stood her ground that day in her bedroom, and I did my best to keep away, but when she hid my pen, it got me thinking. It's hard not to think of her, to erase the sight of her on her yoga mat, in her clingy, body-sculpting gym clothes.

I'm only a man.

And she's become a serious diversion.

And if Rob hadn't shown up so early, what else might have happened between us? Since I'm almost done with my first draft, I'll be able to return to New Orleans. I *should* return. It's what I wanted to do before, but now I'm not so sure. Returning means no more Mari.

When I walk into the kitchen, Rob is sitting on the stool with his back to me, and Mari, standing, looks at me. She's wearing an apron now and I wonder if she's trying to hide her pebbled nipples. I grit my teeth, forcing my errant mind not to go to places that will give me another boner.

Rob turns around, then gets up to shake my hand.

"Hey there."

"Hi." I shake hands but can't bring myself to look at Mari, even though the weight of her gaze feels heavy on my face.

She knows I was taking care of myself, jerking myself to a release, with her in my mind. Shame and embarrassment curdle in my stomach. I am used to not giving much of myself to anyone, but this stranger and I have shared many stolen intimate moments. It seems tawdry. Deliciously so.

"Shall we discuss this outside?" I ask. I need to move away from Mari. I can't be here, in the same house as Mari, and act normal, not after what just happened.

"Outside?"

From the periphery of my vision, I catch Mari lifting her head in surprise. I have never left this house in all the time I have been here. Even when I got my hair cut, I summoned the best barber in Chicago to come here on that day when Mari was out. It's amazing what people will do for vast amounts of money.

"It's lunchtime." I make an exaggerated point of staring at my watch. "We'll go out to eat."

"You don't want me to make lunch today?" Mari speaks up.

"No." It's the first time I've looked at her. A dart of attraction flies through me to her. Can she feel what I'm feeling? Does she think about me the way I think about her?

"You're right," says Rob, getting up again. "He has changed."

It makes me wonder what the two of them have been talking about.

Mari folds her arms. "There's a whole new side to him I didn't see before."

"Thanks for the coffee," Rob says to Mari.

"You're welcome."

"Good to see you again."

"Likewise," says Mari.

"I hope you're taking me somewhere nice for lunch," says Rob. I have no idea where I'm taking him. I haven't been back here for decades. I don't know what type of places there are, or where to go and eat but I've been told that there are some nice restaurants at The Four Seasons.

A short while later, we're sitting at one of the restaurants in The Four Seasons with bottles of beer and burgers.

Except, I'm not very hungry. "To what do I owe this

pleasure?" He can't have flown all the way from New York just to come and see how I am. He called me late last night to say he would be over. That's all I know.

"Sally's aunt is ill." He coughs. "She's on her deathbed. We wanted to come and see her before it was too late."

"Sorry to hear that," I mumble.

"You were only an hour away. I thought it would be a good chance to see how you were doing."

"I'm making progress." Though what happened earlier between me and Mari isn't the type of progress he had in mind.

"Garvey hit number one in the New York Times List," says Rob.

"Great. Good for him." I hardly know the guy, but he's got a good twenty or so years on me. It's not that I hate him. It's that he perceives me as some sort of enemy. I wrote to him when I was first starting out, just as my first book was starting to take off, before it debuted so spectacularly, thrusting me begrudgingly into the limelight, I asked Garvey if he wouldn't mind having a look through my book, and perhaps, if he could, supply me with a quote. This might have been rash and rather presumptuous of me, but I didn't know any better. I wasn't prepared for a letter from his secretary requesting that I never make such a demand again. She went on to say that he had read the first page but couldn't read any more.

It shocked me that an author of his caliber and standing could be so rude.

"Great?" Rob picks up his burger. "The guy's doing well. He's going to stay in that position for a good while and probably hang around in the Top Ten for the rest of the year."

"Great." I don't want to hear any more about James Garvey.

"I'm expecting you to knock him off the list when you release."

"That's a tall order."

"You've made that list before."

I'm not feeling it this time around. I'm not feeling this book. I've been writing, but I'm not getting the feels. I have too many other things to contend with. There are days when I think my head will explode. Or my cock.

"I'll send you the first draft in the next week or so," I tell him.

"You sure?"

"Yes." He looks at me as if he doesn't believe me. "Is that why you're here? To assess me?"

"You had me worried when we last spoke, when you said you wanted to come back home. You're up and down, Ward. You're all over the place."

"I'm making progress."

"You are making progress, but I wanted to make sure you're okay."

"I'm okay."

"I wonder if I did the right thing, putting you all the way out here and then getting you a live-in housekeeper. With your history."

I raise an eyebrow.

"With your mom passing," he says.

"You move me here, and put me in this situation and now you're asking if you did the right thing? It's a little late for that, don't you think?" Now that Mari and I are embroiled in some weird and sordid fantasy.

"I wanted you to get some closure. Let's face it, who else is going to give you that kind of advice? You don't have anyone," Rob reminds me lightly. "I don't want you to fall back down that hole again, and it looked like you were starting to."

"I'm making progress not just with my writing." I flex my muscles. "Can you tell?"

He nods approvingly. "I noticed right away. I noticed it from the moment I saw you. No hair growth on your face either and you finally got a haircut."

I rub my hand along the smooth skin along my jaw. "It was getting too long and knotty."

"You look ten years younger."

I nod.

"You look like a new man. Well," Rob clears his throat, "you look like you did when we first met."

"That was a long time ago."

"Like I said, ten years younger. How many pounds lighter?"

"Enough." I run a hand over my arm, over the biceps and down. Am I pleased with the result? Hell, yeah. It got easier when I started to see progress, much like writing. When I could write for two minutes and it didn't read back like word vomit, I'd write more. Soon, I got to a point where the story poured out of me. It's the same with exercise. At first, I was driven because remembering Trevor's jibes spurred me on. Then I didn't want to give Jamie anything about me to laugh at with her.

Then I reached a stage where I could feel the difference in my body. Could feel it getting hard, not so pillowy. Could see the way Mari looked at me sometimes when I caught her staring.

It was enough to motivate me.

"I saw you fall apart once before, Ward. Saw you unable to write or function. Saw you reduced to a shadow of your former self. I didn't want to see your brilliance wasted."

"I managed to turn it around."

"In time you did. You were also younger, more of an unknown, just starting out. There's more pressure now."

"I had a glitch." I play with my food, not really in the mood to eat.

"You have a gift, Ward, and I don't want you to waste it."

"I don't intend to."

"I have to say, I didn't expect such a dramatic transformation and so quickly. Mari said you were working out."

"Yeah?" I'm curious to know what else she said.

"You look thinner. Fitter. Better. It's a miracle that you're on target with the book, but the exercise?" He cracks a grin. "I wasn't expecting miracles, and yet, you've confounded everyone."

"Everyone?"

"Mari said you'd been in the gym a few times on your own, before the second guy started."

Those were the times that made me notice her. Hard not to notice her on her yoga mat in her various poses. "That was early on," I reply. "When I was procrastinating. Sometimes, hitting the gym is easier than writing."

"And lying around like a couch potato must have been even easier. She says you don't do that anymore."

"Have you been interrogating my housekeeper?" I cry out in exasperation.

"If anyone's going to know what you're up to, it's her."

What else did she tell you? I want to ask him, but I don't. It's better not to turn the conversation around to Mari because then I won't be able to get her out of my head.

"What's the holdup with the first draft?" he asks.

"I'm stuck on a plot point. I'll figure it out. Don't worry, I'm working on fixing it."

"I'm not worried now. Not anymore." We eat in silence before he asks, "Have you visited your old house?"

I'm about to take another bite of my burger, but I don't. "No."

"Any plans to?"

"No."

"Fair enough. Maybe you don't need to."

"I never needed to."

He drops me back home after coffee, but declines my invite to come in. Says he needs to get back, otherwise Sally will start to worry.

When I walk through the door, Mari is in the hallway about to drag the vacuum cleaner up the stairs.

"Here," I stride towards her. "Let me help you."

"I can manage," she insists, one hand on the hose and the other grabbing the handle of the machine. Of course she can. She's no wilting flower. And even if she struggled with it, she still wouldn't want my help.

Our gazes lock and hold. An image flashes past of where we were before Rob showed up. She won't look away, and neither do I. Will she speak first? Will she allude to what happened earlier?

Of course not.

And yet I want to talk about it. I can't pretend that nothing happened when so much has already happened between us.

MARI

. . .

"How was your lunch?" I ask, not wanting his help, but not wanting him to walk away.

There's something unspoken between us, something nebulous and intangible that we can't grasp, even though the physicality was so real.

"Nice. It was a nice change to go out."

In the silence that follows, I rack my brain for something to say but find no words. What words are there for what he did, for what I felt, for what he made me feel?

"I never knew that you were from around here," I say, hoping to get him to elaborate.

"I was born in Chicago."

"You were born here?"

He nods.

"I had no idea."

"Why would you?" he asks.

Why would I indeed? This man is like a blank book with the writing in invisible ink. Impossible to determine by the naked eye, unless you have a means of decoding it.

Ward and I only talk about what he wants for lunch and dinner. Or we scribble notes to one another.

We make small talk. He seems anxious to get away, but I can't pretend everything is normal when it isn't. He has touched me, run his hands over my bare buttocks. Pressed himself against me and I loved it.

Seeing us now, no one would have any idea what we had been doing only hours earlier, and the eerie thing is that neither of us is talking about it.

"Aren't you tempted to go have a look?" I press, now that I have a hook into some new piece of information about his past.

"Tempted to look at what?"

"The place you lived at before?"

He frowns. "I don't ever want to." There's something nonnegotiable behind that sentence. Something I can't get to the bottom of.

"Rob said that had been one of the things he'd hoped you would do."

"You and Rob seem to have had a lot to say about me."

I sense he doesn't like that, and then I get worried when he says, "You didn't tell him ... did you?"

Tell him what?

From the look on his face, it quickly becomes apparent. He thinks I told Rob what happened between us. Surely, he wouldn't think that? "No!" I cry. "I didn't say anything about ... about that. It's none of his business."

His mouth twitches, and I hold my breath, waiting for him to say something. *Anything.* Wishing he would acknowledge what happened.

"I'd better get back to my writing."

"Are you sure?"

Are you sure? I want to slap my hand to my face in embarrassment. What a thing to say. He doesn't reply. He doesn't acknowledge it in any way. His expression offers no insight into what he's thinking. I feel like a fool and hang my head in shame as he disappears out of sight.

I'm reminded of Jamie, and what he thinks of me and my reckless choices.

This need to keep Ward by my side comes from a desperate place somewhere inside me. I don't even know who I am any more. It's this place, and the company, or lack of, it's me being so bored stupid, with my self-esteem in the gutter, that I can't help myself.

CHAPTER TWENTY-FOUR

MARI

Jamie asks me again if I want to go out on the weekend, but I brush him off again by saying that I need to spend time with my mom. Her fall, although minor, has given me a scare, and I want to spend as much time with her as I can.

On one particular day, it's been raining the whole time and I feel as if a storm is brewing. After having my dinner, and noting that Ward hasn't come out to have his, I finish everything and head up to bed. None of this is normal. None of this is ordinary, and yet he and I continue on as if nothing happened. Sometimes I have to think really hard because us getting so close and intimate feels like it could have been my imagination playing tricks on me.

I snuggle up on my bed reading a book, and checking for job vacancies on my laptop. The rain is relentless, and I stop reading and walk over to the window to stare. The rain comes down in sheets. I love the sight and sound of it, especially being inside all snug and warm when it is soaking wet and miserable outside.

Watching the rain reminds me of how stuck I am. Of how nothing has moved on for me in my life. Dale has moved on. His girlfriend must have advanced in her pregnancy. I never did ask him how far along she was. I didn't want to know about that. I haven't heard from him, but I also gave him no reason to seek me out.

Against the background noise of the rain, I can't help but think about Ward and how we went from sixty to zero and fizzled out. And then I try not to think about him, but it's impossible not to, so I turn on the TV trying to keep my mind on other things. When my eyes get all heavy and I can barely keep them open, I go to sleep, even though the rain is lashing down outside.

But I can't sleep. A flash of lightning zigzags through the night sky. Moments later a clap of thunder follows. I yawn, and notice that the TV is still on and a black and white movie is playing. I must have drifted in and out of sleep but now I can't get back to sleep because of the noise outside.

Yawning again, I climb out of bed and tiptoe to the window. A flash of lightning slices across the sky. There's no way I'm going to be able to fall asleep now, so I slip a sweatshirt over my nightshirt and head downstairs.

WARD

When the lightning flashes again, I sit upright on the couch. I have the fire burning, so it's warm and cozy. I knew I wouldn't be able to sleep tonight, so I didn't bother going up to my room to go to bed. I knew sleep would be impossible on a night like this.

I wait it out in the study, but I have the blinds up so I can see the lightning when it comes. I've always needed to face my fears, and tonight is just another test of my fear.

I've tried to read through my work. It's almost there. I'm at the last hurdle, I have an ending in mind but the ending I started with is not the ending I want. It doesn't fit quite right.

The door opens, the sound of it startles me, making me turn. I'm on edge as it is. Mari is in the doorway holding a cup.

"The light was on," she says. "I thought you might have left it on by mistake." She hovers in the doorway, uncertain and unsure. What happened between us makes things difficult. I don't know how to face her or be around her.

I can't trust myself.

And for that reason, I have stayed away from her as much as I can. But she's here now and I don't want her to leave. "I can't sleep," I tell her. The sight of her on a night like this is comforting and very much welcome.

"You're working." It's neither a question nor a statement. She seems hesitant to move. I want her to come in, come closer, but I'm scared she'll walk away and leave if I suggest such a thing.

There is a push-pull in all our interactions and this is the reason I've hit a wall on my ending. It's not just that the plot point stinks, it's that the library of images and emotions and feelings that Mari evokes in me are getting in the way of my creativity. It leaves me unable to finish my story properly.

"Come in," I say finally to plug the awkward silence. What better way is there to spend this gloomy night than with Mari?

CHAPTER TWENTY-FIVE

MARI

"Are you sure? I don't want to disturb you."

"You're not disturbing me."

I can't help noticing that Ward looks so sad in the dimly lit room. A reading lamp is switched on beside the couch, lending a warm glow. Elsewhere in the study, a few other amber-colored lamps are switched on. Ward usually only ever turns two lamps on. Tonight, most of them are on. There's something else that's unusual. The blinds are up. This is odd. *Very* odd. He never has his blinds up. Ever. This is the first time. He must like watching the rain as much as I do.

I walk in, still holding my cup of untouched hot chocolate. I'm tempted to ask him if he would like some, but he seems deep in his manuscript, with the papers balanced on his lap.

"You have your blinds up?" I ask.

"I like watching the rain fall."

We have something in common. "You too?"

He looks at me, his brow creasing.

"I like watching the rain," I confess. "I love the sound it makes. It's soothing."

"You like the rain?" he echoes.

I nod.

"I was waiting for the lightning," he tells me, closing his notebook. A loose sheet of paper floats to the floor. I pick it up and hand it back to him. "Are you stuck again?"

He doesn't talk to me about his writing, and I know better than to ask, but I feel that I can ask him anything. I feel we've reached a point where we can do that. I don't sit down. There's only one couch, and I'm wary of keeping my distance.

"I'm stuck, but I'll figure it out." He puts his work to the side. "Sit down."

"Are you sure?"

"I could do with some company tonight." His admission surprises me, but, like him, I'm glad for the company. I sit down, a small distance away from him and hold onto my cup as if it's my small protective shield.

"I woke up because of the thunder," I tell him.

He turns to face me. "I couldn't sleep because of the thunder."

"Too noisy?"

"Too many bad memories."

"Bad memories? Did you get caught out in it once?" I take a sip of my hot chocolate. He exhales slowly and looks away from me. For the longest moment, he says nothing. "I didn't get caught in it."

I hold my cup with both hands, waiting for him to embellish his story, but I get silence instead. I can see that he wants to talk, but this man who surprisingly has a gift for writing doesn't seem to have the same when it comes to talking. I'm going to have to pull it out of him, word by word. "Then what was it?" I ask softly.

"I hate it."

"The rain?"

"The lightning."

"I've never cared for lightning much," I say. "It's just a flash and then it's gone before you really see it, but the rain." I stare out of his windows. He has two large bay windows and the rain falls like crystal beads, illuminated by the lamps in the garden. "I just love the sound of the rain more, but thunder scares me. It makes me jump."

"Lightning makes me jolt," he says.

"I can see why. It's unexpected."

"It's the fear of what it reveals."

"Reveals?" I turn towards him slightly. "What does lightning reveal?"

He presses his lips together, and I know his moods and mannerisms so well that I sense his reluctance to tell me more. But I want to know more. This might be my only chance. "What does it reveal, Ward?" My voice is almost a whisper.

He coughs, and stares at the fire. "My stepdad used to lock me in the attic when I was a boy."

I hold my breath at the thought of such cruelty. "He used to lock you in there?"

"For a day or two, as punishment."

I almost choke. "For what?"

"Because I didn't like him and he knew it. He was mean. Had an evil sadistic streak in him."

"How old were you?"

"Six, almost seven."

"Oh, Ward. I'm so sorry." I wish he would look at me.

I'm almost tempted to lay my hand against his face and make him turn to me. But I resist.

"He used to lock me in the attic when I was bad."

"Were you a bad boy?" I can't imagine Ward being bad, and then I remember the way he teased and aroused me with the pen. There are many facets to this man.

"When I didn't call him 'dad', or say 'please' and 'thank you' or do what he asked me to do. I wasn't used to him, and I didn't like him coming between us. I didn't like him. It had always been me and my mom. It had just been the two of us until then. And my grandparents. My dad left before I was born. I never knew him."

I blink in shock.

"Then he came along, but we didn't need him."

"How awful for you," I murmur, and realize that I have never heard Ward speak so much in one sitting before.

"She left me with my grandparents and went away for a weekend. Then came back with him. Said they got married."

This sudden insight into Ward's life shocks me. It must have hurt, to suddenly have to deal with a new addition to the family. I sit quietly, and I no longer feel like drinking any more of my hot chocolate.

"What did your mom do when he did this?"

"She disappointed me." He takes a breath in, pauses for a moment before answering. His quivering chin is the only sign that of his unease. "She went from being my world to making him her world. Her silence made her complicit."

"Ward," I say, my heart splits in two. "That's awful."

"She was probably so relieved to have someone take care of her. It wasn't easy for her, being a single mom."

"It can't have been."

"I went from being the apple of my mom's eye to being a piece of shit on the bottom of her shoe."

"No, Ward. Surely not." I'm not a mother, and even I can't believe a woman would be so callous to her child.

"She wanted me to be nice to him, but I couldn't be. I was jealous that he was taking my mom from me. I couldn't help myself."

"You were only a child," I point out.

"He'd grab me by my shirt and march me up the stairs and into the attic, and then he'd leave me there for hours, if not overnight."

"Overnight?" I am horrified.

"Sometimes two nights."

"Two nights? What about food? And going to the bathroom?"

"He'd leave me scraps of food, and give me toilet breaks now and then."

I put my hand to my mouth. "Oh, Jesus." I want to give him a hug. But the cup of chocolate in my hands prevents me. It will spill if I make a move. "That's evil. Downright evil. Did nobody help you? Your grandparents?"

I shake my head. "They didn't know."

"Why didn't you tell them?"

"I was scared."

I let out a cry of anguish, as Ward paints a picture of his life.

"He'd take out the lightbulb so I'd be left in the dark. He'd scare me and get great pleasure in doing so. He would creep up into the attic, and I'd be sleeping, and he would shout, or say something scary. The fucker liked making me jump. He was a complete bastard."

"He sounds like a psychopath." I lean over him to set my cup on the side table, and my breast accidentally brushes against his face. I didn't mean to do it. I wanted to free my hands because I want to hug him, because I feel so sad for him. He doesn't seem to notice. "And then what happened?" I whisper, sitting back in my place.

"It was a night like this when he locked me in the attic once. I wasn't scared of thunder and lightning then. Even as a boy, I found it exciting. I'd watch the lightning, then wait for the thunder, counting how many seconds would pass. But he changed all of that for me."

I am so caught up imagining the young Ward and his evil stepdad that my heart races, and breaks a little for him.

"That night I curled up to go to sleep, expecting to be let out again in the morning, but he changed tactics. He started talking to me in the dark. It was heavy stormy weather. The noise of thunder and lightning filled the air, yet in the darkness I was somehow reassured by his voice. But at the next lightning strike, he stepped in front of me. He was wearing one of the Pierrot doll masks."

I frown.

"The sad-looking clown with the white face and dark eyes," he explains.

I cry out in fear and sorrow and a mingling of both. "He did that to *you*?" I can't wrap my head around this.

"He scared me to death because I wasn't expecting it."

"Oh, Ward." I don't know what to say. I want to comfort him but I'm scared he will push back on it. I can't read him, even when I think I can. We sit in silence but I can't get the image he has painted out of my head.

"It helps with you being here," he says, looking ahead.

I place my hand on his thigh. "I'm sorry for what you went through."

"Not your place to be sorry about something you weren't there for."

"But I'm sorry all the same."

He nods. "I'd been scared all my life. I took to writing horror later as a way of dealing with what happened. I learned that the only way to confront my fears was to write about them, and in time, the things from my childhood days didn't scare me."

I squeeze his hand, feeling grateful that he has shared a hidden part of him. All of Ward is a mystery to me, until he lets me have a sneak peek. Like he did now. I feel I have a better insight into the man. "What can I do to help you?" I consider making him a mug of hot chocolate.

"Just stay here."

In the silence, the weirdness between us amplifies. The things that happened here in this very room, the episode with the pen, him stroking and touching me with it, all of it comes alive in my mind in brilliant color. I consider leaning across him again in order to reach for my cup, but my nerves and recklessness get the better of me.

Instead I take a risk and move over and position myself so that I'm straddling him. And then I wait for him to ask me what the hell I'm doing.

He looks up at me. The light is dim but not too dark that I don't see the element of surprise in his expression. I sit on his lap, my knees on either side of his hips, and just like that, oh-so-slowly, his hardness begins to poke at me.

My hands are on my thighs, one of his arms rests on the armrest, the other by his side.

"If you want me to move, just say the word." My voice is barely a whisper. This isn't me trying to be sultry. This is me being half scared, half bold. It's my next move, following on from his seduction tactic with the pen, which has given me enough confidence to know he won't fire me for this.

He doesn't say a word, but his cock replies with a little

twitch. "Hmm." I mewl. I like the feel of him against me. It's all I've been thinking about ever since I first felt him against me.

My nightshirt has ridden up to my thighs and I'm feeling warm. It's not only because the fire is burning. The heat between us grows. I take off my sweatshirt so that I'm only wearing my strappy nightshirt.

Another flash of lightning cuts through the night sky. Ward's body tenses, and I hold his shoulders. "It's okay," I murmur, just as a burst of thunder follows. I put my hands on his shoulders, can't help but slide them down his arms slowly. I run my fingers over his muscles, loving the feel of his hard-as-rock biceps. There is no stomach between us. I splay my hands over his chest, over his t-shirt. Feel his hard, lean stomach.

"Someone's been working out," I whisper. I long to slide my hands under his t-shirt so that I can touch his skin, but I force myself to go slow.

"You notice the difference?" he asks. I bite my lower lip, then slide my hands back up to his arms. "I've been noticing a lot of things."

"Like?"

"The beard. The hair."

He smiles. "I can think more clearly now that I don't have the weight of all that hair."

I mirror his smile. "It suits you." He hasn't asked me what the heck do I think I'm doing, so I take it that he's okay with me sitting on him like this. Besides, I already have confirmation from the bulge between his legs. Feeling brave, I lift up on my knees, then position myself so that the throbbing between my legs, the slick wetness of my arousal, is directly over the tip of his erection.

An animal growl falls from his lips as I push my hips

into him then rock slowly back and forth gently. He seems to like it. At least, he hasn't complained. I also like the feel of him against me. My panties are so wet, and when I reach down to touch him through his sweatpants, I feel his wetness, too.

"I want to make better memories for you."

I swallow, wishing that we were naked. Wishing I could impale myself on his sweet and sexy cock inch by inch. The more he hardens, the more I rub against him.

"Is it helping?" I whisper, my need to come getting stronger and stronger. The thick tip of his cock isn't going to do it, but it helps in some small way to quell the desire that has been building up inside me for weeks.

"Helping with what?" he asks, his breath ragged.

I close my eyes, wanting all of him and yet forcing myself to hold back. The next move isn't mine to make. He grabs my hips with both his hands as I continue to rock against him.

I don't want a barrier between us, I don't want clothing. I want just him. I close my eyes, and throw back my head back, taking all I can from him in this constrained position. He squeezes my breast, holding it in place as I rub against him. And then he puts his mouth to my other breast, still through the fabric of my nightshirt.

I long to be completely naked. To feel skin on skin, but we make do with this. The sensation below is dulled, but my frenzy makes me ride him harder. I can't help but cry out. I haven't had an orgasm in weeks, and yet I've spent most of my nights thinking of Ward and imagining such a moment as this. I've been a walking, throbbing mess for days.

His cock is upright, and I can't position myself directly over the tip. I need more. As if he knows, he slides his fingers inside me, and I lose myself, thrashing against his hand as he sucks my breast even harder. I lift up, kneeling so that he can move his fingers more freely, and he does, setting up a rhythm with his fingers and thumb. I am light, and dizzy, and weightless in his arms. I'm on fire as I collapse in a heap in his arms.

He's still hard. I slide my hand into his pants and taking a hold of him. For a shock-filled second, my eyes widen at the size of him in my hands.

Sweet Jesus.

I pump him hard and fast, and relentlessly. He comes quickly, with a grunt, his face collapsing on my shoulder. We hold one another, my arms around him, his hands around my waist. He clings to me as another crash of thunder bursts.

"I don't have a good track record with women," he murmurs after a long time. We don't pull apart, and he doesn't look at me.

"I don't have a good track record with men."

And maybe we might just fit together because of that.

CHAPTER TWENTY-SIX

WARD

I'm sticky, and sweaty, and I can feel her wet heat through her panties. I rub my thumb over her nipple, feel it rise beneath the fabric. Feel my own dick slowly rise again like a sleepy giant waking from its quick short nap.

Her soft body curls around my chest, her face buried in the crook of my neck and her arms over my shoulders. I don't want to break the intimate spell which holds us together. I don't want to be left with nothing but the cold, hard reality of my daily life. Mari has unknowingly added a tinge of intrigue and flirtation to my world which has been gray for so long. She has added color.

The thunder and lightning have stopped and the rain seems to have trickled to nothing.

She shifts on my lap and yawns against my shoulder before pulling back.

"See, it's gone," she says. "Nothing to be afraid of." She peels her body away from me, even though we're both still joined at the hip. I touch her hair, running my fingers through her silky locks, wishing I could do that whenever I wanted, instead of snatching a moment like this. "Thank you for changing my memories." She smiles. I want her to stay here all night.

"I should go and shower," she says, ungluing herself from me. We haven't kissed, we haven't seen one another naked, we haven't made love, and yet we have shared a deeply intimate moment, one which sears deep into my soul, and which will haunt me in those fretful hours before sleep. I don't want her to leave. I'm not done. *We're* not done. I want more, and every part of her that I touch tells me she wants more, too.

"Stay." I grab her hand as she stands up.

"I can't."

"Says who?" I want to know.

"Says me."

Our fingers slide out of one another's hand as she turns to go, leaving me with a hard-on and a good look at her delectable legs.

Now that I've had a taste of her like this, I want the real thing. "Why are you doing this?"

She pulls up a strap that has fallen down and exposes a bare shoulder. "I don't know how things will be if I stay here all night."

I rush to reassure her. "We don't have to do anything." I would never expect anything from her. Just like now. It only happens if she wants it to. She cups the side of her neck, as if she's thinking, as if her head's telling her to leave and her heart—her heart or her pussy—is telling her to stay. This is pure lust, but women are more emotional. That's why she's leaving. She's scared she'll get hurt. That's why I stay away from women, because I'm scared

I'll get hurt, too. For two relative strangers, we have a lot in common.

"It would be a mistake," she says.

"This wasn't a mistake." I rise up from the couch. An uncomfortable soggy patch sticks between my legs. She needs to know this wasn't a mistake, and that I'm grateful she came along and changed this miserable night for me. She gave me the relief I needed.

She smiles. "That's good to know."

"I mean it," I tell her.

She turns to face me fully, and I can't help but admire the outline of her full and perky breasts. Just looking at her turns my cock rock hard again. I want to be inside her, I want to make her writhe and moan harder. The thought makes me harden. Her gaze lowers to the telltale signs of my attraction. My tent pole rises once more, bringing a mischievous grin to her face. "Someone's wide awake."

"Then stay."

She bites her lower lip, as if she's thinking about it. "I shouldn't."

"Do you want to stay?" I ask, but she slips out, like a shadow, leaving me alone in the shadows of the crackling fire, with another boner to tend to.

The next morning, our eyes meet across the hallway. Jamie's arrived and he's talking to Mari. He has his back to me, while Mari looks directly at me. A bolt of heat passes through me. Memories of last night, her scent, her arousal, her sighs as she came, all of these things fly through my head.

"Good morning." It's not something I usually say. I'm

not polite and I don't care enough about people to wish them a good morning. But there is something especially good about *this* morning. My mood has been lifted. I *feel* better.

Mari looks at me but it's more through me than at me.

Maybe she's embarrassed, maybe she regrets what happened. I hope not, because I don't.

After my workout with Jamie, I have lunch and try to get back to my manuscript, but I'm still stuck with the ending. And then I start thinking about Mari. She seemed closed off again. I don't want to go back to how things were between us in the beginning.

I want to see where this could lead.

Maybe I'll have my dinner in the kitchen this evening and talk to her then.

MARI

I can stop walking on eggshells while Ward is in the training session with Jamie. A sense of shame rolls over me.

I couldn't look Jamie in the eye when Ward came over. It was out of character, him saying 'good morning', in that over-the-top happy voice. I should be glad that he's not sullen and miserable, but in the cold light of the day I question my actions.

I would hate for Jamie to find out what happened last night. I myself can't understand it, but Ward obviously has an effect on me which turns me to mush. I couldn't sleep last night even after I showered and washed Ward's scent off. All I did was think about him, but I'm worried about what he will think now that there is no fear to confront, no lightning from his childhood days.

He can act it out better than I can. He can be cold whereas I can't hide my emotions because I'm not built that way. I can't hide what I feel, which begs the question, what do I want?

I'm not here for long.

He's leaving soon.

We don't even know one another.

What we have isn't even a friendship. It's an understanding, a raw, carnal, desperate understanding. I thought I knew myself, but Ward brings out a part of me I didn't know I had.

I'm in the kitchen preparing lunch when Jamie passes by after the workout.

"Raleigh's finally having that get-together," he announces. "She got a job and says she's got something to celebrate. Let's go."

"I could do with an evening out." I make a face because she was never one of my favorite people. But maybe what I need most of all is to get out and have fun. Meet people and enjoy life. Otherwise I'll end up making more mistakes like the one I made last night.

"It must get boring being stuck here all day long."

I feel my cheeks grow warm. Being here is a mixture of many things. Boring, frustrating, claustrophobic. Fun and exciting, too. "It is a bit," I say, even though this is not entirely true now.

"Come along. It might be a good opportunity to see what everyone else is up to. They might know of any jobs available."

That is a good idea. I scratch my cheek. "I might come along."

"You said your job search hadn't come up with anything yet," Jamie counters.

"I'm not officially looking."

"This will be over once Ward finishes his book."

"I know."

"So, is that a definite 'yes' for Raleigh's get-together?"

I sigh heavily. "I guess so."

He shakes his head and looks at me with a grin. "I never had to work so hard to get you out of the door before. What's Ward got that's keeping you here?"

I shift uneasily and try not to fidget, but before I can think of something to say—which would have probably been something silly because I'm so paranoid about Jamie knowing—he says, "Ward's getting ambitious. He's outgrown the routines I've created for him, so now we're boxing."

"Boxing?" That surprises me.

"I let him throw some punches while I held up the shields."

"You do look slightly red," I remark, taking a closer look at Jamie's face.

"It was his idea. He's turned it all around pretty quickly."

"Yeah?" He has turned it all around. Last night I found out. His body was hard. His thighs were solid, and his arms were built. He no longer has that belly. I blink and try to force myself to look at Jamie instead of getting pulled back into a replay of me and Ward in his study.

"He's in a good mood," Jamie comments. "Is he close to getting his book finished?"

"Must be."

Jamie sniffs under his armpits. "I need to shower and get to work. Come on Saturday."

"I'll let you know."

"Let me know? You mean I haven't convinced you?"

"I'm thinking about it."

When it comes to Ward and me, anything could happen between now and then. *Anything.*

CHAPTER TWENTY-SEVEN

WARD

I'm harder. Toned and leaner, and I'm making progress. Sparring with Jamie, I can see just how far I've come. I myself can see the changes in my body when I feel my arms and run my hand along my stomach. The flabbiness is gone and in its place are the dips and valleys of muscles which are defined.

Mari likes it. I know she does. She wants me, I can read her so easily. When there's an end goal, a motivation, it's always easier to do the hard work.

I shower up after my session and look forward to having my lunch. Having it in the kitchen marks a new change and it gets me out of being in the study all day long. I've also figured out my ending. It came to me during that boxing bout with Jamie. I now know exactly what to write and how to wrap my story up, and once I'm in the flow and writing, I'll get it done in the next few days.

I want to talk to Mari. Maybe talk is going too far. I'm curious to gauge her mood. See if she feels different, because I do. It's either my story or her. That's all I have in my head these days. Now that I've fixed the problem with my story, my mind wanders over to Mari and stays there. Hard to forget what happened between us. Harder still to not want more.

But as I head towards the kitchen to have my lunch, I hear Jamie's voice. He's still here. They're laughing. I catch the tail end of their conversation; something about a party. As I walk in, there's an awkwardness that wasn't there earlier. My paranoia kicks in. They've been talking about me. That son of a bitch has been laughing at me behind my back. Mari doesn't look my way. Maybe she's been laughing too.

"Is this mine?" I ask, pulling a plate out of the fridge, even though I never ask her. It's a given.

"Yes, that's yours. Did you want—"

"Thanks." I cut her short, take my food and leave.

Screw that lunchtime conversation with her.

I eat my lunch alone in my study, feeling none of the exuberance I felt before. Highs and lows. That's the problem with getting involved. I force myself to look over my final few chapters, but every so often I am reminded of Mari and Jamie in the kitchen and it guts me.

I make an attempt to write the ending down, but it's not that simple now. The words don't flow out. They are stalled and stilted. I pore over every word, every character motivation. Every line of dialog. I doubt myself and second-guess each line. I'm back to being stuck again.

I put a huge line through the page, then crumple it up and hurl the ball across the room. I try to write again and still the words don't come easy. I see Mari in my mind's eye.

She's in her nightshirt, teasing me. I close my eyes and play it out all over again.

Hell, no.

That's not going to help. Determined to push on, I scribble down more words, *any* words, even words that don't make sense.

She's on my lap. Gyrating. Teasing. Playing with me. My fist slams onto the desk. This is not good.

I can't get the vision out of my head. She's sitting on me. My cock in her hand. What would it be like to have her naked beneath me?

No.

I strike a line through the almost empty sheet of paper.

I try again.

Close my eyes.

Breathe deeply.

Try to conjure my characters in my head. Try to see what they do and why, and what it was I had figured out for them. I try to write again. A noise in the hallway catches my attention. I hold my breath and wait. For her.

Mari usually walks around, cleaning, decluttering, polishing as she goes about her daily tasks, but now every noise has me looking at the door, wondering if she will come in.

Waiting for her next move. *Hoping* she will come in, because we need to talk about what happened.

I wait and suck in another breath but her footsteps peter away.

I hiss out a breath.

I can't focus because my mind is consumed by her. I never know when she might come in and tempt me again. I spend my days and nights wondering what she's thinking, what she's feeling, and what she wants from me. Because I know exactly what I'm thinking and feeling and what I want from her.

Fuck.

I smack my pen down. Try some positive self-talk. Tell myself that I'm making progress.

Not when it comes to your writing.

I'm making progress of a different sort. With Mari.

So where is she now? Now that's she's set my blood on fire.

I have another boner I don't need.

This can't go on.

Her.

Me.

Us.

Whatever this hidden, secret, lustful thing between us is.

The angry buzz of the vacuum cleaner kills the quiet, and now I can't work at all. It's not the noise, because that hasn't bothered me before.

It's *her*.

The thought of her in that other room, getting on with her work. Why is she able to get on with her tasks, and I can't?

I need to block her out.

An angry groan escapes my mouth, anger and frustration puffing up like a souffle. I walk around the room, needing to expel the energy that's been building up inside me like a pressure cooker waiting to explode.

Three hours later, I haven't written a thing. I can't focus. I can't think. I can't make progress. That's what counts. That's what matters. A finished book. Not how much stamina or muscle definition I have. Or the number of push-ups I can do. Or Mari swanning around the house and keeping her distance, then turning into a vixen when I least expect it.

This can't go on.

I've turned into a frustrated, horny loser.

I throw my pen down and stand up with such force that the chair is knocked back. I'm going to put an end to this, and now. I walk out towards the source of the vacuum cleaner's noise. She's in the TV room and looks up as soon as I walk in. For a long drawn-out moment, I find myself falling into those dark irises, rekindling the fires of last night. They burn bright. A shiver rolls through me as I recall her breast on my lips, her sated sigh as she came, clinging to me as if she would never let go.

She switches the vacuum off. "Yes?" It's a cold, hard, clinical 'yes'. Almost headmistressy in its authority. She doesn't want to talk about it. She doesn't want to revisit last night. It's off topic.

It propels me to say what I need to. "This can't go on. This—whatever it is we're doing."

Her eyes widen. I can't tell if it's because I've dared to bring up the unspoken, or because of what I've said. "You distract me, and I can't have that."

She's silent, as if the force of my words has knocked the life out of her. I need her to say something. I need her to tell me I'm wrong. I need her to say we can continue. She helped me last night. She helped me make new memories. She listened and was there for me.

Each time I look at this woman, I see something new. She's a good person. A sexy, irresistible woman who cares about me. She's the perfect combination, and I'm still too afraid to go for it. "Do you understand?" I ask her when she doesn't say a word.

She stares at me defiantly. "You make it sound as if I've been the one pushing this."

"I didn't strip down to my shirt," I remind her.

"I was washing myself in *my* room when you walked in," she asserts.

"You stood there letting me have a good look."

She lifts her chin, because she knows I'm right. "You rolled your pen all over me."

"You *took* my pen, and then you claimed you found it."

Her mouth twists. Is it only me who isn't good at communicating with women? I'm a master of the written word, but I clam up when in person. "And because you think I took your pen—"

"Didn't you?" It's the second time she's refuting that and it makes me stop and backtrack. Is there a possibility that she didn't intentionally take it? What if it was an accident, as she claims? Then I'd be left looking like the fool. I only used the pen on her because I believed she was playing games with me.

Fuck. The longer she looks at me like that, as if I'm clearly delusional and desperate, the more I know it was an accident.

My twisted writerly mind jumped to the wrong conclusion completely.

"You came to me in the study," I remind her. I'm grateful that she did. I relive that moment many times. Her skin, her softness, her wetness, her breathless sighs, these very things I can't erase—nor want to.

"I came downstairs because the noise of the thunder woke me up. I made a mistake, and one I sorely regret."

She made a mistake? *I* was her fucking mistake?

"It's not like me to do things like that. I'm not that type of woman."

"I'm not that type of man."

For a reason I can't fathom, she looks nervous. "Are you ...?"

I'm too busy staring at her neck, and her lips and eyes, and the parts I want to kiss, to notice her hesitation. "Am I what?" I ask.

"Are you going to replace me?" The tone of her voice snaps my attention away from her lips and to her eyes. She looks timid. "I can't lose this job."

I tilt my head. "You won't lose this job." Her irrational fear makes her weak. I like her when she's the other way; a woman who knows what she wants and sets out to get it. The woman before me is nothing like her. Mari wrings her hands together.

"I wasn't thinking. I saw you all alone, and you looked sad. I shouldn't have come into the study." There is fear and trepidation in her voice, something new and unlike the wild creature who seduced me.

"I asked you to come in."

She presses her lips together and gives a tiny shake of her head as she looks down. Her heated cheeks are the first sign that she is embarrassed. This other Mari unsettles me. I'm so used to her being bold and brash, and in charge.

In control.

I can't help wondering if this is an act, but then I remember what Rob told me about her getting laid off her other job abruptly. I'm not familiar with that type of life-changing event. I can't relate. "I shouldn't have even been there."

She's so worried about the lousy job. "You won't lose your job. You've done nothing wrong."

She won't lift her gaze to me, but her cheeks are even more red. "Thank you."

"But we can't do this." Even as I tell her this, I don't really mean it. Not deep down inside. Not really.

"You're right," she says, staring at me. "We can't."

"We need boundaries."

"We just need to stop."

Her saying that, making the decision, annoys me.

"I need to finish my book—"

"And I need to finish my chores."

I was about to explain to her that I spend most of my waking hours thinking of her, but she's turned her back to me and switched on the vacuum cleaner again.

MARI

I want to bury my face in shame, but I vacuum away, needing to be busy, and praying that we won't cross paths again today. Ward leaves the room after making me feel like a cheap slut.

I turn on the vacuum cleaner, not because I'm in a hurry to clean the house, but because I need him to know that I'm okay, that he hasn't hurt me, that I don't care.

But he has hurt me.

And I *do* care.

I care very much because nobody has ever made me feel dirt cheap before, yet Ward Maddox has accomplished this so easily. Except he's wrong to think I instigated this turn of events. He can't know and won't ever know that the reason I didn't rat out Jamie was to protect him.

And yet, I haven't been an angel myself. I didn't help things with my look-at-me-in-a-bra move.

Somewhere between Dale cheating on me, and Ward

having some inexplicable crazy-as-heck effect on me, I've lost my self-esteem and become a needy woman. I have become the type of woman I used to scorn; a woman who uses her sexuality to attract men.

But it's less about the attraction and more about the power. Having someone like Ward—a rich, famous and reclusive man who barely knows me—take an interest in me is great for my self-esteem.

After this exchange, I revert to how I was before, with my previous keeping away from him stance. I don't hide from him like before.

These stupid games we play have to stop, but I wasn't prepared for him to stop them now, so soon.

In the days that follow, I keep my distance again. He does, too. He's gone quiet and back to his reclusive self, only without him hanging around in the TV room, slouching all over the couch, making a mess with all the chip packages.

We both get on with this new state of affairs.

When Jamie asks me again about Raleigh's party a few days later, I tell him I can make it. As well as getting me out of the house, it's going to be a great opportunity to see what my friends are up to, and to see if I might have better luck looking for jobs where they work.

On Friday before he leaves, Jamie confirms about the party tomorrow and offers to come by in a taxi to pick me up at eight o'clock. I catch a glimpse of Ward walking past the door, and a sense of smug satisfaction comforts me.

I've already made up my mind to wear my sexiest dress, and I hope he'll be skulking around to see me in it.

WARD

. . .

"When can I expect it?" Rob asks when I tell him that I'm still stuck on the ending. I clutch the phone tighter. "Soon." But I don't know how I'm going to get any writing done today, knowing that Mari is going out with Jamie tonight. I haven't been able to make any progress all day.

"That's what you said last time."

"I'm working on it. There are still some things I need to iron out."

"Sure thing, buddy. I was under the impression that you were almost there." I sense an unasked question lingering behind his words.

"You'll have it as soon as it's done." I hang up. I have made no progress ever since I warned Mari that we had to stop. But now I realize the real issue. It's not that I've stopped thinking of Mari. In fact, the problem is much worse. I have blue balls and I am even more frustrated than ever.

The solution wasn't to avoid one another, it was to get together and talk it out. It was to *do* something about it. The pent-up frustration is now at exploding point and my manuscript is no further along. I grow more miserable and frustrated with each day.

She's doing exactly as I asked, she's keeping her distance, but not seeing her is killing me. Things are so much worse, not better.

I slam the phone down and squeeze the soft padding near my eyebrows. It's full of tension. My eyes feel sore. My neck feels stiff. I can't sleep properly. My brain churns with plot points that I hate again and characters who are too stupid to live.

I hate my story. I told Rob I was almost done, and I was, but now I detest everything I've written. It stinks. It's boring. It's drivel.

Worse, Mari is going out with Jamie tonight.

I blame Rob for putting these two people in my life.

They've caused me more problems than I care to count. Everything about this current situation, about her and him, messes with my mind.

I should burrow away in my writing cave but if I do that, my mind will be on Mari leaving. Jamie said he was coming at eight to pick her up. I resolve to be in the gym at that time, working up a sweat and venting my frustration, but when the time comes, I hover around in the kitchen.

When the doorbell rings, Mari doesn't see me loitering in the hallway when she rushes to answer the door. But I see her. It's pretty fucking hard to miss her in that sexy short white dress with pencil point heels.

I see the back of her dress. It is low enough that it comes down all the way to her lower back. I hiss out a breath. She's not even wearing a bra.

This revelation smacks me in my gut.

She says something to Jamie, and by the time I've realized that her voice is getting louder and that she's coming into the kitchen, it's too late for me to hide.

Too damn late.

She almost walks into me skulking in the shadows. "Oh, sorry. I didn't see you there."

My mouth hangs open. I want to disappear. Before I have time to collect my thoughts and find something to say, she sashays past me again.

I hear laughter, and then the door slams shut. I kick the door closest to me. Screw the gym. I search for junk food to fix my mood and find chocolate, and a bag of chips, and some cans of fizzy drink.

This evening, I'm going to do nothing but eat and watch TV. But as I flick through channels automatically, not watching anything, my mind is in chaos. Soon enough, the floor is littered with wrappers and empty cans.

I stay up until two in the morning, waiting for her to return. I wait and wait, and when it turns to four o'clock, my stomach is in knots. She's with Jamie, probably in his bed and she has no intention of coming back tonight.

Fuck her.

And fuck Jamie.

CHAPTER TWENTY-NINE

MARI

I must be a walking magnet for men to treat me badly, but I never seem to learn my lesson. First Dale, now Ward. Jamie is right. I feel ashamed. Well, I'm going to wash Ward right out of my hair. Just like I did Dale.

I twist and turn as I admire myself in the mirror. These heels are going to be killer to walk in but they make my legs look long, and accentuate my calf muscles. I turn around and glance over my shoulder to check out the dress from behind.

It's low at the back and thank goodness I remembered to bring my backless bra which gives me the confidence to wear this without worrying that I'll have an accident and reveal all. I had to pick my dress up from Jamie's place because I had no going out clothes here. I feel homeless with my belongings scattered between Jamie's and Ward's homes. I need to get my own place and start over.

Still, I'm looking forward to tonight. I haven't dressed

up like this for months and now I've gone all out. But as I take another look at myself, I'm worried that it's *too* much. The dress is too fancy, too sexy, and the heels are killer.

It's only Jamie.

Yet I'm not dressing up for him.

I want Ward to see me before I leave. I rush to get the door when Jamie arrives. His face lights up the moment he sets eyes on me, but I don't pay much attention to his compliments because I'm trying to figure out how to get Ward to see me. I can't walk into the study, which is where he most likely is. But he sometimes hangs out in the kitchen.

"Just a moment," I tell Jamie, and before he can say a word, I head into the kitchen, not because I need something, but because I can almost sense, can almost feel Ward is nearby.

I'm right, because as soon as I round the corner, I almost walk into him.

He was lurking in the shadows.

I just didn't expect him to be so bad at spying.

I apologize and swan past him into the kitchen, but there's nothing I need. He saw me. That's all I wanted, for him to know what he had turned away. Jamie keeps staring at me to the point that I find it annoying. I feel naked and uncomfortable as I step into the cab, wearing my pin-heel stilettoes.

I won't last the night in these and will have to take them off in the club.

"Is it a club or a bar?" I ask Jamie as we settle into the cab.

"It's both. She said it's a new place." His eyes take in my dress again, and he looks at me, then looks away. "You look amazing, Mari. Knock-them-dead amazing." I frantically try to pull down the hem of my short dress. Sitting down, it goes right up to my thighs and I feel even more self-conscious and very bare. While it was worth it, me wearing this sexy little number along with the beautiful satisfaction of having Ward see me in it, I'm now left feeling a little cold and uncomfortable.

"Why are you smiling?" Jamie asks.

"No reason. I just need a good night out."

His eyes sparkle in mischief. "Yeah? You seem uptight. Are you?"

I rest my back against the seat and exhale slowly. "You don't know what it's like being cooped up inside that house all day."

"I said you needed to go out more, didn't I? Well?" he says, running his gaze down the length of my dress. He's ogling me and I slap his arm playfully.

"Don't do that!"

"You look hot."

"Don't say that." It makes me uncomfortable and Jamie has never made me feel uncomfortable before. I wonder what's changed things? Is it because of my foolish entanglement with Ward? Because I don't feel ashamed about it, I don't regret it happening. What I do regret is Ward making out that it was all my doing and reprimanding me for it.

"But you do look hot!" he protests. "I've never seen you in something that short and that ... revealing."

I wince. "Is it that obvious?"

"Is this your way of saying that you're over him?"

"Over who?"

He frowns. "You've forgotten him already, I see."

"You mean Dale? Dale who?" I throw him an exaggerated puzzled expression.

He laughs. "That's more like it. I haven't seen you smiling much lately."

"That's because I haven't had a lot to be happy about." If I was holding out any hope of Ward making me feel better about myself, wanting me, or telling me how much he wants me, that would have been a start. But he obviously doesn't feel that way about me.

"We're going to have a lot to smile about today, you and me." Jamie sinks back into the seat and looks out of the window.

We reach the club not long after, and rush over to the group of our ex-work colleagues who are waiting outside. My heart warms at the sight of them. Familiarity and people I know. Jamie disappears then comes back with Raleigh and we all hug and kiss and excitedly talk all over one another. It's been a long time since we all caught up. We had a great bunch of people working at the hotel, and I miss the camaraderie and friendship. We eventually go into the club where Raleigh greets us. Jamie gets a big hug and a kiss on the cheek, and I get a 'Hey' from her. Which suits me just fine. Apparently, we have a section of the place solely for our group. This is so much nicer than I expected, and I am so glad that I came out tonight.

"I'm getting this round," Jamie says, brushing his hand on my back. "Do you want your usual G & T?"

"Yes, please! Thanks." A G & T is exactly what I need.

He walks away to the bar and Raleigh follows after him. I have a good feeling about this. I'm sure she had a thing for him, but couldn't do anything because he had a girlfriend. I'm also sure she didn't like me much because Jamie and I always hung around together. I hope now that he's single, he'll be able to act on it.

My friends get up and hit the dancefloor, and I join

them, forgetting that I'm wearing dangerously thin sandals. In a crowded club with people sweating, and the air heavy with sweat and alcohol, I lose myself.

This night was exactly what I needed.

Jamie comes over with my drink, but I don't want to sit down, and I don't want to hang onto my glass while I'm dancing, so I tell him I'll find him when this song is over. But I don't go, even when the song is over. I'm having so much fun dancing, and I'm so into the music that I don't want to leave. It's as if I'm making up for all the shitty days I've had these past few months.

All that dancing soon makes me thirsty, and I go to the bar to ask for a glass of water. A hand skims my back, and I'm too dazed to snap to attention immediately. When Jamie perches on the stool next to me, I grin like an idiot at him.

"Want another G & T?" he yells into my ear, trying to get heard over the sound of the music.

"What happened to my other one?" I yell back, directly into his ear.

"I gave it to Raleigh."

I give him a thumbs-up and order a big glass of water instead.

"You're looking ...." I don't hear the entire sentence because the music has suddenly gone up a notch, and the bass reverberates along the wooden floor. I can feel it in my soul.

"What?" I yell, cupping my ear, indicating that I haven't heard him.

"You look ..." He shouts something again, this time up close and right into my ear so that I can feel his hot breath on my neck, but the beat is loud and thumping. I still can't hear him no matter how loudly he shouts.

I shake my head, and he reaches for my hand and then pulls me up. "Let's go outside!"

I grab my glass and totter out with him, with one hand on my glass, trying not to spill the water, and also trying to get my hand out of Jamie's grip. He's pulling me along but I'm in my heels and I can't walk that fast. We head out towards a grassy section with chairs and tables, but I trip in my too-stupid-but-sexy sandals, and fly straight into Jamie's arms. The glass goes flying and lands on the grass, thankfully unbroken.

"Hey," he says, holding me with both hands on my arms as if he's worried that I'll topple over again. "You okay?"

"It's these silly heels," I complain, looking down and examining the ends to see if they were still intact. I wish I'd worn my Converse sneakers.

"What happened?"

"You were pulling me along," I complain. Why the heck he wanted to go outside, I don't know. "What are we doing here?" I ask him as a passing server picks up the fallen glass.

"I couldn't hear you in there."

I fan my face. "It was so hot in there." I need the fresh air. Jamie has suddenly gone quiet, and I look around for Raleigh or some other familiar faces. But I hear the notes of a new song playing. It's one I really like. "Let's go back," I cry.

"Stay out here a while," Jamie pleads. "We've barely had a chance to talk."

But I don't want to talk. I want to dance. "Aw, come on. I like this one."

He makes a face. It doesn't look to me as if he's heading inside anytime soon. I want to go inside and get back to dancing. I look around for some of our friends. "Who are you looking for?" Jamie asks.

"Raleigh. I noticed you two were busy catching up."

He cocks his head, as if not understanding.

"With Raleigh," I say. "She looked so happy to see you."

"She was happy to see us all."

I poke him in the shoulder gently. "She looked especially happy to see you. Have you asked her?"

"Asked her what?"

"Come on, Jamie. Don't pretend. You liked her."

"I did not."

I frown at him in disbelief. "You did, too."

"She's not really the one for me."

I find this hard to believe and fold my arms and frown at him again. "She's besotted by you. Can't you tell?"

He clears his throat and shakes his head. "Nope. Can't see it."

Another group of our friends comes over and we end up talking to them. The conversation soon changes to what we're all doing now and where we're working.

"I'm housesitting," I say, my eyes shifting to Jamie and praying that he won't tell them the truth about me. I don't care that the guy I'm a housekeeper to is a famous author, I care more about my ambition and what my friends will think of me in my new role.

"Housesitting?" someone asks.

I tug at my earlobe. "Um-hmmm."

"Let's go and party at your place then," someone else suggests. The idea is popular with everyone.

"You don't want to do that," Jamie says, "I've seen the place. It's a dumpster. The guy has dogs. Five of them. It's so not a party place."

There is more talk about what to do after the club closes, and someone mentions a few parties that are going on tonight. People umm and aaah about which party to go to with nothing decided. They leave to go back to the bar, leaving me and Jamie outside again. I thank him.

"Why didn't you tell them where you're working?"

"Because I'm fickle and I don't want people to know I'm a housekeeper."

Jamie lowers his voice. "Not even to the great Ward Maddox?"

I shake my head. Hearing Ward's name out loud does something to me. So far, this night has been successful, and losing myself in the music meant not thinking about Ward. I'm eager to know what makes Jamie think Raleigh is not the one for him. I decide to flip this conversation because it could give me some insight into my current dilemma with Ward.

Raleigh is standing over by a tree, talking to some people. I've been watching her and have noticed that she's been glancing in our direction. Jamie's had his back to her, so he has no idea.

"Look at her," I say, tugging Jamie's arm, and trying to be discreet without pointing.

"What about her?" he throws a glance over in her direction and turns back to me.

"She keeps looking at you."

He doesn't say anything.

"Oh, my goodness." I slap my hand to my forehead. "I've messed things up. She thinks you and I are together."

"And what if she does?"

"But we're not. Go talk to her," I insist.

"I don't want to talk to her, I want to talk to you."

"You won't get an opportunity like this again, Jamie."

"I'd rather stay here and talk to you."

"This could be your last chance!"

"I don't want to talk to her," he insists, sounding more

annoyed than he should. I stop pushing and we're quiet for a long time. I'm not sure what's going on with him tonight.

"Do you think this is a sexy dress, or a *really* sexy dress?" I ask.

"What?" he blinks rapidly, as if the question is confusing.

I run my hand down my dress. "Do you think this is tastefully sexy, or slutty sexy?"

His mouth opens as if he's going to say something, but he doesn't.

"Well?"

"You really want me to answer that?" Now I'm worried, because his reaction tells me that Ward's reaction might not have been what I hoped. All of a sudden, I'm pulled down the rabbit hole of what that might be. Maybe my stunt to show him me in a sexy dress isn't as clever as I first thought. Maybe he'll see me as a slut and it might confirm what he already thinks. Maybe he's glad he cooled things down between us.

"Yes, I really do. I need to know. Ward was in the kitchen and he saw me go out in this."

Jamie squints in disbelief. "And?"

"And ... and ... nothing. I mean, I just wonder what he thought."

"Why are you so worried about what he thinks?"

Jamie won't understand it, but what Ward thinks matters to me.

"I don't want him to think I'm some sort of floozy."

"So what?" There's a tightness in Jamie's face. "He's not going to fire you. Why the hell do you care so much about what he thinks?"

"I got into trouble because of you."

How's that?

"I didn't tell him you took his pen."

Jamie's mouth twists as if he's baffled. "Why's that such a big deal? Can't the guy take a joke?"

"You've met him. What do you think?"

"I'll tell him," he says. "I'll tell him it was me."

"No. Don't. Just leave it. He thinks I misplaced it. It's all good."

"It can't be all good, because you're still talking about it." He sounds irritated and annoyed. "You're always talking about that guy. Even now. We're here, in a different setting, meeting our friends and you're still harping on about Ward."

"Sorry." I take his arm. "You know what it's like. I have no other work gossip to talk about."

"Then don't talk about work. Talk about something else."

His anger startles me. "Okay, sure. Let's talk about ...Uh ..." I'm trying to think of something. "I know. Uh, I'm going to start looking for apartments as soon as Ward's job is over. I promise I'll be out of your hair real soon."

"It's not a problem. You can keep your stuff at my place for as long as you need. You can stay at my place if you don't find something you like, you can stay as long as you like."

I squeeze his arm, lean in and plant a kiss on his cheek. "Thanks. You're a darling."

When I pull back, he stares at me and is surprisingly speechless.

"Are the two of you together now?" Raleigh asks, joining us.

"No! We are just friends. It's not like that." I swat Jamie's arm playfully. "He's like my big brother."

I wouldn't usually have more than two words to say to this woman, but I feel the need to explain our situation, especially because I can see the way Raleigh looks at him. I can see it and I have no idea why Jamie is totally blind to it.

"We're good friends," says Jamie.

"Can I grab him?" Raleigh asks.

"Take him, please!"

Jamie's mouth opens, but I take my chances and leave the two lovebirds alone.

I ponder over what Jamie said, about me talking about Ward all the time. I like Ward. I have feelings for him, and I hate that I am this woman who can't stop thinking about a guy even when he doesn't want her.

He's in my pores, in every cell, and every fiber of my being. I can't stop my obsession. I can't stop thinking about how much I want him. When we're in a room, everything is amplified. I sense things, I can smell his scent, gauge his mood, feel him. I'm not normal around him, because my obsession for him clouds my judgment.

Tonight was less about going out than it was to show Ward that I could go out with another man, and be happy.

It was pure luck that he saw me all dressed up, but all the time I've been here, I've been thinking about him.

I hate myself.

"Hey." Someone nudges my arm as I wait at the bar to place an order for my drink.

It's Danny. He used to be in charge of the hotel's amenities.

He joins me and we end up talking. He's got a really good job now, working for another bigger chain of hotels. This is good to know. I tell him I'm looking for work and he thinks he can hit me up with some contacts at his place.

We're still talking by the time the bar closes, and someone comes over to tell us about a party in one of the suburbs.

"Wanna go?" Danny asks.

I look around for Jamie, but the place is still crowded and I can't see him.

"We're going now. Coming?" Danny asks.

I jump up and follow him.

The house party turns out to be a whole lot more fun than the bar and club.

When the house party ends, I get a cab back with the others and it's almost five by the time I get home. I have no idea what happened to Jamie, but at some point during the night I texted him to let him know that I'd left. I sure hope he and Raleigh are having a good time.

CHAPTER THIRTY

WARD

I wake up, not that I slept much, tossing and turning in bed all night, sliding in and out of pockets of sleep. Fragmented images of my mangled plot and Mari in that dress poked and prodded at me all night.

She's probably still with Jamie now. The thought makes me leap out of bed. I need to do a workout, because there's no other way I can vent my frustration better. Pumping iron and doing one of Jamie's harder workouts might calm me and get rid of this restlessness that keeps me awake.

Tomorrow, I will call Rob and demand to return to New Orleans. This current setup messes with my head too much. It gets in the way of my writing, my life and my sanity.

Grabbing my sports towel and a bottle of water, I head for the gym. The last few times after a good workout, I've left on a high. There's some truth to the endorphins and adrenaline after a good workout which leave me feeling happier, more capable and less stressed.

As I walk in, eagerly looking forward to it for probably the only time in my life, I see *her*. Mari on the mat, her hands and feet planted firmly on the floor, and her butt high in the air. She's doing that same goddamn downward dog pose she did the last time.

When the hell did she get back?

I hear her gasp, and then she stands up quickly. Her face is shiny. I can't tell if she's just warming up or is halfway through her practice. An awkward moment drags out into a prolonged stare. Her hands slide to her hips, jarring me with the image of her in clingy leave-nothing-to-the-imagination gym gear. This is quickly replaced by the image of her in her party dress and heels last night.

I pray my cock doesn't stand to attention and salute her.

"I'm nearly done," she says slowly, turning her back to me and standing tall, stretching her arms high in the air, then bringing them down to her chest. When she stands on one leg, planting her other foot against her inner thigh, I don't know where to look. She's calm and composed and balanced—on one leg. I am not. Even standing on two legs and admiring her figure from behind. My insides are in chaos. Bedlam ensues. My nerves are in turmoil. Only my cock is super happy.

The sight of her slim naked waist is a mating call to every cell in my body. She's done it again. Disrupted my best-laid plans. I don't know what to admire more, the fact that she can stand upright without toppling over or the beads of sweat on her back.

"When did you get back?" I ask casually, as I get up and walk towards the treadmill.

"What?" She breaks the pose so that both feet are firmly planted on her mat. She also looks pissed that I'm interrupting her workout, but I need to know. "What time did you get back?"

"Why?"

She's annoyed at me. At first, I'm surprised, but then I remember. I told her we couldn't continue with what we were doing. I more or less laid the blame on her and now I want to make amends. "I'm just trying to make conversation."

"Why?" She takes the top off her water bottle and takes a long sip. With her chin tilted like that, her neck is elongated, and I wonder what it would be like to kiss her there.

I start walking on the treadmill. "Because we're both in here, and I'm trying to be polite."

She doesn't answer. She looks too angry to make conversation, and I should have known better. We get on with our workouts in silence.

Because I need the distance between us, I move away towards the corner where the weights are and lie down on the bench. This is easier, lying on my back on a bench, because it makes it almost impossible for me to look at her. Yet if I tilt my head, I can still see her reflection in the mirror.

Fuck.

This is way worse because now she's lying on her back with her legs straight up in the air. I can't help but watch her. I'm mesmerized admiring her cute butt as she does little crunches by lifting up with her hips.

My heart rate spikes further when her legs fold over her stomach so that her toes are touching the space on the floor next to her head. Crablike.

Fuck, no.

That familiar twitch in my pants is back. Tiny beads of sweat start to slowly form along my hairline.

She's doing this on purpose because she knows how it affects me.

I decide to do the same to her and work through the various weight machines. We work like this quietly, pretending to ignore one another. The atmosphere is strained.

She catches me looking at her as she bends over to pick up her water bottle again. "What?" she snaps.

"Nothing. I was just—" I don't finish the sentence because it would be rude to tell her that I was admiring her figure.

She takes a step towards me. "You were what?"

"Nothing, I was just—" Her gaze dips to my biceps as I continue to pull the weight down smoothly.

Two can play at this game. If she's going to give me something to stare at, I'm going to do the same back.

We've crossed a line somewhere. This isn't how a boss and his housekeeper communicate, but my twitching cock reminds me that that's not who we are any more.

"Why are you in here?" Her face twists. I've never seen her this angry before. "You never come here this early."

"I live here. This is my house." Technically it's not mine, and I wait for her to point this out, and when she doesn't, "You seem angry with me, more so than usual."

"Do I need to spell it out for you?"

I have an inkling but I'd rather hear it from her. "Please do."

Angry lines form on her brow. "I don't want your small talk. You don't have to make polite conversation just because we happen to be in the same room together. It seems pathetic, after what you said the other day."

I knew it. "You're mad at me for saying we had to stop."

"I'm mad at you for implying that I was the one who had designs on you," she protests.

"I can't focus with you around."

That seems to hurt her. Something flickers in her expression and I regret what I've said. I don't mean to say that. I need her around me. I *want* her around. I want something different. I want to say I'm sorry for saying what I did, but I can't. Words like that, in situations like this, don't come easy.

"I'm staying out of your way like you asked me to," she snaps. Simmering rage and resentment heat up the charged pathway between us. A sheen of sweat glistens on her skin, like the beads of perspiration on her face.

"I can't work for you anymore. I... I ... I'll quit. I'll quit as soon as I find something else."

Quit? What is she talking about? She can't quit. But she stomps out before I can say something to make her take back her words.

There's no way I will allow her to quit.

CHAPTER THIRTY-ONE

MARI

I raise a shaky hand to my cheek. Why did I say that?
Silly, silly, silly woman.

I'm in no position to quit and I can't even take it back. I'd rather gouge my eyes out than go begging to him.

But at least I haven't quit with immediate effect. I gave myself some leeway. I had the sense to say I would leave as soon as I found something.

But I wanted to say something. I needed to shock him. How dare he start talking to me as if everything is fine?

How dare he?

I hate him.

I hate that miserable, bad-tempered and rude excuse for a man.

I can't even figure out what it is I feel for Ward Maddox. Is it hate, or something more complicated? I tried to not watch him lifting weights but every so often I'd steal another look at him. I would feel the rush of blood through my veins as I ogled his body. I blame the sight of his muscles pumped to the max as he showed off in front of the mirror.

Even now, I'm a throbbing, pulsating heap of nerves. "What are you doing?" I hiss at myself in the mirror. I tilt my chin. I try to see myself through Ward's eyes. I look slimmer, and more toned in these clingy gym clothes. He saw me like this.

I changed my yoga routine to incorporate some sexy poses that I knew would make him want me. I needed to know if he did, but I'm the one who's turned on. Not him. He'll be back at his desk getting on with his writing before I've even showered.

I stare at my reflection. I am so far removed from the woman I used to be. Losing my job knocked me sideways. Getting this job has made things worse. It's hard, worrying about money, my mom and her health, and having to contend with my plummeting self-esteem. To then have this hate-love thing going on between me and Ward is harder still.

I can't handle it, and I see now that neither can he.

I'm going to call Danny and ask if he wants to meet up. That's what I'll do after my shower. Get out of here and spend my afternoon with a normal guy. See if he meant what he said about finding employment at the place where he is.

I stay in the shower for ages. The water crashing down soothes my mood, calms my beating heart.

I step out and dry myself quickly before wrapping a towel around me and bunching my wet hair up in another towel. I lie on my stomach, on the bed, and check my messages before I call Danny. I have a whole heap of messages from friends with many posting pictures from the party last night.

I'm still smiling when I hear a knock at the door, my mind still on the party and the selfies many of us took.

"Mari?"

I sit upright in a flash.

Ward is outside my bedroom

I jump up and look around for clothes, my frazzled brain trying to figure out why he is here and what he wants.

"Mari? We need to talk. Please."

I hold a hand to my chest, keeping the towel glued to my skin.

"Mari?"

"What?"

"I won't come in."

"Can't it wait?" I ask, even though I'm curious to know what he has to say.

"Don't go. Don't quit." His muffled voice from the other side of the door reaches inside me and grabs a piece of my heart.

Don't get too excited.

He doesn't want you to go because he needs a housekeeper, someone to feed him and clean his house.

I don't know how to answer him so I remain silent. But I also need to see his face. I need to read his expression. So I foolishly open the door and catch a waft of clean, fresh mint and mountain rain.

I fold my arms tightly around me, feeling silly with my hair bunched up in the towel and sitting on my head like a pineapple.

His hair is also wet, and he's changed into a new set of clothes. He stays where he is, hovering just outside my door, not daring to step inside. "Don't leave. You don't have to quit."

I'm touched that this is what he's concerned about. But

I also have to get real. "I can't stay here. I can't work for you anymore."

"You need this job," he insists.

He's right. "I haven't quit right now," I tell him. "I said I'd leave when I found something else."

"But you don't have to find anything else."

His answer knocks the wind right out of my lungs. What does he expect me to do when he leaves Chicago? "I will at some point."

"Just not now."

His voice is softer, like it was on that lightning-filled night. It speaks to my core. My heart softens, the space between my legs getting ready for more of the nice Ward. I've already given in.

I need to face up to him. "You're rude, and ill-tempered, and a jerk."

He folds his arms. "I'm no good with people, but you already knew that."

"You're a difficult man to be around."

"I'm a writer, not a social animal."

"Oh, I know," I say, my sassiness in full swing. The weight of the towel on my head reminds me that I look silly. I whip it off before running my hand through my hair, trying to straighten it.

"Is it that obvious?"

He steals a glance at my towel, the one I hold against me as some sort of defense shield. Not one to miss an opportunity, I take a quick look at his biceps. I love a man with strong arms, and muscles, and those lovely workout veins. Ward is slowly getting those arms.

I look up, but it's too late. He's caught me ogling him. "That's not it, though, is it?"

"What?" I pull my towel even more tightly around me.

"That's not why you're pissed off with me. Why you weren't in the mood to talk to me just now."

I almost choke with exasperation. "You said we should keep away from each other. I was keeping away."

His eyes twinkle. "I've been unkind, and I'm sorry. After that night in the study, I should have thanked you, but I didn't. I pushed you away."

I take a tiny step back, because his words are like an unexpected gust of wind.

"Do you accept it?" he asks. "My apology?"

"I only wanted to help you that night."

"You *did* help me."

"I never intended for that to happen."

"Lap-dancing isn't a skill set on your resume," he acknowledges. If this is his idea of a joke, it's a bad one. As if I don't already feel bad about my reckless behavior.

"Sensual pen massage isn't one on yours," I throw back.

"I can give you another one, if you want."

"What?" My wavering voice manages to utter one word.

"Did you like it, Mari? Me touching you like that?"

My mouth dries up, my throat, too. My heartbeat begins to thump, only it's in the space between my legs, and not where it should be. If this is his idea of a joke ... the bastard. He's giving me hope, and just like that, he can take it away.

"You're cruel," I say. Because he's playing with me. He's so, so cruel. He's feeling horny, so he's come to my bedroom. He wants something. And I want to cry. He wants to use me, and ...

"I can't stop thinking about you, Mari. I can't finish my book because I'm stuck on the story. I can't get the image of you out of my head."

I melt. Literally. My insides hollow out and turn into a great big ball of mush. Ward Maddox can't stop thinking about me. He's a man of two sides. A split personality. A tortured soul.

But you're hurting too, a voice whispers in my ear. *Don't be fooled by his words.*

And now that he has confessed his feelings for me, my nerve endings are jangling wildly. Are they his true feelings for me, or just empty words? I can't tell, because I can't think. Blood rushes to every orifice in my body and I suddenly feel lightheaded.

He's a Jekyll and Hyde character, I remind myself. A beguiling combination of brooding and tortured.

I take another step back, but he doesn't move. He's not a threat, but I move away because I'm in danger of throwing my arms around him, especially now that I know he won't stop me.

"Did you stay with Jamie last night?" he asks.

"Why? Did you wait up?" The few inches between us bristle with sexual energy. I feel it in my core. The pounding in my heart is nothing compared to the throbbing between my legs. My gaze lands on his broad shoulders. I feel the urge to run my fingers over his biceps.

"Yeah." He clears his throat. "I hated that you went with him."

"Why's that?"

"Because I wanted you here with me."

My mouth falls open. I forget to breathe.

"I saw you in that dress," he says, leaning forward. His voice is low and sexy, enticing and warm, like a lover's kiss on a rainy day. His hooded eyes lock onto me, pulling me into him without him even touching me. "I couldn't concentrate. I couldn't write. I was good for nothing."

This new revelation makes me gasp. In the space of a few minutes, Ward has revealed more about himself than ever before. I'm clutching at happy possibilities, wanting to believe all the good things, while pushing all the bad things out of sight. Everything he says makes my insides glow. His words intoxicate me. "So ... so ... you waited up for me, to do what?"

"To see you, to say I was sorry. To make amends."

"Is this what you're doing now, making amends?"

"I don't want you to leave, Mari. I hate that you think it's the only solution."

"Then what do you want?"

"For you to stay."

"But you've already told me you can't concentrate with me being around. Seems like me quitting is the best solution for both of us."

His jaw tightens, the tell-tale muscle flexing at the side. "Please don't leave."

I really don't want to leave, not only because of the money I so badly need, but because there is something about this man which pulls me towards him. I hate him and want him with equal measure.

"I'm not good with people, Mari. I'm not a people person, but it matters to me what you think."

"Why?"

"Because I like you. I care about what you think of me. I want ... I want to stay friends."

The way he's looking at me, all bedroom eyes and sultry voice, the way I feel about him, my heart clattering, my insides on fire—we both know staying friends is a huge, huge lie.

"I'm your housekeeper. I work for you. I make your meals," I point out.

"I'm aware of that."

He doesn't want me to leave. That's a huge load off my

shoulders. I ditch my plans to call Danny. I don't need to look for work. I don't need to get stressed out all over again.

"You said you can't write when I'm around," I counter. "Why are you so eager for me to stay when you know I get in the way of your writing?"

"I'm almost finished writing my first draft. Rob said I could return home once that was done."

We stare at one another, my gaze dipping to his lips.

I want his kiss so much. We haven't kissed yet. There are other things we have done, but not that, and now I want to kiss him all the more.

One of us is going to have to make the first move. He can hold back better than I can—this man who says he's no good with people. I have less self-control.

"Friends?" I say, holding out my hand.

His heavy hand clasps mine. "Friends."

We're still holding hands, and I'm still staring at his lips.

"There will be no more help and support during inclement weather," I say.

He grunts and grips my hands a little tightly. "I can't run my pen all over your body?"

He's putting ideas in my head. I gulp. "Not if I can't reciprocate."

He steps towards me, crossing the line separating the hallway from my bedroom. Now he's in my territory, and my skin tingles with anticipation.

"Just friends?" I remind him, as he inches closer.

"Your call."

A warning pierces through the haze of my attraction: he's blowing hot right now, but what happens tomorrow when he blows cold and leaves me to suffer?

With a playful little tug, he pulls me towards him. That's all it takes. In the next second, he hoists me up in his arms. My legs wrap around him as if they were already an extension of his body. Our lips smooth together, tongues meeting hungrily. He tastes fresh and minty, warm and sweet. I cling to him with my arms around his neck as his kiss deepens and I tumble headfirst into it.

My towel falls off, because my hands are elsewhere, around his neck, instead of guarding my nakedness. We both stop and gasp. I'm completely naked as I stare at his swollen wet lips. He sets me down even though I am panting with need.

I'm naked, and he's in his sweatpants and t-shirt. It's a little one-sided to me.

"Damn it," he growls, devouring me with his eyes.

"How is this going to work?"

He bends down, brushes his hand against my cheek. "We make it work," he whispers, kissing me softly again, his lips pressing against mine as if they belong there. His hands caress my sides, flitting from my waist to my hips and back again. It's sensual, and tickly, and I don't want him to stop. I splay my hands across his chest as we kiss. There's no urgency now, or desperation. This is an acceptance kiss, one that tells him I want this, I'm okay with it. The kiss that leads to other things. The kiss that is filled with anticipation, desperation and lust.

"Did you like my new yoga move"? I ask, trailing my tongue along his lower lip.

"Which one?" He nips at my lip playfully. "The one with your bottom up in the air? Or the one with you standing with a foot tucked against your thigh?"

"You were watching closely." How is it that he's so tender and soft now? Where's the beast gone? The moody, surly man who skulks around?

"I couldn't not stare at you. You're impossible to ignore. God knows I tried."

"Maybe you should have tried harder?" I clasp my arm around his neck and revel in the new thing we've now morphed into.

"I did try hard."

His tongue delves into my mouth, explores, and duels. This is heady, like drinking a large glass of wine. My head feels light, my stomach jittery. I feel blessed that he is here, in my arms, kissing me. It's all I've ever thought about since that day, and now that I know he wants me, the victory is sweet. I nip at his lips, before going for another long, slow, wet kiss. He groans then, and I feel his cock twitch against my belly. I don't have a stitch of clothing on, and yet it feels entirely natural.

"So, you waited up for me last night?" I ask again, needing to hear how jealous he was.

"I hate that you went with him."

"Jamie?"

"You looked so sexy in that dress."

"If it helps you to know, I went to the party with him but it was you I thought about."

This brings a smile to his face.

I touch his jaw, run my fingers over the sharp little hairs breaking through his skin. "I hated you."

"*Hated?*" He kisses me. "Even now?"

"Would I hate you even now if we're doing this?"

He kisses me again.

"Did you come to my room knowing this would happen?" I ask, our lips touching as we talk, his breath and mine mingling as if it is all one.

He holds my face with his hands as if this is extra

important. "I came to apologize. I didn't know you'd be wearing a towel."

I slide my hand into his boxers and clasp my fist around his cock, pumping him gently, watching him wince and shiver. "You didn't? What did you think I was going to do after my workout?"

"I didn't think." He lets out a shaky breath. I pump him some more. His cock grows and hardens in my hand.

"Having a problem getting your words out?" I tease.

He exhales again, his eyes flutter closed as I rub my thumb over his silky tip.

"I felt bad that you said you'd leave," he manages to say. "I want you to stay."

I assess his features, so strange to have him be this close to me. The last time we were like this, it was under the spell of the thunder and lightning in his dimly lit study. It felt not much different from a dream. This, now, in the cold light of day, this seems more real. More intense. More potent.

"You've played with my mind for weeks, and I need this." I give an extra yank of his cock. He grabs my hand and stops me.

"I will come if you keep that up."

"I expected you to have more staying power." His hand stays on my hand which is on his manhood. These close and intimate encounters, with my hands in his pants, fill me with an urgent need. He takes my hand and moves it away, but there's no doubting the size of his hard-on and the fact that soon enough it will need taking care of.

I pick up my towel and go to cover myself but he stops me. "No."

"No?"

In answer, his lips trail down my shoulder and down to my

breasts. He sucks hungrily at one, teasing and nipping gently with his teeth, making me feel loose and wet. Liquid heat swirls around in my stomach and lower. When he turns his attention to my other breast, I run my hand through his damp hair and yank a handful of it, holding onto it as a wave of excitement showers over me. He kisses and sucks, making satisfying sounds deep in his throat, as if he's craved this for a long, long time. I throw my head back, lost in the wet heat that binds us together.

"I haven't had sex for over a year," he states, as if it's the most normal thing to announce at a time like this.

"Over a year?" He'll be hungry for it, and I intend to be the one he feasts on. "That's a long time." His hair is cold and silky against my hand. The harder he sucks my breast, the more I want him. My skin tingles with electric sparks. I am intoxicated by him, by the new and strange turn of events. Knowing he has gone without for so long makes me want him right now.

And then he does something that makes me jolt. He slides his finger inside me. It's so unexpected, so glorious, so perfect, that I cry out with joy. He puts another finger inside. No foreplay, no rubbing or tweaking of my clit, just a straight-up thrust of his long, thick fingers. I want to come so hard. I can't help myself. Ward plays me like an instrument, making me mewl and sigh with abandon. I moan with each tantalizing grope of his fingers.

If he continues, I will come. And I don't want to. Not like this. I reach for the hem of his t-shirt, trying to tug at it hopelessly, so that I can yank it up and over his head, but I can't keep my eyes on the prize, not when he's stroking my clit like that. My brain has fogged over and I'm good for nothing right now. "This isn't fair," I whisper. "You're fully dressed."

Without a word, he stops, moves his hand away and strips down. Completely.

I can't take my eyes off his beautiful body. It's hard, and taut and lean. My mouth waters at the sight of his glorious cock with its glistening tip.

We tumble back on my bed, naked at last, rolling around until he gets on top of me. The feel of him against me, his hot bare skin against mine, his hard wet cock, stabbing and leaving a wet trail where he touches me, makes my heart beat so loud, I'm sure he can hear it.

He lowers his head, our gazes unflinching. "What do you want, Mari?"

That's easy. "All of you."

"All of me?"

"All ten inches," I giggle.

He throws his head back, hooting with laughter. "You sure?"

"Absolutely."

"Like this? Here?"

"Yes, like this, here." I wish he'd stop the questions and get on with the action.

He chews his lip, his expression sobering. I prepare myself for a brushoff. "What?"

"I don't have a condom."

Of course he doesn't. I like that he doesn't carry one around with him.

"Let's take this to your bedroom," I mumble as our lips brush together.

"I don't have one there either."

I huff out in disbelief.

"I didn't think I would need one," he explains, putting his mouth to my breast again.

The fogginess in my brain clears. "I'm clean," I

announce. "And I'm on the pill." He stops sucking and stares at me, his moist lips the only point of focus for me as I dive back into my murky past. "My ... uh ... the guy I was with before, he cheated on me. He got someone pregnant. So I got tested to make sure he hadn't given me something. That's why I know I'm clean. And if you haven't had sex for—"

Ward lifts up on one elbow. "He cheated on you?" I nod, a part of my brain telling me that he's focused on the part of the sentence I least expected. We can fuck now. I won't get pregnant and he won't catch anything. Instead, he presses his lips to mine gently. "I'm sorry someone did that to you."

I kiss him back, because his lips are full and wet, and because I'm hungry for him in a desperate, shameless way. It looks like we get to do this after all.

"Are you sure?" he asks me, and it's the gentlest he's been, reminding me that he does have his tender moments.

"I'm absolutely sure."

His eyes flash with desire. "But you went out with Jamie last night."

"To make you jealous."

He gets up off the bed, then lends me a hand and yanks me to standing. Just as I frown, feeling puzzled and disappointed, he spins me around so that my back is to his chest. "You succeeded." He runs his hands greedily all over my body, massaging and playing with my breasts. One hand trails down my stomach and drops further down. He plants one of my feet on the bed, opening me up a little, before sliding his finger over my folds. The ripples of excitement this causes make me arch my back against his chest.

His cocks jabs my bottom, and my mind doesn't know where to focus. His fingers slide and circle around my clit, and his other hand plays with my breast. I turn to the side. "Kiss me," I beg, needing his lips on mine while I drift in and out of this sexual haze. He meets my lips hungrily, we try to kiss, unable to properly latch on. Even though he is driving me insane with his flexible fingers, it's his cock that I need.

"Do you want me, Mari?" he asks, his voice riddled with need.

"Yes."

"Are you ready for me?"

"Yes."

He's messing with my brain, with his hands in all my erogenous zones, and me at an awkward angle that stops me from exploring him as much as I want to.

He pushes me onto the bed, face-first, doggy style, and makes a sound, low and throaty. The bed dips as he climbs on behind me, his knees on either side of mine. His cock is at the ready, dipping into my wetness.

"Yesss," I beg. A shiver runs through me as he nudges my opening with his thick tip. My hands slide forward and clutch the bedsheets as he tunnels into me. Every thick beautiful inch of him fills me while my stomach and breasts are pushed down flat. I groan in ecstasy, animalistic sounds falling from my lips.

"You okay?" He bends over my back, his hand stroking my clit, making me moan even more. "Oh ... yes ..." I cry, and then he thrusts in deep, one short sharp thrust and he's in to the hilt.

I feel full. It's the strangest sensation, and just as I get used to this blissful feeling, he pulls out. Then starts to thrust, setting up a pace, and every few thrusts leaning over to play with my clit. I whimper, feeling powerless, gutless, boneless. He keeps slamming into me, then pulling out, then does it over and over again. We are white heat, wet, and sticky. His cock inside me is like nothing I've had before.

I bury my face into the mattress, absorbing every feeling, every thrust, every touch.

Until a tinny sound breaks the spell.

It's my cell phone.

I try to locate it with my one free arm, to see who it is because I always worry that it might be my mom. I lift my head. It's Jamie. I let it ring and bring my attention back to myself.

"Aren't you going to get that?" Ward asks, his voice strangely hard. He's still inside me, pushed right to the hilt, as if he's taken up permanent occupation inside my pussy. I'm poised on the precipice of something deep and all-consuming.

My head falls to the bedsheets.

"Aren't you?" he asks again.

I can't answer because I'm about to fall from this precipice.

"Mari?"

"Don't stop," I beg. "Go harder."

He obliges, thrusting in and out of me. I love that he owns me like this, that he wants me, that he makes me feel dirty and delicious with every thrust. It's frightening and exciting, this new stage we've reached. My feelings, ripped and raw, about what this means, and what he thinks of me, fall to the side. All that matters is him, and the pleasure that drips from our oneness.

His hands grip my hips and I cry out, losing myself, forgetting who I am. I'm wasted, limbless and boneless, as he rides out his pleasure. I feel his aftershocks inside me and I push back, trying to squeeze every last ounce from him.

CHAPTER THIRTY-TWO

WARD

This has to be the best sex ever.

I turn my head and observe her side profile. I watch the rise and fall of her breasts, then turn on my side, propping myself up on my elbow so I can look at her properly.

She tilts her head towards me, the corners of her lips curving upwards into an inviting smile which makes me want to take her all over again. "You might just have erased the ghost of my ex completely."

I reach out and run my finger along her lips. "Do you still miss him?"

"Sometimes." She throws an arm across her chest, as if she's trying to cover herself up.

"I've seen all of you," I say, peeling her arm away. I still want to look at her naked body, now that she's lying next to me, instead of dreaming about it. "You. Are. Beautiful," I murmur, bending down to drop a kiss on her shoulder.

She doesn't say anything to that, and the silence stretches out endlessly. I hope she doesn't regret what happened. "You're cold," I say, watching her nipples rise without me having touched her yet. I nod, directing her to see what I see.

"Maybe it's not the cold." A hint of mischief makes her eyes light up. In answer, I shimmy a few inches closer and kiss her on the lips. It soon becomes one of those fevered, urgent kisses, and our bodies seem to have recovered and recharged enough to want to try again.

When I stroke her arms, I notice goosebumps. "How about we get under the covers?" I suggest. I'm not sure if she expects me to leave. I'm hoping she won't discard me now that she's made use of me. I don't want to leave even though it's what I would normally do.

A writer's life is lonely. Mari distracts me, but she also gives me something more. Hope and meaning, maybe. Our roles have reversed. She has needs, and I took care of them. She's a lusty, sexual woman, not a shy wallflower and I like that she takes control.

She jumps up, pulls away the covers and slides in between the sheets. "Getting in?" she asks but she doesn't need to wait for my answer. I dive in and as soon as our bodies touch, we're kissing and stroking one another again.

Her cell phone rings again, and this time I reach for it as its nearest to me.

"Your friend again," I say, seeing Jamie's number.

"Danny?"

Danny? I was worried about Jamie. Who the hell is Danny?

I hand her the phone, while rolling on top of her and planting myself in between her legs. Resting on my elbows, I watch her as she takes the call, and then I suck her breast again. Her conversation is labored, and she's doing her best to sound normal but when I dip two fingers inside her and thumb her clit, her voice turns shaky. She struggles to maintain a normal voice and a normal conversation in a situation which is not so normal. Her back arches, her voice goes up an octave and she squeezes her legs together.

It sounds as if Jamie's asking her about last night. Sounds as if she left without telling him. Sounds as if he wants to meet up with her again today.

I shove another finger inside her. She begins to cry out, then shoves a hand in front of her mouth to stifle her cry.

"Sorry," she wails into the phone. She's trying not to shudder as I make her come. "I ...uh ...uh ... I dropped a ... carton of milk. I need to clean it up." Hurriedly, she tells Jamie she's going to call him later.

I slide my fingers out, but my thumb is attached to her clit and she's having trouble stringing a sentence together.

"Who's Danny?" I ask, shifting myself on top of her and sliding inside her a few inches.

She makes a happy noise. "I love your cock."

"I love your ... womanly parts," I say. What do I call it, so that it won't offend her?

She hitches her hips as if she's trying to sheath me. I pull away, but its murder for me to stay here when all I want to do is slam inside her.

"Danny?" I ask again.

"Why do you care?"

"I want to make sure I'm not treading on any toes."

Her eyes cloud over. "I'm not a cheater."

"I didn't peg you for one," I slide inside her, watch her head press back into the pillow. Her face flushes as I slowly fill her up and she stares back at me as if I'm the only man on the planet.

"Then why would you say that?" she asks, her voice breathless.

"Someone like you, it's hard to imagine that you're single." I push myself all the way inside her and hold there. Her muscles clench around me and I suck in a shaky breath.

MARI

We had sex again, and maybe another time after that. I can't remember clearly. We must have both fallen asleep again. All I recall is curling up in his arms, and it being still bright daylight.

Now it's dark outside. We hadn't drawn the curtains, and the darkness pours in. I turn the lamp on but Ward is nowhere to be seen. Disorientated, I reach for my cell phone but it's completely dead.

Most of all, I'm hungry.

And I wonder where Ward has gone.

I get out of bed, feeling a little sore. I consider going downstairs wrapped in nothing but my bedsheet but I'm worried it might be premature. I don't know who *we* are yet, Ward and I. He said all the right things, but that was when he was in my bed. Out of the bed, in the cold, back to normality, he might say something else and I might not be ready to hear it.

A slight hesitancy creeps into my belly, because with him I never know what to expect. I get dressed quickly, throwing my sweatshirt and jogging pants on and traipse downstairs looking for him.

He's not in the kitchen or the TV room, which means he's likely to be in his study, writing.

Should I disturb him?

He already thinks I'm in his way.

I have to respect his writing time.

Torn, I head back into the kitchen and rifle through the fridge, looking for something quick and easy to make. I didn't even make his lunch today. Or dinner.

I decide to make the simplest dish on the planet. Pasta with sauce out of a jar.

"You're up."

I snap around to see Ward in the doorway, arms folded watching me. My attention goes back to his t-shirt. Um-hmmm. He's turning into a fine figure before my eyes. We exchange an inquisitive stare across the kitchen island. I'd love to know what he's thinking. Whether he considers me a mistake, or a fling, or something more.

I should protect myself. Not dream of making plans. It was just sex. The image in my head of us both thrashing around between the sheets doesn't quite meld with this one of apparent domestic bliss in the kitchen.

"I am. When did you get up?" I check the pasta. It's al dente, just how I like it.

"A couple of hours ago."

I stir the pasta sauce. He comes over, bringing his intoxicating scent with him. I swear my ovaries just jumped for joy. From this moment on, I know that his aftershave will always be a direct call to my core.

I stir the sauce. "You should have woken me up." I wait for his reply but he's busy getting the plates and cutlery out.

I plate up the food and we sit side by side. "You should have woken me up," I say again.

"I didn't want to wake you." There's a softness in his

eyes and on his face that wasn't there before, he's gentler, but for some reason I feel as if I'm on a second date with someone. Even though we've already crossed the sex line, I feel awkward and shy around him.

"You're quiet," he says.

I pause for a while as I consider this. "I don't know how to be around you." I want to be honest. A frown line appears on his forehead.

"What do you mean?"

"I mean just that. I feel awkward. I don't know how to be. I don't know if tomorrow you'll push back and say this never should have happened."

He sets down his fork. "I didn't intend for this to happen, not now, at a time like this and—"

"I didn't mean for this to happen either," I say.

"But it did happen, and I'm glad it did. I want you, Mari. I might not have admitted it before, but seeing you with someone else made me see it more clearly." He takes my hand, and his gesture, his willingness to be more tactile than me, makes me feel warm all over.

"And if you have regrets tomorrow? If you decide we have to stop this?"

He shakes his head. "This was a two-way thing. You're irresistible. I'm ... not." The way he says it confirms to me that he has issues with his past health and weight, not dissimilar from my own issues about needing revenge or wanting to feel that I am attractive after being cheated on. Maybe Ward and I aren't so different after all. He needs me as much as I need him.

"I don't want you to feel awkward." He tucks a lock of hair behind my ear. I examine his face, all of his features as he does this. All I want to do is put my arms around him and lose myself in his embrace. But I want to make sure this isn't the post-sex feel-good hormones still floating around in his bloodstream and making him be all happy.

"I'm your housekeeper," I say, scratching my neck, "You're a best-selling author." I've broached that subject, tiptoed around the boundaries trying to figure out if there is a way forward for us.

He frowns again, moving his hand away from the fork he was just about to lift. "Why does that worry you so much?"

"It doesn't worry me. I'm just saying, that's all." And then I remember there's something else. "Jamie can't know," I say quickly, suddenly remembering that I haven't called him back.

"I wouldn't want him to know either—not because of the status thing."

"What status thing?"

"You seem to be worried, you just said that I'm this high-earning author and you're a housekeeper. What will people say?" He throws his hands up in horror, mimicking fear and shock. I am seeing a new side to Ward now that we've been intimate. I love that he is opening up to me. It's painfully slow going, but at least I'm seeing this new side to him.

"We can tell Jamie, if you want," I suggest only to test his reaction. I sense he doesn't want Jamie to know anything.

"Wouldn't that make things difficult for you? He's your friend and you're the one who has to deal with him."

I don't know what Jamie would think or say, and I don't want to complicate my life further by explaining anything. "We should just keep this as our dirty little secret."

This seems to annoy him because he sets his fork down again, only it's not gentle and makes a hard noise on the plate. "You consider it to be dirty?" he asks, obviously not liking the description.

"Well..." It's not exactly above board. "We didn't meet under normal circumstances. You didn't wine and dine me. We didn't really get to know one another. This isn't normal in any way, shape or form."

"I don't give a shit about normal. I don't care what people think. This feels right. *You* feel right." He leans forward and drops a kiss on my lips. A ray of happiness bursts inside me and warms every part of my body. It's not the kiss that did that but the fact that he's having this conversation with me and admitting how he feels about me. Ward Maddox has done a complete turnaround.

This feels right.

I'm so happy I could cry. "You weren't exactly a cheerful happy-go-lucky guy when I first met you," I say, cupping the side of his face. I can't help but slide my thumb over his thick stubble.

"I'm pretty happy now though." He winks at me. "I haven't had sex for over a year."

"So you keep reminding me."

"I haven't." He drops another light kiss on my lips. The food has taken a backseat. We're facing one another directly, stool to stool.

"Glad to be of service," I say, kissing him right back.

"I might be out of practice."

"Out of practice?" The way he took me, the way I came, he's anything but out of practice.

His hand drops to my neck, then starts to slide lower. "I could do with some more practice."

I jerk in my seat as he cups my breast, runs his thumb over me. "I'm sure we can get plenty of exercise in. I'd be more than happy to create the perfect training environment for you."

He pulls his hand away, and the nerve endings in my chest rise up in protest. "Need to eat," he says, motioning for me to start as well. "You're going to need all the sustenance you can get."

I start eating again, though my focus is less on my appetite and more on getting him back into my bed. "I still don't know a lot about you. You're as mysterious to me as your books are." The most I ever got from him was when he told me about his stepdad locking him in the attic.

"I'm a writer and an introvert. I'm not good with people. You bring me out a bit more."

Is that a compliment, I wonder? I have no idea how he meant it but I'll take it as one. When he kisses my hand, I get another glowy, sunshine feeling in my chest. For a rebound sex thing—which is what I'm going to label our encounter as—this doesn't feel so dirty.

"This is good sauce," he says.

"You like it?"

"I like it very much. I'll have to thank the chef."

"It's jarred pasta sauce," I say, giggling.

"I still have to thank the chef."

We get back to eating.

"No telling Jamie," he says, after a while, surprising me that he's still thinking about Jamie.

"It would complicate things for both of us."

"Why? Were you and him ever together?"

"No!" The idea is absurd. "He's nothing more than a good friend. He's getting over a recent breakup too."

Ward is silent.

"You don't want Rob to know," I say.

"It's none of his business."

How long will we keep this up for? "Boundaries," I say, thinking out aloud. "We'll need rules. I don't want you getting all pissy with me again."

"Do I get pissy with you?" he asks, as if this is news to him.

"All the time. It's like walking on eggshells, being around you."

"I'm that bad?" He seems genuinely shocked.

"You really haven't been around people much, have you?"

He says nothing which makes me think he's going to be like this, choosing only to speak when he wants to.

"Your study is off limits, except when I'm cleaning."

"I wouldn't say its off limits," he's quick to reassure me. "I enjoyed your midnight visit last time."

Ah. So, he doesn't mind me interrupting him like *that*.

"But I can't be disturbed when I'm writing."

I snap my fingers at him. "Gotcha."

He chews his lip. "And it's probably better, you know," he coughs lightly, "uh ... for us to stay in our own rooms after."

This is a slight downer for me, but he has changed so much since I first met him, I let him have this peculiarity. He is, after all, a man of many boundaries and rules. "Sure."

"Don't get upset."

"I'm not," I lie.

"I have a book to finish and submit to Rob before it goes to the editor."

"I understand."

We look at one another, and I don't know about him but my mind has just blown through a montage of everything we did in bed earlier. When his eyes twinkle, and a smile plays on his lips, it's clear to see that he's thinking the same thing.

"Did you reach your goal for today? The pages written or whatever you need to do?"

"I have a goal of writing five thousand words a day."

"And did you?"

"Given the fact that we spent most of the day having sex, then no."

"You didn't write *anything?*"

"Three thousand words. It's slow going."

I'm impressed. "Not bad, given the physical exercise you've undertaken." I lean towards him, reaching for his plate. "If you get five thousand words written, we can have dessert."

"Dessert?" It's takes a moment for him to get it.

I take our plates over to the sink. "In *your* room this time."

"Five thousand it is."

CHAPTER THIRTY-THREE

MARI

He got his word count in, and we ended up in his bed later that night. Not long after, I left the warmth and comfort of his body and returned to my room even though I was tempted to stay. It's better if I just put up with his rules and conditions.

This new turn in our situation makes me happy. It puts a spring in my step, and I see the change in Ward, too.

I still have my chores to do, and he still has the pressure of the book weighing on his shoulders. Although, as he told me when he stripped my clothes off me slowly, now that he has the motivation and a reward at the end, he'll get the book finished quicker.

And then we'll be over. He didn't say that, but I know. It's a fact of life. This is temporary.

Ordinarily, I would never have gotten into this type of arrangement. I have friends who have friends with benefits and hookup type arrangements, but that idea doesn't appeal to me. I'm a romantic fool. It's also why my breakup with Dale hurt me so much. If it had only been about sex, it wouldn't have mattered as much. For me, it was about love. I loved him. For him, it was just about the sex.

"There you are." Jamie has found me. He steps inside and pushes the door shut, but not completely. "You're hiding in here."

I laugh. "What? Why would you say that?"

"You're acting weird."

I laugh again, thereby acting weird. "I'm not acting weird." I forgot to call him again. All of yesterday it was about me and Ward. I never had the chance to call Jamie back.

"Are you avoiding me?" he asks.

"Avoiding you? Why would I do that?" But I can't lie to save my life. All the other times I've been in the kitchen waiting for Jamie and knowing that he will pass by to catch up with me on his way out. Today I've busied myself with dusting the library. It's obvious I've been avoiding him.

"Because you haven't returned my calls."

"Sorry. I got busy."

He frowns. "Cleaning the house, or making his food?" He sounds angry. "Did I do something wrong?"

"No, why?" I stop dusting and force myself to look at him.

"You left the club without telling me—"

"I texted you."

"At 3:27 a.m."

He remembers the exact time. Who the hell remembers the exact time a text was sent? "I forgot. We ended up going to a party, and I forgot. I texted you as soon as I remembered."

"You completely forgot about me?" he asks, his eyebrows shifting north as his disbelief deepens.

I make a face. "I'm sorry." Thinking about it now, what I did was wrong.

"And who's '*we*'?"

"Me and Danny and a few—"

"You and Danny?"

"And a few others."

His eyes are cold and hard. "You didn't think *I'd* want to go? Or you didn't want me to tag along?"

"You were with Raleigh."

"I was with *you*." It's only when he jabs a finger at me that the extent of his rage becomes apparent.

I step back, startled by his reaction. "I'm sorry. I thought you and Raleigh—"

"Screw Raleigh."

I'm guessing from this, his night didn't end well.

"You didn't call back, and when I called you, you said something about spilling some milk. You never called back."

"I'm sorry." The way it sounds, now that he's telling me all of this, it's no surprise he's so angry. "I've just been so busy, Jamie."

"All of a sudden you're too busy to talk to me? Have I upset you in any way?"

"No! Of course not. Don't be silly."

"What are you doing?" he asks as I get back to my chores.

"Dusting." I turn around, so that he can see the duster in my hands.

"Why now?"

"It's my job," I say, laughing falsely and doing it badly.

"I'm shocked that you left the bar without telling me."

"Bar?"

He looks at me in disbelief. "Raleigh's party. Saturday night. Try to keep up." He's more than a little pissed. I haven't even thought about the party. Too many other things have kept me occupied since then.

"Why did you do it, leave like that?"

It's not easy, thinking back a few days before the marathon sex runs Ward and I have had. "Raleigh," I blurt out, because most of that night is a blur to me.

"Raleigh?" Jamie snaps. "What's she got to do with anything?"

"You were both talking. I didn't want to interrupt you."

"Interrupt? We went to that bar together, Mari. You and me."

I scoff. "But we're not joined at the hip, Jamie. We're not together." He looks like he's going to explode. His nostrils flare, and it confounds me that he is so enraged. "You both looked like you were getting along so well."

"And you and I don't?"

I don't understand why he is so annoyed. "I'm sorry. I didn't think you'd get mad about it. I wasn't going to go to the party but a group of us got talking and then Danny suggested we all go to a party."

"So you just upped and left?"

"I didn't do it on purpose. Why are you so mad at me?" After the up and down emotions I've experienced in the last forty-eight hours, I'm ill-prepared to handle Jamie's wrath.

"This isn't like you, Mari. You didn't even have the decency to call and let me know," he asserts.

This is true, and I immediately feel like a bad person. "I wasn't thinking."

"You seem to be doing that a lot lately."

"I've got a lot on my mind."

"I called earlier and you sounded weird then."

I turn to him and examine his face. "What is wrong with you?"

"What's wrong with you? You leave me at a bar and go off to a party with Danny. What's with the interest in him all of a sudden?"

I raise my eyebrow because he has it all so wrong. "Can you hear yourself?" I cry. "*Me and Danny?* Are you insane?" I'm certain that the alternative, the truth about who I was really with, would be so much harder for him to accept.

"Yes, you and Danny."

The door pushes open. "Am I disturbing something?" Ward looks at us. I blink. This looks suspicious. Me and Jamie, here in the library. I hadn't realized we were talking so loudly.

"We were catching up about the events from the party," I say, hoping that he won't get annoyed seeing us together. My gut instinct tells me that Ward's not a huge fan of Jamie.

"Oh, right. The party. Sorry to disturb you." He leaves.

"Why's he so nice and cheerful?" Jamie asks.

I'm not going to tell him the reason why, though I have to laugh, and this time it's not a false laugh. It seems that the pent-up sexual tension has oozed out of Ward completely, such that even seeing me and Jamie talking like this in the library of all places isn't enough to rile him up.

However, the same can't be said of Jamie.

"You've changed. I don't know what it is but you're different," he says.

I do another one of my false laughs, which probably helps push his theory that I am being weird. Because right now, being confronted by him like this, I feel weird. "You're so wrong."

"What the hell is going on?" he mumbles to himself. "Ward's acting weird too."

I start making a list of groceries I need. "He's almost at the end of the book."

"He was telling me how quickly the words were coming now."

Knowing that he's being rewarded with sex, it's not surprising.

CHAPTER THIRTY-FOUR

WARD

I'm having lunch in the kitchen by myself when Mari appears. "Jamie said you were different today." She sits on the stool next to me.

"Different how?"

"You weren't angry or irritated about finding me and Jamie in the library?"

"Should I be?"

She raises an eyebrow.

I stop eating. "Was I really that bad before?"

She gives me a slight nod.

"Well, maybe I have something that he doesn't."

She tucks a stray lock of hair away from her face. I like it when her hair tumbles over her bare shoulders when she's in bed with me. Now she's got it pushed away from her face and in a bun, but every now and then a stray lock of hair escapes. I used to be tempted to want to move it out of the way for her, and now I can.

"He was annoyed that I left the bar and went to a party without him."

"Is that what happened?" There I was thinking something completely different.

She tells me what happened that night, and I have to say, if I were in his place, I would have felt the same.

"It surprises me because that's not like him," Mari continues.

I'm not worried about Jamie or Danny or anyone else. She's with me, for now. "Maybe he hates his job?"

"Working for you?" She shakes her head. "He might not act like one of your biggest fans, but Jamie loves your writing. He was blown away when I told him I was working for you."

I had noticed, because he asks me so many questions, and I don't like to talk about my writing. "Aren't you having lunch?" I ask, when she gets up again to leave.

"I'm in the middle of cleaning the bookcases in the library."

Bookcases? "Mari, this isn't my house. I don't own it. You don't need to clean every nook and cranny."

"What else is there to do?" she wails, sitting back on the stool again.

"Aside from cleaning the rooms we use, I'm not too worried about the rest of the house. Go shopping. Read. Watch TV."

She looks affronted. "I've been cleaning like a fiend for weeks."

"It was in the contract," I remind her.

"It's not like I have anything else to do."

I take her hand. "I'm telling you now, you can go easy on the cleaning." She jumps off the stool, her face one huge smile. "I could read your manuscript and give you feedback, check for errors—"

I cut her off. "That won't be necessary." No way. I get up and take my plate over to the sink.

She rushes over to me. "Why not?"

"You don't read horror. You told me."

"But I could try. Now that I'm sleeping with the author, I wouldn't be so scared of the story."

"You think so?" This clearly makes no sense, and I have to laugh at her simplistic conclusion.

She nods enthusiastically. "Come on, give me a chance. Before you send it over to Rob, let me have a quick read through. I want to be of use."

I can't have anyone read my manuscript. No beta readers or proofreaders. No one. Only Rob gets it in the first instance, before it goes to my editor.

"Are you sure?" she asks me.

"I'm sure." I tap her on the nose. It's her face I want to cup, her lips I want to kiss, but kissing will lead to something else, and that interruption won't help me to reach word count today. Better to get my reward after, when I feel I've earned it.

"In that case, I'd better get back to my cleaning then. I won't be giving you any rewards," she admonishes me.

"Not even if I hit my daily word count?" Naturally, with a specific goal to reach—sex with Mari—I've been hitting my word count with ease. Also, not being frustrated or lusting after her now, because she's all mine, seems to have unblocked whatever was hampering my creative flow.

Now that I know I can have her, I no longer jump and fantasize each time I hear her footsteps. I can focus on my writing, and know that if I'm good, I get to spend time with her.

It works.

She's happy, and so am I.

This calm and steady environment does wonders for my creativity and the following weeks run smoothly. I work better when I only have my words and story to think about. I have never lived like this, with someone around all the time, someone I have feelings for. Someone I have come to trust and open up to. It's been a long time since I've allowed someone in. Allowed someone to get close, someone who genuinely cares for me. I'm in danger of getting used to this and wanting it to be this way forever.

One evening I go to her room, knocking on the door, waiting for her to let me in. She's lying on the bed suggestively in her underwear. "Reward time?" She spreads her legs, and props herself up on her elbows. Her breasts threaten to spill out of her bra cups.

She takes my breath away. I fight the urge to strip and dive onto the bed but my cock has other ideas.

"I hit seven thousand words today," I say, sounding like a schoolkid.

She gets up, flips herself so that she's on all fours, still on the bed. Her dangling breast are an invite. She knows exactly what I want, and what I want is a release. Just not of the bookish kind.

I strip down to my boxers and dive onto the bed. We're a tangle of limbs, of hands, and tongues. I clamp my lips over hers, and kiss her, fucking her mouth the way I intend to fuck her below. We roll around on the bed, fighting for dominance, her wanting to be on top, me letting her for a few moments before throwing her onto her back. She's beautiful, and lush and inviting, and I'm the luckiest man alive. I pull down her bra cup and suck.

"Hey." She grabs a handful of my hair and lifts my head. "Let's go slower."

I glance down at her breast, see the nipple erect. "I can't go slow. I need my reward." I suck her other breast harder, but she's not reacting the way I expect. I lift my head. "I don't get my reward?"

"Why the rush?" Her fingers run through my hair. She loves doing that and I love her doing it even more. "You don't play with me anymore," she says in a childish voice. I lift up on my knees, ready to pull my boxers down. "Play?" I'm desperate to thrust into her. Knowing she'd be waiting, I tortured myself with the wait, and managed to write more than I had intended. The waiting has taken me to the edge. All I want is to explode inside her.

But she's not smiling. "What's wrong?" I toss my boxers to the floor. She sits up, reaches for me, does her magic with her fingers, grabs my manhood and runs her thumb over the tip then begins to slowly pump.

"Nothing," she says, then watches me fall apart while she does her usual magic.

I lie down on the bed, and she shifts position so that she's leaning over me, taking care of me with her hand while she dips her head down and kisses me. It's the softest, most gentle kiss, it's more intimate than her touching and stroking. We stare at one another and I swear I feel a level of connection that sends a shiver through me.

"I wish we could talk more," she whispers.

With her stroking me so beautifully, talking is the last thing on my mind. "We can talk *after*."

Her stroking continues. My breath catches in my throat. She's sad about something. There's a somberness to her mood. I should ask her, find out what's wrong. *Later*. I hiss out a breath when she pumps me harder. Is she going to use her hand to make me come? I had other ideas.

"Something wrong?" I manage to say.

"I wish it wasn't always about the sex."

"You're the one who put the rewards system in place." She speeds up her movements. Oh, fuck. If she continues doing that, I'll explode in her hand.

"How many times have you been in love?" she wants to know.

What? I can feel my eyes rolling towards the back of my head. I jerk, hissing out another grunt because Mari has perfected this art so well.

"In love?" I manage to rasp.

"How many times?" Her hand stills on my manhood.

I can't believe she's asking me these questions now of all times. I push her hand away even though heat flushes through my body. I sit up, even though I'm rock hard.

"You're asking me this now?"

"Now that I have your full attention—who was your first love? Like, a real proper first love?"

"Why are you asking me all these questions now?" When I'm minutes from release. My past girlfriends are the last things I want to talk about *now*.

"Mari," I rasp, wishing she would start stroking me again. My spirits are slowly deflating just like my manhood. "I love ..." I pause, hissing out a breath. What do I love? Her? No, it's too soon. I feel something, because I have given her more than I have others. I miss her, I need her, but this isn't love. Love hurts, and twists, and destroys.

"You love what?" she whispers.

I groan inwardly. This has turned out to be nothing like the evening I had in mind. We've derailed. She looks at me "I love this, what we have."

"Being in bed with me? Is that all?"

She's busting my balls, literally. Why do women want to talk all the time? "I love having you around, okay?"

"I don't want you to get mad at me, I just wanted to know. I feel as if I don't know much about you."

"Maybe I like it that way." This is why emotional entanglements drive me crazy. Women want to get inside my head. They want to know everything. Maybe I don't want them to know everything.

"You're a mystery. I was only asking about your past love life. It's not an unusual question."

"Maybe I don't want to open up the past."

"Is the past so bad?"

This is getting unreal. "You know it is." I sit up and push her hand away.

"I can make it better," she says.

"You have." I walk over to the chair and grab my sweatpants. The mood has turned. I've lost interest.

"Don't go." She jumps up and rushes to me, taking my sweatpants from my hands.

"Leave it," I grumble. "I'm not in the mood. You keep talking." I can't hide my displeasure. I came here to fuck. Not to have a debate about my relationships. I have an erection as long as my arm. Feels like it. She bites her lower lip and leads me back to the bed.

"I was just wondering what happens when you finish the book."

The book? I blink. All I ever think about is the book. I hate it, and like it, and then rewrite it and suffer over it. She is the only one who provides me with something else. "I haven't thought that far. Why?" I don't understand what she's getting at.

"It was just a question. There's nothing deep about it."

"What do you want, Mari?"

She looks as if she has something to say. I'm all ears. "Well?" I prompt, when she appears to hesitate. She shrugs.

"What do you want?" she asks me.

"Sex. That's what I came for." But I'm not prepared for the way her face crumples. I feel like a douchebag. "You devised the system," I remind her. "It spurred me on to write more than usual."

"Then let me give you the reward you've earned." She pushes me onto the bed and strips off slowly. I lie back, rest my arms behind my head and watch her. That's better. She's a tease, and she's so insanely good at it. I lick my lips when she's completely naked. I couldn't have asked for more.

She climbs onto the bed and lowers herself slowly onto me. Desire thickens inside me and I hold my breath, not wanting to take my eyes off her. She has become my salvation, this beautiful woman with a heart of gold. She is starting to erase old ghosts, and as she sits, having taken all of me inside her, she looks at me as if I am her world.

Now that's the kind of reward seven thousand words is worth writing for.

CHAPTER THIRTY-FIVE

MARI

The night ends with us cuddling up in bed after sex. Just like it ends most nights. He hasn't answered my questions. I have a feeling he doesn't want to talk about it.

I'm making the same mistake again. Mistaking sex for love, and foreplay for connection. Ward's been hitting his word count goals, so naturally I reward him with sex. There's no need for him to wine and dine me. No need to build up to anything, what we have is purely physical. I'll take it because it's the only way I can get close to him. I wish he would open up to me, I wish this could be more than just sex, but Ward doesn't seem to want more.

When it comes to relationships, I seem to always be chasing a shooting star. Ward comes to my bed, but other than that, I can't reach him. He's closed off and I know next to nothing about him.

I tell myself that this is something that suits us both. We

were filled with simmering lust before and now at least we get to satiate our needs. This should be enough, but it isn't.

Jamie has calmed down. We are friends again. He asked if I wanted to go out on Saturday night, just me and him, on account of us having had that little disagreement. I told him it wasn't a disagreement, it was him being petty. I also feel that it's too soon, only weeks after Raleigh's get-together. I'm not ready to go out again. The real reason I don't want to go out is because the object of my desire is here at home.

As with most nights, Ward leaves somewhere in the middle of the night, and even though I'm wide awake, I pretend to sleep until I hear him leave and close the door.

I try to ignore the sadness that pinches my heart. This is my fault. I'm the one who made this into a game. I'm the one who started the whole word count and sex reward. I fooled myself into believing that we were on the edge of a new start, having given in to our baser instincts, but there is nothing deeper for us.

Ward, too, is struggling with our arrangement, I can tell. One night he almost fell asleep in my bed. I was curled up against him, nuzzled against his chest, feeling wanted and cherished with his arm around me. I hadn't been held like that in months. I was almost falling asleep when he climbed out of bed. I asked him to stay but he refused, he said something about it being better for us to stick to our boundaries. The clock showed 3:15 a.m. He left even though most of the night was over and I lay in my bed all alone, missing the warm space he had vacated.

I must be careful and guard my heart. It's not something I'm good at. In the space of a few months, I have gone from being cruelly cheated on to finding sexual gratification with a man who seems incapable of connecting.

Lurching from one situation to the other isn't the wisest move for anyone, let alone someone like me with all the things that are going wrong in my life, but at least it's better than being alone.

"Let me help you with that," he says one day when he sees me in the entrance hall about to go upstairs with the vacuum cleaner.

"It's okay. I can manage. You have words to write."

"If only." He takes the vacuum cleaner from me. "I'm stuck."

"Stuck? On what?"

He reaches the top of the stairs and sets the vacuum cleaner down. He winces, shoves his hands in his pockets. He never talks about his writing. Never tells me what exactly he's stuck on. I've tried to pry it out of him, but the man won't give anything up. He plays his cards too close to his chest.

"Just ... stuff," he says, in his usual vague and cryptic manner. "It's in my head but it won't come out the way I want it to."

I make a face. "So, give me some specifics."

Give me something.

He sighs loudly then shrugs, choosing to hold on to the problem, whatever it is, and not wanting to share it with me. I can't help him if I don't know. I also can't mean much to him. But I still want to help him. I hate seeing him stuck and weighed down, and he so clearly is. "How about we get out of the house?" I suggest, since he is clearly struggling.

"Leave the house?"

"Yes. Do the impossible. Leave the house." Being inside all the time can't be good for him. All that stale air in that stuffy room. He needs fresh air, and I'm surprised he doesn't know this. "It will be good for you. I'll come with you, if you like."

"And go where?" At least he's considering the idea.

"To a coffee shop. Or a bar. Or, heck," I throw my hands into the air. "We could even have dinner outside." I should be mad at him for being so uncaring, and yet this is who I am. I do care that he's struggling. I don't want him to be stuck. I want him to get his book done on time. I want him to be happy.

Why can't he act like he wants all these things for me?

"Dinner?" He wrinkles his nose, the idea is clearly not appealing.

I'm romantic and foolish and desperate to move what we have out of the bedroom and have it be more like a normal relationship. "We can do anything you want."

He's not even listening to me. His gaze is somewhere else, as if he's thinking. "Maybe I should go and revisit where I used to live."

This is unexpected, him sharing something personal with me. I leap at the opportunity. "We could do that. We *should* do that. It will be nice!"

"Nothing about it will be nice." He clings to the handrail, his knuckles so tight that the skin is stretched taut.

"Then why do you want to go?" I ask softly.

"Rob thought it would be a good idea."

"You don't always have to do everything Rob says."

"He knows me better than I know myself sometimes."

That hurts. Because I want to know him better than Rob does. "Then maybe we should go. It might help with your writing. Help you to get unstuck."

He starts to go downstairs.

"Is that a yes?" I call after him.

"I'm still thinking about it."

One day, when I've stopped working for Ward and he returns to New Orleans, I'll tell Jamie what went on between me and the author he so admires, but I won't tell him how much he breaks my heart.

CHAPTER THIRTY-SIX

WARD

I've got my writing flow back now that I'm not frustrated or distracted. This new arrangement has been working. Mari's rewards motivate me, as sick and perverted as it may seem. I no longer procrastinate because the carrot she dangles works, but lately, something new bristles beneath the surface of my skin and I can't pinpoint what it is. The words come, but a melancholy sweeps through me and it affects me enough that I consider Mari's suggestion to go outside.

I decide to do the thing I've been putting off. Although my mom died in a hospice far, far away from here, memories of the once happy home of my childhood still gnaw at me. It's time to go face it for one last time. Maybe that will help me put a lid on this part of my life so that I can move on. At least I now have a taste of new things to look forward to: Mari, finishing a book, having a movie release, a return home.

I catch her by surprise at lunchtime when I tell her that I want to go. "Do you want me to come along?" she asks.

"Only if you want."

"I don't have that much cleaning to do."

That settles it. I give her the address and she agrees to drive me there but stepping out of the house together, just the two of us outside of our roles, it feels strange. Is our relationship tied to the confines of the house and, more specifically, the bed, or can I dare to envision something more with this woman?

As she drives, Mari is quiet, as if she too can sense the awkwardness, because she's normally a chatty person.

When we get there, I climb out of the car and stare up at the dilapidated building. It looks so much smaller from how I remember it. The paint is chipped and the door is a different color. The grass is straw-like and a pale, patchy shade of green. I remember how my mom used to take pride in this little patch of green. How she would water it and tend to it, and how I would help her, carrying my plastic yellow watering can while she turned on the sprinkler.

Mari slips her hand into mine, but I slip mine back out and fold my arms. This used to be a happy home and all it took was one man to change the course of my life. "Do you want to go inside?" Mari asks.

I shake my head. One look at this shithole, that's all I wanted.

"But we've come all this way."

"This is enough," I tell her. But just then the door opens and a guy walks out with his hands in his pockets, his eyes narrowed. With us staring at the house, it immediately looks suspicious. "Can I help you?" he asks.

"He used to live here when he was a boy," Mari pipes up.

The guy looks at me as if he doesn't trust me.

"We were just taking a walk down memory lane," she adds. Mari and her big mouth. That woman doesn't think. I turn around and head back towards her car.

"What do they want?" I hear someone say.

I turn around and see that a woman has also come out. "Come on," I hiss to Mari, not sure why she's engaging in a conversation with these strangers. But she waves me over. I refuse to go at first, but then my curiosity takes over and I walk back.

"You lived here?" the girl asks me. I give Mari a death stare.

"He did when he was a child," Mari answers for me. "It would be great if he could take a quick look inside."

Hell, no. I am *not* going inside. I start to walk away again, but she runs up behind me. "They said you could go in."

"I don't want to go in."

"But they said you could."

"I don't want to," I insist.

"Ward. We're here. They said you could go in and have a look around. They don't mind."

Hell, no.

"Come on." She takes my arm, and I begrudgingly head back towards the house with her.

"What did you say to them?" I growl.

"You weren't going to ask so I did." She looks at me with apprehension. "You might not get another chance, Ward. They seem nice people. They said you could have a quick look. Quick, though, because they were on their way out."

I glance back at them. The girl is smiling although the guy still looks at me with trepidation. I don't want to do this.

After he died, I went back, hoping to reclaim the life me and my mom used to have. But she wasn't so happy to have me back. She always blamed me for him dying. Said I punched him so hard it broke him. It broke me. I only lasted a year. Couldn't listen to her pining for the piece of shit who had made my life a misery. Couldn't reconcile this stranger of a woman with the mother I used to have. In the end, I left this hellhole not because of my stepdad but because of my mom.

Mari takes my hand again and this time I don't push it away. The couple watches us warily. Mari turns to them. "Do you want to show us around quickly?"

"Nah, you're good to go. There's nothing much of value for you to steal."

The girl pokes the guy in the ribs. He has his phone out and is looking at it, as if he's reading something.

"You can go in," the girl urges.

I let go of Mari's hand and walk through the tiny living room. I see the miniscule-sized kitchen just off the side. It all looks so much smaller now that I am standing here as a grown man, instead of the six- or seven-year-old I was when we first moved here.

I see my mom on the couch, and my stepdad standing over me. I relive the taunts and shouts. I smell the alcohol and cigarette smoke. My heart begins to pound.

I don't want to be here.

"Is it okay to go into the attic?" Mari asks.

"You want to go into the attic?" the guy echoes. "It's a mess."

"Let them," the girl insists. "But be careful. The stairs are—"

"Narrow," I say. They were always narrow. One time my stepdad scared me so badly that I fell down the stairs as

I left the room. I twisted my ankle and couldn't walk for days.

We follow the girl upstairs. She waits on the landing and I look at the two tiny bedrooms. Both doors are open. Both rooms are a mess. The room that used to be mine is filled with clothes and boxes. I take a closer look and peek my head inside. Nothing of me remains here. It doesn't look like a room as much as a storage space. The wallpaper is different, as it should be, seeing that I left more than two decades ago. My mom got me a wallpaper that was blue with astronaut figures and planets. Now it's been replaced by paint that is stained and peeling.

Mari's hand brushes against mine again, and once again I move my hand away but she manages to grasp one of my fingers. She's trying to be supportive, but I find it too much. All of this is too much. I am drowning in an overwhelm of unwanted memories; suffocating in a sea of ugly emotions that should have been laid to rest a long time ago.

"I can show you the attic real quick," the girl says, suddenly becoming very helpful.

"Lead the way," Mari tells her.

"There's a lot of junk up there," she says, waiting by the stairs. "You go ahead. I'll be downstairs."

I start to head up the stairs and hear Mari say that we'll be quick. I open the attic door, and the dusty, musty, cloying smell of years of old dust and stale air hits my nostrils. Reaching out, I hit the light switch. It's still in the same place. I peer closer to examine it and discover that it's the exact same light switch. At least, I think it is.

I walk inside. The room is littered with boxes, bags and heaps of junk. My heart begins to thump again, just like it used to when I was a frightened boy, huddled together in the dark. I stare at the lightbulb. There's a bulb in it. Not like those scary nights when my stepdad would take the bulb out, leaving me in pitch darkness.

Mari stands in the doorway, watching me. There is genuine concern in her eyes. I should be touched, I should let her comfort me, but I can't. It's not easy to allow someone to do that for me when my own mother couldn't. I react to Mari in the only way I know how—to keep her out.

In the corner is the same old mirror. Dark blue plastic edging that is covered in thick dust, and the mirror itself almost opaque. I walk around slowly, my fingers touching the walls and lighting up my synapses, making the fear come flooding back. The stale stench returns too. I used to sit here, huddled and hugging my knees with my head down and sobbing, wishing that my mom would hear me. But after that first time, I knew it was no good.

She never came to my rescue.

Worse, she never tried to stop that man from dragging me up there. It was as if she gave up on me. I bend down and there, in faded writing, but still legible, are my initials, *WM*, and a long list of dates. These are the dates of my incarceration. Seeing them like this, in print before my very eyes, brings tears to my eyes.

Nothing much has changed in here. The air and ambiance of this room is the same. Details are vivid in my mind, so vivid that when I wrote my first book, it was easy to relive every wretched moment, to remember every minute detail.

Warm hands go around my waist from behind. "We should go," Mari whispers. Her face presses against my back. "They have somewhere they need to be."

"Yeah." I sniff and clear my throat. "We should."

I'm the first one out of the house. I need to walk away and take a deep breath but I can't get away fast enough.

"I thanked them." Mari comes over to me.

"I ... I couldn't .... I had to get out."

She does it again, taking my arm, hooking hers through mine. "I know. I understand." She faces me, her hands taking hold of mine. "That can't have been easy."

I swallow and stare at a point above her head.

She leans forward and kisses my chest. "I'm sorry I asked them. I thought it might help." She looks up at me. I had a feeling she'd said something to them. No one in their right mind would let a pair of strangers come into their home.

"I told them who you were," she says, wincing. "I'm sorry. I thought it was important for you to see it."

I nod. That's why they let us in. That's why the guy was probably on his phone, looking up who I was.

"Did I mess up?" she asks. It's hard to miss the neediness in her voice.

"It's okay," I say. "Maybe Rob knew better. I had to see it. But you pushed me to do it."

"I'm glad I did."

"Thank you," I tell her. This time I take her hand and am rewarded with a smile.

"When were you last here?" she asks as we get into the car.

"I came back at sixteen, after he died, when it was safe to."

"Came back from where?"

"From the children's home."

"You went to a children's home?"

I brace myself. "For a while."

"How long?"

"A few months."

"Why?"

I inhale a long breath. I can't talk about it.

"I'm sorry," she says, understanding.

"I was only there for a few months when the fucker died." I remember hearing the news at the home. I remember being so happy that I thought my heart might burst.

"Oh," Mari gasps. "You've had such a traumatic childhood."

"But that bastard dying was the best thing."

"Do you want to go by and see the children's home?" she asks. "I can take you."

"It's closed down."

"We could walk by, if it might help."

"Help with what?" I snap. We face one another.

"I don't know. I was only trying to help."

She *is* trying to help. She always wants to help. She's not the bad person in all this. "I'm sorry. I shouldn't snap at you."

She takes my hand again. "It's okay."

"I want to go home."

"There's so much I don't know about you, Ward," she says as we drive away.

"It's better that way."

CHAPTER THIRTY-SEVEN

MARI

He's quiet all through the journey home. There are moments when he lets me in, and some moments when he shuts me out. I have no clue as to what I am to him; just a comfort in bed, or something more. It's disconcerting, given the fact that I have always tried to be there for him, even though he hasn't done the same for me.

He goes into his writing cave when we get home. I sense he is going through some pain and I want to make things right again. I want to make him not hurt but I can't help him if he won't let me.

Ward isn't one to let me in on his thoughts and it's a wonder he ever told me about his stepdad in the first place.

I decide to leave him alone and fix dinner. I baked bread this morning. Not just any bread, rosemary focaccia, because he casually mentioned a few days ago that he liked it. He said it was the one last good memory he had from his childhood.

Baking bread is so far from who I am and I barely recognize this new domestic goddess I have become—taking care of Ward, being supportive, being there for him so that he can do his work. This is everything I railed against—being a homemaker and putting my own goals aside for someone else—and yet there is something healing in our current setup. I remind myself that I am going through a journey, as is he. We're just two people taking advantage of a unique situation.

It won't last forever. Soon enough I will get back out there into the world and become a working, independent woman.

I've made homemade vegetable soup to go with it. Just as I finish heating it up, Ward pops into the kitchen. He announces that he is eating in the study, and mumbles something about being behind on his writing.

He's either lying or he doesn't want me to be with him tonight, because I'm certain he told me earlier that he was on target. I understand his need to be alone, so I plate up his food and hand it to him. He thanks me for making the bread, takes his food and hastily leaves.

He has hurt me again. I thought I was helping him, I thought we were getting closer but I'm deluding myself as always.

I crave connection, that of the emotional kind, not so much the physical. The sex is great, but something is missing. Being stuck in here without having other people to bounce things off of is hard. I miss the water cooler conversations at work. I long for friends to catch up with during my lunchtime and coffee breaks.

What Ward and I have is intense. Bottled up like concentrated perfume; overpowering, cloying and almost suffocating. The type of stuff that renders a person unable to breathe.

This house harbors us. It closets and cloaks all of our needs and desires, keeps the secrets of the way he uses me, and the way I let him. We're not normal people in a normal relationship. We don't go out to dinner or hang around outside like normal people. We don't go for walks, or go to the park, or go out with friends.

I try not to have illusions of what this is, but being here alone and with not much else going on with me, Ward provides me with something that is lacking from my life. I'm scared of what will happen when time runs out for us.

Today was the first time we were out together. I was hoping to do something that might get him unstuck and help him to move on but when he hides so much of himself away from me, what chance do I have?

He's hurting.

Visiting a place like that will have an effect. I bring my laptop downstairs and wait for him in the kitchen in case he feels like talking. I look for new jobs online and update my resume. I even consider calling Danny again about that job he told me about. Then I hear a noise and I stare at the door, wondering if it's Ward leaving the study and coming to find me.

It's not. Ward isn't coming. I wish he would talk to me. It doesn't always have to be about sex. I wait for him until just after midnight, and then I go upstairs to bed.

I curl up in bed and just as I find my eyes getting heavy, the door opens. My eyes fly open. A lamp flickers on and Ward stares down at me, looking rougher than ever. I sit up. "What's wrong?"

"I can't sleep. Can I sleep here?"

My heart takes a leap so big, I'm scared it might jump

out of my chest. This is a break from the usual. I move over and pat down the place where I had been sleeping, the bedsheets are warm and slightly ruffled. He climbs in beside me. "Sorry to wake you."

"Don't be sorry." Because I'm not. I'm ecstatic. He lies on his back, his hands clasped behind his head and those sexy, bulging muscles peeking out from the sleeves of his t-shirt. I lift up onto my elbow, loving my new view, loving that he has willingly come to me. Longing swirls in my heart, and my belly begins to quiver. Could I be any luckier? Feel any happier?

After today's visit to his childhood home, I don't expect him to have hit his daily word count but my heart is soft, and I want to smother him with every ounce of love I feel for him. I'll reward him anyway, only this won't be a reward. This will be me taking care of him. I'll do anything to take his mind off those dark times he has suffered.

I move towards him and stroke the sharp pointy strands of his five o'clock shadow. Slowly, slowly, slowly, my hand slides lower but he shifts, moving his arm, and taking a hold of mine. He stops me. "Not tonight. I'm not in the mood."

I put a finger to his lips. "Shhhh." Of all the things he could have said and done, it's this that fills my heart to overflowing. He came to me. He wants to *be* with me, and not just for the sex. He *needs* me.

I want to bury my face in his chest and put my arm over him. I want to nestle against his warm skin. I want to touch his body, but neither I nor he will be able to hold back if that happens. I need to stay away and put a few cold inches between us. So, I lie on my side with my hands reluctantly away from him, and I stare at his side profile, admiring his biceps as if I've seen them for the first time all over again. After a while I switch the lamp off.

I must have drifted off to a good sleep, because when I next awaken, I feel groggy. I'm a light sleeper and I stir and instinctively open my eyes when Ward shifts.

It must be early in the morning because in the blue light of a new day, I find myself staring at his back. He's sitting on the edge. I reach out to touch him but he gets up. I wait to hear the door open and then close. He's starting to mean so much to me, and I hate that he feels the need to leave. I'm scared that he doesn't feel the same way. I am left alone once more and I check the time. It's 5:00 a.m. He's done it again. This man can't settle. He can't *be*. It's his restlessness which takes him away.

I splay my arm out, touching where he lay, and then foolishly, I shift over, and sleep on the side of the bed where he had been.

A few hours later when I see him again, it's in the kitchen and I have his breakfast ready. He looks rough, even worse than he did last night.

"Hey," I say gently. My heart goes out to him. I want to put my arms around him and ask him what's wrong, and then I want him to tell me so that I can fix it. But he doesn't give much away. If anything, he's as distant as ever and back in that faraway place.

"I can't be disturbed for the next few days," he informs me. "I have to get this done."

"What about Jamie?"

"He's still coming. Exercise helps."

He leaves, and I try to figure out if it's just me he wants to push away. I thought after yesterday, things might be different but maybe he's crossed the boundary and gotten too close, become too vulnerable and now he can't handle it. He's pushed me away again, just like that, with a click of his fingers. He's using me, and I'm letting him.

That's how the rest of the week goes. We're back to staying apart, me tiptoeing around him. It's high time I checked out of this situation.

I revert back to being just the housekeeper, hating myself for being in this position. I start looking online with renewed vigor, sending my CV off as many places as I can. And in between, I still visit my mom. She seems weaker each time I go, and her memory seems shakier, but Brenda assures me that this is to be expected. On the weekend, I spend both days with her.

When I return, Ward is sitting in the kitchen. I'm on edge, wondering which side of him I'll see this time. "I went to see my mom," I tell him when he remarks that he's hardly seen me. I tell him that she's in a nursing home.

"And you go see her on the weekends?" he asks.

"Most weekends." I explain about her having Alzheimer's and how much it scares me and how this new nursing home is good for her.

"She used to live with you," he states, as if this surprises him. I explain why I had to move her to a home when I couldn't cope, when she became a risk to her own safety. "I couldn't have her live by herself. I had to take care of her."

"You're a good daughter."

"She's all I have."

"She's lucky to have you."

I walk over to the sink and pour myself a glass of water. "I reached my daily word count today," he announces proudly.

I turn around, sipping my water slowly. "That's good."

He eyes me, as if he's waiting for me to say more, but I won't say more. I won't be his sex on tap. "Goodnight then." I walk out, even though it takes all of my focus not to turn around and walk back to him.

. . .

WARD

Mari's angry with me, and who can blame her? What did I expect? For her to invite me to her room just because I've had a good writing day?

Complications, that's what I am contending with now.

I hate complications, and that's what this little arrangement has become. Neither of us bargained for this. I certainly didn't intend for this to happen.

It. Just. Did.

I'm scared of having feelings for her, scared of what it might mean. If she had agreed, we would be having sex right now and everything would be okay.

I hate that we're like this, not talking. I can do without the sex, but her not talking to me is harder to deal with. I'm going to fix it. I make my way upstairs, and knock on her door. There's no way I'm going in unless she lets me in.

"Mari?" I knock again, four, maybe five times.

She comes to the door and opens it a little. "What do you want?" She sounds tired.

I have no answer because that's not the question I was expecting. "You're angry with me."

"So?" She says it in the tone of a sullen teenager.

"I don't want you to be angry with me."

"You have that effect on me sometimes."

I clench my jaw. I haven't come here to have sex, but I also don't want to get into a conversation about what we have. I don't need the drama. I'm a fucking writer, and there's plenty of drama in my head all the time. I certainly don't need any more.

I want to rest and lately she's the only one who allows me that luxury. She's the only one who gives me that place of calmness. "Can we talk?" I want to lie down and have her cradle my head. I can't explain to her how revisiting my home was a mistake. It's shaken up all manner of dirt and silt. I wish I hadn't revisited the past.

"Talk? *Now* you want to talk?" She tilts her head as if she doesn't believe me, as if I have something else in mind. "What do you want, Ward?" She opens the door and walks away, folding her arms as she hovers by the wall, nowhere near the bed.

I walk in. "You're angry with me."

"You only come to me when you want sex."

"That's not entirely true. I came to you the other night."

"And you left halfway through the night."

"It was almost morning," I protest.

"That's just semantics and you know it."

My mouth twists, but I am cautious of saying the wrong thing, especially because I have no idea what I want any more. "I'm sorry if I upset you."

"You can't rent me by the hour," she cries.

"That's not how I treat you."

"I never know where I am with you. One minute you want me, you need me even, and then you feel guilty and you tell me you need your space." She glares at me. I hover around the bed, then move away, slipping my hands into the pockets of my sweatpants, unsure of how to be.

"What do you want, Mari?" I ask her, against my better judgment. As if I could even give her the thing I suspect she wants. I learned a long time ago that people are not to be trusted, especially the ones you come to rely on and trust the most.

"I don't ...I ..." She stumbles on her words, and I sense that she too is being careful. "I don't, I *won't* allow myself to be used anymore."

"Used? Is that how you see it? I used you?"

"We've used one another."

That much is true. She has needs. She needs me. *Needed* me. "We didn't set out to do this," I remind her. "It just happened."

She nods, but her arms are still folded like a defense shield and nothing is going to get through. Not my words or my actions. I don't plan to do anything tonight. I didn't come here with anything in mind. I just can't operate this way when the way we had started to be was so much better.

I don't want her to go to sleep thinking I'm an asshole. I especially don't want her to think I don't give a fuck, when I do.

Staring at her, with only a few strides between us, I'm blindsided by the notion that I care more about Mari than I allow myself to think. She has always made things better for me. I'm so used to my own company that I haven't needed to think about anyone else but me.

I'm learning, but some lessons are hard to learn when you come from where I do.

"It did just happen," she says, agreeing, but "What is this? What do we have?"

I hate that she's making it difficult. Putting me on the spot. "We have ..." I don't know what to call it. I should have been prepared for her to dissect and analyze everything.

But I, too, have been unfair. I haven't treated her the way she deserves to be treated. I've been selfish, thinking only of myself.

"I can't get close to you and it's not for lack of trying. You don't open up."

Where I come from, with the things that have happened, it's near impossible for me to open up. She's lucky. I have shared more with her than I do with most people. "What do you want to know?"

"Whatever you're willing to tell me."

I'm not willing to tell her anything. She's forcing me to be another way, and I can only be the way I am.

"There you go again," she says, jabbing a finger at me. "You close me off. You only tell me little things here and there."

I came here to talk, and now that she's confronting me, I can't. So much of my past has been shaken up and has been spinning around in my head. "Goodnight," I say, not wanting to push past this.

She doesn't say it back.

Tonight is going to be another sleepless night for me. Instead of returning to my bedroom, I head downstairs to my study. When sleep doesn't come, there's no point lying in bed tossing and turning. I might as well try to write.

CHAPTER THIRTY-EIGHT

MARI

I'm calmer the next morning and Ward seems fine, too. He hasn't shaved and his eyes are ringed with dark circles.

"Did you sleep?" I ask as I pour his cup of coffee.

"Not really. I was writing until the early hours."

We're talking normally, and there's no hint of the drama from last night. I feel bad that he came to me to apologize and we ended up having another disagreement.

A knock at the door signals that Jamie is here so I go to answer it. "I'm seeing Danny this week," he informs me as I let him in.

This reminds me. "I should meet up with him as well," I say.

"You haven't yet?"

"I've been too busy."

He swipes his hand across his chin. "This is a big house,

but you said you can take your time cleaning all the rooms. I don't get why you're so busy all the time."

I shake my head at this typical man's reply. "We can swap roles one day. I'm sure Ward would let us if I put forward my argument."

"What argument is that?"

"That you have no idea what you're talking about." We hover around in the hallway instead of heading into the kitchen. "Why do you need to see Danny?"

"This job is going to end soon, and it's not looking good with where I'm currently at. Danny mentioned he has potential openings where he works."

"When?"

"Sometime on the weekend, unless you're going to visit your mom."

"I can take time out this weekend."

"I'll see what I can do," says Jamie, just as Ward comes out into the hallway. He lifts his coffee cup and greets Jamie who comments, "You look like you're ready to go."

"I am. I'm enjoying my workouts," Ward admits. "Now that's something I never thought I'd say."

Jamie raises an eyebrow at me, then rubs his hands together. "We'll take it up a level then. Are you ready?"

"I was born ready," is what I hear Ward say as the two of them head towards the gym. I can only pinpoint Ward's exuberance down to him being so near the end of his book that any day now he could say to me that he's done and is returning to New Orleans.

I definitely need to meet with Danny. I'll take two jobs if I have to. I'm sick of hanging around for morsels of interest from Ward, sick of wishing he would see me as something more than a physical release. It hasn't all been bad. This man and his moods have kept me on my toes, and for that reason, I've managed to stay on here. Still, I sense that the end is near, and as the days go on, my feelings towards him change.

During the following days, Ward is still nice and kind and polite, and still looking as sexy as ever. Tellingly, he hasn't mentioned anything about meeting his word count goals lately.

Sometimes I catch him looking at me when I look up, and I can tell that he thinks about me as much as I think about him. There's a sizzle in the air even though we aren't sharing the bed.

"How is your book coming along?" I ask him one day after dinner. He's sitting on the stool, taking forever to finish. A part of me hopes that he's dragging out the time so that he can see me. It's only at mealtimes that we seem to get the time to talk.

"I'm on the second read through," he informs me. "Making notes and finding lots of errors."

"You'll be finished soon?" I need to know how long I have here. I don't want any nasty surprises. I don't want him to come to me one day and say 'goodbye', cut me off suddenly and disappear. Even this tawdry thing we've got going deserves a gentle letting go.

"Not soon." His voice is tight.

"But you said you were at the first draft stage and then you could go home."

"I need to ensure that the story makes sense. It needs another read through."

"What does that mean?" I'm trying to gauge how long we have, and he's being vague.

"It means I need more time."

"How much time?"

"Why the need to know?" he asks.

"So that I know how long it might be before I have to start looking elsewhere for work." I *am* sort of looking elsewhere, but nothing promising has turned up. The job market is as stagnant as a dead lake. Hopefully the meeting with Danny will prove fruitful.

Ward seems irritated by my questioning. "I can't give you a time limit. It's not that simple."

"That doesn't help me." I wish he would look at me with longing. Why can't he?

"You sound anxious to leave. Are you?"

I fold my arms and scratch my nose for good measure, trying to act all casual—which is hard because casual is something I don't feel about him and me. "No."

"Then what's up?"

This stops me. His voice is soft again, his gaze softens too. It's almost as if I have the old Ward back. The good old Ward. "You haven't talked about your word count," I say, curious to know what he'll answer.

"We were done with talking about word counts," he says slowly. "You made that clear to me the other night."

"I'm glad you've taken it on board." I'm not glad but I'm in danger of being as clingy and as desperate as I was with Dale. The first time I found out he cheated on me, I accepted his story of a drunken encounter with a woman at work who liked him. Stupidly, I didn't heed the warning, and I took him back.

"I got the message." Ward gets up to leave even though his plate isn't completely empty. It's obvious that he's fed up and eager to get away, because this man has a good appetite and never leaves his plate empty.

"Good." I toss the word at him as he walks away.

"Yeah, good."

A visit to Maplewood to see my mom soon buoys up my

spirits. She's back to her normal self again. Today she was my real mom, and she didn't lapse in and out of remembering. I cherished every second we shared. We talked about my dad, and our family vacations, birthdays, and memorable moments.

And then she asked me about Dale and I almost blurted out that we'd split up and how could she forget?

Until I remembered that I hadn't told her.

She doesn't know.

She doesn't any of it. Me losing my job, or Dale cheating on me and fathering someone else's child, or me getting evicted.

It hit me then, like a wrecking ball to my heart, that the person I had looked up to and gone to all through my life for wisdom and guidance was the woman I could no longer go to with my problems.

With my circle of loved ones shrinking, I feel increasingly isolated and lost.

"We're good, Mom," I tell her.

"That boy ought to put a ring on your finger," she says. Instead, I hold her hand and squeeze it and smile through the pain of what I know. I spend the day with her, helping her to eat, and talking about the past. Being around Ward on a bad day is like walking through a bombed-out site, trying to miss the debris and broken stones and splintered glass. Being with my mom allows me to smell the roses and take in breathfuls of fresh air.

However, the day that had started off so well doesn't end so well as I face my new normal. Desperate for friends, connection and belonging, I go over to Jamie's and break down. I burst into tears as soon as he opens the door and fall into his arms.

He holds me and cradles my weary body against his

chest. He gets out the best medicine: a bottle of wine and chocolates, and we spend the evening on the couch. I tell him everything that was hurting, but I leave out everything about Ward.

I stay over that night and sleep on the couch even though Jamie insists I could have his bed, but I'm not going to put my good friend out like that.

My weekend ends up being wonderful. Like the good old days. We wake up late, have brunch and laze around. Jamie reminds me of all the good things I used to have when I had a life, an apartment, a job and a boyfriend.

I don't want to return to the mansion. I don't want to see Ward. I don't want to get ensnared again into his sticky web. Most of all I don't want to look him in the face with longing and have him stare back at me as if I mean nothing.

Later that afternoon, we meet with Danny at a bar and we end up staying there all evening, until late at night. I'm tipsy, and happy, and for a moment it seems as if I had my old life back.

But in the end, I have to return back to Ward's house. We get a cab and when we got there, Jamie helps me out. Then he hugs me because I keep saying I don't want to do this anymore.

Eventually, I find the courage to go inside.

CHAPTER THIRTY-NINE

WARD

She was away the whole weekend.

The. Entire. Fucking. Weekend.

I looked out of the window as soon as I heard a car pull up. Saw her and Jamie embrace outside. Even kiss maybe. I couldn't bear to look.

Fuck.

I slunk away to bed, but I couldn't sleep. I'm back to staying out of her way again.

When Jamie shows up the next morning, I'm already in the gym working out. He's impressed. Says that I'm a new man.

There's nothing new about me, or how I roll. When women get too close, I freeze up. I can't handle it. I don't want it, and so I tell them to go, and then I miss them.

When Jamie leaves, I take my lunch and head back into the study because I can't face her. I can't bear to be around her.

But once I'm at my desk, I play with my tuna salad. My appetite is lost. All I see is that image of her with her arms around Jamie. I keep staring at the screen, editing and rewriting my words, hating every single word that I've written. I'm in danger of stalling again.

This has to stop. I've decided I'm going home to New Orleans at the end of this week, even if the manuscript isn't as finished as I want.

Mari is playing with me. Messing with my head. Screwing with my writing. I can't have another day of sitting around unable to do anything because I am this close to finishing this book, and yet these last few chapters have dragged on.

I know the reason why. She's in the kitchen, oblivious of the hell she's putting me through. She's left her mark on me. Wormed her way into my skin, burrowed deep into my mind.

I will fix this now. I push away from my desk and decide to confront her but in my quietly simmering haste and rage, I run right into her as I storm out of my study. She's outside my door, carrying the vacuum cleaner. Her large eyes widen, and she springs back, still clutching the damned vacuum cleaner hose.

"Sorry," she cries, breathless and timid, and so unlike her. The shock of brushing against her has a similar effect on my mind. I feel just as breathless and startled but I don't apologize. I'm not in the mood to be nice.

"You were gone the entire weekend."

She tilts her head, lifting her chin in a defiant manner. "And what if I was? You said I have weekends off. I'm sorry I forgot to leave your lunch and dinner."

"I can manage."

"Then what's the problem? Because I can see there is one."

Smart little minx. She's come to know me so well. My moods, my thoughts. It's almost frightening. I grit my teeth. Honesty isn't the way I deal with these things. Not when it comes to being vulnerable, letting myself open up to another person. My past taught me that doing so only breaks you. I want to be unbreakable, and that's why I don't get close. Rob is the closest I will allow, and now Mari wants to know what the problem is.

"I'm careful." I breathe out. Confessing is hard. "When it comes to meeting people, I like to keep my distance."

"Is that all?" she asks, confounding me. What the hell does she mean 'is that all'? I narrow my eyes.

"We're done then." She bends down to pick her vacuum cleaner up again.

I let her take a few strides away from me before hollering. "No. That is not all."

She sets down the vacuum cleaner but doesn't immediately turn to face me. This woman is going to be the death of me. She presses every single button to my moods, turning them as easily as if she were changing channels on a TV remote.

I've never met anyone like her, have never been with anyone like her. I'm at her mercy, and while I like it that way sometimes, I hate giving up my power. I hate her having control of me. Letting others have control of your moods and therefore your well-being isn't the way to survive, and survival is the only game I play.

I walk up to her, and around her so that I'm facing her. She appears calm, even if she crosses her arms again. "I'm not used to this," I tell her.

She stays silent. Now she's playing her game. She's not

going to give an inch. It's all down to me. I can't do without her, so I have to bare all.

"This wasn't supposed to happen, this thing between you and me. I don't get close. I don't open up, but *you*," I lift up my hand, about to jab my finger in her direction, then stop myself. "You put me in a situation that is new and uncomfortable. A situation I didn't want to be in." I stare at her face, at the lips I long to kiss, and I want her to say something. I want her to acknowledge that she heard me.

"And what situation is that?"

"You know what situation," I cry out.

"Then say it," she orders.

I bite down hard. Nobody makes me do anything I don't want to. So why the hell is Mari different? "When you and I ..." I clear my throat. "When we're ..."

"You want sex," she states calmly, as if she's asking me to pass the ketchup.

"You say that as if it's all I want from you," I retort. I want something more, something everlasting; sex is fleeting, transient. I want longevity. I want to take a shot at something even though things never worked out for me before. With Mari, I finally feel like trying again.

"It *is* all you want from me. Have you forgotten out last conversation? You can't communicate. You're a writer, Ward, but you can't talk to me."

All too well, unfortunately. The painstaking silence drags on like a freight train. Heavy and labored. I wish she would say something. Once again, our roles have reversed, how is it that I'm on tenterhooks waiting to hear what she has to say? "I've always told you that I'm not good with people."

"But you'll take the sex, if you can get it?" she taunts.

The muscles along my jaw flex. I'm in danger of

grinding down a few layers of enamel on my teeth because they're so tightly clenched.

"I missed you. When you were gone over the weekend, I wanted you back here."

She lets out a surprised gasp. "You're wondering what I was up to, staying over at Jamie's place. You're wondering what we did. You're wondering why I didn't come home until late the next night."

I watch her lips move, and I remember tasting her sweet little mouth and hate that someone else might have touched her. "Did you fuck him?" I spit out.

A look of revulsion flickers across her eyes, her face wrinkling as if she's tasted something disgusting. "Your imagination is wild. Almost bordering on paranoid, some would say."

I grasp her wrist. It's thin and fragile. I soften my grip not wanting to hurt her. "You behave as if you have a hold on me, Ward. As if I matter. As if you care."

"I *do* care. I care about you." I can't believe I said that to her, and as much as it surprises me, it also seems to catch her off guard. "I do care," I tell her again, thumbing her wrist slowly. "I might not have said the right things the other day, but I was telling the truth."

She snatches her wrist away. "You didn't really tell me anything except that you don't want to open up. You don't want more."

She picks up her vacuum cleaner again, and my anger rises. I'm not done yet. "Where are you going?" We're not done. *I'm* not done. I've just exposed my inner feelings, and she's tossed them away like a week-old bag of salad.

"Thank you for leveling with me," she says. "I appreciate it."

Appreciate it?

Is that all I get? I watch her go up the stairs, only this time I don't offer to help. My ego has been dented and I don't have it in me to be chivalrous.

MARI

I force myself to walk away smoothly, to show that I have it together, but I don't. I'm clutching the vacuum cleaner so tightly that it's sure to leave the imprints in my hand. I feel the heavy weight of Ward's stare as I try to climb the stairs as confidently as I can.

At the top, once I'm out of his sight, I lean back against a wall and inhale. My legs are shaky, my heart thundering like a hundred galloping horses.

Ward Maddox just did the unthinkable. He let down his armor and told me that he missed me. He told me that he wanted me back. He said he cares about me.

Inside, the cells in my body jiggle with joy. A beating, a throbbing, a pulsating orchestra of music starts up inside me all playing in sweet harmony, as if Ward's fingers have plucked the strings to my heart and commanded the rest of me to follow suit.

He just wants sex. An ugly whisper starts up in my head.

No, he doesn't, I tell myself. Those weren't the words of someone who craves *just* sex. Ward is as lonely as me, as broken as me, but for different reasons.

Naturally, I'm in shock after what he said. I would have jumped on him, thrown my arms around his neck, wrapped my legs around his waist. I would have sealed his mouth with my lips and kissed him deeply. We would have probably wound up having sex right then and there in that hallway.

I wanted to.

I could have.

But I didn't.

Who does he think he is that he can come to me when he has a need and expect me to give in?

I will punish him.

He's jealous because he thinks I was with Jamie. I hold my hand to my beating heart. A blanket of warmth wraps itself around me. Ward Maddox misses me and cares about me.

I'm the luckiest woman alive, and this time I'm not going to give in to him as easily.

CHAPTER FORTY

MARI

Dare I believe that things between us are back to normal?

I can't read the book that last night I couldn't put down. I can't watch TV.

Ward hasn't talked about his word count, and I'm aware that he's in editing mode. He seems more miserable than ever and I can't tell if it's because of the state of his revisions or if it's because I haven't responded at all to his startling admission of feelings for me a few days ago.

I took his words and held onto them for a few more days. I wanted them for myself, to replay them over and over again, before Ward's mood changed and he replaced those words with cruel ones.

I have come to know that this is fleeting, and he won't allow himself the gift of happiness for too long. He'll revert back. He's damaged and with a childhood like his, it's not hard to see why.

We're back to having lunch and dinner together, but this time each interaction is fraught with a frisson of sexual tension.

Jamie reminds me about dinner on Saturday, and he does this in front of Ward, not knowingly, because Jamie has no idea about me and Ward. Yet I see the expression on Ward's face change. I enjoy seeing his unease.

Later that evening, after the two of us have had dinner, I get up to load the dishwasher when Ward comes over to help me, even though it's not his job, and even though there are only a few dishes. "You don't have to do this. I can manage."

"I can't sit and watch you and do nothing."

"You used to sit and watch me," I retort, and then, to soften the blow. "It's my job, remember? We signed a contract."

His face darkens and I sense the chill in his mood. He's trying to make amends and be extra nice and I've thrown the word back at him. I'm still not sure if it's his cock or his heart that needs more attention, but I am enjoying this time and milking it for all it's worth.

"Done," I say, closing the dishwasher door. "Everything is done. It's been a good day." I'm feeling especially chirpy, because his silence and subdued mood, and that look in his eyes, tell me he needs me. "Has it been for you?"

"What?" he growls.

"A good day?"

"I've made progress." He stares at me. I wait for him to say it, to tell me that he's had a good day. It's no longer about word counts, because he isn't doing much writing, just the rewriting. He looks pleased with himself, yet he doesn't articulate any of that. Probably because he knows what I would think.

"That's wonderful. Well, goodnight." I start to walk away because I have to reply to the email I have about a job interview.

"Where are you going?"

"I have things to do."

I walk away, even though my body has already prepared itself in anticipation of having him in my bed, but that's not going to happen until I say so.

But as I retire to my room for the evening, I'm at a loss for what to do next. My mind is jittery and I can't settle down. I can't watch TV or read a book, or surf aimlessly online. I should reply to the people who want me to come in for an interview but that would make it all so real. The idea that I could get a job elsewhere means that I would have to give notice here. With things seemingly back on the track with me and Ward, I'm no longer eager to leave. We aren't done. I don't want to leave, and he's already told me he doesn't want me to go.

If I feel this jittery, I can't imagine how Ward feels. I don't even have a deadline weighing on my shoulders. I don't have an editor breathing down my neck, or a competitor's success making me doubt myself.

If this is difficult for me, how much harder must it be for Ward?

I can't do this any longer.

I want to give in.

I want to surprise him.

I want to seduce him.

And tease him in the process.

Arousal surges through me like a freight train, hard and fast and heavy. The more I think of him, the more I want him.

But first, I need something. I slip into his bedroom.

. . .

WARD

Insanity. That's what this is. How can I be creative when my cock has other ideas?

This environment isn't conducive to writing and editing a book. That's what having a housekeeper such as Mari is like. I need Freya again. Life was so much less complicated at home.

Mari's gone to bed, and I was prepared for us to sit and talk for longer. I want her, I crave her, but I can hold back, and if that was all she wanted, to talk and do nothing else, I would have happily agreed. But leaving me like that, as if she can't bear to be around me, that's another level of headfuck I can do without.

Eager to overcome the mounting frustration, I settle down at my desk and go through the printed-out chapters of my manuscript. My heart isn't in it, but the clock is ticking. I told Rob that he would have these last week. And last week I told him he would have them the week before that.

Even he can see that I've stalled again. Exhaling slowly, as if I'm about to prepare for a marathon, I pick up my pen and start to read.

And I hate every single word I read.

It's always like this. I hate what I've written. So I get to work, scribbling notes in the margins, crossing out lines and dialog and prose that is stilted. Words I don't like and putting question marks over things that don't make sense.

How can my manuscript still be so messy when I've

rewritten each chapter so meticulously? I read another page and leave more ugly red lines.

"Why so much red? It can't be that bad."

I look up to find Mari staring down at me. She's wearing my satin robe, the one I used to wear a long time ago.

I didn't even hear her come in, and seeing her dressed like that suddenly gets me hot, as if a wildfire has spread all over my body. My cock stands up elated.

"You ... had ... things ... to do," I say, offering up a lame-ass reply. I stare at my robe, and my initial instinct is to tear it off her. I don't need to wonder why she's here, because that look in her eyes, coupled with her new choice of attire already tells me.

"I've done them all." Her mood is playful, her voice is flirty.

I throw down my pen. "I'm not making progress," I say wearily, and there will be no further attempt at any progress, not if she's going to stand there dressed in that. "It's hard."

She struts over to my side, pushes my chair back and stands in between my legs, before lifting her knee and resting it on the small area of the chair between my legs. Her hand goes straight to my cock. "It *is* hard."

My brain fogs over. My mouth stops working. I stiffen further.

"I love what you're wearing," I manage to say. Her hand squirrels into my sweatpants, and she strokes me over the fabric of my boxer briefs. I stutter out a breath, the sensation so unexpected, it sucks the air right out of my lungs. "You don't have to ..."

"I'm not here for you," she tells me. "I missed *this*." She plucks me loose from my boxers and clasps my dick in her hand. I feel like I could explode right now. But she begins to stroke, gently at first, then slightly harder. My chest constricts, the air in my lungs is inadequate. Her strokes get longer, her grasp harder, and each time she reaches the end, she glides her thumb over my tip, making me jerk because it feels so, so, so damn good.

My head falls back. I have dreamed about this temptress for weeks. I've missed her. I've *needed* her, I prayed she would visit me, would tend to me, but I never expected this.

When I next look down, she's on her knees, her lips sliding up and down, taking me deeper each time. I fist my hands in her hair, scared of letting go, scared of making myself so vulnerable.

MARI

He's at my mercy. Pinned in his chair, vulnerable and wanting me. I've surprised him completely because I've never seen his cock stand to attention so fast.

I slide my lips slowly over him, taking in his entire length slow, slow, slowly. Animal moans fall from his lips. He jerks in the chair. It empowers me each time I hear him grunt and groan.

"Ma...*ri*," he hisses, grabbing my hair, pushing it away from my face as he watches me work on him.

I'm going to take him to the edge. Drive him delirious. I love that I can make him feel like this and I take my time pleasuring him with my mouth, needing him to feel for me what I feel for him. Wanting him to want me, this man whom I have tamed and can now claim as my own. Any moment now, he's going to come in my mouth. That's not what I want. I need him buried deep inside me, but I keep tipping him closer to that beautiful edge.

"Stop ..." he bites out. "I'm going to ..." He tries to move my mouth away, but my lip suction is too strong. It's instant, the consequences my actions have. I can make him writhe and moan. He's almost there, I can feel it. I almost don't want to stop, but I force my lips off him, then wipe my mouth.

His breathing is fast and furious, his head lowered. I stand up slowly, wanting him to see me. Placing my finger under his chin, I lift his face then open the robe, *his* robe, and reveal my nakedness.

His mouth falls open. He reaches out to touch me but his touch isn't what I need.

Not wasting any time, I straddle him, climbing onto the chair, onto him, my legs on either side of his thighs. My breasts hang in front of him, a deliberate temptation. He's craved this for weeks and I have deprived him. He clamps his mouth over my breast and suckles me hard. The sensation shoots straight to my belly, then slides down lower, heat, and liquid snaking around between my legs. I position the tip of his cock at the mouth of my silkiness, and I hold there. He utters a sound somewhere in the back of his throat, a low and dirty sound that calls to my feral nature. I hear it in the base of my belly, feel the reverberations of his desire echo deep inside me.

A non-human mewl, wild and guttural falls from my lips as I slide myself down his thick length. This is pure bliss. I run my hands through his hair, because I can't get enough skin-to-skin contact. He fills me up, consumes and overwhelms my body, top and bottom. I sheath him completely, sitting down on him at last with all of him inside me.

I want to go slow and long, take my time because we haven't done this for a while. I need him as much as he needs me. Energized, I move up and down slowly, savoring the feel of him as he fills me completely.

He growls, then puts his hands on my hips. We can't wait. There is a desperation and urgency to our union. I move up and down, but his hands give me more momentum. Blood courses through my body, amplifying everything, heightening every feeling I have for this man. We use one another, draining and squeezing and taking every last drop of pleasure, until we come together. When I stop convulsing, when the aftershocks of our lovemaking subside, I rest my head on his shoulder, and he holds me, as if he never wants to let me go.

CHAPTER FORTY-ONE

WARD

I'm a hot sticky mess, but she's in my arms, sitting on me and I don't want to let her go.

I am drawn to this woman and I can't reverse it. I don't want to be a stranger anymore. I don't want to spend my life in my study writing all day and seeing nobody but Freya.

She moves, lifts her head off my shoulder and looks at me with her dark bedroom eyes. Then she kisses me. It's a light press of her lips against mine, but it's enough to rouse the cells in my body. I stand up still holding her, and her legs tighten around my waist. The robe has slipped off one shoulder and I pull it back on again.

"This suits you," I whisper as I walk upstairs with her.

"Maybe I should borrow more of your clothes."

"I prefer you with no clothes."

She plants playful kisses along my neck, then squeals, "Put me down. You'll fall."

"Don't trust me?"

Her leghold around my hips tightens in answer and my manhood is fully awake again.

I enter her room and throw her onto the bed. She lies back, shrugging out of the robe, widening her legs enticingly.

I wasn't planning to leave her tonight or get any sleep; I was planning to take a shower first because her scent is all over me. She catches my hesitation as I rake my gaze up the length of her body.

Quick as a flash, I flip her onto her stomach and thrust inside her. We both moan at the same time. She is sweet, and hot and tight. She fits me like a glove. I kiss her shoulder, emotions swirling around my heart, making me feel things that have long been buried. She giggles, and I drop another kiss. It's a gentle gesture, unlike the shitstorm of feelings I have for her. Pressed against her, buried deep inside her, we are skin to skin. I own her. She belongs to me. I drop a spattering of kisses on her back, and when she squirms again, I thrust into her. She writhes and moans, and I begin to thrust harder and harder.

The next few hours pass by in a blur. Everything I've been holding in, my feelings for her, my desire, my need, pours forth. We take a bath together. Ordinarily I wouldn't indulge in such time-consuming activities, but Mari insists. There's a playfulness around her, which is contagious. Sitting in the bathtub with her between my legs, and with her back to me, I enjoy the sensation of soaping her, of exploring every inch of her body as she lies against my chest. Under the water, I pleasure her with my fingers, kissing her wet skin as my other arm locks around her. She jerks to my touch, and I bask in the heat of our union. I don't want to think about all the things that could go wrong.

They always do. I won't let the past gnaw at my gut and I allow myself to enjoy this precious time.

She wants to know when my book will be done, she seems to need a date for when she needs to find a new job by. I'm in no hurry to leave now. I can stay here for longer, until the entire book is done, perfecting it once it comes back from the editor. I'm in no hurry to rush back to New Orleans.

But I want very much for her to come back with me, at least for a while, to see the city I love. I'm not ready to let her go so fast. I didn't plan for this, but now that I have her, I want her with me for as long as she wants to stay. I ask her.

"Come back with you to New Orleans?" She turns her face to look at me, but it's not easy, given the way she's resting against my chest.

I massage her soapy breasts, feel her nipples rise like pebbles. "Why not? I was going to courier the document to Rob, and in that week where I have nothing to do, why don't you come back with me? I'll pay you."

"You already have a housekeeper."

"I won't pay you to be my housekeeper."

"Then what will you pay me for?"

I have to be careful with what I say. This setup is so precarious. I can't *not* pay her, because I know she needs the money. I'd rather have her with me than not. "I'll pay you to be my personal assistant."

She likes the sound of this because she squeals, though it could be because my fingers are rubbing against her folds. She presses against me, her breath hitching in her throat. "What does that entail?"

I thumb her clit, and it no longer seems to matter as she shudders to my touch.

Later, when the birds begin to sing, I curl up against her

in bed, breathing in the scent of her hair. I haven't lain with a woman like this in years. I haven't let anyone come this close.

"Goodnight," I whisper.

She's quiet, and I'm not sure if she heard me. I kiss the top of her head. After a while, she asks, "Are you staying?" in a groggy voice, on the edge of sleep.

"Yes."

She huddles closer to me, then flings one of her legs in between mine until we're a tangle of warm bodies.

"Ward!" Mari hollers directly in my ear. I am so bone-weary, I can't even open my eyes. "Ward!" She shakes me roughly. "Get up!" She sounds hysterical. My eyes fly wide open. I reach for my bedside table, trying to find my watch, and failing.

"Get up!" Mari cries, rushing around the room in a frenzy. My attention immediately fixates on her. I sit up, so caught up in her nakedness that it takes a moment or two for me to realize I'm in her bed, in her room. I blink a few times, then look up at the ceiling, look at the room. Memories of last night flood back.

"Get up," she cries, swiping my robe from the floor and throwing it on. She flies towards the door.

"Where are you going?"

"Jamie's here. We overslept!"

She disappears just as I'm about to tell her to ignore Jamie. I have a workout in mind, but it's not with Jamie. "Mari!" I yell after her, not understanding why she's rushing to answer the door. We could pretend we went out.

But of course, that wouldn't be so plausible in the light

of day. I'm still groggy with post-sex haze. I have a growing boner, and Mari isn't here.

Swearing under my breath, because we could have been doing something better than a goddamn workout right now, I make myself get out of bed.

There's nothing worse than getting ready for a workout I don't want.

MARI

Jamie's here and he won't stop ringing the doorbell.

I didn't want to get out of bed. I could have lain in Ward's arms all morning. I could have had more of what we had last night. I rush downstairs as the doorbell rings again.

I open the door and Jamie stares at me in shock, his gaze going from my face and trailing down the length of my body.

"What are you wearing?" he asks. His voice is harsh, severing the bubble of last night's memories I had been floating in.

Oh, god.

I forgot. I put my hand to the robe, securing the edges so that it doesn't gape open. Somehow, I manage to tighten the sash that's holding the outfit together. I wish I'd stopped to think before I raced downstairs.

He looks at me, suspicion black like poison in his eyes.

"I washed it, and I ... it ended up in my pile of clothes," I stammer, knowing that he isn't buying any of this.

"You've overslept," he says, making it sound like an accusation instead of a statement.

"Good morning!" Ward's voice behind me is good-humored and bright. I'm shocked by the speed with which he got ready and came down. I don't dare turn around even though I'm curious to know how he looks, and whether Jamie will put two and two together.

"I'm heading straight to the gym," Ward says, "You two catch up." He disappears, leaving me with a grouchy looking Jamie.

"What's going on?" Jamie asks, his gaze slipping to my neck. I pray that Ward didn't leave any tell-tale kisses there, that Jamie can't read the guilty look I'm trying so hard to hide. I'm useless hiding things.

"Nothing is going on," I cry, trying to sound exasperated that he would ask me such a thing. I'm failing miserably. I walk into the kitchen, knowing that there is nothing casual, or normal about me coming downstairs wearing Ward's robe and having overslept, and with Ward coming downstairs after me. None of this is normal, and Jamie isn't stupid.

"He's annoyed with me," I say to Jamie, making up a story on the go, and struggling to make it sound believable.

"He didn't sound too annoyed."

Jamie doesn't follow me into the kitchen but hangs around in the doorway. He doesn't want to talk, but I am desperate to prove that nothing happened last night, even though all the evidence points to the contrary.

"He's annoyed with me, you remember how he was with the pen?" I'm trying to buy more time so I can figure out a better excuse. Instead, Jamie raises an eyebrow.

"Coffee?" I say, putting the coffee maker on.

"Since when do I have coffee before the workout? And

since when does Ward ever go to the workout before me?" Jamie snaps.

I pick up a wooden spoon as if to make a point. "I'm fed up. I hate this job. I'm sick of answering the door, and cooking, and cleaning, and I'm sick of tiptoeing around on eggshells around that man. I'm better than this."

Jamie blinks at me as if I've had some sort of meltdown. I have. But it's a completely different type of meltdown. Again, he's not buying this. I can see the cogs of his brain turning and trying to piece it together. "I need to speak to Danny," I say. "One of his contacts emailed me to arrange a job interview."

Jamie's face twists. He then turns and leaves.

I wait a moment before I allow myself to breathe out. My ruse was pathetic. It didn't work. He knows. He knows what I've been up to, and he's already judging me. This makes me angry, and I rush upstairs to shower and get ready. After that I rush back to clean the study first while waiting for Jamie to finish.

But after the workout, Jamie doesn't stop for our usual chat and he leaves without saying a word. I won't even know where to begin in order to explain how this, me and Ward, happened.

"What did he say?" I ask Ward when he comes back downstairs after his shower.

His face breaks out into a dirty grin "He said I was getting big." He flexes his arm and proudly shows off a bulging bicep. The tease. Does he know what the sight of his muscles does to me? I could indulge in innuendo and entice Ward back to bed in the middle of the day—this would be a new challenge—but I am determined to find out whether Jamie was suspicious.

"But what did he say? About me wearing his robe? And us not opening the door. Didn't he find it odd?"

"He didn't say anything."

"He knows," I say, wringing my hands. It shouldn't matter, but it does. In all the time he's known me, I've made bad mistakes. I've been hurt and I messed up, and then I got hurt again, and now I'm doing this.

He can't know the truth of me and Ward.

"Why are you so worried?" Ward's hand grazes my cheek, but it doesn't settle there. He moves his hand away and pours himself a cup of coffee. This is what I expect from him. He's not going to daydream about the things we can spend time doing, even after the night we've had. He's focused and goal-oriented and he's already thinking about the book and everything he's got to do today.

He's not thinking of me.

I'm about to answer, but he's walked out. His mind is elsewhere and I've lost him already.

CHAPTER FORTY-TWO

MARI

My life flips on its side. Things are going well with Ward, but Jamie is the one who is now giving me grief.

He's not being outright rude, but he's ignoring me. Barely says 'hi' when he arrives and then rushes out so fast that I never catch him in time to confront him.

Ward and I have settled into another routine. There are no rewards this time, not like before. He doesn't always sleep in my bed, but on those nights he does, it's not always about the sex. We talk.

He's also starting to open up to me. Telling me things from his childhood and how he got into writing. I learn things about his stepfather that make my blood boil. I discover how much his mother let him down. I come to understand him better.

He tells me about how he took to writing when he was in his teens and a teacher at school encouraged him.

"She said she loved my writing, and that I had a gift, and she told me I should put it to good use."

"You loved to read?" I ask him.

"More than most boys. I would get lost in books. It was the perfect escape."

"And what did you write about?"

"Anything. High school essays and stuff, I did well at them. I found that I could express myself through my words and having someone believe in me was such a revelation."

He's lying on the bed, and I'm propped up against the headrest. We're fully clothed, and I have his head on my lap. Staring down at him, it's so clear to see how much he has changed. The mountain-man beard went a long time ago. Today he has a four-day growth, and I prefer him like this. I skim my hand over his jaw, stroking his almost-beard as if it's a much-loved pet. He's shirtless, of course, wearing only sweatpants, so I get to run my hands over his muscles and his hard, toned body.

"She believed in you because she could see how gifted you were," I say, stroking the side of his face.

"Having someone believe in you makes a world of difference." His brows push together. He's thinking, and I know better than to ask him what he's thinking about. With Ward, I've learned that he will tell me when he's good and ready. It's impossible to pry stuff out of him. He'll tell me when he's good and ready.

He's been talking about his New Orleans home and says he wants me to come back with him for a week or so while Rob looks over the book. He says he often needs a break when he's done with the first draft of a book because it's so intense and he needs to switch off completely. Usually he would go away, out of state somewhere because he needs to unwind. This surprises me because after all his talk of being a recluse and wanting to stay at home, I never assumed that someone like Ward would want to travel much. But he assures me he does. Only now that he's been here in Chicago, he wants to go home for a break. His plans have changed, and I don't know how much I've influenced them. For all his talk of leaving here, he now has plans to come back and do the edits.

It means I get to work for him for a little while longer.

One day Ward is busy in the study rewriting his crucial end scene. He woke up early and told me he still wanted to do the workout with Jamie but he had to write the new ending first and he didn't know how long it would take.

When Jamie shows up, I tell him that Ward is busy and asked if he could wait around for thirty minutes or so because Ward doesn't want to miss his session. I joke with him about how much Ward has changed but he doesn't laugh. Instead he stares at his watch in annoyance. "He wants me to wait here?"

This wouldn't be a problem. It would mean more time for me and Jamie to talk, but we haven't been all that friendly since the day I answered the door wearing Ward's robe. Our relationship seems to have stalled and sputtered just as mine and Ward's has blossomed.

It doesn't stop me from trying to make amends. "Have a cup of coffee," I say, with more optimism than I feel. When he starts to follow me, I go over to the coffee machine and pour him a cup. "Ward loves his workouts so much now. You've obviously had a good effect on him."

"Not as much as you."

I twist my mouth, thinking of something to say. I can no longer deny that anything has happened. It's too late for that.

"Why are you still so angry with me?"

At first, he looks so choked up that he can't speak. "What is it?" I ask, alarmed and worried that there's something bothering him that I don't know about. I move towards him and touch his elbow. "Jamie?" I wonder if there is something else, something I've missed. I've been thinking he's annoyed at me, but maybe it's something else entirely.

"You," he hisses. "You can't help yourself."

It is me and I don't even know how to answer to that. He's so red in the face that he's starting to scare me.

"This is Ward Maddox. I thought you might have been able to keep your legs closed for him."

I gasp, as if he's punched me in the stomach. "What ... why ..." I can't bring myself to ask him what business this is of his because I'm still reeling from his words.

Jamie talking to me like this is unheard of. He jabs a finger in my direction. "You can't help yourself. Any man who pays you any attention, and you lose the ability to think."

I open my mouth. Then close my eyes. He's thinking of Dale, but this is different. "This is different. This isn't what you think."

"He's Ward Maddox. He's supposed to be a recluse. How did you manage to ensnare him?"

His accusations bring tears to my eyes. I'm as hurt by his words as I am by his tone. The man I thought was my friend is speaking to me with so much venom.

Even you, I think to myself. It's bad enough having a lover cheat on you and hurt me the way Dale did, but I never imagined my good friend would hurt me.

"Do you know what he did to his girlfriend?"

I cock my head, certain that I didn't hear right. "His girlfriend?"

"He killed her."

I feel a double hit to my body, to my stomach and my chest. I struggle to breathe. "No ... that's not true ..."

It's not true. It can't be.

"You said she died under mysterious circumstances."

"It came down to her word against his, and she's dead." Jamie slams down his coffee cup.

"But ... I checked. I ... I couldn't find anything." I checked once, and I didn't find much on him. I would definitely have remembered something like this.

"He's a powerful man. It's all buried."

"It would have come out."

"It's his word against ..." Jamie turns his hand, palm side up, as if asking me to dispute this further.

I refuse to believe it. "Ward wouldn't. He's not capable of such a thing." I might not know everything about him, but I know he wouldn't do something like this.

"He's messed up in the head, Mari. Deep down you know it."

"That's not true. You don't know what sort of a childhood he's had."

"He got sent away from his parents, because he smacked his dad's face so hard, his jaw cracked."

My mouth opens. No way. This is a lie. It didn't happen like this.

"You're in bed with a monster. Only someone like you would find someone to fuck, even when you should have known better."

He rushes off, then comes back. "Tell him I had to go."

The door slams hard and Ward appears. I've been standing comatose for goodness knows how long. "Where's Jamie?" he asks, looking around. I stare at his face, Jamie's allegations fresh in my mind.

"Mari?"

"He ... he... he said he had to go. Something came up."

Ward scratches his head. "That's a shame. I rushed to get finished."

"You can do a workout by yourself," I tell him, even as doubts and worries screech around in my head. There is so much I don't know about this man. At first, I thought it was because he was an introvert, wanting to keep to himself, but now I wonder if it's because he has much to hide.

CHAPTER FORTY-THREE

WARD

"I've told you about Dale," she says, sipping from a glass of water. We've had dinner, sitting at the kitchen island, and now we're having our end of day discussion. "Tell me about your former lovers."

Not again.

She takes my hand, entwines her fingers in my hand, moves her stool a little closer.

"Why do you want to know?"

She sounds exasperated. "Because you know all about me." She volunteered that information. I hated her last boyfriend, but maybe because of him, I got to meet her.

"Some people are closed books," I say, kissing her hand. "While some of us can be read as easily as a Dr. Seuss book." I raise an eyebrow and smile.

"You take that back," she says, laughing. "I am *not* easy to read."

"If that's what you want to believe, you can." She told

me. It was as if she wanted to get it all out of her system. He sounded like a bastard boyfriend. I'm glad he's her ex now. She deserves better, and I want to try and be that someone better.

"You've always said you like to be alone, and you prefer your own company, so I want to know. How long?"

"How long what?"

"How long ago have your past relationships been?"

She's not going to give up. We had this a few weeks ago, but she's now started asking me again. My past is my past, and I want to look forward, but I sense she won't give up asking, so it's better if I tell her. I've had short relationships. There was the editor's assistant. The woman who arranged a book signing in Santa Monica. The secretary at the Arts Council in Montecito.

Short. As in a couple of weeks. There have been others, of course, but no one I wanted to be around long enough. No one I cared enough about to open myself up to. No one I could trust.

"You really want to know?"

"Yes, I really want to know."

"It's embarrassing."

She laughs, then stops laughing and looks at me, as if she can't tell whether I'm joking or not. "A week, maybe two. I have encounters." That's probably a better word for it.

"Encounters?" She gives me an are-you-kidding look.

"I don't like being with people, not the whole time."

"But...pfft." She puffs out a surprised breath. "A week or two? What is that?"

"Sex is what it is."

Her expression sobers. She's connecting the dots. "Is that what you and I are?"

"This has been longer than a week or two, hasn't it?"

She looks pensive. "Is that why you and I were stop-start in the beginning?"

I nod. "I didn't want to get involved, but I couldn't resist you. I struggled with it, I couldn't be with you, and then I discovered I couldn't be without you."

She seems satisfied, but I don't get a cutesy cuddle or kiss, which is what I thought my confession would earn me.

"So, when was your last 'encounter?'"

"Just over a year ago. Thirteen months, to be precise."

"Thirteen months," she echoes, sitting forward. I can see the top of her cleavage and it sets my pulse racing.

"I don't get to meet people," I protest. "You've seen me. I sit at my desk all day long. Writing is a solitary profession."

"You poor thing," she says with much pitying exaggeration. "Tell me more."

I snort. "Why do you want to know, Little Miss Inquisitive?" I lean forward and give her a kiss.

She kisses me back. "I want to know everything about you."

"That's impossible," I say.

"Impossible to want to know everything, or impossible for you to tell me?"

"Impossible given the boner you're giving me." She has that effect on me every single time. I talk to her, we get close, kiss and hold hands, and I want to throw her over my shoulder and take her upstairs.

"I can take care of your needs," she says, seducing me with her bedroom voice all over again. My breathing steps up a notch. "But I want to know things about you. You're like a black box, Ward. I want to know if you've ever been hurt ... like I was ... Dale."

All I want to do is take her clothes off and make love to

her. I press my forehead against hers. "What's the point of talking about the past? I've been hurt, but I don't want to dwell on that." Mari is something new and exciting for me. It's been a long time since I've felt this way about anyone. I never thought I would ever find this type of connection again, and yet, here it is. I just wish she'd stop with the one hundred questions.

She thumbs my lower lip. "I just want to make things better for you."

"And you do." I stare at her, our faces so close together that we are breathing in one another's breath.

I slide my tongue into her mouth and give her the longest, deepest kiss. My insides throb with excitement as I stand up and swoop her up in my arms. There's only one way this night is going to end, and it's not with an interrogation.

CHAPTER FORTY-FOUR

MARI

Because of Jamie, I've looked things up online, things about Ward and his past.

There are photos of book signings, and a few rare pictures of him shaking hands with various literary people. I even find a few pictures with Rob. There are none with women though. Like a stalker, I googled his past girlfriends, and only found a mention of Lisa Dooley. She died but there is no mention of how she died. If it had been suspicious, surely it would say. What I did read was that Ward went on to have some sort of breakdown. It was after the success of his first book. He couldn't write for years after that.

I don't want to believe Jamie's words. He's annoyed and he hates me, and he thinks I'm a slut for being with Ward. Who the hell is he to judge me?

When I look back on all our interactions, I see things differently now. He behaved more like an older protective boyfriend, which is something I don't need. The more I think about it, the more obvious it becomes, his questions and preaching about my boyfriend choices.

He thinks I'm making a mistake with Ward, but he doesn't know the half of it. Ward isn't messed up, he's hurting. No one understands this better than I do.

I decide to avoid Jamie, and no longer hang around the kitchen for our daily chat. I find it odd that this is a situation I never thought I would be in—growing closer to Ward while being at war with Jamie. I don't want to make up with him. He's being awful sulky about something he knows nothing about, and he's too overprotective for my liking.

We need a break. We've worked together, and then continued to see one another through this job, and with both of us going through changing relationships and job losses, and adjusting to a new life, it's no wonder things are difficult.

If Ward and I are seeing one another, I shouldn't need to hide it from one of my closest friends. My attempts to get Ward to open up aren't always successful. I'm finding out things slowly, but chipping away a little at a time. He's had a lot to deal with and I'm trying to be gentle with him.

This will take time. I love being with Ward, I love what we have, and no one is going to ruin this for me. I want to tell my mom because I'm so happy and I want to share my happiness with her but I don't want to risk confusing her because she doesn't even know about Dale and me splitting up.

I head towards Ward's study to clean it while he's showering. The fire is burning as usual. He must have been up early to get some work done before Jamie arrived.

I wipe down the desk, taking care as always when I lift his notebooks and piles of paper, his pens and pencils, to wipe away the dust before neatly putting them all back in order, just the way he likes it. I see a scribble on a piece of paper and, curious, I take a peek.

Ward has scribbled my name again, in bold, beautiful, elegant letters. He has beautiful handwriting for a man. I stare at my name—there are no love hearts or doodles, or scribbles—it's just my name, but it's enough to send me into a tailspin of happiness.

He *thinks* of me.

He thinks of me even as he sits here trying to get words down. I'm always in his thoughts. It's the most reassuring and comforting feeling.

I think of him almost all the time. It's like I can't ever get enough of him. Most nights, he's also in my bed, it's like he can't bear to be apart from me. As if he can no longer bear to be alone.

I shove the sheet of paper back again in with the others and tidy up the piles before I begin wiping his lampshade, but my curiosity gets the better of me. I've never read any of his work. I don't even know how he writes. Jamie's always said that he's a gifted writer, but I don't know. Maybe taking a little sneak peek might give me another window into this elusive man?

I move away a few stray sheets of paper, and find page one of his manuscript. The title says, '*The Unseen Face-DRAFT*'. I get a tingle in the pit of my stomach knowing that I'm looking through something that only Ward has seen. I leaf through the crisp white pages, unbound and loose, and glance at the pages of neatly typed prose.

This is his new book. The one he's been working on the entire time I've been here. I wonder if being with me has shaped any of his thoughts and his words. It's a conceited thought to have, but I'm curious.

My breath stops in my throat. My heart thunders.

I'm *so* tempted to read it even though he has warned me not to. I don't read horror, but my fear is less due to that than because Ward told me not to.

I bite my lower lip as I turn the first page. My eye catches the first sentence: *She took my heart and broke it; hurling it against a stone-cold wall so that it splintered into a thousand shards.*

Who is *she*? And why did she break his heart?

I want to know.

My gaze flies across the next line, and the next, and the next. My skin begins to crawl as I read the first paragraph. I try to find myself in this protagonist. Is it a protagonist or is she the victim who dies?

I am already captivated, even though I promised myself I wouldn't read books like this. I like Ward's style. His words hold me captive and I can't stop reading. I go to the next page, the plot reeling me in, the descriptions of the old house making me feel as if I'm there. I hold my hand against my thundering chest.

I should put this away.

I should put it away right now. A fear of Ward catching me mingles with the fear crawling up my spine as I read. Thump, thump, thump beats my heart.

I read on and on. One more page, and then another.

I *need* to stop. But I can't.

It's not entirely scary, *not yet*, though Jamie said Ward's horror isn't exactly gory, it's more the type that messes with your mind.

Jamie.

He might appreciate a glimpse. I could give him a sneak preview. Just of the first page. It could be a peace offering.

Ward doesn't need to know, and what he doesn't know won't hurt him.

Sliding my phone out of the pocket of my pants, I get ready to take a picture and then I stop. I can't do this. What am I thinking? My desire to do right by Jamie—and validating it with the weak excuse that Ward won't know—has clouded my shaky judgment. No way. I can't do this to the man I love.

"What. The. Fuck?" Ward's snarl bites through the air and the phone I was about to put away almost slips through my hands.

"What the *hell* are you doing?" he bellows.

Fear shuts down my vocal cords. It's not what he says, it's the way he says it. It's the twisted look on his face.

"Well?" he yells, walking towards me with a menacing stare. My heart slips through my chest and trickles out of my belly. Ward's gaze, once warm and inviting, now turns to ice.

"What did I tell you? Why the fuck are you snooping around?"

The sheets lie spread out on his desk, blatant evidence of my crime. "I ..." I open my mouth but words fail me. He wants answers and I can't even begin to explain this.

He snatches the papers off the desk and I'm suddenly scared. I violated his rules. I'm the one who's at fault. "I can explain."

"You ..." His face twists, his voice thick with revulsion. "You conniving, lying little ..." He can't bring himself to spit the rest of the words out and then grabs something and hurls it across the room. It hits the wall with a SMACK. It's only when it lands on the floor that I realize it's my cell phone.

"What have you done?!" I cry out, rushing to pick it up.

"What the FUCK have you done?" he roars back. His face is so red. I've never seen him so mad. I need to explain. I need to say something, *do* something. "I'm sorry. I ... I didn't mean to but ..."

Ward walks over to the fireplace and throws the pile of papers from his desk into the fire. All of it.

"Noooooo!" I yell, my jaw goes slack. What has he done? He's flipped. All his hard work. "Ward!" I rush over to his side, see the fire greedily swallowing up his neat white pages. It's the finished manuscript. What was he thinking? I stare at him because I'm worried that he's gone mad. He shows no emotion. His face is calm.

I don't know whether to reach in and save what I can. "This is your book. What you've been working on." I grab the poker and try to move some pages to the side, away from the heat source, but they all crumble like orange dust. "You've ruined it." A cry of anguish steals up my throat.

"*You* ruined it," he says coldly. The chill in his voice guts me. It's like an ice pick straight in my stomach.

"Ward," I touch his shoulder.

"Get. Out." His voice is deathly quiet.

"I'm sorry. I'm so sorry." The enormity and craziness of his actions unnerve me. "Your writing sucked me in. It's brilliant. I couldn't stop—"

"Get. THE FUCK. Out."

Even though he's angry, I feel for him losing his manuscript. I've seen him toil over this. I've come to understand his pressure. Rob will go insane. "You didn't need to burn it."

"I told you," he bites out slowly. "I warned you."

I touch his arm, but he shrugs it off with a violence that catches me by surprise. I don't understand the big deal of me reading a few pages. Rob was going to read it. Why is me reading it any different? Besides, this was just the paper version. He has it all on his computer. He can easily print off another copy.

"You have to believe me. I didn't mean to read. It was just so good—"

His hard eyes turn on me. "Are you deaf? Get. Out."

I take a step back, because this is more than a warning. This is an execution order. He's back to being how he was before. A bully. Feral. Neanderthal. Scary.

In this moment, Jamie's warnings don't seem so out of place. Fearing for my life, I back away, because now I'm starting to get really scared. "I only read the first few pages, Ward. I'm sorry."

He's staring into the fire. I try to turn my phone back on but it is lifeless. I press the on/off switch frantically but I can't get to turn it back on. "You broke my phone," I cry, all the sympathy I felt for him suddenly vanishing.

"You broke my trust."

"It's only a story," I say, staring at him evenly. Does he understand that? "It's only a story, and I only read a few pages. I'm sorry I did."

"I told you not to."

"I ... didn't mean to. I ... I shouldn't have. I'm sorry. I made a mistake."

"So did I."

I stare at him in disbelief. He has a backup of his manuscript, but I don't have a backup phone.

My mom.

The nursing home.

I need to have constant contact with them. He can print his manuscript out again. He can make it so that this isn't a big deal. He can man up. I have to get my phone fixed. Right now, there is no way for anyone to contact me. My anger inflames. "You're making such a big deal of this," I hiss under my breath. "You can print off another copy."

"You've seen it now. It's no good."

"What?" I shriek. Maybe Jamie was right. Maybe Ward is more messed up than I thought. *He's messed up in the head. He killed his girlfriend.* "It's only a book. It's not the end of the world."

"*Only* a book?" he hollers, striding towards me. I flinch as I stumble back. He hasn't apologized once for my phone, and I've said sorry numerous times. He's only concerned about his lousy manuscript. He doesn't care about anything or anyone else.

I was naïve to think he had changed.

"Leave!" he roars.

I intend to. He can die in hell. "Don't worry. I quit," I yell back. "I quit right now."

He doesn't seem the least bit shocked by my announcement. "Then get the fuck out."

In that moment, I no longer want to be here. "You never speak about Lisa," I manage to say. How I dredged something like that up from the past I don't know. Maybe the desire to hurt him made me brave.

His eyes widen with shock. He looks as if he's been hit by a baseball. The color drains from his face.

"What did you do to her?" I back away. I sense him wavering, sense him weakening, sense that I've hurt him.

He shakes his head, his eyes narrowing to slits as he creeps closer. "What? How do you know about her?"

"Lisa Dooley." I lift my head up high. I'm getting something from him, even if it's a truth I don't want to face. "How did she die?"

"What are you asking?" His voice is barely audible.

"I want to know."

"*What* do you want to know?"

"How you killed her." My fear turns into foolish courage, and my body starts to shiver, but it's not from the cold. He puts his hands on my shoulders. "What makes you think I killed her?" he asks softly. His whispered voice freaks me out.

"You never talk about her."

His fingers dig into my flesh. I hear the blood pounding through my ears. I shrug, but he doesn't move his hands away. "She's someone you don't need to worry about."

The tremor begins in my knees and crawls upwards, every cell in my body quaking with terror. I wish Jamie were here.

"Why do you want to know?"

"I ... I... I'm curious." I swallow. His questions ring alarms bells in my head. I try to move back but the corner of the mantelpiece digs into my back. I shrug, trying to shift his hands off but his grip is pincer sharp.

I'm so very afraid.

"That's the problem with you, Mari. You want to know everything. You snoop, and dig, and sneak." He bares his teeth.

"You're hurting me," I cry as his fingers dig in some more. He doesn't seem to take notice. I shrug again, but his grip is tight, so I try to yank one of his hands away but I twist awkwardly and slip, still clutching my cell phone. I hit my head against the mantelpiece then stumble back in pain. A sharp pain slices through me. He grabs me and pulls me away with such force, I'm thrown onto the couch.

Shocked, and terrified, I jump up and run out. Out of the study, out of the hall, out of hell.

My heart beats so fast, and adrenaline surges through my blood. I sprint across the street as if my life depends on it. I'm now convinced it does. And then I run and run and run until I flag down a taxi and beg the driver to take me to my friend's house. I lift a hand to my head and see blood on my fingers.

"Get in," he says.

CHAPTER FORTY-FIVE

WARD

His laughter cackles in my ears and I'm sixteen years old all over again.

My stepfather roars with laughter as he reads my story. It's something I've never been able to forget. I labored over this piece, spent hours perfecting it and rewriting it, and making it the best I could make it. Then I gave it to Mrs. Fennelly, my high school teacher who always encouraged me. In fact, all of my teachers did. I got more love and acceptance from them than I did my own mother. Mrs. Fennelly said it was perfect. She had high hopes, she was excited. I took it home to copy it out neatly before submitting it.

But the bastard found it, and read it, and laughed about it. He made more fun of it because it was my work, and he took joy in making me feel small. Then he read it out loud to my mom, making fun of me, saying nasty things. She took his side. Laughed as well. Asked me what I was thinking when I wrote this. She said she didn't understand it.

He was a stupid man, and when he didn't understand something, he made fun of it. I expected more from her, even after all those years when she had let me down, I still held out hope that she might have taken my side. That she might one day come to her senses and see that man for the loser he really was.

She never did.

I'll never forget his jeering voice saying my words out loud, making my story sound like a piece of trashy overblown prose.

He laughed and said I was a stupid, soft, gay boy. My mom didn't say anything. But when he ripped it up and said it was pile of horseshit, I lost it. I went for him. Lunged at him and socked him once in the eye, then smashed into his face.

This wasn't the first time. Ever since I'd turned thirteen, when I started to be as tall as him, he turned physical, slapping me around when locking me in the attic wouldn't scare me. We'd come to fist fights before, but that day, when he laughed at my competition entry and then ripped it up into shreds, that was the worst. It went beyond a simple scuffle. I went for blood. I wanted to kill him and I almost did.

Those shreds of paper were a metaphor for my life with this man. He made me feel useless and discarded.

But I'd never hit him as hard as I did that day. I'd spent my life taking his crap, being locked up, watching my mom sit around and do nothing. This was the final straw, the thing that pushed me over the edge. I smashed into him, his face and ribs, and he didn't hesitate to hit me back.

Social services got involved. My mom called the police, and I was sent to Grampton House for a while.

That's why I never let anyone read my manuscripts. Only Rob and the editor. Professional people. Catching Mari betraying me so sneakily took me back to that moment when my stepdad ripped up my work.

She won't ever understand. I can't ever make her see. She brought it all back, those buried, painful memories I've always strived to push out of my life.

I stare at the flickering fire. It crackles as my hard work turns to ash. Something dies inside me.

It might not have been so bad if I'd only caught her reading, but to find her taking pictures. The sight of her snapping away, doing that, going behind my back, did something to me. It was sneaky, and I had finally come to trust her. Who was she taking pictures for? She never explained why and my anger stopped me from asking.

And worst of all, she talked about Lisa.

Lisa.

Lisa.

She dredged it all back up again, the unwanted past with all its grime.

I wasn't prepared for her questions. Wasn't prepared to hear that name again. Wasn't prepared for Mari to make those types of accusations.

CHAPTER FORTY-SIX

MARI

I take the cab straight to Jamie's place. I have nowhere else to go. I have no one else to turn to.

I haven't warned him, or asked him, or prepared him and I turn up on his doorstep, feeling as if my whole world just caved in, because it has. The cab driver must have taken pity on me because he left without taking payment.

Jamie stares at me in shock, and then his gaze goes to the cut on my forehead.

"What happened?" Concern creeps into his expression and he takes my arm, leading me inside. "Mari?" His tone is sterner now. "What the hell happened?"

The cut isn't deep because it's stopped bleeding now, but it looks bad. I managed to get a look at it in the cab's rearview mirror.

It's then that I notice he's dressed up, as if he's going out for the evening. "I banged my head." I press a tissue to it and am relieved that there's only a small blotch of blood that comes off. "Can I stay the night, please? There's no place else for me to go." If I could have gone elsewhere, I would have.

"Sure, you can. You can stay anytime you want."

"But you look like you were on your way out."

He ignores my questions and leads me over to the couch and sits down beside me, his face hardening as he surveys my wound again. "He did that?"

"What? No. It doesn't matter." I'm not in the mood for talking about it. I don't want to tell him what happened, even though he was right about Ward.

I'm not ready to deal with it myself. I need the night to process everything that happened today, everything Ward said and did. I've put a Band-Aid over it for now, but the wound is still deep and sharp.

I've messed up again, spectacularly fallen flat on my face with a guy *again*. I blindsided Ward when I poked around about Lisa. I touched a raw nerve and wandered into dangerous territory I should never had stumbled into. He was holding me, and I got scared. He had me pinned in place and I couldn't shake him off.

"I'm sorry to drop in on you like this."

"It's okay."

"You look like you were going somewhere. I would have called, but he smashed my phone."

"Who?"

I don't give him an answer, but he seems to know. Who else could it be? Jumping up, he puts a fist to his mouth as if to stop himself from smacking it through the wall. "*Ward* smashed your phone?" His voice drips with rage. I stare at my hands, then at my knees.

"What the fuck?" he growls. "Tell me what happened."

I shake my head because I don't want to talk about it,

but it's not fair for me to expect Jamie to take me in like this when he must have a million questions.

"Are you going to tell me what happened, Mari, or should I march over there and smash his face?" He grabs his keys and heads towards the door.

"No. Don't!" The last thing I need is for him to go to Ward's place and confront him. I look at my phone, pressing the buttons, willing it to start working again but it's dead. "I'll tell you if you come back here."

"Stay put." He returns seconds later with a wet washcloth and a jug of water and begins to clean my wound. I wince as he wipes the dry blood away.

"I'm trying to be gentle," he says, his voice softer.

"Thank you."

He doesn't say anything at first, then "How do you explain this?" he asks, pointing to my gash.

I don't know where to start.

"I swear to god, Mari, if you're still going to defend him, I will have no choice but to kick the crap out of him. I don't give a shit who he is. He's a fucked-up guy, and you really picked a bad one this time." Anger flashes across his eyes. I wish I hadn't come here. I wish I'd gone to someone else, but the number of people I can rely on these days I can count on three fingers.

I start to tell him what happened, about how I started reading Ward's manuscript even though he'd warned me plenty of times not to. I tell him that I only did so because I saw my name scribbled on a sheet of paper.

"Your name?" Jamie asks with disdain. I tell him how I read one page, and hadn't intended to read any more, but I got sucked into the story, and then I had the bright idea to take a picture for him.

"For me?" Jamie puts away the damp washcloth and jug on the coffee table.

"You and I haven't been getting along and I thought you might like it. You asked me to once. Do you remember? I never thought he'd catch me. I was hoping to take the pics for you, because you asked me before—"

"Don't go blaming me for this," he says, getting up, his face turning red.

"I'm not." I rush to reassure him. "I'm trying to explain why I did it. I thought I could make it up to you." I stare up at him sheepishly. "Anyway, I didn't do it. I didn't. I stopped because I knew it was wrong but he walked in just then and I guess he got mad and then he must have thought I was taking photos."

"You took a stupid crazy risk, even for someone like you."

I stare at the floor.

"He hit you because you read his manuscript?"

"He didn't hit me. I banged my head."

He laughs, a cruel, disbelieving laugh.

"He didn't hit me," I insist. "We ... I ..." I don't want to think about that moment because it scares me. He held me in place and I tried to get away but he shoved me, and I can't bear to think about that. What it means is too horrific for me to deal with. I also decide it's better not to tell Jamie this. "I slipped and my head hit the mantelpiece."

"You just slipped? Next you'll be telling me that his floor is an ice rink."

"I swear, I slipped."

"I don't know what to believe. You're hiding something, defending him because you can't face up to what he is. Just like you took a risk getting involved with him." Jamie glares at me, and it's the first time he's addressed it, that Ward and I were together.

I can't look at him. I can't meet his eyes. He's judging me worse than ever. He won't understand how I found a part of Ward that I could tame, a part that was hurting and that I could kiss better. He won't understand that I found him attractive and sexy and I needed him. "He went crazy when he saw me."

"That doesn't surprise me," he says, scrubbing his hand over his face as if he's trying to make sense out of it. "How stupid can you be?"

The way he says it makes me want to leave. Aside from Jamie, I have no one. My mom is in no position to help me.

My mom. I need to find a way to contact her and the nursing home and to give them a new contact number, probably Jamie's number. I tell Jamie about Ward throwing my phone against the wall and breaking it, and then how he burned his manuscript.

"He set fire to it?" he asks, shocked.

"He scooped up all the papers and threw them into the fire. He's been working on that for months."

Jamie mutters something under his breath, something that sounds like a swear word. "The guy is a nutcase."

I bite my lip. Examining Ward's behavior, I see that Jamie isn't far wrong. "I quit," I tell him.

"You what?"

"He told me to get out. He was so angry, Jamie. You should have seen him."

He is quiet, then looks away. I feel uncomfortable. I've imposed myself on him, and I've messed things up. He is dressed up and he definitely looks like he had other plans. "I shouldn't have come here," I say, getting up. I should have checked into a hotel.

"What? No." He rises with me. My mind is in disarray. He's not exactly distant or cold, though I can sense his rage. He's never really liked Ward, I don't think, even though he's been in awe about his books.

These last few weeks, I've sensed a hardness in Jamie. It might even have been around the time Ward and I got together.

But I've also done wrong by Jamie. He's always been there to pick up the pieces, he was there for me when Dale cheated on me, and when I didn't have a place to stay, and he's here for me now. I've come to rely on him when I have no right to.

His phone rings and he turns his back to me. I try not to listen in, but I can't close my ears, and he's being overly sneaky, which makes me even more suspicious. "I promise I'll make it up to you," is the only thing I hear him say clearly.

"You did have plans." I feel guiltier than ever.

He doesn't look at me. "It's only Raleigh. It can wait."

"Raleigh?" I sound even more surprised than I should. The possibilities flood my mind. "You were going to see her? Then you should go," I tell him. "*I* should go. I shouldn't have come here. I'm sorry." I mean it this time. I feel like an extra leg on a four-legged table—unnecessary and out of place.

Clutching my phone, I head towards the door, determined to leave and to let Jamie get on with his life. I have much to think about, not least of all getting back to Ward's place to get my bag, my purse, my money, and my belongings.

I didn't think.

I just fled.

I need solitude. I've suppressed what happened

between me and Ward earlier, but I need to process it properly. I'm so messed up and broken that I can't think straight, but I've done the wrong thing by coming to Jamie and expecting him to put me back together again.

"I asked him about Lisa Dooley."

He looks alarmed. "Why the heck would you go and do a stupid thing like that?"

"I wanted to know the truth."

"And you expected him to confess, just like that? Are you insane, Mari?"

I feel suddenly claustrophobic. There is too much emotion in this room. Too much going on. Too much to think about. Too many things I don't want to face. "I should go, Jamie. Let me."

"I've just canceled with Raleigh."

"I heard, and I'm sorry, but I didn't ask you to cancel on account of me."

"You showed up on my doorstep looking like that. What was I supposed to do?"

I take in a slow and steadying breath. I've messed things up for both of us, our beautiful friendship most of all. "I'm sorry for messing up your plans."

"Stop apologizing and sit down." He moves towards me, which prompts me to do as he says.

"Don't worry about Raleigh, I was only going out because she called me."

"You can still go out, if you have plans. I'll stay here. Unless you were going to bring her back home afterwards."

"After what?"

"Your date."

"And what would you think if I brought her back here?"

"Huh?" I frown, not sure what he's asking.

"What would you do if I did bring Raleigh back?"

"Naturally, you need privacy so I would check into a hotel for the—"

"But what would you *think?*"

I don't understand what he's asking me. "I'd be happy for you. She's liked you for the longest time and now that you're single ...."

"You don't even care, do you?" he snarls, his tone catching me off guard.

"If you're that pissed off at me for ruining your night, why don't you let me go? I can check into a hotel." What is his problem exactly?

"I've canceled, and it's not a problem," he says tightly. "Sit down. I'll order us take-out."

I'm about to tell him that I have no belongings, or money, or purse, but I'm suddenly exhausted by the events of the day and I don't even put up a fight.

CHAPTER FORTY-SEVEN

WARD

I didn't sleep. I tossed and turned like I was having spasms. Came downstairs in the early hours to write, and then I remembered there was nothing to write.

It's burnt. I can print it out again, but I can't get over the deception. Her fucking deception. She broke my trust.

I'll print off another copy and send it to Rob, because he's expecting it, but the book is tainted for me. I've already lost interest in it. Mari went against my wishes and did what I specifically told her not to. There's no way I feel the same way about it now.

She won't understand. Many won't. It takes blood, mental anguish and sweat to write something that people might want to read, to produce words that some might remember, if only for a few moments, once they have finished reading it.

She didn't just taint it, she tainted us. I misread her. Had her down for a warm and wonderful woman, sexy as hell, and caring, too. Someone who helped me to heal. What I didn't expect was for her to be conniving, devious and deceptive.

People change, people lie, they deceive. I expected her to be different but she disappointed me. I can't trust her.

And yet. And yet another part of my head, or maybe it's my heart, tells me that Mari isn't like my stepdad. She didn't read my words out loud and laugh her head off, nor did she say they were trash. She didn't demean me. She said my writing sucked her in. Said it hooked her so completely that she couldn't put it down.

That's a good thing.

But the betrayal is deep, and the deed is done. I need to move on. Rob is waiting for this, but I can't send this to him. For me, this manuscript has been ruined.

True to form, I slip back into my earlier state. I eat all the junk I can find and I slouch on the sofa, watching mind-numbingly crass TV. This is what I have to do to take my mind off the whole sorry saga.

The doorbells rings, and rings, and rings. It takes me a while to rouse myself to get up off the couch. The noise is so loud, and I'd only just made myself comfortable. The disruption pisses me off and I'm even more annoyed by the time I open the door.

I blink at Jamie. I'm in no mood for a workout. I search his face for signs of unease, something to confirm my suspicions that Mari went running to him. I was so convinced that she had, and that she had told him everything, that I hadn't expected him to show up here ever again.

"Hey," he says in that annoyingly upbeat voice of his. He stares at me a little more intently than usual.

"She went to you, did she?" There's no way she's gone to him and not told him what happened.

"And what if she did?"

I leave the door open and go back inside, returning to the couch. Jamie follows me. "What's going on?"

It's only when I see his gaze flicker over the floor that I see the floor properly for the first time myself. Cans and wrappers from chocolate bars and potato chip bags litter the floor along with a box of half-eaten donuts.

"What did she tell you?" I ask as I start cleaning the trash from the floor because now I'm embarrassed by it. I wish I hadn't let him in. I should have turned him away from the door, but he holds the key to Mari, and it's her I want to know about.

He folds his arms. "Let's cut the crap," he says. "Do you want to tell me what happened?"

"I'm sure she's filled you in."

"She didn't mean to read your book," he snaps. "She got curious."

That snags my attention. "Curious?"

He explains, saying something about how the two of them had had a disagreement and how Mari had wanted to make it up to him. He says he'd asked her once for a sneak peek at my book because he loved my writing, but she had refused.

This pisses me off tenfold—the fact that she made such a colossal mistake all for this loser. That's why she was taking pictures. For him. It still doesn't make sense. She knew how protective and paranoid I am about my manuscripts. She knew this, and yet she still went ahead and did what she did.

"She was going to take pictures for me, but she—"

"I don't need you to make excuses for her." I throw him

a hateful look. If he's trying to make her look good, I'm not interested. I continue picking up stuff from the floor. I'm shocked by it, now that I'm the one who has to clean up. I really binged out like a madman. I'm in danger of falling back into a rut again, and this time I won't have anyone to pull me back out.

"What happened to you?" Jamie asks, probably because the room looks like a crime scene. "You look like shit."

"I had a rough night."

"Mari didn't look too great when she showed up. She had a cut on her forehead."

"I didn't hit her, if that's what she told you."

"She didn't say you did," he counters.

I stop what I'm doing and look at him. I hate this guy. I've always had a sneaky suspicion about him. "Does she always go running to you?"

"She has nowhere else to go. You smashed her phone."

"I was angry."

"You're always angry."

"What's that supposed to mean?" I ask. When he doesn't answer, I ask him why he's here. "You're obviously not here for the workout."

"No."

"That suits me because I'm not in the mood for exercise either."

"I don't care what you're in the mood for. I came to get some of Mari's belongings."

I turn around and survey his expression. The guy is pissed about something. This guy, I realize suddenly, has feelings for Mari, and she has no idea. It surprises me that he's been able to keep up the daily workouts knowing that she and I had a thing going on. "Then you'd better hurry up and get her things."

"She left everything behind, didn't even grab her purse."

"She couldn't get out fast enough," I tell him. Now that I've had time to think about it, it was fear that I saw in in her eyes. She was scared of me.

Jamie gives me a hard stare. "If I find out you hurt her," he jabs a finger at me.

"What are you going to do?" I stand up straighter, pulling myself up to my fullest height. Crazy, pining douchebag. I can see right through him. Must have killed him to know that she was in my bed most nights. I don't hurt people. I would never raise my hand to a woman, but he's not going to believe me, and I'm not even going to try to convince him. Still, I begin to wonder what he must think of me. What she must have told him.

He presses his lips together as if stopping himself from saying something. Besides, he's in my house, and I have the upper hand.

"I need to grab a few of her things. Can I?"

"Upstairs. Hers is the first room on the left."

"I won't be long."

"Might as well take all of it," I growl. I can't imagine she'd ever want to set foot in this place again. I'm not sure it would be good for either of us.

"She's sorting stuff out and needs her purse, and credit cards. She's getting her phone fixed, the one you broke."

"It was an accident."

"I'm sure you have a lot of those," he says, moving towards the stairs.

Goddamn cocky little shit. What does he mean by that? I wonder what lies he's been feeding her. "Get her things, then get the hell out."

CHAPTER FORTY-EIGHT

MARI

My cell phone starts beeping. Text messages from an unknown number flood in and just as those stop numerous voicemail messages pour in. I haven't been able to pick up because my phone had stopped working. I stare in horror because so many messages means something is wrong.

"Are they all coming through now?" the tech assistant asks me.

"They seem to be." I laugh nervously as I check through the texts.

Call me

Call who? These can't all have come from yesterday.

Jamie dropped me off at the mall while he went to Ward's place to get some of my belongings. I should have gone with him but I needed to get my phone fixed. Truth was, I couldn't bear the thought of seeing Ward again so soon.

"Is there anything else I can do for you, ma'am?"

I don't recognize the text message numbers and I have at least a dozen voicemail messages from the nursing home number.

My insides freeze.

"Ma'am? Was there anything else?"

"Uh ..." I look up, my mind fractured. "N-No, thank you." I hand him Jamie's debit card to pay. I have no money, no cards, nothing because I sprinted out of Ward's house. Jamie gave me his card, and his PIN number and told me to get everything figured out. He trusts me implicitly and I don't know what I would do without him. I promised to pay him back as soon as I got my purse back.

I rush out of the store and stand over by a wall as I call the nursing home. I have a feeling I'm going to need something to lean on. My stomach doesn't feel right. There's no point in wasting time checking each message. Something is clearly wrong. I call the nursing home instead.

The moment I get through and ask for my mom, my worst fears are confirmed.

"A stroke?" The word smashes into my solar plexus. I hit the wall and slide down, ending up sitting on the floor. I am broken. "When? Why didn't you call me?" The voice at the other end isn't one I recognize. The person is saying something so fast I don't understand exactly what happened. She's bumbling and I'm trying hard to listen, to process.

If it had been Brenda on the line, she might have delivered this news as softly as she could have. This caregiver gives me the cold hard facts.

She tells me that my mom had a massive stroke last

night and she's been in the hospital all night. They tried to get a hold of me but couldn't and they repeatedly tried all the numbers they had for me. With me having moved, and my phone being broken, there was no way they could have reached me. I had meant to call them when I got to Jamie's, and then I forgot. I never even thought to give them Ward's or Jamie's number at any point because I never expected to be without a phone.

And now my mom is very sick. The news shatters my already fragile world.

"You need to come quickly." The nurse gives me the hospital address, and I try to remember it. It's not difficult, but I'm so numb and so lost, it's easy to forget who I am. I rush outside the mall and run over to where the taxis are.

It's only when the cab driver asks me if I'm okay that I realize I'm crying. "My mom's had a stroke," I say, wiping my tears. "Can you drive fast?"

I close my eyes and think of my mom. Guilt sinks into every pore. I should have gone to her immediately. I would have, had I known. I would have, had it not been for Ward.

How is this even happening on top of everything else?

As soon as we get to the hospital, I jump out and charge through the hospital doors. I head straight to the ward where my mom is. I pray that she'll be okay. I've never prayed harder.

She's here, I tell myself. She's here, and I'm here, and she's going to be okay. I pray that she'll be happy to see me, and she'll be sitting up and smiling at me as I walk in.

And then I remember. It hits me like a water cannon. My mom has had a massive stroke. I don't know what this means. Nobody has actually told me how she is and I have no way to gauge the enormity of this news until I see her.

I'm hysterical by the time I reach the nurses' station. I'm

rambling, unable to formulate a complete sentence, unable to think coherently until a nurse tries to calm me down. I don't mean to make a commotion but a doctor soon comes over, and when they realize who I am here to see, they take me aside.

The doctor says something about it not looking good, and that my mom's condition is progressively worsening.

This isn't real. He's talking about someone else. "Let me see her," I cry, begging them. I'm crying at the same time and not talking clearly. My cell phone rings, and I turn it off completely because the only person I needed to hear from, the only person who mattered, is here.

My mom is the only rock I have and I feel suddenly bereft.

A nurse leads me to the ICU. My mom is asleep. Her eyes are shut. She looks peaceful. I would give anything to have her wide awake, even if she didn't know who I was, even if she thought I was a complete stranger. I crave her smile and for her eyes to see me. I crave for my living, walking, talking mom to come back and say something.

"Mom," I whisper. The strangled word comes out sounding odd. I take her hand. Thankfully, it's still warm. "Mom," I say again, leaning over to place a kiss on her cheek. "Mom, wake up."

"She can't hear you," the nurse tells me.

I don't even bother looking at her. How does she know my mom can't hear me? Who knows what my mom can hear or feel right now? I squeeze her hand gently again, rubbing it ever so softly between my hands. "Mom, it's me, Marianne. Your Mari. Remember, Mama? I'm here now." She still doesn't move. Her eyelids are motionless. She doesn't give me a sign. I begin to pray again out of sheer desperation, willing and wishing for any movement.

But there is nothing.

I have so many questions, but I don't want to ask them yet. I don't want the nurse to say anything in case my mom hears. Thankfully, she leaves the room so that it's just me and my mom.

I sit by her side all night, and I must have nodded off, because at some point, my mom's room is full of people. I'd fallen asleep. I jump up, but I can't see her because there's a wall of three, maybe four, medical staff in front of me, blocking my view.

"What's going on?" I cry.

They're working on my mom. There is noise and confusion, machines beeping. Ominous sounds of desperate people. A flurry of thoughts blasts at me like a tiny tornado and my hopes spiral to their death. I feel as if I am going to faint and everything inside me threatens to shoot up through my throat.

CHAPTER FORTY-NINE

MARI

She's gone

My mom went peacefully, they tell me, but to me it seemed like anything but peaceful. They worked on her and tried to revive her. It was noisy and a hive of commotion. She had a heart attack in the end and they did all they could, but they couldn't save her.

Standing on the edge, watching, praying, wishing, it didn't help one bit. My mom passed anyway, and it seemed anything but peaceful to me.

I'm all cried out now. I begged for them to leave me with her, and they did. I clung to her warm hands for as long as I could. I sobbed my heart out, falling into pieces that will never be whole again. I lost my dearest, oldest friend, and I feel so empty that the slightest breeze could pick me up, carry me away and set me someplace else and I wouldn't care. I don't belong anywhere now.

As I leave the hospital, the birds are singing. I've never

hated the sound of birdsong as much as I do now. What right do these creatures have to sing when I've just lost my mom, the only person who really cared about me? She was the only person who loved me unconditionally, no matter what. Her love was unparalleled; unlike the type of love I've had from others.

I return to Jamie's place, and on the way I call and give him the news. I also apologize and tell him that I've been using his debit card. It's such a trivial little thing to worry about in the grand scheme of things, I remember thinking this even as I said it to him.

Looking back, I don't understand how I had the presence of mind to call Jamie and tell him that my mother had passed, let alone tell him about the cab fare.

But that's the thing about life. It still goes on, and even though my mom has passed, the rest of the world carries on as normal.

I am numb during the entire cab ride. Each second I get further and further away from the place where my mom rests makes me feel as if I'm deserting her even though she left me first. I will never see her smile again, or have her gray-ringed eyes on me. I'll never be able to put my arms around her frail body, and I'll never go searching for the scent of lavender again.

I wish I'd spent more time with her. I wish I'd gone to see her every weekend. I wish I hadn't been scared of her lapsing in and out of forgetfulness. I would give anything to have my mom alive, even if she didn't know who I was.

As soon as the cab parks outside Jamie's place, he comes running out and settles the fare. He's been waiting for me and looks as if he hasn't slept a wink. He must be exhausted. I'm feeling the exhaustion now, as it sinks into my pores and deadweights me.

I've been trying to be brave, trying to hold it together, but upon seeing Jamie, the strength drains out of my body. He opens his mouth to say something, but then holds back, his face softens and he holds out his arms and lets me fall into them. He hugs me tightly, and it's exactly the type of hug I need.

This is what a true friend does and how a true friend behaves. Jamie is my rock.

"My mom died," I say, even though he already knows. The saying of it out loud makes it true in a way that not saying it never did. He holds me for the longest time, still standing in his doorway, before he pulls me inside, where his arms go around me like a protective blanket. He doesn't ask any questions, he just holds me and lets me cry.

We sit on the couch, and I sob because my heart is broken, and because my mom was the only constant in my life. Jamie lets me be, gives me time, lets me get it all out. I cry until I have no more tears and my voice is hoarse.

He asks me if I've eaten, if I need a drink of water, or something hot, or alcohol. I shake my head. I haven't eaten since I left this morning, or was that yesterday morning? This day has stretched out so long, it feels like a week.

He fetches me a glass of water nonetheless, and I gulp it down, then sit back against him, against the couch, not wanting to move, not wanting him to move. I tell him slowly, because he deserves to know, this man who waited up for me until the early hours. I tell him how I saw my mom in the ICU, and how I sat with her for a few hours, and how I fell asleep only to be woken up when the doctors and nurses came running in.

I tell him how when they could do no more, when she had passed, I held her hand, and told her I loved her, and asked her to forgive me for not being there sooner and for not visiting her more often.

"That's not your fault, Mari," he says, hugging me to him.

"I could have gone. I could have spent more time with her, instead of wasting it with ..." I stop and think. *Instead of getting all wrapped up in Ward's little web.*

"It's easy to have regrets," he says softly. He's trying to make me feel better, but I feel wretched. I chose to spend those weekends with Ward, because weekends were the only times he'd take things slower, ease up on the writing, give himself a break. I wasted precious time with my mom for sexy times with a man who I don't really know, and a man I now hate.

I think back to our argument. It was only yesterday, and yet it seems like weeks ago. I turn to Jamie. "If he hadn't smashed my cell phone, the nursing home would have contacted me right away. I would have gone to my mom sooner. I could have had more time with her."

"Woulda, coulda, shoulda, these are words of regret, Mari. Don't beat yourself up wondering what might have been." His arm squeezes my shoulder in a reassuring hug. I shift my legs so that I'm sitting on the side with my legs tucked under me, and I'm resting against Jamie's chest. It feels a little too familiar. I remember doing this with Ward not so long ago.

Jamie kisses the top of my head. He's the only person that I can rely on and trust. "I have to find a job," I say, remembering that I have now quit working for Ward.

"Don't worry about that."

"I have to figure out the funeral."

The funeral.

How is it that today I'm talking about funeral

arrangements, and yesterday my main worry was reading a few pages from Ward's manuscript? Life can change in the blink of an eye. So fast that even now, I feel I've got whiplash.

It will be a small affair but arrangements will need to be made.

"You need to sleep first," Jamie says. "And worry about the other stuff tomorrow. Don't ever think you're alone, Mari, because you're not. I'm here for you."

WARD

"It went up in flames," I tell Rob when he calls to tell me he still hasn't received my manuscript. He is used to this, my timelines slipping, especially when it comes to my first draft. It's almost like a game but I've never said this to him before. There is silence at the other end. I can almost see the dumbfounded look on Rob's face.

"In flames?" His upbeat voice tells me he's not sure if I'm joking or being serious. This is the first time I've hit him with something like this. A manuscript on fire. He's had to deal with me being late many times, but not dangerously late, and definitely not this.

"I threw it into the fire." I look at the floor, at my desk, trying to locate the damn box of donuts.

"You're not kidding me, are you?"

"I swear I'm not. I threw it into the fire."

"You needed to get it to me, Ward. It needs to go to the editor next week."

"Shame about that."

"Should I ask why you threw it into the fire?"

"Probably not."

"Print off another copy. Send me that."

"I can't do that."

"Why not?"

"I can't use this manuscript."

"What?" he shrieks. This is another new thing he's heard from me. He makes another low-rumbling noise which is a cross between disappointment and rage.

"What do you mean you can't use this manuscript?"

"I can't."

"Why are you talking in riddles? What's going on? Is Mari there?"

"She's gone, too."

I hear a deep grumble at the other end. "What have you gone and done? I'm about to catch a flight to the Bahamas. It's supposed to be an anniversary present for my wife. I was *supposed* to enjoy this trip because I thought I would've received and read your manuscript by now."

"Sorry."

He huffs out loudly. It's the sound of exasperation, frustration and downright giving up.

"Say it," I taunt him. "Say you've given up on me. Tell me I'm useless." Others have. I sniff, then take another sniff of my armpits. I wrinkle my nose in disgust. The room stinks. The blinds are still drawn. I haven't showered since ... since that argument with Mari

The TV room is a mess and so I've come into the study even though writing is the last thing on my mind. I can't make out if it's daylight or night outside and I don't want to find out, either.

"You make it hard for me to want to work with you, Ward."

"Then don't. Walk away."

"What happened?" he asks. I can hear the concern in his voice. I know Rob. He probably wants to walk away but can't. He's too decent, too caring. I should be lucky to count him as a friend.

"I got bored," I reply. I got bored of giving a fuck. I got sick and tired of being let down.

"You miss this deadline and it's going to cost you," he threatens. "Don't mention your fans getting pissed off, think of all the people working to get this book to market. You might feel okay about letting yourself down, but you're letting down whole departments of people."

"As many as that?" I mumble, stretching out on the couch and looking around, trying to find something to eat. Then I see it, the box of donuts. Only, it's lying on the floor near the fireplace and it looks almost empty.

I don't even remember finishing it off. I don't even know what day it is. A weekday or the weekend. It wouldn't be so bad if I was suffering a bad hangover, because alcohol would have helped numb my feelings. I don't care for alcohol, but it would probably be way cooler than overdosing on a box of donuts. Food coma has always suited me. Maybe because there is a deep-seated urge to feed myself, to not go hungry. Food signals comfort. No food signals terror.

My own mother didn't care that I was up in the attic starving and scared. She was happy for her husband to leave me there for days without food. How could she not care?

"What caused this?" Rob asks. "Was it revisiting your childhood home?"

"No. Wasn't that." I wish I hadn't mentioned it to him.

"Because you were fine. You were on target up until then. What happened?"

What happened? I fell back into the spiral again. Couldn't help it. Couldn't save myself if I tried. Despite my outward shell, my world within is fragile. I can plummet in a second.

I *have*. "Stuff happened," I answer. I consider ordering more donuts. I've come to love the expensive donuts from that fancy bakery in town. I blame Mari for that. She's the one who introduced me to them. I blame her for everything.

Rob huffs out loud enough for me to hear. He's incensed. "I can't do this anymore, Ward. I need to be someplace else."

"Then don't."

"I treated you like a friend but I can't do anymore for you. I can't save you if you won't save yourself." The line goes dead. The bastard hung up on me.

Somewhere in the fog of my thinking, I am aware that I need to get myself out of this rut. But knowing and doing are two different things. I'm stuck back in that spiral I can't climb out of. Even if I try to put a leg forward, I get sucked back into the vortex. Not that I've tried too hard just yet.

Maybe I should just go home. There's no need for me to be here anymore. I've angered a whole heap of people. My publishing house is going to write me off. Rob has given up. I haven't taken my editor's calls. I don't care that James Garvey is riding high in the bestseller charts. He can take my crown.

I'm sick of writing, of the relentless schedule. I'm sick of making words mean something when life itself has no meaning.

I reach across the floor trying to grab the bag of potato

chips lying just out of my reach. I stretch over, reaching out for it, and fall off the couch, hitting the floor with a thud.

Crap.

I knock over a half-full can of Pepsi. The coffee-colored liquid sinks, bubbles and all, into the beige carpet, leaving an ugly stain.

I growl in annoyance. She's not even here to clean it up.

The doorbell rings, but I'm not expecting anyone. I ignore it and climb back onto the couch with my bag of chips but the doorbell rings a few more times, and pisses me off even more. Eventually, I drag myself up to answer it.

"I'm coming!" I holler when it rings again. There's a persistent fucker on the other side of the door. Who the hell could it be? Jamie knows better than to come here.

Mari?

Has she come to make amends?

But when I open the door, it's Jamie's ugly face I'm staring into. "What the hell do you want?" I snarl.

His eyes narrow. He doesn't look too enamored to see me either. "I need to get some more of Mari's clothes."

I sneer. "She sent you again? What are you, her lapdog?" I open the door to let him in.

"I'm here because she never wants to see you again," he says, telling me something that is no surprise at all.

I scowl. Didn't he just take some of her things last week? "Take everything. Take the whole goddamn bunch." I really don't want to see him here again. Or her.

I walk up the stairs, he follows. Even though he knows where her room is now, I feel the need to see it again for myself.

I haven't stepped foot inside here and as soon as we enter, I catch a hint of her floral scent. The dresser has a few things still on it. Jamie walks over to a closet and grabs a few clothes.

"Take it all," I bark.

"She only needs a few business suits."

I don't want him here and I don't want any memory of her. "Take. It. All."

Jamie's face hardens. "I don't have time for that. We're busy. She's busy." It's the way he says it that catches my attention. They are busy doing what?

"How is she?" I ask. I'm curious to know, now that he's pushed all thought of her to the front of my mind. I'd buried all thoughts and feelings about her. Pushed them to the back, trodden on them and kept them down, and now he's brought them all to the forefront again.

He doesn't answer, but instead, pulls out her clothes. *What does she need business suits for?* "Did she find another job?" Or maybe she has an interview. I hope she gets the job because she needs the money.

He throws a few things into his bag, and picks up suits on hangers. His silence troubles me. "Is she okay?" I ask.

"As if you care." He gives me a dirty look.

I *do* care. I'm in a bad place right now, but I do care.

"You've got sugar all over your beard," Jamie points out. I wipe it away quickly with the back of my hand. Then I smooth down the front of my t-shirt because I'm suddenly conscious that I must look like shit. That I probably smell, and that he knows it. I look like a slob. I *feel* like a slob. He'll go back and tell Mari what a train wreck I am.

"What's happened to you?" he asks. "You look like a mess. Do you miss her that much?"

I run a self-conscious hand across my beard, hoping to wipe away all traces of sugar, donut crumbs and anything else there might be. "I need to know that she's okay."

"You don't need to know anything," Jamie hollers, brushing past me as he walks out of the door.

There's something he's keeping from me.

He likes her.

I always suspected.

He stops when he gets to the bottom and glares at me. "Her mother died, you asshole. She died and the nursing home couldn't get in touch with Mari because you," he stabs a finger in my direction, "you smashed her cell phone, you fucking freak." He slams the door as he leaves.

Mari's mom died? They couldn't get a hold of her? I try to ignore the sharp pain that slices through me, spreading from my chest to my back. Her mom died and the nursing home couldn't get a hold of her?

Because I smashed her cell phone.

I sit on the stairs in shock, feeling the force of this blow more acutely than when my own mother died. I feel for Mari, and what I did. The guilt climbs up through my stomach and into my throat, until I choke on it.

I want to do something. I want to help her. I know what her mom meant to her. She will be devastated. She'll be heartbroken. I can't have her break down.

CHAPTER FIFTY-ONE

MARI

I haven't been able to get out of bed. Jamie gave me his bed again and he's been sleeping on the couch. He's been working and comes back in the evenings, but he calls and checks in on me many times throughout the day.

I like that I'm here alone. Even making conversation is hard. Luckily for me, Jamie understands. I don't have to pretend to be something I'm not, and what I am right now is a mess.

I can't function. I can't eat, or sleep, or think. I can't do anything. I don't want to do anything.

I want to curl up and sleep for years.

My mom's funeral takes place next week. We've got the date, and I've let a few friends and family members know. I wouldn't have been able to do this without Jamie's help. I wouldn't have been able to function even in the tiny capacity that I am had it not been for him.

I've sent him to get some of my business suits. I'm supposed to be working on a speech but I can't find it in me to write the words I have in my head. I can't express how much love I have for my mom. *Had.* The love I *had.* I can't encapsulate it in words, what I feel for my mom, what I *felt.*

It is an overabundance of feelings, a myriad of emotions. Her smile, her touch, her voice. There are so many precious fragments of things I remember; her picking me up from school, and sending me away to college, her nursing my heart when my first boyfriend dumped me, and then doing it again over the years when all the others did. It was the pride in her eyes when I got my first job, and her elation for every job I got after that.

I feel her through images and emotions, not words. It makes it impossible for me to write it all down.

Ward could have helped with that.

The reminder of him sets me crying again. Not because I feel sad or miss him. What I feel is hate, so much hate, but crying is the only emotion I have. I seem to only operate in two states: crying or not crying. There is nothing else in between.

I'm staring out of the window when Jamie returns. He'll be home all day today, it being the weekend, so I will have to try extra hard to convince him that I am coping.

"Hey," he says, walking in with a bag of my clothes. He's carrying the jackets and skirts on hangers, and he disappears into the bedroom presumably to hang them up.

I turn my writing pad upside down so that he can't see.

"How are you doing?" he asks, coming over and sitting down on the far end of the couch. I lift up my feet, hunching up my legs to clear him a space.

"Good." I smile as if to prove it.

"Get anything down?" He swipes the notepad before I can stop him. He turns it over and stares at the blank page. "Want me to help?"

I shake my head.

He nods. "You've got time. It will come."

Will it? I don't want to say the last goodbye, that's what makes this so hard. I swallow, trying to push back the huge lump that forms in my throat. "Did you get everything?"

"I picked up what I could. I had to do it quickly because he was hanging around watching."

I clear my throat.

"I told him," says Jamie. "He kept asking how you were. I wasn't sure if you wanted him to know, but he kind of put me on the spot."

"It's fine." That man can be overbearing. I know how hard it is to be around him.

"I told him it was his fault that you couldn't get to your mom fast enough because he broke your phone."

I lift my head, feeling a sense of satisfaction. "Thanks." I wait for Jamie to tell me more, but he doesn't say anything else. He gets up. "I'm going to cook us a nice dinner tonight."

"I can help," I say, getting to my feet slowly. I want to help. I need to. I have to do something to get out of this funk.

"Hey, no." He ruffles my hair. "You don't have to do a thing. You just take it easy, Mari. I've got this." He disappears into the kitchen only to return moments later with a bar of my favorite chocolate. He's stocked up on these, I've noticed.

"This will make things more bearable."

I reach out for the brand-new unopened bar. "Thanks."

"I'd better get started on dinner."

"What else did he say?" I ask him as he walks way.

"Who?"

"Ward."

"Nothing else."

CHAPTER FIFTY-TWO

WARD

It wasn't easy getting hold of Rob again, but after the fifth message I left for him, he finally called me back. If he was hoping for a miracle from me regarding the manuscript, he must have been sorely disappointed because I asked him to send me the work contracts he had drawn up for Mari and Jamie. It's how I got Jamie's address. It's the reason why I'm on his doorstep on Monday morning.

Just as I had hoped, it's Mari who opens the door. I'm hoping it's because he's at work.

She looks haggard. Her skin is pale, her eyes hollow. She seems thinner, fragile, as if she's about to break.

"I'm so sorry for your loss," I say. I fumble around, not sure what to do with my hands and wishing I had brought something. Flowers, a card, but I'm not sure of the etiquette. I'm not sure she wouldn't throw the flowers back at me, or rip the card up in front of my face. She stands there, not letting me in, not moving a muscle. Just staring.

"May I come in?" I ask her. She continues to stare at me as if she's in shock. This concerns me, because the sassy and in control woman, the one I later came to know, isn't here. She's as broken as I am.

"Please," I beg. This might be my only chance to reach her.

She doesn't want me to come in, and she's too polite to say it, so I push the door open, making the decision for her. "I won't stay for long." I hover near the closed door, mindful of taking up her time, and invading her personal space. "I'm so sorry about your mom, Mari. I didn't know. I—"

"I didn't get to her on time," she says, walking away, standing over by the window, as if she needs the distance between us to feel safe. "I missed out on being there for her because of you." Her anger returns and spikes in an instance. "All because of you." She jabs a finger in my direction, her face twisting with rage. I have failed her. I've messed up in a way that is irredeemable. "What happened, in the end?"

"She died."

Of what, I want to know but I don't think she will tell me. I take a step towards her needing her to know how genuinely sorry I am. "Tell me how I can make it up to you."

"You can get out. Leave. Never show your face here again."

She's angry. Lashing out, wanting to hurt me. These are feelings I understand completely.

What becomes apparent to me is that my anger vanished the moment Jamie told me about her mom. It stopped being about me, and the manuscript, and the donuts and my own funk. Hearing about Mari's tragedy pushed me into action in a way that nothing else could have. Now that I've seen what a state she is in, I desperately want to help her but she won't let me. I can try and try again until she gives in.

"You're angry. You hate me. I don't blame you but—"

"I never want to see you again."

"I understand but—"

"I'm shocked that you have the audacity to show up here."

"I *needed* to see you." I look at her forehead. There's a tiny scar where she hit her head. "That looks like it's healed," I say, raising a finger to touch her but she flinches.

"Jamie took care of it."

"I'm sure he did."

She stares at me motionless. "What were you trying to do, kill me?"

I lower my head, brows pushing together, the weight of her accusation settling hard and heavy on my heart. I am aware how deep hatred can run, but I'm still not prepared for the depth of Mari's hate for me even though she has every right to abhor me forever. "I was trying to protect you."

"By grabbing me and hurling me to the couch?"

"You slipped and I was worried you were going to trip and fall into the fire."

"That's not what happened."

I blink, confusion rendering me speechless for a few moments.

"That's not what happened," she insists.

"What do you think happened?" I ask, slowly.

"You had your hands on me. I tried to shrug you off but you wouldn't budge. You *scared* me."

"I didn't mean to take a hold of you, Mari. I was angry. You *betrayed* me."

She laughs cruelly. "By reading a few pages of your book?"

"Yes." She won't understand, ever, and now is not the time to tell her. I doubt I ever will. "You hurt me and I reacted in the only way I know how."

"That's worrying," she throws back.

"I'm not perfect and I have a temper, but I would never hurt a hair on your head."

She looks stunned.

"When you tripped and hit the mantelpiece, I was scared you were going to fall into the fire. You were holding your cell phone in one hand." She stares at me as if she's replaying that scene in her head again, as if she's unsure whether to believe me or not. "I let someone go to her death once and I've lived my life blaming myself for it. I wasn't about to risk you falling into the fire, so I grabbed you and hurled you as far from it as I could. I should have been gentle but my main concern was for you not to get hurt."

She seems to believe me—she should believe me, because it's the truth. There's a softness in her eyes for the first time. Then, "Did you hit your daily word count?" she sneers. "Is it sex you want now?"

The blow hits below the waist and my brain stutters, trying to make meaning from this. All those important bodily functions, like the heart beating and blood circulating, lungs breathing, they all slow down. She's another one who means the world to me, but now she's pushing me away.

"Is that the reason you're here?"

I care about her is the reason I'm here. This isn't me, this isn't what I do, come groveling to someone, but this is exactly what I'm doing and she's throwing it back in my face.

But I also understand rage. I fool myself into believing that she doesn't mean what she's saying. "It stopped being about the sex a long time ago."

She scoffs, then shakes her head. "That's what you'd have me believe. You're incapable of emotion. Of feeling, of empathy. You think about yourself and no one else."

"That might have been true once."

"It's true now."

"If I could turn back time and take that day back, I would do things so differently."

"Would you?" she snarls, showing her teeth. "What would you do differently, Ward? What?"

I didn't come here to talk about me. I came here to find out what I could do for her. But since she's asking. "I'd take a step back. I'd ask you why you were reading my manuscript. I'd ask why you were taking pictures. I would behave a whole different way."

"Like a normal person?"

"I never said I was a normal person," I raise my voice without meaning to. She knew that about me from the start. I'm shaped by my past. Most people are.

"You're so far off the normal spectrum, I think about us and wonder what I saw in you."

That's another blow below the belt. I'll take it. I'll take anything she wants to hit me with because it means she's getting her anger out, and she needs to. Built-up anger can poison a person as surely as strychnine.

"I don't regret a thing," I tell her.

"That's because you got sex on tap." She almost smiles, but it's the type of smile that makes my blood run cold. Still, I take another step towards her, determined to get through to her. "That is not true. What we had was starting to be more than sex. You made me see things the way I should have. You made me *feel.*"

"I should never have gotten involved with you."

"Getting involved with you was one of the best things I ever did."

She stares at me in open-mouthed silence. That seems to have hit a nerve. I advance a step closer.

I consider telling her the truth, that I've fallen for her. But if I told her now, it would be taking advantage of her delicate state and I won't do that. "I care about you and I feel bad that I hurt you."

"I can't see you feeling bad about anything, unless you've run out of donuts."

I look at her in surprise. I have changed a lot these past few months. I managed to get out of my rut and she had something to do with it. I'm not that guy anymore.

"I'm truly upset about your mom passing," I say, ignoring her stab at me. "And I blame myself for breaking your phone and for you not finding out right away."

"You should blame yourself, because it's your fault."

"I'll take this to the grave with me. You cared a lot for your mother and she was lucky she had you."

She jabs a thumb in her chest. "I'm the lucky one. I was lucky that she was my mom." She sounds as if she's fighting back tears. I want to put my arms around her and hug her. I want to tell her that I'm going to take care of her and be there for her, but she twists the knife in deeper. "I'm just so sorry that I met you. I wish I hadn't."

I refuse to give up. She will always blame me for what happened, and it's something I have to live with. I can't turn back time, but I want to make things right for her, if she will let me. "Tell me what I can do to make things better. Let me help you in any way. Let me pay for the funeral."

Her face drains of color. "Get out!" she yells with an animosity that knocks the air out of my lungs and leaves me struggling to get mouthfuls of air. "Don't think this is me being emotional, and all over the place. I hate you, Ward. I regret that I ever met you."

I shake my head, refusing to believe that this is it. That it's over.

"Get out and never contact me again," she begs.

I was going to tell her to ask me anything she wanted and I would answer all of her questions, all those many questions she used to ask me before, all those questions about Lisa. I was prepared to answer everything, but the hate in her eyes rolls off her body in the same way that her desire once used to. I step back. "If that's what you want."

"It is."

I nod. "I'm so sorry for your loss."

As I walk to the door, she stops me. "I need you to know about the pen."

I turn around.

"I didn't misplace it. I never took it. I never touched your things. Jamie took your pen. I didn't tell you because I didn't want you to fire him like you did Trevor."

At first, I want to believe that she's lying. Everything I did, touching her the way I did, all the assumptions I made were based on her taking the pen. I thought she was playing games with me. I believed she had picked up on the unbridled energy I could feel between us.

I can't speak because her words have tasered me.

"I wouldn't lie about such a thing," she assures me, fixing me with a hard stare. My gut tells me this is the truth. I wouldn't have laid a finger on her had I known this then. Believing she wanted me was the thing that gave me the courage to make my move.

CHAPTER FIFTY-THREE

MARI

I manage to get through my mom's funeral somehow, but it feels as if my body has been through a meat machine, ground into a million pieces, chewed up and regurgitated at the other end.

I am still hollow but most of all, I am bone tired. I'm also still at Jamie's place, almost three weeks after my mom passed, but I don't remember each day clearly, or each week. I know of two events, when my mom died and the day of her funeral.

And now I am supposed to somehow get back to normality, only I don't know what normality is.

Jamie is as kind and as accommodating as ever, but in some far corner of my mind, when I get a few moments of clarity, when the fog lifts temporarily, I can't stay here like this forever. I need to get another apartment and a job. I also need to take care of my mother's affairs, go back to the nursing home and get all her belongings. I have to see how much money I have.

I can't rely on Jamie's good nature.

He tells me he needs to go grocery shopping, and I manage to get out of bed and rise to standing. Lying around in bed all the time has wasted my muscles and killed any strength I had.

"I'll go." I stand up, but the look in his eyes--fraught with worry and concern--tells me more than if I looked in a mirror.

I smooth down my t-shirt, try to pull the hem down so that it will reach further instead of hovering just below my panties. I should put some more clothes on, but I still haven't gone to Ward's to get the rest of my belongings and I've gone through the few clothes I had. They're all lying in a dirty pile in a corner of the room.

"I should go," I tell him, standing up straighter, trying to convince him that I am capable.

He walks over to me and sits me down, then he crouches on the floor. "I'm worried about you."

"I'm fine. I'm going to be fine. I'm going to make plans."

He shakes his head. "You haven't had breakfast. You haven't had lunch."

"I'm not hungry."

"And that's why I'm worried."

I bite my lip. "I'm not hungry because I'm lying around in bed all day. I can go shopping. I can be of use."

"Not now."

"I need to do something."

He stands up. "Fine. But let me go shopping, and when I get back, you can cook."

"Deal."

I reach for my purse which is on the bedside table. "Let me pay for this."

"No."

"Please," I beg.

"You can do it when you get yourself back up on your feet. When you've got a job. When you are able. There's no rush."

"Okay, fine. Have it your way. But I'm cooking."

"And I'm looking forward to it. I'll be back soon."

I collapse back on the bed when I hear the front door close. I have to start looking for work again. Someone from Danny's place arranged an interview for me but I couldn't go. It was the week of my mom's funeral and I forgot to email to let them know. Danny says they weren't too happy about it. He explained the situation to them, and they said they'd get in touch again but they haven't, so I need to chase that up again.

I also need to get my belongings from Ward's place. I might just go with Jamie sometime in the next few days and make sure I get everything.

I lie back on the bed, then pull the covers over me. This is all I can handle for now.

This. Lying here, remembering, revisiting, regretting.

The doorbell rings, and I don't move. When it rings again, I groan and get up. Jamie gets a lot of packages delivered. He's a typical guy always ordering his tech gadgets. It's the one thing I can help him with, being his personal package receiver. I rush to the door before the mailman disappears, but when I pull open the door, Ward's eyes stare back at me.

Dark and hypnotic, they make my insides jump. From shock, maybe, or maybe from surprise. Unlike the last time he came, when he looked so rough, like he'd barely slept, this time he looks so much sharper. His hair is neatly cut, he hasn't shaved, but there's that light dusting of hairs around his jaw that I once used to love.

I open my mouth to say something, but his eyes start to dip down the length of my body, until he quickly manages to bring them back up to my face again.

Old habits die hard.

The old familiar heat begins to snake inside my belly.

"I waited for you to get your stuff, but ..." he starts. It's then that I notice the bag at his feet.

My belongings. "There's another one in my car, I wasn't sure you would be in."

"You packed everything?"

"Everything. I took the liberty. Hope you don't mind."

He hands me over the bag. "I'll go and grab the other one." He disappears and I rush into the bedroom and slide on a pair of jeans and throw on a sweatshirt.

When I return, he's standing in the doorway. "Here you go." He puts the bag inside, but doesn't walk in. We look at one another warily. Each time I take in his face, and his build, and his countenance, I can't help but wonder how he has managed to turn things around.

He's not the one who lost a mother, though.

But I remember, now that I am connecting the dots, that his mother had died not so long before we met. Knowing what I have been through, and knowing a little about his past, I find myself wondering about him and how he would have dealt with something like that.

"You can come inside. I don't bite," I tell him. He seems reluctant to take me up on my offer. "I'd rather not have you standing in the doorway like that."

He walks in and shuts the door, but doesn't move far from it.

"I was going to come around with Jamie and get everything," I tell him. "It's been busy here with my ..." I still can't bring myself to say it.

"It was last week?" he asks.

"The week before that."

"It must have been a hard day."

I clasp my hands together as if I need the strength to hold myself together. He has packed my things and brought them to me so I should at least thank him. "Thanks for these, but I would have come over eventually."

"I wanted to see you, and I needed an excuse." His confession confuses me. While I'm not so sure that I hate him as much, I'm trying to move on and forget him. Words like these don't make this easy. "An excuse?"

He doesn't smile but there is a twinkle in his eyes which I remember very well. "I had a feeling you weren't going to let me in if I came without your belongings."

"Why did you want to see me?"

"To say goodbye."

Goodbye? Why am I so shocked? It was going to happen at one point, I just never expected it would happen like this.

"I'm going back to New Orleans next week."

"What happened to the book?"

"I manned up like you suggested, and printed another copy off, and sent it to Rob. He got it a few weeks later than planned, but ... he got it. My editor is still talking to me. Looks like I might have salvaged things."

"Good for you."

I recall our argument and the good time before that. Rollercoaster times some of them, but unforgettable times, too. We are extremes, he and I.

Deep dirty passion, reckless friendship, extreme hate.

He kept me on my toes. He was what I wanted, what I

am drawn to: risk, and danger, not average or nice, or boring. For my sins, these are the types of men I am drawn to and Ward Maddox fit the bill one hundred percent.

Looking at him, my heart begins to flutter, and just as quickly I am reminded that we have too much bad history between us to fix anything.

"My dry cleaning," says Jamie, pushing the door open. Ward steps out of the way, but the two men are eye to eye as Jamie walks in, his face growing ugly as he fixes his gaze on Ward. "What are you doing—"

"He came to drop off my things," I say quickly, all too aware of the growing animosity between these two men.

"How do you know where I live?" Jamie asks, but he looks at me. "Did you tell him?"

"Mari had nothing to do with it," Ward says smoothly. "I should have brought everything over the last time I came—"

"He's been here before?" Jamie shrieks. His anger isn't directed at Ward, it's directed at me.

"He ... he came once ... when he found out about my mom."

"You never thought to tell me?"

"There was nothing to tell," I reply. I am sick of Jamie policing my every move.

He scoffs. "You're going to take him back?"

"Jamie!"

"I always said you were a pushover. Don't you ever learn?"

"Stop it." He's embarrassing me. Thankfully, he marches into the bedroom, and I hear him banging the closet doors.

"He doesn't like me," Ward states when it's just the two of us again.

"You don't have much affection for him," I point out.

"I wonder why." The way his eyes burn into mine, I can tell he wants to say something but Jamie interrupts the quiet as he stomps back through the room. He's carrying his business suits. He's got a few interviews lined up this week, which is more than I can say for myself. Without a word, he leaves, slamming the door behind him.

Ward's gaze locks onto mine, and then he says something that I wasn't expecting, not in a million years. "Lisa Dooley."

The muscles in my stomach tighten. A ball forms, like days-old stale oatmeal sinking to the base and making everything heavy.

"Lisa Dooley?" I repeat.

"You asked me about her," he puts his hands in his pockets. "You made accusations, if I remember correctly."

"I was told something."

"I need to explain."

I wonder why now, and what difference will it make? He starts to tell me, so I listen.

"I loved her, but our being together was a passionate clusterfuck of disaster. She was good for me, in a bad way, and I was bad for her, in a good way."

I want to ask him to elaborate, but he gives me a dismissive look and I can only surmise that it was to do with sex. I taunt myself with the unwelcome thought.

"Our being together didn't work," he says, moving on quickly, "not if I was being honest. I wanted to walk away. She wouldn't let me. My first book was close to releasing. I had tons of pressure. I needed to prove to myself and to the world that I could do this writing thing and make a living. I didn't have time for her. We argued, and I told her that I wished I'd never met her. She jumped off a building and died. I blamed myself. I always have."

"But that's not your fault."

"She threatened to jump off a building. I told her to go ahead. And she did. She killed herself. How is that not my fault?"

"You were being flippant."

"I should have known better. I should have gone easy on her. She wasn't well, and while I didn't know the extent of her problems until later, there were plenty of times when I suspected something was wrong. I was so preoccupied in my writing that she came second. But the more she clung to me, the more I grew angry. We argued all the time, until eventually, even she could see there was no point in trying to pretend we were happy together. I thought that would be the end of it. But a few months later, she called and told me she loved me, and that she couldn't live without me and she made the threat."

"Obviously you didn't believe she would do that, something so crazy." I need him to see that this wasn't his fault.

"But I told her to go ahead. I loved her, and yet that's what I said to her."

"Ward!" I shake my head. I can see what it has done to him, the weight of this blame, along with everything else that he has carried throughout his life. It has broken him beyond repair. I can't see this man disintegrate before my eyes. I won't allow it. I take a step towards him, but he steps back, as if he needs the distance between us.

"And then what happened?" I ask, staying put where I am.

"I couldn't function. I couldn't promote the book or start writing the sequel. I couldn't write a word. I was a mess. I moped around, not showering, not getting out of bed, just eating myself silly and watching TV. But I wasn't watching it, I needed the noise and the pictures in front of me, but I didn't watch a thing. I didn't do a thing. If you think I was in a state when you first started to work for me, it was nothing compared to the mess I was then. That's when Rob came onto the scene. He's seen me at the lowest of my lows."

He's gone from telling me nothing to all of this, and it's almost too much to take in. Like being waterboarded. I can't even speak.

"I didn't kill her, Mari. I'm no murderer."

I finally find my voice, even though it's a whisper. "But Jamie said ..."

"He said what?"

"That she died under mysterious circumstances." I don't tell him that Jamie said Ward killed her.

"People can have all kinds of opinions about the way in which Lisa died. I've tried to protect her family, and I've tried to block everything online about it. It wasn't fair to her loved ones, all these nasty things people were saying. The police confirmed what happened. There was no foul play. Lisa wasn't well. She had problems, but it hurt her family to have these problems printed and published for the world to read. I don't mean to blow my own trumpet, but a lot of interest in her was because she was my girlfriend. For an up-and-coming horror writer, which was what I was then, to have a girlfriend who killed herself, well, news like that was ripe for the picking."

I let this sink in. My fear of Ward was amplified because of what Jamie had told me. He gives me an are-you-satisfied stare, which makes me look away at the wall, feeling foolish.

"There's one more thing. One more explanation."

My heart sinks. The sadness that lingers around me—for my mom, and for everything I couldn't fix and make better—deepens with every word Ward says. He is ripping my emotions to shreds in order to clear his name. He deserves to, because I have made and assumed way too much. He's not a calculating man, like I feared at first. He's brusque and upfront, and reveals who he is. That's why he scared me at first, from the moment I met him, because his roughness was in plain sight.

I feel sad because we could have had a lifetime of talking. Now he's giving me piecemeal bits about all the things I wanted to know about him back when we were together. It's too late.

"What other thing?" I ask, my voice shaky.

"I got mad that day, really mad, when I caught you reading my manuscript. My reaction was out of proportion to the thing you had done."

"I'm sorry about that." I really am. I've never had a chance to tell him, but now that I've had plenty of time to think about it, and I've had the distance to view my actions through the filter of time and space, I can see that I wasn't entirely blameless.

He looks away, out of the window, at a point in the distance. "What you did, it took me back to the house, to my stepdad, to that time."

I want to rush to him, but I'm scared I might end up wanting to touch him, and I'm also scared that he will push me away, so I fold my arms. "I betrayed you," I say. "I did the very thing you asked me not to. No matter how good your writing was, I shouldn't have read those pages. I'm so sorry."

He narrows his eyes at me, as if he's not sure of my sincerity.

And then I remember, something he said the last time he was here and which I forgot to point out. "About the photos, I didn't take any. It crossed my mind for a few reckless seconds, I considered taking them but I knew I couldn't. I knew it was going too far. The reason I even thought of it was that I'm a people pleaser. A pushover, like that. Jamie has often said that I always try to please."

"You wanted to please him?"

"I ... I wanted us not to fall out. We'd fallen out, and believed I could appease him if I gave him a sneak of your pages."

"And betraying me even more?"

I feel the throb of my shaky heartbeat. "I don't think, sometimes, with my head, and this was one of those times."

"So you didn't take any photos?"

"None. I swear."

"I shouldn't have lost my temper like that. Hurling your phone and breaking it. I scared you and that's another thing I'll regret forever."

We're moving towards an understanding, taking tiny steps towards forgiveness. "You're particular about your writing. You want things a certain way. You have rules and I should have respected that. I'm sorry."

"The reason I reacted the way I did," he says, taking a huge breath and scratching his neck, "is because you reminded me of a time, a very painful time, with my stepfather."

I wince, feeling uncomfortable already. I am aware of how much suffering that man inflicted on Ward. Reminding him of his stepdad is something I would never willingly do.

"I started writing when I was thirteen," he continues, "when a teacher at school encouraged me. I applied myself and did well. I was good at something. She later encouraged me to enter a writing competition. She loved the piece I wrote and thought it had a good chance. But my stepfather read it, and he laughed and mocked me. To cut a long story short, he ripped it up, and we got into a fight. That's when I ended up in the children's home for a while. Things had been getting bad at home but this particular incident topped it all. Aside from Rob or my editor, I've never been able to have anyone read my work before it's published."

My heart lurches. Everything about him, every single thing from his past is filled with hurt. We are broken people, he and I, and we could be whole again if we allowed ourselves to help one another. I venture another step towards him but he motions for me to stay where I am.

He's pushing me away. While I'm not about to leap at him with open arms, it breaks my heart the way he's keeping me at bay. "I'd better go, before Jamie gets back and gets upset."

"We're not together," I say, needing him to know. "We never have been."

"Much to his annoyance, I'm sure."

I detest his sarcasm and am about to say something when I suddenly realize it's the truth.

"He likes you, and he can't stand that you're with me. That you *were* with me." Ward walks towards the door, but I don't want him to leave. I want him to stay and talk. "I blame myself for breaking your phone. I blame myself for putting you through the anguish of not reaching your mother sooner, of never having that chance. The guilt will always linger with me. It's mine, not yours, to hold onto."

He opens the door and stands in the doorway. "I know how you feel, Mari. Lost and bewildered. Numbed and paralyzed into inaction. If you let yourself spiral in so deep, no one and nothing will be able to pull you back out. The price of inertia is too high. Believe me, I've been there."

Don't go, I want to scream at him, but I manage to stop myself while regret cleaves my heart and I watch him walk away forever.

CHAPTER FIFTY-FOUR

MARI

The atmosphere between me and Jamie has become more strained ever since Ward showed up here with my belongings last week.

I've managed to get a job at Danny's place and now I can make plans to leave Jamie alone and find a place of my own. I don't want things to get so bad between us that we can't bear the sight of one another. Jamie has helped me in many ways, but he also makes me feel claustrophobic. This is something I never noticed before.

Taking Ward's advice to not get sucked into a spiral of depression, I try to make a pointed effort to get my affairs in order. It also easier to do this now that I have a job and will have money coming in.

I can finally start to make plans and this afternoon I plan to start looking for an apartment.

It's only when I finally get around to looking at my

finances that I discover I'm still getting paid for the housekeeping job. I'm not getting paid the same amount, I'm getting paid *double*. And there is a suspicious payment of a few extra thousand dollars.

I peer closer, thinking I'm the target of some sophisticated scammer who has planted money in my account and will somehow siphon it away later. It's difficult for me to believe that good things can happen to me, but after a phone call to the bank, I learn that the payments are legitimate.

I call Rob and ask him.

"Good to hear from you, Mari. I'm very sorry to hear about your mother. This must be such a terrible blow."

"It was unexpected, to say the least. I'm not sure I've recovered."

"Something like this is difficult to recover from. Ward said you were taking time away."

"I needed to."

"That's completely understandable. I was going to call you at some point," he says. This immediately fills me with dread. He's obviously noticed the overpayment and wants to rectify it. "You can come back whenever you feel ready."

It sounds to me like Ward hasn't told him I quit. I decide to come clean. "Uh ... I quit, actually."

"You quit?"

"Almost six weeks ago. There's been a mistake because I'm still getting paid for it."

"Ward insisted, he said it was only right that you get paid, especially after such a difficult time."

"Okay," I say slowly. So, he's choosing to pay me even though I quit? "But I've been paid too much."

"Too much?"

"Yes, way too much," I tell him. He must find this odd. I find it odd, because I'm sure many people would keep quiet about such a thing but I consider myself to be an honest person.

"You'll want to take that up with Ward. I hired you, but the rest is on him."

"Oh."

"Sorry, Mari. I've got a call on the other line. Things are going crazy here. Seems like all the pieces of the puzzle are finally coming together now that the book is done and ready to publish."

"He got the book in on time?" I ask quickly.

"Just about. I think it's his best yet. Have you read it?"

"I don't read horror."

He chuckles. "Maybe you should watch the movie then when it comes out. You can close your eyes at all the gory parts."

"I might just have to do that." I can hear the other phone ringing in his office. "I have to go," he says.

"One more thing," I rush to ask him before he hangs up. "Where's Ward?"

"Still in Chicago. He comes back in a few days' time."

"Thanks." I hang up.

WARD

I'm about to go downstairs, when I decide to take one last look at her bedroom. Pushing open the door, I survey her room. The empty dresser, the unslept in bed. I close my eyes and try to catch a hint of her scent. But it's gone. Just like everything that was good between us has gone.

I take my bags downstairs, and I sit on the stairs waiting for the taxi to arrive. I'll be back home by this time tomorrow. Back to normal. No drama, no nothing.

The doorbell rings, and I answer it, thinking that the driver has shown up early. But it's like I've been punched in the stomach when I find Mari on the other side.

It's a shock seeing her again, in the place where we had a lot of good times. There were bad times, too, but the good things always overshadow the bad times. It's something I've had to learn, a new and better way I've tried to be. Focusing on the good things pushes the bad things away and out of sight.

"Hey."

"You're still here?" she asks, looking puzzled. It's as if she expected me to have left.

"I'm waiting for the taxi. It should show up any moment now." I open the door and let her in, thinking how nice this is, her being here. It's been so long since she was here. So much has happened, so much *could* have happened if she had stayed.

"You've overpaid me," she states, confusing me entirely. Foolishly, I'd thought that maybe she'd come to talk, but her visit appears to be based on financial matters. Arrangements. Not affairs of the heart.

"You were still employed."

"I quit."

I wince. "Technically, you did, but I felt bad about everything that happened and you didn't let me pay for the funeral costs or help you in any way. I didn't know how to make it up to you so ..."

She gives me a careful smile. "That's very generous of you, but I don't feel as if I've earned it."

"Please take it. I can't make things better for you and this is the only way I know that might help you in a small way."

She makes a face as she stares at the floor and shakes her head. "I was in a bad place when my mom died. I hit back at you. I lashed out. I wanted to blame you, but the truth of it is that my mom having a stroke was nothing to do with you. It wasn't your fault."

"It wasn't yours."

She looks at me as if I've removed her flimsy façade, the one that covers the real her and disproves that she has it altogether.

She doesn't. I know this because I too have lost people I've loved and I'm painfully aware of the damage it can do. "You blame yourself, but you had nothing more to do with what happened that night than I did. I'm talking about your mom and the stroke, Mari. There is no way you could have prevented that." She looks as if I've winded her. "Hey," I take a step towards her, wanting to hold her face in my hands and talk her through this. But it's too late for all of that. Sadly, I feel that our time has passed.

"You haven't just paid me, you've *overpaid* me," she points out.

"I paid you what I thought you were worth. What I thought I could get away with without you noticing."

"Pfft. You think I wouldn't notice almost an extra $10,000 in my account?"

"It's for the money you would have earned had you stayed here. Had you not quit, had none of the bad things happened. The payment is for that, plus a little bonus."

"I can't accept it, Ward."

"I want you to have it."

When she looks as if she's about to protest, I push back. "Please, take it. *Please.* I have more money than I know what to do with. I'm not trying to buy you out, before you accuse me of such a thing. It would just make me happy to know you have it in case you need it."

"It would make you happy?" she asks.

"It would make me very happy."

"But it's too much."

"You've helped me more than you know."

"I've helped you?"

"Rob forced me to come here because he believed it would get me out of a funk—not unlike the one you're in. I too had lost my mom a few months before."

"I'm sorry."

I take a sharp inhale of breath. "I'm not so sure I am. She stopped being the mom I remembered and needed her to be."

"I'm still sorry."

"When I visited her on her deathbed, needing for her to tell me that she had been wrong, needing her to confess that she had made a mistake and regretted how she had treated me, do you know what she said?"

Mari shakes her head.

"She told me that if she could have picked between my stepfather and me, she would always have picked him. Even then, on her deathbed, that's what she said." My voice turns shaky thinking about it and I clear my throat, willing myself to stay strong.

"I'm so, so sorry, Ward."

"Sorry doesn't fix a thing," I tell her. I tried so hard to

make my mom change. Even after I left, I would still go back and visit her from time to time. But we were never able to get our relationship back. She pined for him. All that time I'd been hoping she would change back to how she used to be, she didn't. That's when I resolved never to get close to anyone. I keep all of this to myself. There's no point in sharing my past with Mari. Not now. "Hearing your own mom say something like that breaks you," I tell her. Hearing a car pull up outside, I bend down to grab one of my bags.

She looks as if she wants to say something, but the time for saying things has passed. I look at the door in anticipation.

"Do you have to leave now?" she asks, her anxiety making her sound breathless.

"I have a flight to catch and I'm all packed and ready."

She looks deflated, so much so that I say, "If you wanted to talk, I wish you had come earlier."

"I only saw the discrepancy in my bank account a few hours ago."

I hate that we have run out of time. "Will you keep the money? For me?" I very much want her to have it. I don't want her to struggle. I want only good things for her.

"If you insist."

"I do."

"Thank you."

True to form, a car honks outside and I open the door and hold out my hand, indicating to the driver to wait. I could assume things—about her and me. I could put a stop to all this now. I could tell Mari I can stay and that I want to hear what she has to say, but I have learned that despite what I want, or how I need things to be, it has to come from her.

I could never understand why my mother stopped

loving me, why she switched her attention to a monster in a heartbeat and forgot that I ever existed. I now have a fear of this happening again, and I won't ever allow myself to be hurt like that. "You're lucky. Your mom wanted you, Mari. She loved you. You can hold on to that kind of love because it stays with you forever."

The taxi driver honks again. I reach for the other bag and see that Mari has picked up the third one. "You don't have to do that."

But she does it anyway and we walk out toward the cab silently. The driver takes my luggage and puts it in the trunk. I shove my hands in my pockets. They are safer there than out, where I run the risk of taking her face and touching her again.

"You being here helped me. Don't tell Rob. This was all his idea and I don't want to give him the satisfaction of knowing he was right."

She sniffles. "I wish you had opened up before. All those times when I wanted to know things."

I manage to give her a smile, and then I do it anyway, because I can't resist. I give in and put my hand to her face. The velvet softness of her skin is warm against my hand and memories flood back of the scent and feel of her against me.

I wish she had come sooner. I wish we had figured things out so that we could have moved to a better place together instead of moving apart. "I'm falling in love with you, Mari, but I have learned that love is a dangerous, precarious thing." The confession tumbles from my mouth before I have a chance to rein it in. Her eyes widen and turn glassy and if she looks at me like that any longer, I will want to wipe those tears before they fall. I walk away.

"It doesn't have to be that way," she calls after me. I stand on the other side of the taxi, my hand on the door, about to open it. I pause and take in a snapshot of her face in case this is the last time I will ever see it.

"You don't have the right to say that to me and leave," she yells.

"Look me up next time you're in New Orleans."

I hope she does, but that is entirely up to her.

CHAPTER FIFTY-FIVE

MARI

He said those things and walked out of my life, ripping through me like a tornado that twisted and broke everything in its wake. Trust Ward to do that to me. He left me thinking, and wishing, and hoping.

I watched the taxi drive away and a collage of our rocky past hurtled by me. We could have reconciled. We could have had a good thing, a *great* thing, before everything was ripped away from us.

It was fortunate that I started my new job soon after. It gave me a reason to move forward every day but, compared to before, everything about my new working life dimmed. It was like looking at a paler shade of a painting that had lost its color in the sun.

My life had no allure. I was grieving for my mom, and that was hard. Harder still was living alone, where it was just me with my melancholy thoughts. I tried to heed the warning Ward had given me about being sucked back into an abyss of nothingness.

I'm not sure I managed to heed it well. It was work that saved me, that gave me a reason to get up and out of bed, and to be useful and pretend to function for the eight hours I was there. But it wasn't easy, forcing myself to get through each day, stumbling from Monday to Friday to Monday again.

On the weekends, I would stay in bed, listless and feeling useless. Jamie tried to help, but I was so aware of his feelings for me, I pushed him away, made it clear to him that I didn't feel the same.

After a while, he stopped trying to help me.

I fell deeper into my malaise.

It became a pattern. I would function during the weekdays and fall to pieces during the weekends.

I kept willing for Ward to contact me but he never did. And I, mindful of Jamie's words that I was a magnet for men and relationships that weren't good for me, forced myself never to contact him.

Even though the temptation was strong, I made myself believe I was weaning myself off an addictive drug.

One month passed.

Then two.

And still I thought of Ward. I forgot about the bad times, and only remembered the good ones.

Three months passed, and I still found myself thinking of him every time I went to sleep and every time I woke up.

I had to do *something*. I wasn't succeeding at all in getting him out of my system. Maybe it was because I needed him more than ever.

I bought a ticket to New Orleans. I called Rob before, and got Ward's address, telling him I wanted to send Ward a card. This was how I found myself one day getting a cab from the airport to Chesterton Heights, Ward's home.

As I look through the heavy black and gold wrought iron gates, I begin to feel claustrophobic. I begin to feel as if I've made a terrible mistake.

What if he has forgotten me? Worse, what if he's with someone else?

Twice I walk away and get my phone out to call a cab, and twice I walk back to the gates and look through them at the huge ornate mansion. I debate once more, trying to will myself to press the buzzer and announce that I am here.

But I am very scared and doubtful and resent having flown all the way here. His home looks like a castle. A beautiful haven. It's so far from anything I have known. He has surprised me again, just like he always did.

My heartbeat is so rapid, I'm scared I'll have a heart attack and collapse outside these gates. Now, that would be a sight. Something ghoulish for him to discover.

The intercom I've been too afraid to touch now buzzes and clicks, catching my attention. Someone speaks. "How long are you going to stand out there?"

It's him.

He's seen me, and now I'm doubly embarrassed. He's probably seen me walk away and come back and walk away and come back.

"Mari?"

His voice, thick and velvety, sends goosebumps breaking out all over my skin. My heart jumps to life again. It's truly frightening, the surge of excitement that courses through me, as if his voice, as if *he,* is the only elixir I need.

"Should I come in?" I ask, becoming that unsure, hesitant woman again. Why does he always reduce me to this? But I realize now, it's not because I'm scared of him, it's because I'm crazy about him and I'm terrified he won't feel the same.

"Do you want to?"

"Do I want to what?" I ask him.

"I don't know, Mari. Do you want to follow through on why you're here, maybe? Why are you here?"

"I came to see you."

"You can see me a whole lot better if you come inside."

He lets me in, and I walk along his long, beautiful driveway, staring at the magnificent house and trying not to hyperventilate.

I barely get a chance to raise a hand to the door knocker, when an elderly woman opens the door. "You must be Freya," I say, seeing the crinkles in the corners of her eyes as she smiles at me.

"And you must be Mari."

I raise an eyebrow. "Yes, I am."

"He hasn't stopped talking about you," she says, opening the door to let me in. *He talks about me?* This isn't like him, the man who holds every minute detail close to his heart. I'm too shocked to speak.

"What did he say?" I laugh nervously.

"That you used to write him little notes. Food notes, he called them." She chortles with laughter. "I don't know what you did to him, but he's a whole lot more bearable these days. He's in the conservatory, let me show you the way."

I follow her through richly carpeted hallways and note the stained-glass windows, and rich dark wood paneling. I lose count of the number of sparkling chandeliers.

This place is steeped in a bygone time, but it feels strangely comforting, strangely luxurious and decadent. I would never have expected this to be Ward's home, but now that I know it is, it doesn't seem so absurd. Coming from where he has, I understand why he is here, in this magnificent home.

Freya opens the door and motions me to go in. There, in the middle of the room, is Ward. He's standing expectantly, with his hands in the back of his jean pockets, as if he's waiting just for me. He looks thinner than last time. Smarter, too. More dressed up without wearing anything fancy. No sweatpants, but jeans, and a t-shirt. Smart shoes. He looks drop-dead gorgeous. It's too much for me to take in. His surroundings and him all at once.

My brain fogs over in a mist of desire. I'm irritated and annoyed with myself for not having an ounce of resistance. This man's effect on me is potent and resisting him is not an option.

"You look good," I tell him, keeping it cool, or trying. Holding back while I can.

"Thank you. You look ...," he pauses, "You look as though things are getting better."

I raise a hand to my hair. I had it cut and colored before I came and now I'm self-conscious. The months haven't been good to me, but I am hopeful and more optimistic than I was when we last met. I've lost weight, I don't sleep well, and I'm aware that Ward is being kind to me. A haircut and color can only do so much. It can't completely hide the scars of all that has happened.

I stare around the room. It's all glass with a few comfy chairs and a couple of tables. Flowers and plants decorate every corner. It's light and airy, nothing like the writing cave I remember him in. He must sense my surprise because he says, "I write here most days."

"That's unusual," I remark.

"I can write better here. It's still enclosed but I can see out."

I glance outside. His grounds are a place of beauty. "It's very bright." I recall how he never had the blinds up, how he would never let any light in.

"It suits me these days." He walks towards me and my body starts to cheer. Cells jumping like preschoolers at play. My heart swoons all over again as he takes my hand in his big strong one, lifting it to his lips and pressing his lips against it. A shaky breath falls from my lips, as if I've run out of air. I'd hoped he'd have kept that distance between us, because I can't take so much of this so soon.

His aura, powerful and overwhelming, and his presence, commanding and strong, are enough to unnerve me. I had schooled myself into toughness the entire trip here, and yet, here I am, weak and vulnerable, and all he had to do was kiss my hand.

His eyes are dark and dangerous, but our gazes lock steadily and I feel the warmth that emanates from them. His lips curl up into a smile and my heart floats away. This is intoxicating, him still holding my hand, rubbing his thumb over the back of it while his gaze burns into me. "How have you been?" he asks.

"Oh, you know, getting by."

"You can do better than getting by."

"It's not always that easy," I shoot back. It has been a struggle.

"I know." His thumb on my skin is comforting, and a reminder of the good times we've shared.

"I've missed you, Mari. I've been looking out for you every day."

I try to swallow, but can't, because my muscles have gone on strike. "Every day?" I manage to say, finally.

"Every day."

He holds my gaze, that look alone making me shake and throb with excitement. I had forgotten how strong it could be, the electric sizzle that rolls in the air whenever he and I meet; how much desire and yearning can coexist in the few inches between us. He kisses my hand again. "I couldn't be happier to see you."

"I *needed* to see you," I tell him, my stomach sinking then rising, as if it's on choppy seas with no sign of land in sight.

"Needed?" He dips his head, amusement twinkling in his eyes, as if this makes him happy.

I can't remember what I was supposed to say to him. I'd been working on my lines all the way here, hoping to come across all casual and unaffected as if I had strolled by all the way from Chicago to New Orleans.

"Needed, Mari?" he asks again, as if he needs to know. There's an intensity in his voice that I pick up on.

"Needed," I confess. "I tried to forget you but I couldn't. I tried so hard to shut you out of my thoughts, but you always crept back in."

This wasn't how it was supposed to go. I wasn't planning to do what I always do, tell him how I feel, state my feelings first. I'd hoped I would be stronger, more together, but Ward has unraveled me. He did that right from the start and nothing is going to change that.

My gaze falls to his lips, then up to his eyes, then to his broad, broad shoulders. I'm a goner. The space between my legs, the part that belongs only to him, aches with lust.

He smiles, and my heart is in danger of bursting through my chest and flying right out of his floor-to-ceiling glass walls.

"You're in my thoughts every moment, Mari. I never stopped thinking about you and I could never forget you."

"But you waited for me to come to you?" I protest. "What if I hadn't, then what?"

"I had plans to return to Chicago and write the next book. I was going to ask for my trusty housekeeper to come back and work for me."

"Trusty?" I wonder how he can use that word after what happened.

"Trusty, sexy, caring." He slides his hands around my waist. "I love you."

My need for this man intensifies exponentially. My lungs now join my heart and fill, fill, fill, as if they too will burst from too-muchness. Too much happiness, too much joy, and too much gratitude.

I slide my hands around his neck. He dips his head, claiming my mouth as his tongue sweeps in and dances with mine and we kiss feverishly, as if we're afraid to let each other go. His strong, powerful arms wrap around me tighter, making me feel safe and wanted. After losing my way, wandering restlessly in my maze of no hope, I finally feel as if I have come home. With Ward, I am home. He is the thing that completes me. He swallows me up and makes me his and I don't want anyone else because no one else compares.

"I love you," I tell him, and we kiss again, making up for the long, lonely months and holding on to one another, never to let go again.

EPILOGUE
A YEAR LATER ...

WARD

When she came to me, almost a year ago now, standing in my conservatory looking thin and gaunt, I had to fight my initial urge to hold her. She looked frail and brittle and it was plain to see that she wasn't coping.

I didn't intend to touch her, or kiss her, or tell her how much I missed her—not on that first day—but Mari has a hold on me that I don't fully understand. My determination to stay composed and in control lasted all of ten seconds. I couldn't hold back. I had to tell her I loved her, because I did.

She had looked me up and come to me, and that was all the validation I needed. Not a day had passed that I didn't think of her. It got so bad that I had made plans to return to Chicago when I started writing my next book. Chicago has different memories for me now, and if I hadn't heard from her when I did, I was going to seek her out.

But after a lifetime of holding back, keeping my thoughts and emotions to myself, I no longer have to do that, not with Mari. She is my soulmate and we fit together to make the perfect whole.

"How many words?" she asks, her hand skimming over my head. I glance up and watch her float by in a sexy turquoise bikini. She returns to her desk and gets back to work.

There goes my goal for the day. My fingers hover over the keyboard. I won't reach five thousand words. Not now.

Our temporary castle for the next two months is a luxury apartment nestled high up on steep cliffs overlooking the Aegean Sea. In Santorini. This sparkling Greek island with its cool-white-and-deep-blue buildings is one of the most beautiful places I have ever seen.

I only have to look up from my couch to see the tangerine sunset above an azure blue pool that glistens under the sun. The wide-open doors let in a cool breeze but Mari has a desk fan on as she works in full sight of me. I take a moment, maybe ten, to admire her side profile.

How she expects me to reach my daily word count is beyond me.

We don't often get out of bed until noon. Then we have breakfast outside in the huge veranda dotted with terracotta plant pots and pink bougainvillea flowers striking a contrast against the bright white walls.

This is my version of paradise, but it's Mari who makes it so. I could be anywhere and I would be happy, as long as she's by my side. I need nothing and no one else.

I save my document then close my laptop. She hears the sound and glances at me. "Packing up so soon?" she asks, then gets back to her work, typing away on her laptop. She's my unofficial marketing person and assistant and manager. She's the help I needed all along but refused to take.

Rob loves her, because she's taken all his worries away and given him his life back. That and because he can see how good she is for me. These days, there is no reason for him to babysit me or to worry about my deadlines.

I reach my targets and goals, most of the time, and my next book is on track to be finished in time so as not to give Rob a heart attack.

My TV interviews are bearable because Mari is waiting in the wings. Knowing that she's there gets me through the interviews, laughing at the talk show hosts and pretending to be at ease when I'm clearly out of my comfort zone.

I'm only truly at ease when I'm in my home, my castle, a place of comfort—with Mari by my side. Everything that was tough for me before is now bearable because of her.

The Unseen Face became an instant bestseller and from that point on, everything turned crazy. The runaway success of the book was something I was unprepared for. Usually, my books hit the bestseller charts and then drop back down after a few months. This one has stayed high up in the charts and it's still riding high even now.

James Garvey, eat your heart out.

Readers have said this book was different, that it wasn't just all horror and that it had a sense of redemption. Perhaps because *The Morbid* trilogy loosely mirrored my own life.

The Unseen Face was written during a time when I had finally grasped at the possibility of laying my ghosts to rest. Because Mari had given me the happier future I had never dreamed of and a sense of belonging I hadn't ever really had.

"I'm not in the mood for writing," I say, eyeing her side profile as she taps away at the keyboard.

"Your daily word count," she says, in a singsong voice. "You need to meet it."

"If you're going to parade around in a bikini all day, we might need to revise and lower my goals."

She turns and fixes me with a serious stare. "I like to swim laps in between working, but if it's causing problems with your concentration, I can change into something else."

Seeing my expression sour, she gets up and walks over to me.

I move my laptop to the side and let her climb onto me, straddling me.

"No need to change," I tell her, snaking my hands around her waist. "I'll find my motivation, don't you worry."

"That's better," she whispers, splaying her hands on my naked chest. She's good at keeping me in check. It doesn't help that she's sitting on me, or that I'm in my swim trunks. My excitement throbs and pokes her, tellingly. She lowers her head to my chest then drops tiny kisses all over. This isn't going to help me one bit.

"Did you want me to reach my goals for the day?" I ask her, because at this rate, it's just not going to happen.

"Yes." She drops a kiss on my lips, while her soft fingers skim all over my arms and chest. She loves the feel of me, of my muscles and my tautness. My workouts and exercise are more for her than for me. "We've gone through your deadlines and your timetable. You know what you have to do." As if to confuse the heck out of me, she kisses me deeply, her sweet mouth melting into mine and giving me other, different ideas.

My arousal presses against her. I only have to pull the string of her bikini and it will begin—another hot sultry evening that lasts for hours. There will be no more words written today. "Can't it wait until *after?*"

"No," she says, her expression schoolteacherish. "You're getting nothing until you meet your targets."

By targets, she doesn't only mean the words, but the laps I have to take in the pool and the exercises she makes me do. The push-ups and jumping rope and some other cardio moves she lined up for me.

She's my Jamie, Trevor and Rob all rolled into one.

I can't imagine life without her, and I hope I never will. I grab her hand, the sparkling engagement ring flashes in the sunlight streaming in. I push up my thighs, poking her with the signs of my arousal.

She squirms. "Ward, you can poke me all you want, but nothing happens until you finish *everything.*"

My plummeting disappointment is soon replaced by new energy. Now I will be forced to get everything done super, super fast—which is probably why she's sitting on my lap in the first place, dangling the carrot of her sexy, sensual body in front of me.

My gaze takes in her face, rounded and full now that all the worry has been vanquished. I stare at her, hoping to entice her into going easy on me today, but I know it won't work. It never does.

There's no danger of me slipping into an abyss with her around. Mari keeps me in check.

I don't need beautiful, exotic locations to be happy. For me, Mari is my own happy place. She makes sure I never hit rock bottom, and I cushion her so that she never does either.

I love her and she loves me, and it's really as simple as that.

Thank you for reading THE PRICE OF INERTIA. I hope you enjoyed Ward and Mari's story as much as I loved writing it!

THE OTHER SIDE OF GREED is the next book in THE SEVEN SINS series. This is about a billionaire who goes undercover for the wrong reasons.

Greed, lust and sizzling chemistry …
Brandon Hawks has set his sights on a plot of land from which he stands to make millions. The only problem is Kyra Lewis, a champion of the underprivileged and owner of a nonprofits organization based on the same piece of land. And she's not going anywhere.
But Brandon always gets what he wants, no matter what it takes.

SIGN UP FOR MY NEWSLETTER to find out when new books release!
http://www.lilyzante.com/news

Read an excerpt from THE OTHER SIDE OF GREED below.

Happy reading!

Lily

EXCERPT: THE OTHER SIDE OF GREED

BRANDON

"The scent of money is intoxicating." I hang up the phone and signal a chef's kiss. "Another deal done." I savor the glow of warmth that spreads through me. There is nothing more satisfying than sealing another deal.

It's better than sex.

"We should celebrate." Neville, my lawyer, shuts his briefcase and looks hopeful. Because this deal has put another couple of million dollars into my coffers, he expects that I will celebrate with an expensive meal in one of Chicago's finest restaurants.

Ordinarily, I would, but I have other plans. "Jessica is expecting me at the art gallery. I should show my face."

Neville raises an eyebrow. "Are you dating yet, or are you still keeping this purely platonic?"

I pull at my shirt cuffs. "We're good friends, for now."

"Still just good friends? You disappoint me, Brandon. You've been sniffing around her long enough."

"I don't sniff, Neville." And certainly not around someone like Jessica Montrose. A socialite and an art gallery owner, she is smart, polished, rich and powerful, all thanks to her father who once operated a hedge fund in the city.

I have recently taken over Hawks Enterprises, a conglomerate which my father founded many decades ago. He has recently retired due to ailing health—heart surgery has taken its toll—and he has passed the mantle to me. While I have enjoyed not being in the limelight—and I still prefer to fly under the radar—the idea of having this much power and wealth is overwhelming.

I have my eye on Jessica because she is perfect wife material. It's one reason why I haven't jumped into bed with her yet. I want to take things slowly. I'm taking them so slowly that I haven't even made it to first base yet. I'm not inspired to. There's no chemistry, *yet*. She's ... polished. Good for me and my brand. The perfect trophy wife.

"We'll celebrate another time, then. A five-million-dollar deal is nothing to be taken lightly, even for someone like you."

"Some other time," I tell him, glancing at my watch. I want to go home and shower before I go to the art gallery.

Neville rises slowly, as if his portly and round body is too heavy for his knees. His jowls hang around his neck, giving him a St. Bernard Dog air. His love of red wine, blue cheese and rich foods have no doubt helped.

He gets rich off of people like me but he lacks the killer instinct that I have, which is why he's a lawyer charging me by the hour, and why I'm where I am. Making deals, and obscene amounts of money, being driven by the urge and greed to possess, these things run in my blood.

Strange, because that wasn't how my life started.

While I also like the finer things in life like fine dining, thousand dollar bottles of wine and whiskey, and watching sunsets from my private jet, making money is what truly makes me happy. Amassing *things*, possessions, properties.

Emma, my PA, who is smarter and sharper than I give her credit for, notices that my newfound interest in Jessica has a similar trait to my desire to own things. "She's not a building or a commodity, Brandon," she said to me when Jessica first came on the scene, "she's not a 'thing' that you can own or possess; she's a person." I beg to differ. People, like things, can be bought, and owned and possessed. I believe that after much wining and dining, and whisking away on exotic holidays, after gifting her expensive trinkets, and clothes, and accessories, there will come such a time.

My lawyer grabs his briefcase by the handle and swings it off the table, then pauses.

"Greenways. Have you given it some thought?" His greedy little eyes settle on me awaiting orders for my next project. A fun project, I think, before I step into the limelight as Philip Hawks' successor.

"I have."

Neville cocks his head expectantly. "Care to share your plans with me?"

Greenways is a plot of land I am interested in acquiring. It's a prime piece of real estate even if, to the unknowing eye, it looks like an eyesore. Once ignored and forgotten, the area is slowly becoming gentrified—due to money being pumped into the infrastructure in the surrounding areas.

It will be worth a hell of a lot in years to come. Naturally, I want it. My contact, Charlie Stagg, in the city's planning and development department, is available to help as and when needed. The land presently houses a few factories and stores and it's just a matter of getting business owners to move. The problem is, getting them to move isn't easy; they're stubborn, but Stagg can help us.

Reaching out to them in the hopes of coming to some sort of financial agreement isn't going to work. I've seen other companies fail. I've come up with another strategy—which Charlie will help to facilitate by designating Greenways to be a redevelopment project area due to blight. Then the city can rehabilitate it later.

'Later' is when Hawks Enterprises will be given the contracts to build new condos. We'll make a shitload of money in the process.

"I told you, I want to try another way," I tell Neville.

When Neville's thick caterpillar brows meet angrily in the middle, I try to assure him. "Don't look so worried, Neville. I've got this."

"That's what I'm worried about." Neville's brain has short-circuited, and he seems to have forgotten who I am. When I broached this idea with him before, albeit briefly, he didn't sound so eager.

"You are crazy to think you can change Kyra Lewis's mind."

"Shhhh." I hold my finger to my lips. I scratch my chin, bored by this talk of worrying what the peasants at Greenways may or may not like. "Let's not talk about her right now." I've read up about this feisty little upstart. This poor girl do-gooder. Someone needs to warn her that I eat people like her for breakfast. "I want to have some fun with this." I put on my jacket and adjust the cuffs of my shirt.

I'm also eager to be on my way. Working late is the norm for me, but tonight is a rare social evening. Art galleries are not my forte. I find them boring, but if my future wife-to-be is involved in that world, it's something I'm going to have to get to like.

Though the door to my office is open, Emma still knocks on it and hovers, not coming in. "I have some paperwork for you to sign. It's urgent."

"Don't you worry about Lewis," I tell Neville. "I'll update you in due time." I motion for Emma to come in, then survey the sheaf of papers she hands me.

Neville doesn't look amused. "You underestimate people sometimes, Brandon. The Greenways store owners are a different breed."

Emma chortles. "You can say that again."

I give her a not-you-too look before flicking through the pages. She has thoughtfully put bright blue and green stickers on the pages I need to look at. I continue signing as if I don't have a care in the world.

Because I don't.

Worrying is Neville's problem. Not mine.

I've learned from my father, and he is the best. All business deals, all the projects, deals and proposals he was involved in, he's always managed to come out on top. It has benefited him in some way. That's how he operates, and that's what he's taught me. He created opportunities and made boatloads of cash by taking buildings, then breaking them up, and selling them for parts. I watched and learned from him as he took land, bulldozed the crap out of it, and built something better and more upmarket in its place.

Newer and better. Upscale buildings, exclusive enclaves. That's what we build and we've never *not* been able to do as we please.

"I've told him," I hear Emma say to Neville as I skimmed the fine print. "He doesn't take her seriously."

"You don't need to worry," I tell Emma.

"Share it with me, your proposed plan, and then we'll

see how much we need to worry." Neville is about to set his briefcase on the floor when I shake my head.

"I don't have time."

"He has an appointment." I can't figure out if Emma's tone is sarcastic or if she's being serious.

I tilt my head and look from one to the other. These people should know me better than that. I always get what I want, and I always win. "If my plan doesn't work, burning the place down will ensure Lewis and her crew leave."

Neville nods his head as if he approves. "That's something we could revert to as a last resort."

"I was joking, Neville." I may be a lot of things, but criminal isn't one of them. Though, technically, what I'm about to do to Kyra Lewis might be deemed as such to some.

Emma snorts loud enough for me to hear as Neville disappears. "I shouldn't have to listen to this," she mutters, giving me a disapproving glare. "I swear, it's like working for the mafia sometimes."

"Surely I'm more palatable?" I suggest, winking at her.

"Did you sign them all?" She ignores my remark and shuffles through the pile of papers I've left on my desk.

"I signed everywhere you indicated."

She nods appreciatively, clutching the papers to her chest. "Date night with Jessica?"

My jaw tightens. "Not quite." Looking at paintings that make no sense, sipping champagne and picking at canapes isn't what I would call date night. I'm not the type of guy who wastes time and money chasing skirt, but Jessica Montrose is a worthy endeavour. These things take time and there is no rush.

Emma clutches the sheaf of papers to her chest. "*Just* an appointment, then." There is a glint of amusement in her eyes. For a PA, she's upfront, and takes risks in the way she addresses me. She says things that many wouldn't dare. She would be my social conscience if I possessed such a thing.

An appointment.

I open my mouth to put her in her place but I raise my eyebrow instead. She's only a couple of years older than me, but behaves as if she's thirty-four going on seventy.

But she's not far wrong. These sterile-as-a-science-lab encounters I have with Jessica are closer to an appointment than anything else. The pursuit of this socialite is slow, and not exactly fun. It often seems like work.

Kyra Lewis and Greenways? Now, *that* to me seems like fun. Emma moves towards the door. "Have you had a chance to read the notes I collated for you on Kyra Lewis?"

"I skimmed through them." I know enough about the woman to go ahead with my plans.

"If anyone is going to stand in your way, it's her, and, to be clear, I disapprove of your plan."

"You don't know my plan."

"I know *you*, Brandon. Enjoy your evening." She saunters away before I can say a word. I replay her cautionary advice to me. No one stands in my way. Because I'm fucking invincible.

THE OTHER SIDE OF GREED is available at all major retailers

BOOKLIST

**Buy Direct from Lily at
https://shop.lilyzante.com**

The Seven Sins:(New Series) A series of seven standalone romances based on the seven sins. Steamy, emotional, and angsty romances which are loosely connected.

Underdog (prequel)
The Wrath of Eli
The Problem with Lust
The Lies of Pride
The Price of Inertia
The Other Side of Greed

The Billionaire's Love Story: This is a Cinderella story with a touch of Jerry Maguire. What happens when the billionaire with too much money meets the single mom with too much heart?

The Promise
The Gift, Books 1-3
The Offer, Books 1-3
The Vow, Books 1-3

Indecent Intentions: This is a spin-off from The Billionaire's Love story. This two-book set consists of two standalone stories about the billionaire's playboy brother. The second story is about a wealthy nightclub owner who shuns relationships.

The Bet
The Hookup
Indecent Intentions 2-Book Set

Honeymoon Series: Take a roller-coaster journey of emotional highs and lows in this story of love and loss, family and relationships. When Ava is dumped six weeks before her Valentine's Day wedding, she has no idea of the life that awaits her in Italy.

Honeymoon for One
Honeymoon for Three
Honeymoon Blues
Honeymoon Bliss
Baby Steps

Italian Summer Series: This is a spin-off from the Honeymoon Series. These books tell the stories of the secondary characters who first appeared in the Honeymoon Series. Nico and Ava also appear in these books.

It Takes Two
All That Glitters
Fool's Gold
Roman Encounter
November Sun
New Beginnings

A Perfect Match Series: This is a seven book series in which the first four books feature the same couple. High-flying corporate executive Nadine has no time for romance but her life takes a turn for the better when she meets Ethan, a sexy and struggling metal sculptor five years younger. He works as an escort in order to make the rent. Books 4-6 are standalone romances based on characters from the earlier books. The main couple, Ethan and Nadine, appear in all books:

Lost in Solo (prequel)
The Proposal
Heart Sync
A Leap of Faith
Misplaced Love
Reclaiming Love
Embracing Love

Standalone Books:

Love Among the Ruins
Tomorrow Belongs to Us
Love Inc
An Unexpected Gift

ACKNOWLEDGMENTS

I owe a huge thanks to the wonderful ladies in my proofreading group for their patience and support, as well as their tolerance for my ever-changing deadlines. They check my manuscript for errors, typos, inconsistencies and the many strange words and phrases which often find their way into my stories.

They give me the confidence to release each book and I am eternally grateful for their help and support:

Marcia Chamberlain

Carole Tunstall

I would also like to thank Tatiana Vila of Vila Design for creating the awesome cover.

ABOUT THE AUTHOR

Lily Zante lives with her husband and three children somewhere near London, UK.

Connect with Me

I love hearing from you – so please don't be shy! You can email me, message me on Facebook or connect with me on Twitter:

Website **|** Email | Newsletter sign-up